Dear Friend,

Many of us feel nostalgic when remembering a favorite childhood summer vacation. I've been fortunate enough to go back to the same home on the Potomac River every summer from the age of four right on up to today. I won't say how many years that's been now, but my home in Colonial Beach, Virginia, is filled with special memories. Just sitting on the front porch with a good book and a spectacular river view is all that's required to take me back in time.

It was on that porch that I first conceived the idea for the *Rose Cottage Sisters,* a series about four strong women who each return home to Rose Cottage when facing a crisis in their lives. They come to this beloved house soul weary and in search of peace. What they find is a sanctuary and love.

In this volume, you'll read about Melanie D'Angelo in *Three Down the Aisle* and Maggie D'Angelo in *What's Cooking?* In the second volume, *Return to Rose Cottage,* coming soon, you'll meet their two sisters and the men who change their lives.

I hope each of you has a special place like Rose Cottage in your life, one that brings back fond memories or brings you peace in times of trouble. If not, I hope this visit to Rose Cottage will bring just a little of its magic and serenity into your life, as well.

All best,

Sheryl Woods

SHERRYL WOODS

Home at Rose Cottage

MIRA®

Recycling programs for this product may not exist in your area.

ISBN-13: 978-0-7783-2751-6

HOME AT ROSE COTTAGE

Copyright © 2010 by MIRA Books.

The publisher acknowledges the copyright holder of the individual works as follows:

THREE DOWN THE AISLE
Copyright © 2005 by Sherryl Woods

WHAT'S COOKING?
Copyright © 2005 by Sherryl Woods

For questions and comments about the quality of this book please contact us at Customer_eCare@Harlequin.ca.

www.MIRABooks.com

Printed in U.S.A.

CONTENTS

Three Down the Aisle

Prologue

The tears on her cheeks were still damp and her temper was still hot, when someone—no, not just someone, the family calvary—pounded on the door of Melanie's Boston apartment. Before she could drag herself off the sofa, the door burst open and all three of her sisters swooped into her tiny studio looking a bit like outraged avenging angels.

If Melanie hadn't been so completely and totally miserable and humiliated, she might have managed to smile at their ready-for-anything attitude. Had her sisters gotten here before she'd kicked Jeremy the weasel to the curb, he'd probably be quaking in his two-hundred-dollar designer loafers.

The D'Angelo sisters were something else. Singly, they had their own distinctive personalities and achievements, but united they were a force to be reckoned with. And nothing united them like a common enemy—in this case the man who'd lied to Melanie for more than six months.

Maggie and Jo settled on either side of her, patting her hands and murmuring inept but well-meant platitudes about how things would improve, how she was better off without the lying, cheating scoundrel and on and on until Melanie wanted to scream.

Ashley, she noticed, was saying nothing, but her agitated pacing and the flags of color on her cheeks suggested that an explosion was in the offing. Ashley took her duties as the oldest and most successful of the D'Angelo sisters seriously. She also had their father's volatile temper. Melanie eyed her warily.

"Ash, maybe you should sit down," she suggested quietly. "You're giving us all whiplash trying to follow you."

Her big sister responded with a frown. "I don't think so. I'm trying to decide whether to haul this Jeremy's sorry butt into court or just hunt him down and pound him to a pulp."

The rest of the sisters exchanged a look. With Ashley, neither option was entirely out of the question. She had a law degree, a powerful sense of justice, a protective streak and a right hook that deserved respect.

"What good would any of that do, Ash?" Jo the peacemaker inquired cautiously. "Getting your name splashed in the papers along with the whole tawdry reason for your behavior would only prolong Melanie's pain and humiliate her in front of the entire world. Then everyone would know that the creep pulled the wool over her eyes for months. Do you actually want Dad to find out about this? You'll be in court defending him on a murder charge."

Ashley sighed. "True."

They all fell silent, considering Jo's warning. Their father was a lusty, boisterous Italian who'd put the fear of God into more of their dates than any of them cared to recall. And those were the *nice* guys. Jeremy the weasel wouldn't stand a chance against their father's outrage.

Ashley peered intently at Melanie. "Are you sure you

don't want me to do something? There are lots of ways to get even that don't involve bloodshed."

"Nothing," Melanie assured her hurriedly. "It's bad enough that you all know that Jeremy managed to hide a wife and two kids from me, that I believed him every single time he evaded my questions about why we couldn't see each other on the weekends, why we spent so little time in public. He made it all sound perfectly reasonable."

"What made him get around to telling you tonight? A guilty conscience?" Maggie asked.

"Hardly," Melanie admitted. "I ran smack into him while they were all out buying new sneakers for the kids. Even then, he tried to drag me out of sight and tell me some lie about how he was just being dutiful, that it didn't mean a thing, that the marriage was on its last legs. Blah, blah, blah. Idiot that I am, I probably would have listened, too, if his wife hadn't seen us and given him a look that would have frozen anyone else on the spot. Something tells me that this isn't the first time Jeremy's been caught straying by his wife. Her radar was on full alert. How he managed to get away from her to come over here to try one more time to explain is beyond me."

"You didn't listen to a word he had to say, did you?" Ashley demanded.

"Of course not. By then you all were on your way. I wanted him long gone when you got here." She sighed. "How stupid was I? I should have done the math on this months ago."

Jo grinned as she nudged Melanie in the ribs. "You always were lousy at math."

"Not funny, baby sister," Melanie retorted. "What am I going to do now? I certainly can't continue work-ing at Rockingham Industries. If this isn't proof that you should never get involved with someone at the same company—even a company as huge as Rockingham—I don't know what is. My stomach twists into a knot just at the thought of seeing him again. And to think that only a day ago, I did everything I could to bump into him in the hallways."

"You need to get away, take some time off," Maggie said, her expression thoughtful. "And I know the perfect place."

"I need to get another job," Melanie corrected. "I know I wasn't exactly on the fast track at Rockingham, but that receptionist's job did pay the rent."

"You don't need to look right away," Ashley insisted. "If you're short on cash, I can lend you whatever you need."

"Says the high-powered criminal defense attorney who's rolling in dough and has no time to spend it," Jo said. "The rest of us will chip in, too."

"Agreed," Maggie said at once.

Ashley nodded. "There, that's taken care of. And I think I see exactly where Maggie was going a minute ago. You should go to Grandma's cottage, Melanie. We always thought it was magical there. I can't imagine a more perfect place to get your head on straight."

"We were kids," Melanie pointed out. "It was summer vacation. *Of course* we thought it was magical. Notice that none of us has been back since we grew up. Not even Mom goes down anymore, now that Grandma's dead. The place is probably a wreck."

"All the more reason to go," Ashley said, obviously warming to Maggie's idea. "Fixing up the cottage will be just what you need. It's probably worth a fortune. If no one's ever going to use it, maybe we can talk Mom into selling."

"She'll never do it," Maggie said. "You know how sentimental she is about that place."

Ashley waved off the comment. "Beside the point."

"What is the point?" Jo asked. "I'm losing track."

"Fixing the house up will keep Melanie's mind occupied all day, and by night she'll be so exhausted, she'll fall right to sleep," Ashley explained. "The rest of us can take turns going down weekends to keep her company."

"Am I such an embarrassment that you can't wait to get rid of me?" Melanie asked plaintively.

She wasn't sure she wanted to go away someplace where she'd be all alone with only her thoughts for company. Grandma's place, Rose Cottage, was on the banks of the Chesapeake Bay at the tip of Virginia's Northern Neck. With the recent growth of the region, she doubted it was as isolated and tranquil as it had once been, but by Boston standards it was still rural. She doubted there was a movie theater or a mall for miles, much less a Starbucks.

"This isn't a banishment," Ashley insisted.

"But why should I give Jeremy the satisfaction of running away?" Melanie argued. "He's the scumbag."

"She has a point," Jo said.

Ashley scowled at both of them. "So, what are you suggesting? You'll face him down every morning when he walks in the front door at Rockingham? That sounds like fun."

Actually it sounded like hell, Melanie was forced to admit.

"Come on, Melanie. You know I'm right," Ashley persisted. "This is a chance to heal. You'll have time to decide what you want to do next. It's about time you put that college degree of yours to use. You were wasting your talent at Rockingham on the off chance that someday there would be an opening in the marketing department. This could be the best thing that ever happened to you, if it finally gets you to find the right job, instead of something safe but boring."

At the moment, with her heart aching and her pride wounded, Melanie couldn't quite see tonight's turn of events as any sort of blessing, but Ashley usually knew best. "If you say so," she said bleakly.

"Would you rather sit in this apartment and mope?" Ashley demanded.

"No," Melanie said firmly. She'd never moped in her life, and she didn't intend to start now, not over the likes of Jeremy Thompson of the Providence and Nantucket Thompsons. How had she let herself be fooled by that impeccable breeding? Charm and a pedigree didn't mean a man had character.

"Good. That's settled, then," Ashley said. "We'll help you pack. You can leave first thing in the morning. It's a long drive, and you'll want to get there while it's still daylight."

"I haven't even turned in my resignation at work," Melanie protested. Not that she had any great desire to show her face around there as long as there was any chance at all she could bump into Jeremy.

"Fax it in," Ashley said curtly. "If anyone questions it, tell them to take it up with Jeremy. Let him explain. Maybe they'll fire his sorry butt. Or, have them call me, and I'll explain a few facts about sexual harassment."

"It wasn't—" Melanie began, only to have her big sister cut her off.

"It was close enough," Ashley said. "He dangled the prospect of a better job in front of you, didn't he?"

"Yes," Melanie admitted. Even so, despite the appeal of a little vengeance, she still wasn't entirely convinced.

They'd all been brought up with a strong sense of duty and responsibility. Responsible people gave two weeks' notice before walking out on a job, even a job they hated, even a job that clearly had never had any future. Surely her sisters had learned that lesson, too.

"But—" she began.

"No buts," Ashley said firmly.

Melanie sighed. "Okay, then. How am I supposed to get the key from Mom without telling her the whole ugly story?" she asked, grabbing at straws to keep from facing the inevitability of this trip. Their mother, to all outward appearances, might be a gentle Southern belle, but she had the same kind of iron will their father had. She was every bit as capable as Max D'Angelo of making Jeremy's life hell. She'd been inspired by *Gone with the Wind,* so much so that three of her four daughters had been named after characters and the author. Only Jo had escaped that fate. They teased Jo all the time that it was only because their mother has secretly thought of herself as Scarlett.

"Don't worry about Mom." Ashley dug into her huge purse and pulled out an old-fashioned key attached to a piece of rose-colored satin ribbon. "I keep a spare in my purse," she said, looking vaguely embarrassed.

Melanie, Jo and Maggie stared at her. "Why?"

"It's like a talisman," she said defensively. "Whenever things get really, really crazy and frantic at work, I take it out and remind myself that there *is* life after court. There are days when *I* would go to Rose Cottage if I could."

"But you haven't been there in years," Melanie said, bemused by this rare display of sentiment and frivolity in her hard-as-nails big sister.

Ashley winked. "Obviously just knowing it's there works like a charm."

Melanie sighed. If only the cottage would hold a few of

those magical healing properties for her, she'd be eternally grateful. Right now, with the image of those kids and his wife's icy disdain in her head and Jeremy's stinging admission still ringing in her ears, she had her doubts.

1

Every morning when Mike drove his daughter to school past the old Lindsey cottage, he bit back a sigh of regret over its decrepit state. It was like a neglected doll's cottage, abandoned by a fickle child who'd moved on to other toys. The screens on the side porch had been torn by vandals, the front steps sagged, the paint was peeling. One dangling shutter slapped against the side of the house whenever there was any sort of breeze.

The house sat on a valuable piece of property that backed up to the Chesapeake Bay. From the road, the view was all but invisible thanks to the overgrown grass and shrubbery, but it had to be incredible. That anyone could abandon such a place and leave it to the elements to be destroyed was a crime. If they weren't going to use it, they should sell to someone who'd take proper care of it.

But if the sorry state of the house bothered Mike, it was the garden that made him want to leap from the car with his pruning shears, rakes and shovels. Landscape design was his passion, and he could tell that once upon a time, this place had been a garden showcase. Someone had nurtured the roses that struggled to bloom there now.

Someone had given thought to the placement of the lilacs right beneath the windows where the fragrance would drift in on a spring morning.

Now, though, the roses were out of control, tangled with thorny vines. Honeysuckle had taken over the lilacs. The paint on the picket fence was peeling, and parts of it were close to collapse under the weight of the untamed bushes. A few perennials continued to struggle against the weeds, but the weeds were winning. It made him heartsick to see it all gone to ruin.

He'd wanted to buy it himself at first sight six years ago, but the real estate agent said the owner wasn't interested in selling. Apparently the owner wasn't interested in anything having to do with the house, either.

"Daddy," Jessie piped up from beside him. "Why are we stopping here? This place is scary."

Mike glanced over at his six-year-old daughter, who, at the moment, looked like a Victorian painting of a blue-eyed, blond-haired angel. There were no smudges on her cheeks, no tangles in her hair, no rips in her clothes. In fact, she was having a good morning so far. There had been no tantrums over which dress to put on, no battles over the scrambled eggs he'd set in front of her for breakfast because they were out of Cheerios. Days like this were so rare, Mike had learned to cherish them when they came.

Not that he would trade one single second of the time he spent with her, tantrums or not. Jessie was his precious girl, his little survivor. She'd been through way too much in her young life. She'd been born addicted to the drugs her mother hadn't been able to quit, drugs Mike hadn't even realized Linda was hiding from him. When doctors at the hospital had told him his irritable, underweight baby girl was going through withdrawal, he'd been stunned.

He'd spent the next six months after that battling with Linda, trying to get her into rehab, trying to make her see that she was destroying not only her own life and their marriage, but their daughter's life, as well. Unfortunately, nothing he'd said had gotten through to her. The drugs were far more powerful, far more alluring than his love or the needs of their baby girl.

Finally, filled with despair, he'd gone to court, gotten his divorce and full custody of Jessie, and left. Linda's folks knew where to find them, if Linda ever got her act together and wanted to see her child. Until then, though, Linda was out of their lives.

Linda's heartsick parents had agreed that he had no choice. That, at least, had given him some comfort, knowing they believed he'd done what he'd had to do. They visited regularly, but Linda's name was rarely mentioned, especially in front of Jessie. Now that she was old enough to understand, when she asked the inevitable questions about her mother, Mike answered as honestly as he could, but it broke his heart to see the hurt in Jessie's eyes.

Being a single dad would have been hard under any circumstances, but dealing with Jessie's lingering behavior problems was enough to test the patience of a saint. As a baby, she'd screamed her dissatisfaction night and day. Now she was simply unpredictable, sunny one minute and hysterical the next.

Most days Mike was up to the task of dealing with her mood swings, but there were times when it was all he could do not to break down in exhaustion and weep for the damage that had been done to his beautiful little girl.

That was one reason he'd chosen the small town of Irvington on the Chesapeake Bay. There was plenty of work to be had here, but the pace was slower and less demanding than it would have been in a major city. If he needed to spend extra time with Jessie, he could do so without feeling he was shortchanging his clients. And, because his reputation was excellent, he could pick and choose among those who sought his services, making sure that each of them understood that Jessie would always be his first priority.

"We need to go *now!*" Jessie commanded. Even at six, she had the imperial presence of a queen commanding her subjects. She lowered her voice and confided, "I think ghosts live here, Daddy."

Mike grinned at her. It wasn't the first time she'd expressed a negative opinion about the rundown place, but the addition of a ghost was something new. "What makes you think that, pumpkin?" he asked.

"Something moved at the window. I saw it." Her lower lip trembled, and panic filled her eyes.

"Nobody lives here," Mike reassured her. "The house is empty."

"Something moved," Jessie said stubbornly, clearly near tears. Whether she'd actually seen something or not, her fear was real. "We need to *go!*"

Rather than argue, Mike accelerated and continued on to the school. Any logical response he could have made would only have escalated the tension, and the rare serenity would have been shattered.

As soon as they were away from the house, Jessie's shoulders eased and she gave him a tremulous smile. "We're safe now," she said happily.

"You're always safe when I'm around," Mike reminded her.

"I know, Daddy," she said patiently. "But I don't like that place. I don't want to go there again. Not ever. Promise."

"We have to drive by it every day," Mike said.

"But only really, really fast," Jessie insisted. "Okay?"

Mike sighed, knowing that reasoning with his daughter when she was like this was a waste of breath. "Okay."

"Have a good day, pumpkin," he said a few minutes later when he left Jessie at the front door of the school. "I'll be right here when you get out this afternoon."

He'd discovered early on that she needed to be reassured again and again that he would be back, that he wouldn't forget about her. The psychologist he'd spoken to said Jessie's need for constant reassurance was yet another effect of not having her mother in her life, of knowing that Linda had abandoned her. Some days he wondered if he shouldn't have lied and said Linda was dead, if that wouldn't have been less cruel, but he hadn't been able to bring himself to do it. Maybe he'd naively held out hope that someday Linda would straighten herself out and want to be a part of their daughter's life.

"Bye, Daddy." Jessie turned away, then looked back at him, her expression filled with worry. "You won't go back to the bad house, will you? I don't want the ghost to get you."

"No ghost is going to get me," Mike promised, sketching a cross over his heart in the way he always did to reassure her that he meant what he said. "I wear ghost repellent."

Jessie giggled. "You're silly," she told him, though genuine relief flashed in her eyes.

Then she was gone, racing to catch up with a friend. Mike stared after her, wishing it could always be this easy to calm her fears. Some nights there was no consoling her. Some nights she had nightmares she refused to describe, calming only when he held her.

When Jessie was finally out of sight, he turned on his heel

and went back to the car, already planning his jam-packed schedule for the few hours till school let out again.

But instead of heading toward the job he had land-scaping a newly completed house overlooking the bay, he drove back to the Lindsey place, drawn by something he couldn't quite explain.

Had Jessie actually seen something move? Or was he simply reacting to her too-vivid imagination, caught up in the mystery of the deserted house that had fascinated him from the moment he'd arrived in town? Whichever it was, it wouldn't take more than a few minutes to put his mind at rest and satisfy his curiosity. Maybe then he'd be able to put his mild obsession with the place behind him once and for all.

Melanie was standing in her grandmother's kitchen in-effectively battling cobwebs, when the front gate creaked, sending her already jittery nerves into a full-blown panic attack.

Only a few minutes earlier she'd thought she heard a car stop on the isolated road, but when she'd peeked through the curtain of her upstairs bedroom, she'd seen only a glimpse of sun on metal before hearing the car drive on. The incident, which would have been common-place enough in Boston, had been oddly disconcerting here.

With her heart pumping and her pulse racing once more, she crept into the living room and edged toward the window she'd thrown open to let in the cool spring breeze.

"What the hell?"

The very male voice just outside had her plastering her back to the wall, even as her heart ricocheted wildly.

"Anybody here?" the man shouted, rattling the door-knob.

This wasn't good, not good at all, Melanie decided. Her

cell phone was across the room, just more proof that she wasn't thinking clearly of late. Even with all the recent development she'd noticed as she drove in, the nearest neighbor was a quarter-mile up the road. There were a few boats on the bay this morning and sound did carry near water, but would anyone get here in time even if she shouted for help?

She tried to think what Ashley would do. Her fearless big sister would probably have a firm grip on a lamp by now and be in attack mode by the door. Picturing it, Melanie reached for the closest lamp with its heavy marble base and tested its weight. This sucker could do some real damage, she concluded, suddenly feeling more confident and in control.

"Who's there?" she shouted back in what she hoped was a suitably indignant tone. "You're trespassing."

"So are you."

She was so taken aback by the outrageous accusation that she swung open the door and scowled at the interloper. It was amazing how much braver she felt with that lamp and a little indignation on her side.

"I most certainly am not trespassing," she said again, trying not to let her voice waver at the sight of the hulking man on the threshold.

At least six-two and easily two hundred pounds, he was all muscle and sinew. Even though it was barely April, his skin had already been burnished gold by the sun, and his dark brown hair had fiery highlights in it. His T-shirt stretched tightly over a massive chest, and his faded jeans hugged impressive thighs. An illustration of Paul Bunyon immediately came to mind.

At any other time in her life, she might have been more appreciative of such a gorgeous male specimen, but in recent days anything driven by testosterone was the enemy. That didn't seem to stop her heartbeat from skipping merrily at the sight of him. Given his obviously sour mood, her instinctive response was doubly annoying.

. "Cornelia Lindsey is dead," he announced, his blue eyes steady and unrelenting as he challenged her to dispute that.

"I know," Melanie said. "She was my grandmother. She died seven years ago this month."

He nodded slowly. "You've got that much right. You're a Lindsey?"

"Actually I'm a D'Angelo. Melanie D'Angelo. My mother was a Lindsey until she married my father."

"Cornelia Lindsey was Southern through and through, according to the neighbors. You don't sound like you're from around here."

"I'm not. I'm from Boston."

"You have any ID?"

She regarded him with a mix of amusement and defensiveness. "None with my family tree printed on it. Who *are* you? The local sheriff or something?"

"Just a neighbor. This place has been empty a long time. Someone turns up out of the blue like this, I just want to be sure they belong here. If you are who you say you are, I'm sure you can appreciate that."

It was evident to Melanie that he wasn't going to budge without some sort of proof that she wasn't a stranger setting up housekeeping in an abandoned property. He was right. She ought to be grateful that a neighbor would take such interest in making sure the cottage was secure.

"Stay there," she muttered, then stared at the lamp she still held clutched in her hands. She set it back on its table, then crossed the room to grab her purse and several of the framed snapshots sitting on the old oak sideboard.

When she returned, she handed him her driver's

license, then a photo of a grinning girl with freckles and hair bleached almost white by the sun. "That's me at six," she said, then showed him the rest. "My sisters, Maggie, Ashley and Jo with our mom. And this one is of all of us with my grandmother, Cornelia Lindsey, just before she died. Did you know her?"

"No," he said, taking the photo and studying it intently.

To her surprise, he barely spared a glance for her sisters, all of them long-legged beauties. Instead, his gaze seemed to be focused on something else in the picture.

"I knew it," he mumbled, then scowled at her. "You all should be ashamed of yourselves."

She flinched at the outrage in his tone. "I beg your pardon!"

"The garden," he said impatiently. "You've let it go to ruin."

Melanie sighed. She could hardly deny it was a disgrace. She'd all but had to chop her way through it to get inside. She was pretty sure her car was likely to be swallowed up by aggressive vines if she didn't move it on a regular basis.

"I noticed," she conceded mildly.

His frown deepened. "Now that you're here, what do you intend to do about it?"

Melanie shrugged. She could have told him it was none of his business, but she didn't have the energy to argue about something so unimportant with a total stranger. Nor was she inclined to defend their neglect of the house or the garden. It really was indefensible, given the way their grandmother had loved this house and doted on her roses.

"I don't know," she said eventually. "Something, I suppose. First, though, I have to air this place out and chase out seven years' worth of spiders and bug carcasses."

The man on her doorstep regarded her with undisguised disapproval. "Don't wait too long. Now is the time of year to fix it." He dug in his pocket and handed her a card. "When you're ready, call me. It needs to be done right, and something tells me you've never gotten your hands dirty." He shot a disdainful glance toward her pale, smooth hands. "I'll show you what to do, so you don't make things worse than they already are."

Before she could reject the ungracious offer, before she could even muster a suitably indignant retort, he'd turned on his heel and gone, crashing through the overgrown weeds and vines like an intrepid explorer in alien jungle territory. He stopped several times to examine the rosebushes with a surprisingly gentle caress or to tug violently at a choking strand of honeysuckle, muttering to himself in an undertone. Melanie had little doubt that whatever he was saying was unflattering.

Annoyed by his judgmental attitude, she was about to rip the card to shreds, but something about the delicate artwork in one corner caught her eye. It was only a line drawing, but the combination of seagrass and roses reminded her of the way Rose Cottage had been in its heyday. He was right about one thing. Her grandmother would be appalled by the garden's sorry state of neglect.

Her gaze moved from the drawing to the name.

Stefan Mikelewski, Landscape Designer, the card said simply, along with a phone number.

Okay, so he was abrupt and abrasive, but he apparently had actual expertise she could use if she was to make any headway at all in the disastrous garden. She tucked the card in her pocket, then went back to the kitchen, hoping to brew a cup of tea so she could start the day all over again.

One look around, though, told her that even the simple task of boiling water was entirely too daunting to contemplate on an empty stomach. It could take hours to get the stove clean enough to set a teakettle on one of the burners. Coffee was out of the question with no sign of a coffee grinder for the special-blend beans she'd brought with her. Maggie, with her gourmet mentality, had instilled a love of perfect coffee, along with a taste for haute cuisine, in all of the sisters.

Melanie consoled herself that she wasn't really running away from all the work that needed to be done. She had to go into town anyway so she could stock the refrigerator with groceries and spend a fortune on cleaning supplies. The fast-food dinner she'd had before she'd arrived the night before had worn off hours ago, and she was definitely going to need stamina to tackle the thorough cleaning the house required. Last night she'd done little more than sweep out the attic bedroom she and her sisters had always used and make up the bed with the fresh sheets she'd brought with her.

Turning her back on the mess was perfectly sensible, she concluded. "It'll be just as much of a disaster when I get back," she told herself, grabbing her purse and heading for the door.

In fact, something told her she could spend the next week scrubbing the place from top to bottom and she'd barely make a dent in the cleanup effort. As much as she'd hated Jeremy a scant thirty-six hours ago, her sisters were about to join him on the short list of people Melanie didn't want to see anytime soon, not unless they came wielding dust rags and brooms.

Her cell phone rang just as she pulled into a parking

space in Irvington's small downtown district, where she'd noticed a promising coffee shop the night before.

"Relaxing yet?" Ashley inquired cheerily.

"Remember what you said about being so exhausted from cleaning I wouldn't have time to think?" Melanie muttered. "It took two hours to clear a path to the bed last night."

"Uh-oh," her sister responded.

"Triple whatever image you have in your mind, and you'll have some idea of the work ahead of me. And that's inside. The yard's worse."

"That bad?"

"And then some."

"How's the weather?"

"Don't change the subject. I want you to know just how annoyed I am with all of you right now. I feel like Cinderella, left behind to deal with the mess her wicked stepsisters didn't want to touch."

"Hey, it sounds like this is working out just fine," Ashley countered.

"In whose universe?" Melanie retorted.

"You're not thinking about Jeremy, are you?" Ashley said. "Gotta run. I'm due in court. Love you."

Melanie tossed her cell phone back in her purse. Much as she hated to admit it, her sister was right. She hadn't thought about Jeremy the scumbag all morning, except in passing. Whether that was due to the daunting prospect of cleaning Rose Cottage or the equally daunting encounter with Stefan Mikelewski was hard to say.

"Blame it on the cleaning," she muttered to herself as she headed for a coffee shop down the block. Thinking about doing battle with dust bunnies was a whole lot safer than remembering the way the landscaper had made her blood hum through her veins, especially when he'd deliberately taunted her about the condition of the garden. Maybe that was a reaction to his arrogance and nothing more, but she didn't want to test the theory with another encounter anytime soon.

As she drank her coffee and ate an entire huge cinnamon roll, she considered how fortunate it was that she had days and days of work ahead of her inside the house before she could even begin to contemplate doing anything outside. That would give her time to decide if she wanted to tackle it on her own or ask for help from the disconcerting Mr. Mikelewski.

Or maybe just hightail it back to Boston and forget the whole thing.

Now there was an idea, she thought happily—until she remembered the reason she'd left in the first place. She swallowed hard and steeled her resolve to stay right here.

After all, no amount of dirt and grime, no tangle of weeds, no judgmental scowls from Mr. Mikelewski could be awful enough to drive her back to the city where Jeremy was contentedly living with the wife and two children he'd neglected to mention to her until she'd caught him red-handed.

The memory of her total humiliation was a terrific motivator, she concluded, as she made a whirlwind trip through the grocery store and exited with a cart piled high with comfort food and antibacterial scrubbing supplies.

She was going to wash years of dirt out of Rose Cottage and toss every last memory of Jeremy out with the filthy water...or die trying.

2

It had been a week now, and Mike hadn't been able to shake the image of Melanie D'Angelo standing in her doorway clutching a heavy lamp and facing him down without the slightest hint of trepidation. Of course, there had been shadows in her cornflower-blue eyes and smudges on her pale cheeks, but she'd shown absolutely no fear in the face of his intrusive, skeptical questions or his condemnation of the garden's sad neglect. He'd been impressed, to say nothing of intrigued. Now, thanks to that unexpected encounter, he was more drawn to the Lindsey cottage than ever.

It was the shadows in her eyes that had gotten to him. They were evidence of the kind of vulnerability he tended to avoid like the plague these days. He had all the emotional upset in his life he could cope with. He didn't need to go taking on some stranger's woes, even if she did have skin like silk and a body that all but begged for a man's attention. He still hadn't forgotten the way her blouse had gaped slightly to reveal a slight hint of cleavage or the way her jeans had clung to the curve of her hips and her endlessly long legs.

He didn't need a woman in his life, especially not one who all but shouted that she came with complications.

Hell, he had all the work he could handle, too. He didn't need to go looking for any more, especially of the unpaid variety. She hadn't called, so obviously she didn't think she needed his help untangling that mess in her yard. He should forget all about Melanie D'Angelo and the Lindsey cottage. They were someone else's problem.

But then he remembered the photo she'd shown him. Oh, he'd noticed the four gorgeous teenagers and their handsome mother and smiling grandmother, but his heart had done a little stutter step at the sight of the climbing pink, white and red roses, the heirloom tea roses, the brilliant orange tiger lilies, the stately hollyhocks. Someone—Cornelia Lindsey, obviously—had tended that garden with love, and it deserved respect by those who followed. Her descendants *should* be ashamed for not nurturing such an incredible legacy.

That was one of the things he liked most about his work. If a man spent time nurturing a garden, planting carefully, watering, weeding and fertilizing, he could count on it to offer beauty and behave predictably.

Nature had its whims, of course. Hurricane Isabel in 2003 had wreaked havoc on many of the stately old trees around the area and carved up riverbanks and shorelines. Even so, in Mike's view people were far less reliable, no matter how much nurturing they received. Linda was testament to that. And for all of the dedicated nurturing he gave to Jessie, the results were unpredictable, as well. That didn't mean he would ever stop trying, but he needed one part of his life—his work—that he could count on and control to some degree.

Each day when he drove past Rose Cottage, he looked for evidence that Melanie D'Angelo had clipped back the first rosebush, but so far the garden was as much a disaster as ever. Despite his own best advice to stay the hell away, it grated on him that she'd done absolutely nothing. It was almost as if she were deliberately defying him. But that was absurd, of course. Why would a stranger's opinion matter to her one way or the other? She was clearly perfectly comfortable with the overgrown surroundings. Maybe she didn't intend to stick around long enough for any of it to matter.

When he pulled off the road in front of the house, he told himself it was only because he had an hour to kill before his next appointment. He told himself he was only being neighborly, reassuring himself that Melanie hadn't been overcome by dust, squeezed to death by a tenacious honeysuckle vine or attacked by a stray water moccasin.

When she didn't respond to his knock with that lethal lamp in her hand, he went looking for her. That it also gave him a chance to explore the rest of the property was purely a side benefit.

As he'd expected, the view was magnificent, with crabbing boats on the horizon and sunshine glittering on the gentle swells of the bay. Old oak trees and a line of weeping willows near the water's edge dappled the overgrown lawn with shade. There were more eyesores, though. A now-dead oak had been ripped from the ground by the hurricane, its roots exposed and as tall as a house. It had lain there so long it had destroyed everything beneath it. Other trees had been split, most likely by lightning, and should have been trimmed back long ago if there was to be any chance to save them.

At first, with so many downed trees and plants to draw his attention, he almost missed Melanie, but he finally spotted her at the back edge of the lawn, sitting on a weathered glider, her shoulders hunched, one foot tucked under her, the other pushing the swing idly to and fro. She looked so thoroughly dejected and defeated he almost turned and left her to her obvious misery, but he couldn't bring himself to do it. Six years after learning the hardest lesson of his life, and he was apparently still a sucker for a vulnerable woman.

"Melanie?" He spoke her name softly, but she jumped just the same, sending tea splashing out of her cup and onto her long, bare legs.

"Damn, I'm sorry," he apologized, offering her a handkerchief to wipe up the mess.

"Do you intend to make a habit of starting my day by scaring me half to death?" she inquired irritably.

"Apparently so," he said with a shrug. "Sorry. Want me to leave?"

She actually took her time answering, which told him she was seriously weighing her options.

"No, I suppose not. Now that you're here, you might as well sit down," she said grudgingly. She slid over to make room for him on the swing.

Mike hesitated. The swing wasn't all that wide. Sitting beside her would put her a little too close for comfort.

"If you don't sit, I'll have to stand," she said eventually. "Looking up at you is giving me a crick in my neck."

Since there was no alternative other than the overgrown lawn, Mike sat on the swing, keeping a careful distance between them. "You haven't done much work on the yard yet," he noted, figuring he'd be safer if he put her on the defensive.

"I don't even know where to begin. Besides, I'm still trying to deal with the house."

He regarded her skeptically.

She immediately bristled. "Hey, don't look at me like

that. I *have* been working. In fact, once I got started, I decided the living room could use a fresh coat of paint and maybe some new curtains. That's made everything else look shabby, so the whole project has gotten out of hand. I've done nothing but paint for days now."

He didn't even try to contain his surprise. "You've painted the entire house since I last saw you?"

"Most of it," she said. "I haven't gotten to the attic bedrooms yet."

"When? How?"

She grinned. "Don't tell me you're actually impressed with something I've done."

Mike didn't want to concede that he was. "Haven't seen the job yet, have I?"

"Oh, come on, admit it. You didn't think I was going to lift a finger to put things right around here, did you? You probably thought I'd turn a blind eye to the work that needed to be done or, worse, just give up and run away."

"To be honest, that thought did occur to me. Why didn't you?"

"No place else I wanted to be," she admitted.

Her eyes were filled with that same sorrow he'd noted on his last visit. It made him want to hold her. To fight the urge, he balled his hands into fists and dug his nails into his palms.

"What's wrong with home?" he asked.

"If you're referring to the place where my parents live, there's nothing wrong with it."

"You're still living with your folks?"

She gave him a wry look. "You're going to keep poking at this, aren't you?"

"Just being neighborly."

"Well, then, let me make it as plain as I possibly can. I don't want to talk about Boston or my past."

Mike could understand that kind of reluctance all too well. "Okay. Then that brings us back to this place."

She gave him a faint grin. "Actually, Mr. Mikelewski—"

"Mike."

"Mike, then. When it comes to this place, I think you'll find I'm full of surprises. Once I get around to these gardens, I intend to see that you're awed and amazed. By the time I leave—"

He gave her a sharp look. He'd expected as much, so he was surprised by the disappointment that slashed through him. "You're not here to stay?"

"Nope. Just passing through."

That made her willingness to do anything at all to bring the place back to its former beauty all the more remarkable. He should have felt a wave of relief at the news that she wasn't staying, but he didn't. He told himself it was because there was no way she could turn this garden around on some two-week vacation or whatever she was taking here.

"That makes it even more important that you consider my offer of help," he told her. "You won't be able to accomplish much on your own during a brief vacation."

She gave him a long, steady look, then nodded. "I'll keep that in mind. And for the record, I'm not exactly on vacation. It's more like a sabbatical."

"How long?"

"I'm not sure."

He saw her evasiveness as just more evidence that she couldn't be counted on to make a real difference here. "Say you do all this work," he said, regarding her curiously, "who'll look after it once you're gone? Or do you plan to abandon it again?"

"To be honest, I hadn't thought that far ahead," she told him. "Right now I'm barely planning this afternoon, much less tomorrow or next week."

"Drifting's fine for a time," he said. He'd done his share in those first weeks after he and Linda had separated. Only Jessie's demand for attention had kept him focused at all. He glanced at the woman next to him and added, "But making it a way of life is dangerous."

"Oh?" she asked, her tone edgy. "Do you have a lot of experience drifting along?"

Mike thought about the question before responding. When it came to emotional drifting, he'd become a grand champion, but having Jessie hadn't allowed him to drift in any other way for long. She forced him to live in the moment, since plans could get scrambled in a heartbeat on one of her bad days.

"Everyone needs goals," he said at last.

She regarded him curiously. "What are yours?"

The conversation was getting way too serious and increasingly personal. Mike grinned, taking that as his cue to leave before he did or said something he'd regret. "I only have one goal that concerns you…getting you to fix up this garden." He winked at her. "See you around."

On his way back to his car, Mike couldn't resist taking a peek in the front window. His jaw dropped. Melanie had indeed painted. The walls, which had been a dingy cream on his last visit, were now a sunny yellow. The trim was white, and the sheer curtains billowing at the windows were fresh as a breeze. A blue-and-white spatterware pitcher held a bouquet of daffodils. If every room had been transformed like this one, Melanie D'Angelo was going to bring Rose Cottage back to life.

He couldn't help wondering, though, what it was going to take to put a sparkle back into her eyes.

"Not my job," he told himself grimly, then wondered why the hell he'd needed to utter the obvious warning. It should have been a given.

Maybe it had something to do with the fact that the whole time he'd been sitting in that swing he'd wanted to haul her into his arms and kiss her until that sad mouth of hers curved into a smile. That was damn dangerous thinking for a man who'd vowed never to get involved in another relationship that could break either his heart or his daughter's.

Melanie was feeling inspired. The living room at Rose Cottage had turned out so well that she was ready to tackle the rest of the house. She'd gone through a dozen different decorating magazines and turned down the corners of every color scheme that appealed to her.

Now she was on a mission to see what she could find in the local stores to use as some sort of centerpiece— a piece of pottery, a painting, throw pillows—in each room to set the tone she wanted to achieve. Since she was unemployed and using her dwindling savings to accomplish the makeover, she had to be frugal. Fortunately, there were all sorts of antique shops tucked away in the Northern Neck, and not all of them dealt with high-end items she couldn't possibly afford. Besides, she liked the idea of bringing in things with a history.

For her own room she was looking for the shades of the sea—blue, soft green, pale gray—but she couldn't quite resist an occasional burst of orange or pink or even red in an old picture for the walls or a pillow that could be tossed on the bed. After all, even the tranquil bay turned brilliant shades of orange at sunset.

She'd just emerged from a shop in the neighboring town of Kilmarnock, feeling triumphant about finding a cobalt blue pitcher inside, when she spotted Mike's truck across the street. Her heart did a little stutter step of anticipation. Because of that, she would have hurried on, but he came out of the real estate office and immediately spotted her.

Crossing the street with his long stride, he studied her with his usual solemn expression. "You look pleased with yourself," he concluded.

She lifted the bag containing her treasured pitcher. "Successful bargain hunting," she told him. Because she couldn't resist, she pulled the dark blue pitcher from the bag and held it up to the light, which made the old glass sparkle like sapphires. "Isn't it amazing?"

His gaze was on her, not the pitcher at all, when he echoed, "Amazing."

Her heart skipped a beat under that intense gaze. "You're not looking at the pitcher."

He shrugged and dutifully shifted his gaze. "It's a nice one, all right. It would look good with flowers in it."

She laughed. "Do you ever think about anything besides gardens?"

"Sure."

"Such as?"

"Have lunch with me and I'll tell you."

The faintly flirtatious words seemed to catch him by surprise as much as they did her. Melanie was tempted to refuse, but the idea of another lonely meal back at the house held no appeal. Even the company of this dour man with the one-track mind was more intriguing than eating one more tuna on rye by herself.

"Sure," she said at last.

When they walked into the brightly lit café, it was

already crowded with a mix of locals and tourists, each type readily identifiable. The locals wore slacks, long-sleeved shirts and ties or dresses and heels, while the tourists were armed with cameras, maps and local guidebooks.

Mike spotted a table in the back and led the way, pausing to greet several people he knew. By the time they'd reached the vacant table, he'd introduced Melanie to so many friendly people, many of whom had known her grandmother, that the names were a jumble in her head.

A pretty blond waitress in her late twenties made a harried pass by their table to drop off menus and water. Melanie noticed that, rushed as she was, the woman managed a warm, lingering smile for Mike. He, however, barely seemed to notice.

"The crab cakes are good here," Mike told Melanie without bothering to pick up the menu himself. "And the burgers."

"How's the grilled-chicken caesar salad?" Melanie asked and got a raised eyebrow in response. She chuckled. "Too girlie for you?"

"Hey, I burn a lot of calories in my work. I need more protein than some little chicken breast and a bunch of lettuce leaves for lunch," he said disdainfully.

"And the fries that go with the burger, are they an important source of sustenance, too?"

"Absolutely," he said, poker-faced. "But it's the chocolate shake that really keeps me going."

To Melanie's surprise, after days of having very little appetite, her mouth was suddenly watering. "I'll have that, then."

"The shake?"

"No, all of it," she said decisively.

His eyes widened. "All of it?"

"Burger, fries and shake," she confirmed. "If the pies are homemade, I might have to have dessert, too."

When the waitress returned, she gave Melanie only a passing glance before focusing her attention on Mike.

"How've you been? I haven't seen you and Jess in here in ages."

Mike seemed vaguely uncomfortable. "We've been busy." He gestured in Melanie's direction. "Have you met Melanie D'Angelo? She's living at the Lindsey place. Cornelia Lindsey was her grandmother. Melanie, this is Brenda Chatham. She owns this place."

Brenda barely spared a nod in Melanie's direction—acknowledged and dismissed—before giving Mike another broad smile. "How about that dinner I've been promising you? I have an awesome recipe for barbecued ribs."

Mike frowned. "Thanks anyway, but my schedule's pretty tight right now. Speaking of that, we'd better get our orders in so I can get back to work."

Brenda didn't even try to hide her disappointment. "Your usual?"

Mike nodded. "And Melanie will have the same. How do you want your burger, sweetheart?"

Melanie ignored the endearment, because she saw exactly what he was trying to do, create an intimacy between them that would finally get Brenda's attention. "Medium rare," she told Brenda.

"Sure thing," Brenda said.

After she'd gone, Mike regarded Melanie with a rueful expression. "Sorry about that. Brenda has some crazy idea that we'd make a good couple. I've tried to set her straight, but she's persistent."

"Have you considered just telling her you're not interested?"

He looked horrified at the thought. "Wouldn't that be rude?"

Melanie couldn't help chuckling, though she should have found his lack of candor troubling. "Actually I'd prefer to think of it as being honest, assuming you really aren't interested. She is an attractive woman, after all."

He stared in the direction of the kitchen, looking perplexed. "Is she?"

A man who didn't notice a willing blonde with huge brown eyes and a gorgeous figure? Melanie shook her head. She hadn't realized such men existed. Of course, maybe his lack of interest had something to do with the mysterious Jess Brenda had mentioned. "Who's Jess?"

Mike seemed taken aback by the question. "My daughter," he said eventually. "She's six. Most people call her Jessie."

Memories of Jeremy and his silence on the subject of his very real family slammed into her. "When were you planning on telling me about her?" she asked tightly.

His gaze narrowed. "It's not as if she's a secret. Most people in town know I have a child."

"I didn't."

"Okay, then, now you know. I have a daughter."

"And a wife?"

"No," he said tersely, almost as visibly tense now as Melanie was. "Let's talk about something else."

"Such as?"

"Boston and why you ran away from it," he suggested.

Melanie immediately saw what he was doing. She had her off-limits topics and so did he. She couldn't shake the feeling, though, that she at least needed to know if Jess's mother was completely out of the picture or not.

"One last question and I'll get off the subject of your personal life, okay?"

He gave her a grim look. "You can ask, but I reserve the right not to answer."

"Are you and Jess's mother divorced?"

"Yes."

Relief, out of all proportion given the circumstances, flooded through her. Whatever secrets Mike had about his family, at least she knew they weren't likely to come back and bite her in the butt the way Jeremy's had. Of course, the tension in his shoulders and the dark shadows in his eyes suggested there were things he *was* hiding.

So what? she chided herself. It wasn't as if she were dating the man. This was a casual lunch with a near stranger who'd offered to save her from another lonely meal. Nothing more. She was only here for a few weeks, anyway. Nothing would come of it, even if she were inclined to let another man into her life—which she wasn't.

The burgers arrived just then. Brenda plunked Melanie's down with a little less care than she did Mike's. It also looked suspiciously as if it had been deliberately burned to a crisp. Melanie put ketchup and mustard on it without comment.

"Trade with me," Mike said at once, his expression grim.

She stared at him. "Why? You didn't order yours burned, either."

"No, but yours came that way because of me. I'll eat it."

"Mike, it's okay. Really." She bit into the burger to prove the point, then chewed the tough-as-leather meat as if it were the best she'd ever eaten.

He sighed, then looked around till he caught Brenda's

eye. "Brenda, there's a little problem here. Melanie's burger is beyond well done. She ordered medium rare. So, since we're both on a schedule, here's what we'll do. Her meal is going to be on the house, okay? And the next time I bring her in here, you're going to go out of your way to see that her food is prepared exactly the way she orders it."

Melanie wasn't sure whether her mouth or Brenda's dropped more, but they were both obviously startled by Mike's deadly serious tone.

"You think I did that on purpose?" Brenda demanded, using indignation rather effectively.

"I know you did."

"I'm not the cook," she reminded him.

"But you do write the tickets, and Boomer wouldn't do a thing on that grill except what you tell him to do," Mike said. "He knows you'll fire him otherwise."

Brenda forced a tight smile and turned to Melanie. "Sorry about the mix-up. The lunch is on me."

"That's not necessary," Melanie began, only to have Mike interrupt.

"Oh, yes, it is," he said. "Brenda wants all of her regular customers to go away happy, don't you?"

"I pride myself on it," Brenda said, not looking any too happy herself.

"Thank you, then," Melanie said graciously. "I know anyone can have an off day in the kitchen. I'm sure that's what happened here."

"Exactly," Brenda said, seizing on the proffered out. "Boomer's a little distracted today, that's all it is. I'd better go have a talk with him."

After she'd gone, Melanie frowned at Mike. "You didn't need to make such a big deal out of it, you know."

"Yes, I did. Weren't you the one who said Brenda deserved honesty?"

Melanie bit back a grin. "I was referring to your disinclination to go out with her."

He shrugged. "Honesty is honesty. I'll work up to the other thing."

"You're just afraid if you tell her, once and for all, that you're not interested, she'll start burning your burgers," Melanie accused.

"Damn straight," he agreed without the slightest sign of repentance.

"Can I ask you another personal question?" When he didn't immediately shake his head, she went on, "She's an attractive woman and she seems nice enough. Why aren't you interested?"

"My life's complicated enough. I'm not looking for a relationship."

Melanie could relate to that. "And I imagine it's a whole lot easier to give a rosebush what it needs than it is to deal with a woman."

His lips quirked slightly. "Couldn't have said it better myself."

Even though she could relate all too well to where he was coming from, some traitorous little voice deep inside her couldn't help murmuring, "Lucky rosebush."

Mike regarded her oddly. "What was that?"

Oh, Lord, had she really said that out loud? "Nothing," she insisted, her cheeks burning.

"I thought you said something about the rosebushes," he persisted.

She feigned confusion. "Really? I was thinking about what you've been saying about what bad shape they're in. Maybe I said something about that without thinking."

A grin tugged at his lips. "Now who's being dishonest, darlin'?"

"I'm not your darling," she said irritably.

"I notice you didn't deny being dishonest, though. Maybe you're just telling a little white lie to spare my feelings."

She frowned at him. "Are you always this impossible?"

He laughed at that. "So they say." He stood up and grabbed the check. "Gotta run, darlin'."

She was about to utter yet another protest at the endearment when she spotted Brenda heading their way. To Melanie's shock, Mike leaned down and brushed a kiss across her lips. No doubt it was only meant to add to the impression that they were a couple, but Melanie's lips felt singed, anyway. She couldn't have uttered a word if her life depended on it. Instead, she grabbed her shake with trembling fingers and drank the last drops of thick chocolate. It was still deliciously cold, but it wasn't half as frosty as the look Brenda gave her when she finally managed to make her exit. She had a feeling that through no fault of her own, she'd just made her first enemy in town.

3

It was the scent of lilacs that brought Melanie out of the house on a rainy Saturday morning the second week in April. It had been years since she'd smelled that aroma, and it never failed to remind her of her grandmother. For all the showy roses in her grandmother's garden, it was the lilacs she'd loved most. She'd filled the house with huge vases of them during the short blooming season. And, rain or shine, she'd thrown open the windows for yet more of their sweet scent.

Now, though, the clusters of lavender flowers were fighting for breath on the overgrown bushes that had been invaded by the twisting vines of honeysuckle. Melanie stared at the mess with dismay, understanding fully for the first time why Mike was so thoroughly disgusted by the neglect. These once-thriving bushes were about to be destroyed.

Inspired to save the lilacs, she went inside, found the key to the garden shed, then headed outdoors with some trepidation to see what tools were available. With any luck, she wouldn't find any snakeskins dangling on the hooks along with the clippers and rakes.

It took several tries to get the old key to work in the

rusty lock on the shed, but inside she found every gardening tool imaginable, all kept in pristine condition aside from way too many spiderwebs to suit her. She gingerly selected one and wiped it off with the old rag she'd brought with her, then went outside to begin the daunting task of putting things to rights in the garden.

Oblivious to the light rain, she began snipping the honeysuckle vines, then tugging the endless strands out of the bushes and piling them into a garbage can. Yanking the roots from the ground was an even more thankless task, one that quickly had her sweating and cursing a blue streak.

She'd filled three cans when she heard the crunch of tires on gravel and a car engine cut off out front. A door slammed, then there was a low murmur of voices suddenly punctuated by a scream.

"No, Daddy! No!"

Melanie dropped her clippers and ran to the front to find Mike bent over beside the car trying to extricate a screaming, kicking child.

"What on earth?" she murmured.

Mike's head snapped up and hit the edge of the door frame.

"Don't get any wild ideas," he said, looking thoroughly defeated. "My daughter's terrified of this place for some reason. She thinks it's haunted."

Melanie took in his weary expression, then glanced at the stricken child whose sobs were finally beginning to lessen as she eyed Melanie with wariness. Nudging Mike aside, Melanie said, "Let me give it a try, okay? I assume this is Jessie."

"Right."

Melanie gazed into deep blue eyes, several shades darker than her father's. They were glistening with tears.

Her fine blond hair was slipping free of a bright-pink scrunchie.

"Hey, Jessie. I'm Melanie," she said quietly. "I live here."

The little girl stared back solemnly, taking in that news. Melanie waited.

"Are you a ghost?" Jessie finally asked in a voice barely above a frightened whisper.

Melanie bit back a smile. "I don't think so. Want to find out for sure?"

Jessie looked intrigued. "How?"

"Pinch me."

"Really?" Jessie glanced up at her father, who shrugged.

"Won't it hurt?" she asked Melanie, her brow creased in a worried frown.

"Not if I'm a ghost."

Jessie reached out with her dainty little hand and gently pinched Melanie's arm.

"Ouch," Melanie said with an exaggerated grimace.

"I'm sorry," Jessie whispered at once.

"It's okay. I guess we know now that I'm not a ghost, right?"

"I guess so," Jessie said, though she still sounded doubtful.

"Want to come into the house?" Melanie asked. "We can check to see if there are any ghosts inside, and your dad can chase them away. What do you think?"

Jessie nodded shyly and held out her arms. Melanie released the seat belt, then lifted the girl out and set her on the ground. She immediately clutched Melanie's hand.

When they stepped through the gate, Melanie caught the look of surprise in Mike's eyes when he spotted the cans filled with vines.

"Been working, I see," he said.

"For hours."

"It's a start," he said grudgingly.

Melanie stared at him. "That's all you have to say?"

A smile tugged at the corners of his mouth. "That's all you've done."

Because Jessie was regarding them with another worried frown, Melanie held back the sharp retort she wanted to make. Instead, she asked, "Why are you here, Mike? Did you stop by just to annoy me?"

"Actually we came because we're going to a nursery over in White Stone. I thought you might want to ride along and get some ideas."

Melanie gave him a wry look. "Don't you think I should get rid of what I have before I start thinking about what to put in the ground?"

"Never hurts to plan ahead. Bring that picture you showed me. I'll show Jessie the swing while you get it."

His arrogant assumption that she would fall in with his plans was almost enough to force a rebellion, but something about Mike Mikelewski's quiet determination to restore her grandmother's gardens got to her. Since he hadn't asked for a dime for his advice or his help, she had to assume it was because he genuinely cared about setting the neglected landscape to rights. She'd be foolish to ignore such an offer out of pure stubbornness.

Even so, a cautionary alarm sounded in her head. Mike might be divorced, but his tense tone the other day suggested there was not only an ex-wife lurking somewhere, but quite possibly an ex-wife who liked to stir up trouble. Melanie wasn't inclined to get tangled up in the middle of that kind of complicated situation.

She'd make this innocuous-enough trip to the nursery with Mike because it was something she'd need to do sooner or later, anyway. But after this, she vowed, she'd discourage any further contact between them.

Not that Mike had actually shown one iota of personal interest in her, she was forced to admit. But every time she looked into his eyes, she suddenly wanted things she'd sworn never to allow into her life again. And that wouldn't do. It wouldn't do at all.

"I promised Jessie a tour of the house," she told him. "We're ghost busting."

His lips quirked at that. "Then, by all means, let's go inside."

"You're in charge of banishing any ghosts we find," Melanie added.

He nodded. "Got it."

Jessie peered up at him. "Are you scared, Daddy?"

"Nah," he said. "No silly old ghost is a match for me."

While Mike was showing Jessie around and conducting dramatic searches of closets and cupboards for signs of ghosts, Melanie took the time to wash her hands and run a brush through her tangled hair.

"No ghosts," Mike eventually hollered from downstairs. "We're going out to the swing."

"I'll be right there," Melanie called back.

On her way out, she grabbed the photo of the garden. Outside, she could hear Jessie's squeals of delight echoing from the backyard. Obviously, her earlier fears had been calmed by her father's ghost-busting expedition.

Melanie rounded the house and spotted the little girl sitting atop Mike's broad shoulders as he stood at the water's edge. She had her hands fisted in his hair in a way that had to hurt like the dickens, but he wasn't complaining.

"Daddy, no!" Jessie shouted, giggling.

"You don't want to go for a swim?" he teased, taking another step toward the bay.

"No!"

Melanie listened to them for several minutes, enjoying the banter and feeling just a little like an outsider. Oddly, it reminded her of the way she'd felt when Jeremy had finally admitted the truth about his family. Aside from the burst of anger, she'd immediately known he had something important that was missing from her life, something she might never have. It was as if she were being taunted by possibilities, and the unfairness of it had hurt.

Mike chose that moment to turn around, and the laughter on his lips promptly died. He studied her intently. "Everything okay?"

Melanie forced a smile. "Fine."

"You saved me," Jessie told her. "Daddy was going to make me swim in the water and it's too cold."

"Oh, I don't think you were ever at risk," Melanie told her. "Something tells me your dad takes very good care of you."

Jessie nodded. "He does, but he's not a mom. Moms know it's too soon to go swimming."

Melanie didn't miss the tiny flash of hurt in Mike's eyes, but he didn't respond.

"Dads know stuff like that, too," Melanie assured Jessie. "My dad used to take my sisters and me to Cape Cod in the summer, and he knew all the important stuff about swimming. My mom never even got her toes wet."

Jessie studied her solemnly, as if she were trying to process such a thing. "Not even once?"

"Never," Melanie told her. "So, you see, it seems to me like you haven't been giving your dad nearly enough credit."

Mike gave her a grateful look as he tucked Jessie into the backseat and snapped the seat belt.

"My dad knows lots about flowers and stuff," Jessie volunteered proudly, obviously eager to jump on the bandwagon about her father's unique talents. "People pay him to make their gardens grow. He's teaching me."

"And do you have your own garden?" Melanie asked her.

Jessie nodded. "I will this summer. It's gonna have squashes and tomatoes and beans for the bunnies."

Melanie chuckled. "I thought people ate beans."

"They do, but bunnies like them better than I do, so I'm growing them just for the bunnies. I got it all planned out. We're gonna buy seeds today. I get to pick 'em out." She peered intently at Melanie. "What are you gonna plant in your garden?"

"I'm not sure," Melanie admitted. "Your dad's going to help me figure that out."

"You probably need to grow some beans, too," Jessie advised her. "There's lots and lots of bunnies and I can't feed 'em all."

Melanie chuckled. "I'll think about that."

"I think we're going to concentrate on flowers for Melanie's garden today," Mike chimed in. He glanced at her. "And maybe think about an herb garden."

Melanie envisioned how happy an herb garden would make Maggie. "Definitely," she said. "Though I don't recall my grandmother having one."

"You don't have to recreate what she had exactly," Mike said. "Gardens evolve over time. Personally, I like a combination of the beautiful and the practical, but not everybody cares about growing their own food or herbs, not when there are farmer's markets all over this area offering fresh produce."

"I wouldn't mind growing tomatoes," Melanie said, thinking of how fabulous it would be to pick one for dinner and slice it to serve with mozzarella cheese and fresh basil, also from her own garden. Never mind that she was unlikely to be here when the time came to harvest the tomatoes.

Mike gave her a lingering look. "There you go," he teased. "You're beginning to envision the possibilities."

"How long does it take for a tomato plant to produce its first ripe tomato?" she asked.

"Sixty days or so, depending on the variety and the weather," he replied.

"Too long," she said, unable to contain a sigh of regret.

"Maybe you'll decide to stick around."

She shook her head. "Impossible."

"You have a job to get back to?"

"No."

"A boyfriend?"

"No."

"Then what's to stop you from staying till you pick your first homegrown tomato?"

"I don't have an endless supply of money," she told him frankly. "Sooner or later I'll have to go back to Boston and find another job."

"Find one here," he said. "There's lots of seasonal work, if you don't want something permanent. Hell, Brenda's always complaining that she can't find good summer help for the restaurant."

Melanie laughed. "Yes, I imagine she'd be absolutely delighted to hire me, since we got off to such a great start."

"I could put in a word for you," he offered.

"Thanks, but if I should happen to decide to stick

around, I'm capable of finding my own job. And having you intercede for me with Brenda would only add fuel to the resentment she already feels toward me."

"You have a point," he agreed. "What field were you in before?"

"My degree's in marketing, but I took a job as a receptionist when I got out of college."

He shot her a disbelieving look. "How long ago was that?"

"Not that long ago," she said defensively. "I worked my way through college—waiting tables, as a matter of fact—so I've only been out a couple of years."

"You have a degree in marketing, but you've been working as a receptionist? Are entry-level jobs in marketing that tough to find?"

"Actually this one was supposed to lead to a promotion, but it didn't work out that way," she said, unable to keep a defensive note out of her voice. She could hear how ridiculous it sounded that she'd wasted so much time waiting for the right chance to come along, instead of making it happen.

The management at Rockingham Industries had dangled the prospect of a marketing position in front of her, but she realized now that she'd made herself all but indispensable as a receptionist, doing the job so well that they'd left her right where she was. Jeremy had repeatedly promised to remind the executives that she was a good candidate to move up into his department, but somehow it had never happened. What a fool she'd been!

Fortunately Mike pulled into a parking lot at the nursery just then, so she didn't have to try to defend her decision. She scrambled out of the car and would have gone on ahead, if Jessie hadn't demanded that Melanie be the one to take her out of the car.

Mike gave Melanie an apologetic look. "Would you mind? Once she gets an idea into her head, there's no peace unless I go along with it. Some things aren't worth arguing over."

"No problem," Melanie assured him, helping Jessie out of the car. When the girl tucked her hand trustingly into Melanie's, something in Melanie's heart flipped over.

"Can you help me pick out seeds?" Jessie asked. "I know where they are."

"Wouldn't you rather have your dad do that? He's the expert."

"I want you to do it," Jessie insisted. *"Please!"*

There was an unmistakable edge of hysteria in the little girl's voice that caught Melanie by surprise. She glanced toward Mike.

"It's okay," he said. "If you don't mind taking her, it might be easier. I'll fill you in later."

Melanie nodded. She smiled down at Jessie. "Okay, then. It looks as if you and I are on a mission, Jessie. Show me those seeds."

When Jessie tugged her off in the direction of the seeds, Melanie glanced back and caught Mike's expression. He looked almost as bewildered and dismayed as she felt.

"Over here," Jessie said, giving Melanie's hand another tug. "See? Look at all the pretty pictures." She headed straight for a selection of vegetable seeds. She studied them as intently as another child might contemplate a video choice, then gave a little sigh.

"Is something wrong?" Melanie asked.

"I like these," Jessie admitted, "'cause you can see what they'll look like."

"Is there a problem with that?"

"Daddy says the best ones are over there, in those

bins," Jessie explained. "There aren't any pictures, so how can you tell if you'll like them?"

"Experience," Melanie said. "I imagine farmers know which ones produce the best crops, so they don't need to see a picture every time." Melanie took her over to the bins of seeds. "See, right here it says these seeds are for Silver Queen corn. I've had that, and it's the sweetest and best ever. I don't need to see a picture to know it's good."

Jessie regarded her with wide eyes. "We could grow corn?"

Melanie laughed at her amazement. "If you have enough room in your garden, you can."

"Daddy never said that, and we've got lots and lots of room. I want some of those seeds," she said at once.

Melanie filled a small bag for her, then labeled it. "Now what?"

"Read me another sign," Jessie commanded. "One for beans."

Melanie found several bins of bean seeds and read the labels.

Jessie peered at them worriedly. "Which ones do you think the bunnies will like best?"

"I imagine they'll be happy with whichever ones you choose," she said honestly. "But I'd pick these."

"Okay," Jessie said readily, reaching for the scoop and a bag that was way too big.

"Whoa!" Melanie protested. "Not so many. You just need a few."

"But I told you, we got lots and lots of bunnies."

"Even so, a few seeds will give you more than enough beans." She handed the child a small bag. "Fill this one up. Then let's go and find your dad."

When they found Mike, he was pushing a cart over-flowing with small plants and shrubs. Melanie eyed it warily. "You've gone a little overboard, haven't you? We never talked about planting bushes."

He laughed. "I do have other jobs," he told her. "Some people actually hire me to do this."

"Of course," she said at once, chagrined. "Is any of that for me?"

"I picked out some perennials for you. I went by what I saw in the picture. These are hollyhocks," he said, showing her a half-dozen plants. "And summer phlox." He gestured toward a larger plant. "Foxglove. And back here are some daylilies we can plant in clusters. It's not much, but it's a start. I didn't want to get too much until we've cleaned out more of the weeds and gotten some decent topsoil in there." He met her gaze. "What do you think?"

"That I'm completely out of my element."

"Which is why I'll be around," he said. "That is, if you want my help."

She gave him a wry look. "I think we can both agree that it's going to be a necessity. We'll have to discuss your fees, though."

"No charge," he said at once.

"Mike, that's not right. You're a professional. I have to pay you."

He returned her look with a stubborn gaze. "Let's just say you've earned at least one afternoon of my time."

She gave him a perplexed look. "How?"

He nodded toward Jessie, who was sitting on the edge of the large cart contentedly counting out the bean seeds. "Keeping her occupied was a huge help to me."

"But all I did was help her pick out some seeds," Melanie protested.

"Which you apparently managed to do without her having a tantrum," Mike said. "I've never once accomplished that. In case you haven't noticed, Jessie can be headstrong."

"Most kids can be," Melanie said. "It just takes a little finesse to work around that."

"Finesse and patience," Mike corrected. "Sometimes I'm woefully lacking in both. Let's just say I'm grateful and leave it at that, okay?"

Melanie studied him and thought she detected sincere appreciation in his eyes. She wasn't entirely sure she understood it, but it was clear he thought he owed her.

"Thank you," she said at last. "I know wherever she is, my grandmother thanks you, too."

He chuckled. "And Lord knows I can use an angel looking out for me. Now let's pay for this stuff and get out of here while peace reigns."

"How about I treat us all to ice cream on the way home?" Melanie offered.

Jessie's head shot up. "Chocolate?"

"If that's what you want," Melanie agreed. "And if your dad says it's okay."

Mike grinned. "You'll never hear me saying no to ice cream, especially not chocolate, right, Jess?"

"That's 'cause it's the bestest," Jessie said solemnly.

"I agree," Melanie said. She leaned down. "You know how it's best of all?"

"How?"

"With hot fudge on top," Melanie said.

Mike groaned, even as Jessie's eyes lit up.

"Sundaes!" Jessie shouted.

"*You* are cleaning up the mess," Mike warned Melanie, his expression dire.

"No problem," Melanie said cheerfully.

He gave her a long, hard look, then chuckled. "That's what you think."

4

Mike couldn't get over the fact that Jessie seemed to have taken such an instant liking to Melanie. She'd been on her best behavior for most of the day. He knew from bitter experience, though, that her good mood could end in a heartbeat. Even as he parked in front of the ice cream shop, he had this gut-deep sense of dread that they were testing his daughter's limits.

Still, once Melanie had mentioned ice cream, there had been no way to bow out of the excursion gracefully. That would have caused a scene, no question about it.

On the entire trip back to town from the nursery, Jessie had debated whether she wanted whipped cream and a cherry on top of her sundae. To her credit Melanie had shown endless patience with the drawn-out discussion. In fact, she'd seemed equally eager to decide on the merits of the extra toppings. Most people would have jumped screaming from the car after the first ten minutes. Hell, Mike was about ready to leap from the moving vehicle himself.

"Have you two decided yet?" he asked hopefully as they went inside. Thankfully the weather was cool enough that not too many people were interested in ice cream to beat the heat. The three of them had the place almost to themselves. He'd been here far too many times when the line had been long and Jessie hadn't been able to make up her mind which flavor she wanted. The decision-making process had taxed his patience, as well as that of most of the people in line behind them.

"I'm having chocolate ice cream and lots and lots of whipped cream on my hot-fudge sundae," Melanie said at once. "How about you, Jessie?"

"Me, too," The six-year-old responded eagerly, looking to Melanie for approval.

"Good choice," Melanie praised. "How about you, Mike?"

Stunned by the success of her clever tactic, he said, "Let's make it easy and make it three. You two find a table and I'll get the ice cream."

"No way," Melanie said. "This was my idea and my treat."

Jessie peered up at her. "But boys always pay when they take girls on a date, right, Daddy?"

"This isn't a date," Melanie said a little too firmly.

Her quick response made Mike all the more determined to act as if it were. "Close enough," he insisted, then gazed into her eyes. "Unless you want to arm wrestle me for the honors." He deliberately flexed his muscle, barely containing a grin as her eyes locked on his arm.

"Show-off," Melanie muttered, tearing her gaze away with unmistakable reluctance. "I won't create a scene and humiliate you by taking you on." She lifted her gaze to his. "But we will debate this later."

He nodded. He had a hunch he'd pushed the limits of her independent streak today. There was a spark of fire in her eyes that he'd never noticed before. He figured that had to be a good thing, given her apparent despondency and lack of interest when they'd first met, but it was probably something he didn't want to stir up too often.

Melanie led Jessie to a table and got her seated with an ease that once again surprised him. Maybe what Jessie had needed all along was a mother's touch. Maybe he was the one at fault all this time, the cause of her tantrums. Lord knew he'd made a lot of blunders while he'd been getting a grip on being a single dad.

But even as the thought occurred to him, Mike knew he was being foolish. Melanie was merely a novelty. She was giving Jessie the kind of undivided attention the child craved. His daughter's good behavior had nothing to do with Melanie's parenting skills versus his own, he reassured himself.

But as reasonable as that explanation was, he still found it irritating that Melanie seemed to have some sort of knack for calming his daughter. Realizing he was actually jealous of the woman, instead of being grateful and admiring, he bit back a curse at his own stupidity.

When he arrived at the table with the ice cream, Jessie was chattering like a little magpie about school and her friends. Mike learned more in five minutes than he had on a dozen rides home. Once again that nasty little trace of resentment crept over him, but he forced it back down and concentrated instead on his sundae.

"I dropped it!"

Out of the blue, Jessie's voice rose to a wail, drawing the attention of everyone in the shop.

"It's okay," Melanie murmured, wiping up the spoonful of ice cream that had fallen into Jessie's lap before Mike could react.

"No, it's all ruined," Jessie insisted, throwing her spoon across the room. "I hate ice cream."

She was about to knock her bowl from the table, when Mike snatched it out of reach.

"That's enough," he said firmly.

"But it's mine," Jessie screamed, trying to hit him.

For just an instant, Melanie looked stunned by the unexpected burst of temper. Mike waited for her to announce a sudden need for a trip to the bathroom or some other escape, but instead, she calmly pushed her own bowl of ice cream away.

"I've had enough, too," she said as if more than half of her sundae weren't still in the bowl. "Jessie, why don't you and I go outside and wait for your dad?"

Mike started to protest, but she gave a slight shake of her head.

"Come on, Jessie. I think I saw some really cool books in the store next door. Want to go look at them?"

Jessie sniffed and blinked back tears, clearly torn between escalating her tantrum and the offer of a trip to the bookstore. She looked at Mike as if he might say something that would tilt the decision one way or another. Instead, taking his cue from Melanie, he simply waited silently for Jessie to make up her mind.

Eventually she scrambled out of her chair and tucked her hand in Melanie's. "Can I get a book about crabs?" she asked hopefully.

"If they have one," Melanie promised.

Jessie beamed. "They do. It's a whole series. I have two, but there are more."

"Then we'll find one," Melanie said.

And then they were gone. Mike stared after them, not sure whether to sigh or laugh. He couldn't very well allow Melanie to bribe his daughter every time she threatened to throw a tantrum, but he had to admit that it had worked like a charm just now.

Or maybe it wasn't the promise of a bribe at all, but simply the distraction. Melanie had taken Jessie's attention off of her frustration and focused it on something else. Maybe there was a lesson for him in that, if he wasn't too busy feeling jealous to learn it.

He contemplated that as he slowly ate the rest of his sundae, barely tasting it but enjoying the brief reprieve. How had a single woman gained so much insight into his daughter in such a short time, when he spent most of his life being totally at a loss?

It was the novelty of it, he concluded once more. It had to be. Melanie could have endless patience because this was the first time she'd had to deal with Jessie's whims. His own patience was threadbare. Maybe he and his daughter needed to take more breaks from each other, but he'd avoided leaving her with sitters, mostly out of guilt. Without a mother in her life, Jessie needed his constant attention—or so he'd convinced himself. Could it be that he'd been wrong about that? Had she needed to be exposed to more people and more social situations than he'd permitted?

Whatever it was that gave Melanie such endless patience, he was grateful. Too bad she wasn't sticking around. Summer was just around the corner, and he was in desperate need of day care. He'd hire Melanie in a heartbeat, if she were willing. Jessie had pretty much worn out her welcome at every child-care center in the region, and taking her with him on jobs had proved to be frustrating for both of them.

The temptation to broach the subject anyway was almost too great to resist. What stopped him was the realization that it wasn't all about Jessie. He'd been more at peace today than he had been in a long time. There was something soothing about Melanie's company that worked its magic on him as well as his daughter.

And sharing the responsibility of caring for Jessie, even for a few hours, had shown him what life might have been like if things had turned out differently with Linda. He'd gotten a taste of being a real family, and the pitiful truth was, he'd liked it.

Was it possible that he'd been waiting all these years for someone like Melanie to come along? Someone who'd take them both on?

No, he said staunchly. Absolutely not!

But even as he mentally uttered the disclaimers, he could hear that they weren't ringing the least bit true. On some level, something had shifted today. Seeing Melanie had stopped being all about fixing up the Rose Cottage garden and had somehow gotten to be about healing his and Jessie's wounded hearts.

Jessie was a complicated and troubled little girl. Melanie had picked up on that even before Mike had hinted at it. The tantrum at the end of a long day wasn't that unusual, but there'd been plenty of other signs, including the way Mike tiptoed around his daughter as if he'd do just about anything to avoid an outburst. Naturally Jessie, being a smart kid, had caught on to that, and she knew just how to play him and his single-dad guilt.

Despite all the problems, Melanie couldn't help being charmed by the six-year-old. She hadn't been around many children, but she'd discovered today that she loved the way Jessie's mind worked, the way her imagination knew no bounds. It was also a boon to her wounded pride to have the little girl regard her with undisguised adoration.

Of course, Melanie warned herself, it wasn't healthy to get too attached or to allow Jessie to become too attached to her. This was a one-time outing, not the start of something.

Still, she couldn't help liking the way Jessie snuggled against her as they sat on the floor in the children's section of the bookstore and pored over the selections.

"I like this one best," Jessie said, after they'd looked at a dozen or more choices. "Are you sure I can have it?"

"Absolutely. It's a present," Melanie said.

Jessie studied her worriedly. "You and my daddy are friends, right?"

"Yes," Melanie said, not sure why that was relevant.

"Then it's okay," Jessie concluded happily. "I couldn't take it if you were a stranger."

Ah! "No, you couldn't," Melanie agreed. "But we can check with your dad, if that would make you feel better."

Jessie eyed the book with longing. "He might say no," she said hesitantly.

"Leave your father to me," Melanie told her with a confidence she had no right to feel. She'd taken a lot for granted today. The mere fact that she'd insisted on bringing Jessie to the bookstore to avert a tantrum was probably more interference than some would have tolerated. But after an initial show of reluctance, Mike had actually looked relieved. She had a hunch he'd been at his wit's end with Jessie for some time now.

Suddenly Jessie jumped up and bolted, clutching the book. "Daddy, look at the present Melanie's getting me!"

Melanie gazed up into Mike's turbulent eyes and guessed that she'd overstepped. "It's just a book. And she read me the first page all by herself, so I thought she deserved it."

His gaze faltered at that. He hunkered down in front of Jessie. "You read the whole first page?"

"Uh-huh. Want to hear?"

"Absolutely."

She plopped right down on the floor in the middle of the aisle and opened the book on her lap. "Chadwick," she began, then looked at her father. "Remember him, Daddy? He's the crab."

Mike grinned, pride shining in his eyes. "I remember."

Jessie went on to read an entire sentence, slowly but without a single mistake. She gazed up at Mike. "Is that right?"

His smile spread. "Absolutely perfect. I guess the book is yours, but I'm buying it." He pulled some money from his pocket and gave it to her. "You take it up front where I can see you and pay for it."

"Okay," Jessie said happily and ran off.

"I would have bought it," Melanie told him. "I'm the one who made the deal with her."

"I know, but it's better this way."

"Why?"

"Because I don't want her to start to count on you."

"It's a book, Mike, not a commitment."

He regarded her with troubled eyes. "Not to Jessie. Don't make promises to her, Melanie. Not when you're leaving."

Suddenly she understood. "You're comparing me to her mother."

His expression turned dark. "You're nothing like Linda," he said bitterly. "But you will leave. You've told me that yourself. I have to protect her from that kind of disappointment. Kids tend to think abandonment is all about them, no matter how often you tell them otherwise."

He walked away before she could think of anything to say. Besides, it wasn't the time or the place to pursue the subject, so Melanie simply followed him as he went after Jessie.

They drove back to her house in silence. Jessie had fallen asleep in the backseat, so Mike left her there and unloaded the plants quickly.

"Keep 'em watered till we can get them into the ground," he said when everything was out of the back of the truck. "I'll be by to help when I have some time."

"Sure," she said. "Thanks for taking me along today."

He gave her a curt nod, then strode back to the car and drove off, leaving Melanie to stare after him and wonder about the woman who'd hurt him so badly he didn't trust Melanie not to do the same. Worse, she wasn't sure she wouldn't. The only way to be sure was to avoid getting involved with him and Jessie in the first place.

Melanie wasn't all that surprised when Mike showed up on her doorstep on Monday morning, most likely right after dropping Jessie off at school.

"Do you have a minute?" he asked, looking vaguely uneasy.

"Sure. Come on in. I just made coffee. Want some?"

"Coffee sounds great."

He took a seat at the kitchen table, but when Melanie had handed him his mug of coffee and seated herself across from him, he avoided her gaze. She could have let the silence go on, but it was beginning to get on her nerves.

"I suppose you came by to warn me again about getting

too close to Jessie," she said. "I've thought about it, and I can see your point."

"Actually I came to apologize," he said, meeting her gaze. "I made it seem as if you'd done something wrong, when you'd been nothing but kind to her all day long. Most people wouldn't have jumped in to take charge when she was about to throw a tantrum. They'd have run for the hills."

"It wasn't a big deal. She's a great kid."

"She's a troubled kid," he corrected. "I'm sure you figured that out."

"Because you and her mom are divorced," Melanie said.

"That and…" He seemed to be struggling to find the right words. "Well, because her mom was addicted to drugs when Jessie was born. It's affected Jessie. She was born addicted, too."

"Oh, Mike, I'm so sorry."

"She's okay for the most part, but there are lingering effects, like the tantrums over nothing. One minute she's fine, the next she's out of control. It's like living with a time bomb, only I don't have any idea when it's set to go off."

Melanie's heart ached for both of them. "That must be incredibly frustrating for both of you."

He frowned. "I didn't come here so you could pity me. I just thought you should know why I'm so protective of her. Keeping Jessie on an even emotional keel is hard enough without people coming and going in her life."

Melanie wanted to argue that children needed to learn that people would always come and go, but how could she? Not only was it not her place, but it was probably entirely different for a child who'd lost her mother. Having that relationship severed at such an early age had to be traumatic. Additional losses would only bolster Jessie's fear that it was unsafe to give her love to anyone. It could have a lasting effect on her emotional well-being.

Before Melanie could think of what she could say, Mike stood up. "Well, that's all I wanted you to know. I'd better get going. I have a delivery at one of my jobs this morning, and I need to be there to supervise getting all the plants into the ground. I should be able to get by here to help you by midweek."

"Whenever it's convenient," she told him. "I just appreciate your willingness to take this on."

Melanie walked him back to the door. Impulsively, she reached up and touched his cheek. "You're a terrific dad, especially given the trying circumstances. I hope you know that."

Surprise flickered in his eyes. "What makes you say that?"

"You remind me of my own dad and, believe me, there's not a better one on earth. You're protective and attentive and you listen to Jessie. Most of all, it's obvious you adore her. She may miss having a mom in her life, but she's very lucky to have you."

For an instant this hulking, strong man looked flustered. "I don't know what to say."

Melanie grinned at him. "It's a compliment. All you need to say is thank you."

Instead, to her astonishment, he leaned down and kissed her—just the slightest grazing of warm lips against hers, but it was enough to send heat spiraling through her.

Then he was out the door. He was halfway to the street when he finally glanced back and caught her with her fingers against her lips. He winked.

"Thanks," he said.

Now she was the one who was flustered. "Anytime," she whispered, but only when he was too far away to hear her.

This visit to Rose Cottage was supposed to provide her with a whole new level of serenity, but suddenly Melanie was feeling anything but serene. She'd felt more clear-to-her-toes shock waves from that innocent little kiss than she'd ever felt in Jeremy's arms. Now wasn't that interesting?

And dangerous.

Mike had worked like a demon all day, pushing himself in the vain hope that sweat and hard work would make him forget all about that kiss. It had happened on impulse, just a quick little brush of his mouth over hers, mostly to see if it would rattle her half as much as her kind words and solemn expression had rattled him.

The joke had turned out to be on him. His blood had been humming all day long, and the scent of her had lingered with him. Apparently there wasn't enough perspiration on the planet to overpower it.

"Hey, Mike, we're supposed to provide the labor," Jeff Clayborne shouted.

"I'm just helping out a little," Mike responded, pausing long enough to wipe his brow with the already-soaked bandanna he'd stuck in his back pocket.

"You help out any more and we'll be out of jobs," Jeff retorted. "Take a break, man. I've got a Thermos of iced tea here that I'll share with you."

Mike knew all about Jeff's tea. It was so sweet it was enough to send most people into a diabetic coma. Jeff said the key to getting it that way was to boil the sugar right into it. Mike shuddered at the thought.

"I'll pass on the tea, thanks, but I will take a break.

I've got bottled water in my truck." He grabbed a bottle from the cooler in back, then joined the other man in the shade of an oak tree.

Jeff glanced over at him. "Something on your mind?"

"No. Why?"

"You usually work this hard when there's a problem with Jessie. Otherwise, you loaf around and supervise the rest of us."

"Very funny," Mike commented. "And you're totally off the mark. Jessie's great, actually."

"I imagine that has something to do with her new friend," Jeff said, his expression innocent.

Mike saw where this was going and wondered how word had gotten around so quickly. Then again, this was a small town.

"What new friend would that be?" he asked, keeping his own expression neutral.

"I heard blond hair and big blue eyes and legs that wouldn't quit." Jeff grinned wickedly. "Oh, wait, she would be *your* new friend, right?"

"Go to hell," Mike muttered.

"Heard she's new in town, that she's Cornelia Lindsey's granddaughter and that the three of you were over at the nursery on Saturday, then at the ice cream shop and then the bookstore."

"It's a damn good thing we weren't trying to sneak around," Mike muttered irritably.

Jeff laughed. "Yeah, well, you definitely picked the wrong place to live if you ever hope to keep your personal life a secret. Besides, an awful lot of people have been trying to set you up ever since you moved here, including my wife. You've turned 'em all down. Naturally they're curious when you managed to find someone all on your own. The staff at the nursery couldn't wait to report to Pam and me."

"Melanie doesn't have anything to do with my personal life," Mike insisted, figuring he would eventually burn in hell for the lie. "She's a client. Sort of."

"How does someone get to be a 'sort-of' client?" Jeff taunted. "Especially since you told me last week you weren't taking on any new jobs for a while."

"I'm helping her get the garden fixed up at her grandmother's place."

Jeff regarded him with amusement. "And I imagine she's 'sort of' paying you for your help. Am I right? What's the going rate for that kind of help? Dinner? A roll in the hay?"

Mike scowled at him. "It's not like that, dammit."

Jeff held up his hands. "Hey, okay. Don't get all worked up. I was just teasing."

"Yeah. That's the kind of teasing that can ruin someone's reputation. Knock it off."

Jeff's gaze narrowed. "Do you really have a thing for this woman?"

"No, absolutely not!" Mike responded fiercely.

Jeff studied him intently, then burst out laughing. "Oh, pal, you are in one helluva state of denial."

Mike glared at him. It was probably true, but his friend didn't need to be quite so gleeful about it. Mike stood up slowly, deliberately took his time over the last swallow of cool water from the bottle, then tossed it in a nearby trash bin. Only then did he meet Jeff's gaze.

"You don't know what you're talking about," he said quietly.

Jeff laughed. "Sure, I do. I said exactly the same thing about Pam till about fifteen minutes before the wedding ceremony. Denial's second nature to us, pal. Women know it, too. They just ignore our protests, and the next thing you know, *bam*, wedded bliss."

"Not gonna happen," Mike insisted. He'd been there, done that and lived to rue the day. Except for Jessie, he reminded himself quickly. She was worth all the rest.

She was also the reason why he'd never let things with Melanie go anywhere. Period.

He didn't waste his breath saying any of that to Jeff. Why spoil his gloating? Jeff clearly didn't believe any of his denials, anyway. Hell, after the impact that sweet, innocent little kiss had had on his system, Mike wasn't sure he believed them himself. Besides, perhaps the rumor of his interest in Melanie would finally get Pam off his case about going out with every available woman she ran across. Maybe that trip to the nursery hadn't been as innocent as he'd believed it to be. Maybe he'd subconsciously known that it would stir up talk, the kind of talk that could save him from all that unwanted matchmaking.

Jeff gave him a knowing look. "You're thinking this will get Pam to stop meddling, aren't you?"

"It crossed my mind," Mike admitted.

"Ha! This kind of rumor is all the motivation she needs to kick her campaign into high gear. You're matrimonial toast, buddy. Accept it now and save yourself a lot of aggravation."

Mike bit back a groan. "Can't you control your wife?"

Jeff gave him a sympathetic look. "You really don't know the first thing about women, do you?"

"No question about that," Mike agreed. "No question at all."

5

On Monday night the skies opened up, and the April showers began in earnest. They continued straight through the day on Tuesday and again on Wednesday. Dull gray clouds dumped sheets and sheets of endless, cold rain, turning the yard into a mud bath.

Melanie sat in the dreary kitchen, sipping a cup of tea, eating a freshly baked chocolate chip cookie that was burned on the edges, and regretting that she'd ever agreed to come to Rose Cottage. She was bored. She was lonely. Worst of all, she was daydreaming about yet another man she couldn't have.

There was little question in her mind that, despite his single status, Mike wasn't available. He'd clearly dedicated himself to raising his daughter and maybe to nursing whatever resentments he still felt toward his former wife. The very last thing Melanie needed in her life was a man whose heart wasn't free, whatever the reason.

She ought to pack up and head back to Boston before the appeal of that one kiss made mincemeat of her common sense. She ought to go back, find her dream job, maybe move into a new apartment and definitely throw herself into enough hobbies that she'd forget all about her knack for finding the wrong men. The D'Angelo women had been taught to be independent. She didn't need a man in her life.

Of course, watching the way her parents still got a little gleam in their eyes when they saw each other and their freely given affection with each other had made all of them long to achieve what their parents had. Colleen and Max D'Angelo made marriage look easy.

But even after convincing herself that it was time to go, Melanie reminded herself that it would be a shame to leave Rose Cottage before she finished doing something with her grandmother's garden. She'd studied that photo Mike had found so fascinating, and she was beginning to envision making the yard look like that again. It was the least she could do in her grandmother's memory.

Of course, if the rains kept up like this, it would be summer before the ground dried up enough for her to get the first flower planted. Melanie wanted to be back home before that, making plans, embarking on her new life.

She bit into another too-crisp cookie, then tossed it aside in disgust. If only she had Maggie's talent in the kitchen. Instead, she was an absolute disaster. Who else could manage to destroy slice-and-bake cookies?

Her pity party was in full swing when someone knocked on the front door, startling her. Melanie was so relieved by the prospect of a distraction, she practically ran to the door, then faltered when she glanced through the window and spotted a dripping-wet Mike and Jessie on the porch. The little twinge of excitement that formed low in her belly was a warning. She was way too eager to see these two. A smart woman would leave the door firmly closed.

Since she tended to listen to her heart, not her head, she opened the door. "Did you two come by boat?" she asked, standing aside to let them in. Jessie clung to her father's hand and regarded Melanie silently.

Mike grinned. "You sound edgy. Getting a little cabin fever?"

"Something like that," she admitted. "Hi, Jessie."

Jessie peered up at her and finally smiled. "Hi."

"I thought for a minute a cat had got your tongue," Melanie teased.

Jessie looked perplexed. "There's no cat here."

Melanie chuckled. "No, there's not. It's just an expression. Here, let me take your coats. Can I get you something hot to drink? Maybe some hot chocolate, Jessie?"

At last Jessie gave her a full-fledged smile. "I love hot chocolate. So does Daddy."

Melanie met his gaze. "Is that so?" she asked him as she led the way into the kitchen. She hung their coats on the drying pegs beside the back door, then glanced once more at Mike. The rain had put a bit of wayward curl into his hair, which gave him a rakish look that was even more appealing.

"Are you sure you wouldn't prefer coffee or tea?" she asked him.

"Whatever's easiest. We just stopped on the way home from school to make sure you hadn't floated away."

"As you can see, I'm still here. Since I finished up most of the work I can do inside the house, I've been reduced to baking cookies." She gestured toward the plate. "They're a little overdone, but help yourselves."

Jessie gave her father a hopeful look. At his nod, she grabbed one and took a bite. Melanie waited for some comment about the burned edges, but Jessie climbed onto a kitchen chair and munched happily, seemingly oblivious to the cookie's flaws. Melanie turned to Mike. "What about you? Are you brave enough to try one? I know they don't look like much."

He laughed. "Actually they look a lot like mine—right, Jessie?"

"Uh-huh," Jessie said, her mouth full. "Daddy burns everything."

"Not everything," he protested indignantly, then shrugged. "I'm great with cereal."

Melanie laughed. "Since you have such low expectations, maybe I'll risk inviting you to dinner."

"Tonight?" Jessie asked hopefully. "Daddy was gonna make spaghetti from a can."

"I definitely think I can improve on that, if you'd like to stay," she said, meeting Mike's gaze. "Maybe real pasta with some garlic bread. Of course, the sauce will be from a jar, but that's still better than canned spaghetti, right?"

"Anything's better than that," Mike agreed. "But if we're staying for dinner, then no more cookies, Jessie. You'll spoil your appetite. Besides, you've already had enough sugar for one afternoon."

Jessie seemed about to argue, but Mike's steady gaze never wavered and she backed down.

"Can I watch TV?" she asked instead.

Melanie glanced at Mike for permission. At his nod, she took Jessie into the living room and left her happily watching a PBS children's show.

"I really only came by to check on you," Mike said, when Melanie got back to the kitchen. "Not to invite ourselves to dinner."

"Believe me, I'm glad of the company," Melanie told him honestly.

"Too much time on your hands to think?" he asked.

"Way too much."

"Want to talk about whatever brought you here? You've listened to me. I'm willing to return the favor."

She shook her head. "It was bad enough wallowing in all that self-pity by myself, I don't want to inflict it on you. I'd rather have you talk to me. Tell me about your latest project or how you ended up here at the end of the earth. You're not from around here, are you?"

"End of the earth?" he inquired. "Isn't that a little bit of an overstatement?"

"It's not Boston."

"But apparently Boston hasn't been all that great to you lately," he reminded her. "Maybe you should think about giving a place like this a chance, instead of dismissing it out of hand."

"I am," she said. "At least for the short term, but I was asking about you. Were you born here?"

"No. I came from Richmond. I actually started my business there, but when Linda and I split up, I realized Jessie and I needed to get away, not just to put some distance between us and my ex-wife, but so I wouldn't be so consumed with work that I couldn't spend enough time with Jessie."

"What made you pick this area?"

"It's beautiful. It's near the water. There's a lot of building going on, so there's a need for a good landscape designer. It's not that far from home, so Jessie can see her grandparents from time to time. It's been a good fit. I like being part of a small, growing community."

"Had you been here before, or did you just drive around till you found a place that suited you?"

"Actually I have a friend who's in the nursery business here, Jeff Clayborne."

"That was his nursery we went to the other day," Melanie recalled.

"Exactly. He was out on a job, or you would have met him." He gave her a rueful look. "Actually he's heard all about you."

She regarded him with surprise. "Really?"

"Word travels fast around here. When I saw him Monday, Jeff had already heard about Jessie and me being at the nursery, the ice cream shop and the bookstore with a gorgeous woman. I'm pretty sure he's up to speed on your entire family history by now, too."

"Now, there's one of the obvious disadvantages of small town living, don't you think? Everyone knows your business."

Mike shrugged. "Seems to me like gossip gets around in a big city, too—at least to your own family and circle of friends and business associates."

Melanie thought of how a fear of gossip had sent her scurrying out of Boston and realized he was exactly right. "I guess 'good' gossip does circulate wherever you are," she agreed.

"So, what do people back in Boston say about you?" he asked.

"Hard to tell," Melanie said evasively. "I try not to give them much to talk about."

"You told me once before that there's no special man in your life, right?"

"None," she said tightly.

He studied her closely. "Something tells me there's a story behind that. You're too beautiful to be alone."

"I was with the wrong man. It ended. That's the whole story."

"In a nutshell," he conceded. "Someday I'd like to hear the unabridged version."

"Why?"

"Isn't that what friends do? Tell each other their deep, dark secrets?"

She laughed. "*Girl* friends might do that. I'm not sure I've ever shared my deep dark secrets with a guy. What about you? Do you pour out your secrets to, say, Brenda?"

"Not exactly. Not that she hasn't tried to pry them out of me. And Jeff's wife, Pam, is a master at the poking and prodding game. Her degree's in horticulture, but you'd think she graduated magna cum laude in investigative reporting."

"How does that make you feel?"

"Edgy," he admitted. "Uncomfortable."

Melanie smiled. "There you go. That's exactly how your poking around makes me feel. Why don't we move on? We could discuss whether or not you're any good at all at making a salad."

Mike looked as if he might argue, but then he gave her a chagrined smile. "Whatever you want. I happen to be excellent at making salad. There's no cooking involved."

"Perfect," she said. "And Jessie can set the table."

Mike opened his mouth, no doubt to argue, but Melanie cut him off. "The dishes are old. If she drops something, it's no big deal."

"Then by all means, let her set the table," he relented.

Melanie regarded him curiously. "Doesn't she have chores at home?"

"Sure. She makes her own bed. It's not pretty, but she does it. And I'm teaching her to do laundry. We're a little shaky on the sorting process, which is why I'm sometimes wearing pink underwear."

"I'd like to see that," Melanie said without thinking.

He gave her an amused look. "Oh, really?"

She frowned at the glint in his eyes. "You know what I meant."

"Of course I do," he said, though he couldn't seem to stop grinning. He stood up. "Where's the salad stuff?"

"I generally keep my salad 'stuff' in the refrigerator. How about you?" Melanie teased.

He scowled at her. "I meant the bowl you want to use."

"Ah, that would be in the cupboard over here," she said.

But just as she opened the cabinet door, Mike stepped in behind her and reached over her head. She could feel the press of his legs along the backs of her thighs. His hips cradled her derriere. The intimacy sent a wave of longing washing over her, to say nothing of the kind of heat she'd sworn to avoid.

He set the bowl on the counter in front of her but didn't back away. Instead, he sighed.

"I swore I wasn't going to do this again," he murmured just before he pressed a kiss to the side of her neck. "Damn, but you smell good. I couldn't get this scent out of my head all day after I kissed you on Monday. It about drove me crazy."

Melanie trembled, as much from the helpless dismay she heard in his voice as from the touch of his lips on her skin. She knew precisely how he felt, understood exactly what it was like to have sworn off something only to be unable to resist it.

In fact, she was clinging to the counter with white-knuckled determination right now to keep from turning in Mike's arms and transforming that tender kiss into something filled with heat and urgency. There was no mistaking the press of his arousal against her or the wanting in his voice. She understood all of that, too.

Slowly, inevitably—and all too soon—he backed away. "I'm sorry," he muttered, avoiding her gaze.

Melanie had lived with too many regrets for too long now. She didn't want another one—her own or his—on her conscience. "Don't be," she said harshly. "We're both adults here. Sometimes things just happen. The only mistake would be in making too much of it."

He faced her then. "Just a kiss, right?"

It was like equating an earthquake with a little shiver, but still she nodded. "Just a kiss."

He smiled, his eyes smoldering in a way that told her he understood the depth of the lie as well as she did.

"Maybe we'd better get Jessie in here now," he suggested. "Before I get any other bright ideas."

Melanie laughed and the intense moment was broken… for now.

Mike had never thought of himself as the type to play with fire, but apparently he'd been mistaken. He was playing with a whole damned inferno when it came to being around Melanie. She could send him up in flames in a heartbeat.

He told himself it was only because he'd been a celibate saint since he'd moved to town. After all this time, it was perfectly natural to assume that sooner or later some woman was going to set him off.

Unfortunately, it just happened to be a woman who was hurting and vulnerable, rather than someone like the very willing Brenda, who could fend for herself. If he took advantage of the chemistry between him and Melanie and wound up hurting her, he'd feel like a first-class jerk. And if he let her into his life, already knowing she was going to run out on him in the end, it would prove him to be an even bigger jerk.

That meant he ought to be steering clear of her, avoiding her like the plague, maybe finding some new route to get to work that wouldn't take him directly past Melanie's house every morning and night. Instead, he punished himself for his wayward thoughts by driving by Rose Cottage and testing his willpower.

Since he appeared intent on pulling into her driveway not two days after lecturing himself on avoiding her, apparently his willpower sucked almost as much as his judgment.

Mike slogged through the mud, telling himself he wouldn't stay long. He'd tell her that it was still too wet to plant the flowers they'd picked up last weekend, despite the sliver of sun that had finally worked its way through the clouds on Thursday afternoon and seemed to be struggling against this morning's gloom, as well. Then he'd leave. No big deal.

Famous last words.

He found her outside whacking at the rosebushes with an oversize pair of hedge clippers and a deadly gleam in her eyes. The sight of it horrified him on so many levels it had him tearing across the lawn to snatch the clippers away from her before she did any more damage.

She stared at him as if he'd gone mad. "Why'd you do that?" she demanded indignantly. "Aren't you the one who's been carrying on about getting these bushes under control?"

He barely contained a groan. "Under control, not murdered in their sleep."

She scowled at him. "I'm not murdering the damn bushes. I'm trimming them back."

"Heaven save me from amateurs," he murmured. "Where are your garden tools?"

"In the shed over there," she conceded grudgingly, then followed him when he stalked off in that direction, still muttering.

"Whatever you're saying about me, say it so I can hear it," she said.

"You don't want to hear this," he retorted, yanking open the door and staring at the excellent collection of gardening implements. It was yet more testimony that Cornelia Lindsey had been an expert gardener who'd cared for the tools she used as well as she had for the garden itself.

"Ever heard of dusting?" he grumbled, as he found some first-class pruning shears.

Melanie glowered at him. "In the house. Not in a tool shed."

"The same rules apply." He shook his head. "Never mind. Just come with me. Try not to get in my way."

"If you're this charming when you're teaching Jessie, I'm not surprised she rebels," Melanie said.

There was a little too much truth in the observation, so Mike chose to ignore it. Instead, he led the way to the rosebush Melanie had been attacking. "Watch and learn," he said as he began gently shaping the bush, snipping carefully so it would flourish, not wither and die.

"Why is that one bit different from what I was doing?" Melanie asked after watching him awhile. "It's just going to take longer."

He rolled his eyes. "It's one of those times when patience will be rewarded. If you chop at it the way you were doing, you'll destroy it. See here? There's new growth. And here."

He showed her the markers he was using in making

each careful cut. When he'd trimmed one entire bush, he handed the pruning shears to her. "Your turn."

She accepted the shears gingerly, then frowned at the bush. She immediately reached for a branch and was about to lop it off, when he winced.

"What?" she demanded, shooting him a look of disgust. "It's dead."

"Not entirely. Look again." He pointed to a nodule that would eventually produce new leaves. "See? If you cut above that, the new leaves will appear anyday now."

"This is going to take forever," she said, but she diligently cut where he'd told her to. "What about this branch?"

He grinned. "You tell me."

She bent over to study it, giving him a very nice view of her lovely derriere. He was so absorbed he almost missed the quizzical look she was giving him as she pointed out where she thought she ought to cut.

"Looks good to me," he said, enjoying the flash of triumph in her eyes. It was almost as bright as the sun that was finally beating down from a clear, blue sky.

She'd made several more careful snips without any need for his interference before she finally turned and frowned at him. "You could help, you know."

"I am helping."

"How?"

"I'm supervising. Without me watching over you, who knows how much damage you might do?"

"Very funny. How many rosebushes do you suppose there are in the yard?" she asked plaintively, wiping the perspiration from her brow and leaving behind a streak of dirt.

Mike had to work hard to resist the desire to brush away that streak on her forehead.

"Enough to keep you out of trouble for a good long while," he said cheerfully. "How about some iced tea? Now that the sun's back out, it's hot out here."

"I'm surprised you noticed, since you're standing around in the shade doing nothing."

He ignored the sarcasm. "Keep at it. I'll bring you a sandwich along with your tea."

"You trust me enough to leave me alone for ten whole minutes?" She feigned shock.

"Thirty actually. I'm going to pick up lunch in town." He gave her a stern look. "And no sitting down on the job the minute my back is turned. I expect one more bush trimmed when I get back."

"It's my damned yard!" she shouted after him.

He laughed. "I know. That's why you're doing the work."

The one good thing about keeping her good and mad at him, he decided as he headed into town to pick up lunch, was that even if he was tempted to kiss her, she'd probably slug him and pretty much destroy the impulse.

"You're mean and arrogant and controlling," Melanie accused as she sat next to Mike in the swing in the backyard, reveling in the welcome breeze off the bay. "I think I could hate you."

"That's nice," he murmured, not sounding especially distressed by the charges. He glanced sideways at her. "The yard's starting to look good, though, don't you think so?"

Melanie could barely turn around to follow the direction of his gaze. Every muscle in her body ached, including a few she hadn't been aware of having. She tried to view it through his eyes. All she saw were a bunch of stubby-looking rosebushes. There were at least as many that were still growing out of control.

"Are you sure they're going to grow back?" she asked. "Right now they just look denuded."

He laughed. "They'll grow back. You'll have so many roses later this summer, the scent out here will overwhelm you."

She regarded the garden wistfully. "Too bad I won't be here for that."

"Stay," he said, not sure why he was so determined to change her mind when he knew the risks involved to his own peace of mind.

"I've already told you that I can't."

"No," he said with exaggerated patience. "You told me you *won't,* not that you *can't.*"

"Same difference."

"Not really. One's a choice you're making."

Melanie sighed. It was true. She was making a choice to go back to Boston, but it was the only choice. That was home, and eventually she did have to go back there. This was an interlude, nothing more.

As if to prove that peaceful moments like this couldn't last, the silence was split by the sound of a powerful car engine, then the cutting of the motor and an eruption of laughter.

"Oh, my God," she murmured, recognizing first Ashley's voice, then Maggie's, then Jo's.

Mike regarded her with consternation. "What?"

"My sisters," she said, aware that she sounded as if disaster were about to strike. "They didn't tell me they were coming."

Amusement flickered in Mike's eyes. "And that's a problem because what? There are no clean sheets on the beds?"

"You know perfectly well that's not the issue," she grumbled, jumping out of the swing as if it were on fire. "I need to get out there before they..." Her voice trailed off.

"Before they see me?" he pressed.

"Yes, if you must know."

"Ashamed of me?" he pressed, his expression suggesting the remark wasn't made entirely in jest.

"Don't be absurd. It's just that they'll make too much of you being here."

He laughed. "So?"

"You don't know my sisters," she said grimly. "Stick around and you'll see exactly the kind of inquisition of which they're capable. You think Pam asks a lot of questions? Have I mentioned that Ashley is a highly successful criminal defense attorney? She never loses. She could cross-examine anyone and get them to admit to things they'd never even *considered* doing."

"Ah, I think I'm starting to catch your drift. You think they'll take one look at you and me, all sweaty and flushed, and assume we've been up to something besides gardening," he said in a deliberately provocative way that made her palms sweat.

"Exactly," she murmured, her throat suddenly dry.

He bent down and gave her a hard kiss that took her breath away. When he released her, she swayed.

"Why the hell did you do that? Didn't you hear anything I said?"

"Every word," he said, sauntering off just as Ashley, Maggie and Jo emerged from the house. "I figured since they were already staring out the window, they might as well get the whole show."

Melanie clenched her fists at her side. "You're a pig," she shouted after him.

He merely waved and went on, leaving her to deal with the fallout. He really was a pig, albeit an incredibly sexy one.

Melanie sighed, then sucked in a deep breath and prepared to face her sisters.

6

"Here for three weeks and she's already met the sexiest hunk in the entire Northern Neck," Jo taunted Melanie Friday night after Mike had disappeared around a corner of the house.

"Sexy?" Melanie asked innocently, determined to minimize Mike's attributes, determined not to get drawn into any discussion about him at all. "I hadn't noticed."

"Oh, God, Jeremy blinded her," Maggie lamented. "She's ruined for life."

"Worse, he robbed her of all feeling," Jo added. "If a man kissed me the way that guy just kissed Melanie, I guarantee I'd understand the meaning of *sexy*. Who is he, by the way? Just in case I happen to bump into him while we're in town, I want to be able to greet him by name and check out his kissing technique for myself."

Melanie felt Ashley's curious gaze on her, but avoided meeting her big sister's eyes. Ashley had always been able to read her better than the others. She fought to keep a perfectly neutral expression on her face.

"His name is Stefan Mikelewski, but he prefers to be called Mike," she said grudgingly. "And if you do happen to run into him in town, I expect you to cross the street, if need be, to avoid him. You're not to take it upon your-selves to cross-examine him, and you *most certainly* are not to experiment with kissing him."

Jo laughed, looking triumphant. "Thought so. She is so into the guy."

Melanie tried to ignore the teasing. "Why are all three of you here?" she grumbled. "I thought you were going to take turns. I also thought maybe you'd actually let me know you were coming."

Ashley grinned. "Something you have to hide, sis? Say, a new relationship? Your protests so far are not all that convincing."

Melanie glared at her big sister. "No, I do not have anything to hide, but there's not enough food in the house to feed you guys and, frankly, I could have used a little fortification before facing even one of you, much less all three of you at once."

"We decided you'd only tell us you were just fine and try to put us off if we called first," Maggie told her. "Be-sides, Ashley wound up a court case yesterday, so she needed a break. I finished the food spread for the July issue of the magazine, so I was ready for a change, too. And you know Jo—she'll go anywhere, anytime."

"Are you saying I'm easy?" Jo inquired testily.

"No, we're saying you're energetic and fun," Ashley soothed.

"Now, Mel, tell us all about the handsome Mr. Mikelewski who just snuck out of here to avoid meeting us."

"There's nothing to tell," Melanie insisted. "And he didn't sneak out. He was already on his way out when you arrived."

"Yeah, I always try to steam up the windows right before I walk out the door, figuratively speaking," Ashley commented dryly. "You mean there's nothing you want to share with us."

"I mean I don't know anything about him except that he's a landscape designer and he's livid that we neglected Grandmother's garden. I've taken more grief from that man than I have from anyone in my life, with the possible exception of Jeremy the scoundrel."

"Is this Mike divorced? Married? Children? You don't know any of that?" Ashley asked, looking horrified.

"He's a single dad, and his daughter's a bit of a handful," Melanie replied, realizing that she was not going to get out of giving them a few tidbits about Mike to chew on. Otherwise they'd pester her to death or, worse, track Mike down for the answers they were after.

"Where's his wife?"

"I have no idea. He doesn't say much about her. She's not here, I do know that much." She was not going to tell them about the addiction. It was none of their business. It certainly wasn't her story to share.

"Are you sure he's not carrying the torch for the ex?" Maggie asked.

"I'm relatively sure of that much," Melanie said. The real issue was whether he'd ever get past the resentment he felt toward the woman who'd put his daughter's life at risk. "Although I suspect he still has some issues to work out."

"Relatively sure? Issues?" Maggie echoed, looking dismayed. "You need to ask the man about these issues. Don't leave anything to chance, Melanie. Not again. Otherwise you're liable to get in over your head the same way you did with Jeremy, then find out you missed some important truths."

"Didn't you hear me? Not if I assume there are unresolved issues between them. That's warning enough for me," Melanie retorted. At least it should be. However, every time Mike kissed her, the warning bells dimmed just a little, until now she could barely hear them.

"But then you might be losing out on the best single, totally available man in the region," Jo countered.

"Not interested," Melanie said firmly.

"Uh-huh," all three of her sisters chorused skeptically.

"Blind and dumb," Ashley added.

Melanie scowled at the lot of them. "Pizza or crab cakes?" she asked testily. "I'm starving."

For a moment she thought her mention of food had fallen on deaf ears, but eventually Ashley took the hint.

"Crab, by all means," Ashley said, then had to spoil it by adding, "and then a few more answers about the intriguing Mr. Mikelewski for dessert."

Mike was still distracted when he picked Jessie up at school. He couldn't seem to shake the feeling that he'd made a mistake kissing Melanie and then leaving her to explain things to her sisters, especially since she was already afraid they'd make too much of finding him there.

"Daddy, you're not paying attention," Jessie accused.

"What? Sorry, baby."

"I said I got an A on my reading test. The teacher said I was way ahead of everybody else in class. That's 'cause you and me read every night."

He gave her his full attention. "That's because you work very hard at it," he told her. "I am so proud of you. This deserves a celebration—what would you like to do tonight?"

"See Melanie," she said at once. "I want to tell her about my test."

"We'll have to do that another time," he said. "She has company."

Jessie's face clouded over. "What kind of company?"

"Her sisters surprised her this afternoon. They came all the way from Boston to visit."

"We could still go," Jessie said, her expression determined.

"Not tonight. We'll tell her about the test on Monday, after they're gone."

"But I want to go *now!*"

Mike lost patience. "Jessica Marie, stop that right this second, or we won't celebrate anything."

She immediately fell silent, but a single huge tear rolled down her cheek. Mike was instantly assailed by guilt and the desire to take back his sharp words, but he settled on another tack.

"I'm sorry you're disappointed," he said quietly. "What about going out to dinner? We could go to the crab shanty and get a dozen crabs."

"I don't like crabs," Jessie grumbled.

Mike had to struggle once again to hang on to his patience. "You do too like crabs. They're your favorite, especially when you get to pick out the crabmeat yourself. You love hitting them with that mallet."

"Well, I don't want to do that tonight," she said stubbornly.

Mike could see in her eyes that she desperately wanted to give in and say yes, but she would rather spoil her evening than say yes, now that she'd dug in her heels. He knew a lot about stubborn pride. It was a trait they shared.

"Okay," he said at last, coming up with a way to make it easier for her to give in. "Then you can sit there while I eat. If you're not hungry, you don't have to eat a thing."

"But it's *my* celebration," she protested.

He shrugged. "It's up to you," he said, pulling into the parking lot of the waterfront seafood restaurant that specialized in casual dining. It was a favorite of theirs because no one cared how messy Jessie was. No one could pick crabs neatly.

As soon as they entered, Lena Jensen greeted them with a huge smile. Lena had been running the place for her brother for thirty years. There wasn't a person in town she didn't know and very little gossip that didn't reach her ears.

"It's about time you came to see me, young lady," she scolded Jessie. "I've missed you. Heard you did real well on a reading test today."

Jessie's eyes turned round. "How did you know?"

Lena winked at Mike. "My grandson's in your class," she reminded Jessie. "Not much at school or around town I don't hear about." She gave Mike a pointed look. "Heard you've been helping out over at Cornelia Lindsey's cottage. That granddaughter of hers is a looker, isn't she? At least, that's what everyone is saying. I remember Cornelia bringing all those girls in when they were young. Can't say I recall which was which, but all four of them were real beauties. It's Melanie who's here, is that right?"

Mike had only caught a glimpse of the others this afternoon, but it had been enough to know that Lena was exactly right. Each one was gorgeous. "Actually they're all here. The others arrived this afternoon for a visit."

"Well, isn't that nice?" Lena said. "I imagine they'll be in before too long. This was the first place they came whenever they hit town to visit their grandmother. It was a tradition I doubt they'll break."

Mike bit back a groan. He hoped she was wrong about that. Melanie would not be pleased to find him here.

"Daddy, are we gonna eat? I'm hungry."

He glanced down into Jessie's upturned face. All traces of her moodiness had vanished. "Lena, you can forget about the menus. Put in an order for a dozen steamed crabs for us, one soda and a beer. It's a nice night. We'll find our way to a table on the deck."

"I'll get the order in right now," Lena said. "You're in luck. It's still early in the season, so supplies are low, but we got in some beauties this morning."

Mike and Jessie made their way to the outdoor deck and chose a table with a good view of the mallards and gulls on the water. In another hour or two, the deck would be packed with locals and tourists, here for the excellent food and the spectacular sunset reflected off the inlet from the bay.

For now, though, Mike and Jessie had it to themselves. Lena brought their drinks, then hurried back to greet the next batch of customers.

"Daddy, do you think that duck is lonely?" Jessie asked plaintively, pointing to a female mallard drifting on the water apart from the others.

Mike gave the question the serious consideration Jessie expected before shaking his head. "No, I figure she's just taking a break. She's probably been pestered all day long and needs some time to herself."

Jessie nodded, her expression thoughtful. "That's what I think, too."

Mike studied his daughter closely and realized that she still wasn't entirely satisfied. Something else was clearly on her mind. "Something bothering you, kiddo?"

"I was thinking," she began, regarding him earnestly, "it would be fun to have sisters."

Mike gulped. "Really? What on earth put that idea into your head?"

"Melanie has sisters. You and Miss Lena said so. And my friends at school have sisters and brothers, too. Sometimes they're pests, but sometimes a pest is better than not having anybody around."

"Are you lonely?" he asked, his heart in his throat. He'd convinced himself that they didn't need anything more than what they had—each other. "I thought Lyssa Clayborne was your best friend. You two arguing or something?"

"Friends are different. They don't live with you," his daughter explained.

"Then you *are* lonely," Mike concluded.

As if she sensed that she had somehow hurt his feelings, Jessie shook her head. "I'm just saying sisters would be fun—better than brothers, probably, but brothers would be okay, too."

He grinned at her. "You think there's a store where we can pick out a few?"

"No, Daddy!" she protested, giggling. "You can't buy sisters."

"Oh, right," Mike said. "I forgot."

"No, you didn't. You were teasing me."

"Only because I like hearing you laugh," he said. "Sorry I can't be more help when it comes to the sister thing."

"That's okay," Jessie said, sounding resigned. "Maybe someday we'll get a mom and some sisters."

Eyes stinging, Mike turned away. It was thoroughly frustrating to discover that he couldn't give his child one of the few things she really wanted. Feeling inadequate, he looked up just in time to spot Melanie and her sisters emerging onto the deck. She spotted him and halted in her tracks.

"Maybe we should sit inside. It's cool out here," he

heard her tell her siblings, trying to jostle them back through the door.

Unfortunately, one of her sisters caught a glimpse of him and realized exactly what Melanie was up to.

"Oh, no, you don't," she said to Melanie. "Perhaps we can join your friend and his daughter."

She was past Melanie and across the deck before Melanie could react. Hand outstretched, she greeted Mike. "Hi, I'm Ashley D'Angelo, Melanie's older sister. And this is Jo. Maggie's back there, trying to convince Melanie that it's too late to run."

Mike grinned. "And why would she feel the need to run?" he asked, though it was perfectly obvious from the curious glint in her big sister's sharp, intelligent eyes.

"You tell me," Ashley suggested. "Maybe it has something to do with that kiss we caught when you knew we were watching."

"Were you?" Mike asked innocently. "I had no idea."

Ashley laughed. "You'd make a lousy witness, Mr. Mikelewski. You get this little tic at the corner of your eye when you lie."

He deliberately rubbed his eye. "Must have gotten something in it. There's a lot of pollen around. Maybe you should sit inside."

"Not a chance," she said, already maneuvering another table over to theirs. She frowned at him. "You could help with this."

He shook his head. "I'm waiting for my cue from Melanie. She seems reluctant for this to happen."

"She doesn't trust me not to go poking around into your personal business," Ashley said unrepentantly. "She'll get over it."

He laughed, liking her honesty. "Frankly, I'm not sure

I trust you, either. She says you're hell on wheels in a courtroom cross-examination."

Ashley gave her sister a long, considering look. "Did she really? I wonder why she'd do that. I guess I'll just have to work that much harder to catch you off guard, now that I know you've been forewarned."

Melanie arrived in time to overhear the last and groaned. "Could we please sit somewhere else?" she begged, giving a look of silent apology to Mike.

"Not on my account," he said. "Besides, Jessie is bursting to tell you her news. She wanted to come by a little while ago, but I talked her into coming here to celebrate instead."

All four women turned their eyes on Jessie then. She squirmed under all that sudden scrutiny, and for a moment, Mike thought her shyness would get the better of her. But then Melanie pulled out the chair beside her, and Jessie immediately scrambled into her lap.

"Guess what?" she said excitedly, her gaze on Melanie's face.

"What?"

"I got an A on my reading test. Isn't that the best news ever?"

"That is fantastic news," Melanie agreed. "In fact, it might be the very best news I've heard in a long time. No wonder you're celebrating."

"Daddy's getting crabs so we can hit 'em with a mallet."

Maggie chuckled. "Sounds energetic."

Mike met her gaze. "You have no idea. The safest seat is at that end of the table, as far from Jessie as you can get."

Jessie's gaze was intent on Melanie's face. "Are these your sisters?"

Melanie nodded and introduced them.

"I was telling Daddy that I wish I had sisters," Jessie announced. "And a mom."

Mike choked on the sip of beer he'd just taken. "Yes, well, we all have our impossible dreams," he said, as three women studied him with absolutely fascinated expressions. Melanie merely looked as if she'd like to crawl under the table.

"What's so impossible about that?" Ashley inquired, regarding him intently.

Melanie scowled at her sister. "Leave the man alone, Ashley. He's not on trial."

"Just curious," Ashley said. "Aren't *you?*"

"No, I am not," Melanie said firmly.

"Ha!" The chorus came from Jo and Maggie.

"If you all don't behave, I'm leaving you here to walk home," Melanie threatened.

Ashley grinned. "It might be worth it."

"Yeah, we'd have Mike all to ourselves," Jo agreed. "Who knows what secrets we could pry out of him?"

Melanie turned to Mike. "Ignore them. I love them, but they're pains in the butt. They have absolutely no idea of boundaries when it comes to social conversation. It's a trait they picked up from our father. Since it drove all of us nuts when he did it, you'd think they'd know better."

He laughed. "I think I can handle your sisters."

This time she was the one who muttered, "Ha!"

To prove his point, he turned to Ashley, who was clearly the leader of the pack. "Tell me, how's your social life these days?"

"As if she has time for one," Maggie murmured.

"Ah, not so hot?" Mike guessed, picking up on the comment. "I have some friends I could introduce you to while you're here. They're a little rough around the edges, but I imagine you could whip them into shape in no time."

"I'm not here looking for a project," Ashley said haughtily. "If I wanted someone in my life, I'm sure I could find a suitable candidate in Boston."

He chuckled. "If I didn't know better, I'd say that sounded downright snobbish, Ms. D'Angelo. Something wrong with a blue-collar guy?"

"Not as long as it's an Italian-silk-blend blue collar," Maggie taunted.

Ashley frowned at her. "I am not a snob," she said, promptly rising to the bait.

"But a blue-collar guy wouldn't suit you, isn't that what you just said?"

"No. I said…" Her voice trailed off. "Oh, never mind. You're only doing this to prove you can hold your own. You don't give two hoots about my social life."

"Sure I do," Mike insisted. "You're Melanie's sister. I want you to be happy."

"And Melanie?" Ashley asked tartly. "Are you trying to make sure she's happy, too?"

"Doing my best," he said easily. "Of course, she'd be a lot happier if I stopped pestering her about getting that garden at Rose Cottage into shape, right, Melanie?"

"Absolutely," she said at once. "In fact, now that my sisters are here, why don't you make them help? They're as much at fault as I am for the disaster the garden's become."

"Good idea," he said at once. "What time should I be there in the morning? Say, six? It should be just about daylight then. With all of you working in the garden, we can get the job done in no time. I hope none of you mind getting your hands dirty."

Ashley glanced at her perfectly manicured nails, then stared at him in horror. "Not a chance, Mr. Mikelewski. Besides, isn't Melanie paying you to take care of the garden?"

"Nope. I'm a volunteer supervisor."

Surprise registered in Ashley's eyes. "Is that so? And this is your profession, landscape design?"

"That's right."

"Then why would you offer your services for nothing?" she asked. "What exactly are you expecting in return?"

"A garden that looks like it did in its heyday," he said simply. "That's my only mission."

"Told you," Melanie muttered to her sisters.

Oddly enough, she didn't look especially pleased to have whatever she'd told them confirmed. Mike figured he'd think about that later. For right now, it was enough to know that he'd apparently thrown the skeptical, inquisitive Ashley off the scent.

"Then what was that kiss about?" Ashley demanded. "Don't you dare toy with her."

"Ashley, that's enough," Melanie said, blushing furiously.

"It most certainly is not enough," Ashley retorted. "I won't allow this man to take advantage of you."

"Don't yell at my daddy," Jessie whispered, catching all of them by surprise.

Ashley immediately looked chagrined. "Sweetie, I am so sorry. I didn't mean to yell at him."

Jessie regarded her skeptically. "Then why did you?"

"I lost my head for a minute, that's all."

"Where'd it go?" Jessie asked, drawing a laugh that broke the tension.

"Hard to say," Ashley told her. "But I promise I won't open my mouth again till I find it."

That drew the biggest chorus of hoots yet from her sisters.

Mike couldn't help getting a kick out of them. They were all so damned protective of Melanie, yet so straightforward and blunt with each other. He admired that kind of honesty and loyalty. With no brothers or sisters of his own, he'd never experienced anything quite like it. He'd hoped to find it in his marriage, but look how that had turned out.

"No need to stay quiet on my account," he told Ashley. "I can take whatever you want to dish out, as long as you're not afraid of Jessie. She's as protective of me as you are of your sisters. It's not a bad trait to have."

Ashley met his gaze, then slowly nodded. "You'll do," she said at last.

Mike faltered at the note of approval in her voice. What the hell had just happened here? Had Ashley given him her blessing? He gazed around the table to see three women regarding him solemnly and one looking as if she'd rather be anywhere else on the planet.

He didn't want Ashley's damn blessing. That implied that he was seriously interested in a relationship with Melanie, which he absolutely was not. Not that kind of a relationship, anyway.

And the kind he was interested in—hot, passionate and fleeting—was definitely not in the cards.

A part of him wanted to make all of that very clear, so there would be no misunderstandings, but he valued his life too much. He could just hear himself explaining that he only did casual flings and finding himself tossed straight over the railing of this deck. It wouldn't be pretty.

"Maybe we should change the subject," Melanie suggested firmly.

"To what?" Ashley asked, her gaze still steady on Mike.

"Something safer and less controversial," Melanie said. "Say, politics or religion."

Mike stared at her and realized she was perfectly serious. Or desperate. He could relate to that. The truth was, right this instant, surrounded by D'Angelo women and a daughter who'd just announced a need for a mom, he was feeling pretty damn desperate himself.

7

"That was interesting," Ashley declared when they'd returned from dinner and her unexpected opportunity to grill Mike. "Let's have ice cream and discuss what we found out about the intriguing Mr. Mikelewski."

"Let's not," Melanie said, wishing for the moment that she'd been an only child. Having sisters wasn't always all it was cracked up to be, especially sisters who thought they had a God-given right to meddle. "We were all there. We heard every word you and Mike exchanged. I don't think we need to do a postconversation analysis like those TV guys who feel a need to dissect a presidential speech the entire nation has just heard."

"But there's a lot to be learned from comparing notes, seeing if we all got the same impression," Ashley insisted. "That's what makes the jury system so effective."

"Now the three of you have turned into a jury?" Melanie asked. "That's comforting."

"No, I only meant that two heads are better than one, or in our case four heads," Ashley replied.

"Make that three. You all can compare notes to your heart's content. I'm going to bed." Melanie headed for the stairs. "And by the way, your beds aren't made. You'll have to do that yourselves. The clean sheets are in the closet. Try not to wake me."

"Do you get the feeling she's not happy with us?" Ashley asked before Melanie had hit the bottom step.

"You," Jo and Maggie replied. "She's not happy with *you.*"

"Me? What did I do?"

Melanie leaned against the wall and grinned as she eavesdropped. Ashley really was oblivious to the fallout when she was on a self-righteous mission. She expected everyone to see that she had their best interests at heart, no matter how intrusive her behavior.

"Let's start with embarrassing her in front of her new friend," Jo explained patiently.

"And making more of this relationship than either she or Mike thinks there is," Maggie added. "How would you like it if we spotted you having lunch with some casual acquaintance and then plopped ourselves down at the table and proceeded to cross-examine him?"

"You'd never do that," Ashley declared confidently.

"No, we wouldn't, but that is what you do," Jo said. "It really can be annoying. Melanie got it just right at dinner. Remember how we hated it when Dad did that to our dates? You're even worse. You've got all that hard-ass courtroom experience going for you. If you ask me, Mike held up pretty well. I'm just surprised he didn't deck you. If it had been me on the receiving end of that interrogation, I might have."

"Seriously?" Ashley asked, sounding genuinely perplexed by their assessment.

"Yes, seriously," Jo and Maggie confirmed.

"Oh, God," Ashley moaned. "I am so sorry. I'd better go tell her."

Melanie barely made it to the top of the steps before

she heard her sister coming after her. She dived into bed and pulled the covers up to her chin.

Ashley appeared in the doorway. "Mel, you asleep?"

"What?" Melanie replied, injecting a note of grogginess into her voice.

"Oh, stop it," Ashley said impatiently. "I know perfectly well you were listening on the steps. I heard you racing to beat me up here." She grabbed a corner of the covers and yanked it away to reveal the fact that Melanie was still fully clothed.

Melanie scowled at her. "If you knew, why'd you bother asking if I was asleep?" she grumbled.

"I had high hopes that you'd be honest with me."

"It was a test?" Melanie asked incredulously.

"I thought it might indicate if you would be willing to tell me the truth about what's really going on with you and Mike."

"I have told you the truth. There is nothing going on. I'm not an idiot, Ashley. I'm only here for a few more weeks at most. Why would I get involved with someone, especially someone with a child who could get hurt if things don't work out?"

"Then you do see all the possible complications and consequences?"

"Of course I do."

"Just the same, I'd feel a whole lot better if you knew more about his situation with his ex-wife," Ashley said, her brow knit in a worried frown. "I don't want his unresolved feelings to come back and bite you in the butt."

"I'm not going to let that happen," Melanie assured her. "Sis, I appreciate your concern, I really do, but give it a rest, okay? Otherwise this is going to be a very long weekend."

Ashley looked as if she might argue, but she finally sighed and gave Melanie a hug. "Love you, kid."

"I love you, too. Now let me get out of these clothes so I can get some sleep. Yard work is damn hard, and Mike maintains a grueling pace. You'll find that out for yourself tomorrow."

Ashley shuddered. "I am not working in the yard."

Filled with a sudden desire for retaliation, Melanie grinned. "Wanna bet?"

Melanie regarded her three half-asleep sisters with amusement. They were not morning people. That's why she'd deliberately rousted them out of bed at six.

"If you drink your coffee, you'll feel better," she assured them. She'd made a very large pot of it. She wafted a cup under Maggie's nose, knowing that the scent of her favorite brew would get to her.

"What the devil's gotten into you?" Maggie muttered, even as she made a grab for the cup.

"It's revenge," Jo said. She frowned at Melanie. "Isn't it?"

"Let's just say I'm taking advantage of an opportunity that's come my way to share the pleasure of putting this place in order again."

"Couldn't I just scrub a floor or something, maybe later this afternoon?" Ashley pleaded, her head resting on her arms on the kitchen table. "It's bad enough that I have to get up at the crack of dawn to be in court, but this is supposed to be a break."

"The floors have been scrubbed and polished," Melanie pointed out. "The walls have been freshly painted. The windows have been washed. This place is a veritable showcase inside, thanks to me. All that's left is the yard and the outside of the house. The house can wait. The yard needs to be done now, according to Mike."

"Where the heck is he? Has he shown up?" Ashley grumbled. "I thought he was the garden drill sergeant. I had no idea he'd designated you to pinch-hit for him."

"If he's smart, he's miles and miles from here," Melanie responded cheerfully. "I am, indeed, taking over for him. Now come on, ladies, let's get busy. All that weeding isn't going to happen by itself. If we finish by lunchtime, I'll take you into town."

"And if we don't?" Maggie asked warily.

"It's grilled cheese sandwiches and canned soup," Melanie told her. "And more weeding this afternoon. I think we're going to need a scythe to get through the overgrown brush down by the water. There are probably snakes in there, too. You're not scared of snakes, are you, Ashley?"

Her big sister gave her a sour look. "You've turned into a mean, vindictive person since you've been here."

Melanie laughed. "Possibly, but I'm feeling better by the minute. I think I'm just about back in control of my life."

"Heaven help us," Ashley muttered, but she got to her feet. "Lead on. Let's get this over with."

Melanie put them to work on the messiest, most exhausting tasks she could think of, then settled into the swing with a cup of coffee. She could see why Mike enjoyed supervising so much. There was something downright relaxing about sitting around with the sun beating down on her shoulders and a good cup of coffee in hand while other people did her bidding.

She wasn't all that surprised when he turned up about nine, glanced around the yard, which was looking about eighty percent improved, and gave her a thumbs-up. "I see you've been busy. Nice work," he said.

"Not me. I'm supervising."

"Who exactly are you supervising?"

She took a quick glance around and realized that her workers had vanished. How had she missed seeing them sneak off?

"Well, they were here," she said with a shrug. "I must have closed my eyes for a minute, and they seized the opportunity to escape. Where's Jessie?"

"Visiting a friend. I thought I'd stop by and see how things were going over here."

"You mean whether they'd let me off the rack?"

He stared at her blankly. "What?"

"Torture," she explained. "They came home last night filled with more questions than ever."

He laughed. "Yes, I imagine they did. Were they satisfied with your answers?"

"No more than they were with yours. I'm hoping to exhaust them, so they'll forget they ever laid eyes on you."

"Has that worked for you?" he asked, his gaze filled with amusement.

"Not so much," she admitted candidly. "But I'm working on it. It's hard, since you keep popping up around here."

"Want me to stay away?"

The offer startled her. "You'd do that?"

"Now that you're actually getting the garden under control, yes." He searched her face. "If that's what you want."

Was it? Melanie honestly didn't know. It was what she *should* want. It was what she'd promised Ashley the night before—that she'd keep things between herself and Mike cool and impersonal. Keeping him away from the house was probably the only way she'd accomplish that, since he had the uncanny ability to get her all hot and bothered even when she was most determined to resist him.

"You probably should keep an eye on things," she said finally. "I could wind up planting hollyhocks on top of daffodils and spoiling everything."

He grinned. "You have a point, but I should probably take off now, before your sisters get back from wherever they're hiding," he said. "No point in getting them all worked up again."

She lifted her gaze to meet his. "I'm sorry they put you through the wringer last night."

"Actually it was kind of fun. Kept me on my toes."

She stared at him. "You enjoyed it?"

"Sure, why not? It was harmless. I like that they're so protective of you. Of course, it's made me wonder why they think you need protecting."

"Long story." She deliberately took a sip of her now-cold coffee and avoided meeting his eyes.

"And you're still not ready to fill me in?"

Melanie wasn't entirely sure why she'd kept quiet, beyond not wanting Mike to lose all respect for her judgment. After all, she had been duped for months by a married man. Yep, that was the reason for her silence, all right. No woman wanted a man to see her for the pathetic idiot she was.

"I doubt I will ever be ready to tell that story to another living soul, especially you," she said honestly. "I'm trying to forget about it."

"Some things you can't forget about until you deal with them," he said.

"The way you've dealt with what Linda did to you and Jessie?"

His expression sobered at once. "Touché," he said grimly. "No more prodding, but I will listen if you ever change your mind, and I won't pass judgment."

"I'll keep that in mind," Melanie said just as her sisters reappeared, showered and looking as fresh and crisp as if they'd never done a lick of work.

"We're ready for lunch," Maggie announced.

"The job's not finished," Melanie pointed out.

"We don't care," Ashley said. "We're going to lunch, anyway. Do you want to come, or do you have better things to do?" She grinned pointedly at Mike.

"Mike was just leaving," Melanie said firmly. "I'll come to lunch with you as long as we stick to a preapproved list of topics."

"Where is this list?" Ashley demanded. "I haven't seen any list." She glanced at Jo and Maggie. "Have you seen a list?"

"I believe it will be easier if you just take note of the one exclusion," Melanie said.

Three pairs of accusing eyes turned toward Mike.

"Hey, it's her rule, not mine," he said. "If a bunch of gorgeous women want to talk about me, I'm okay with it. It'll probably do wonders for my reputation."

"Well, there you go," Ashley said. "No exclusions."

Melanie gave them all a sour look. "We'll discuss this in the car."

"Want me to come along to referee?" Mike inquired.

"No!" four voices chimed emphatically.

Melanie grinned at her sisters. "At least there's one thing we can agree on. Sorry, Mike."

"No problem. I'll just go and track down some of the guys. See what they're saying around town about the D'Angelo sisters."

He sauntered off before any of them could comment.

"Do you think he was serious?" Jo asked, looking surprisingly worried. "Will people be talking about us? About the fact that we're all here?"

"More than likely, especially since we saw Lena last night at the restaurant. She's like a one-woman newscast," Melanie said. "It's no big deal. After all, what could they possibly have to say about us?"

"I'm not very hungry," Jo said. "I think I'll stick around here."

"Jo, you can't do that," Ashley protested.

"I most certainly can," Jo retorted.

"But there's nothing to eat," Melanie reminded her. "We never did get to the store."

"You said there was stuff for grilled cheese sandwiches. That'll do."

Something in Jo's tone told Melanie that she wasn't going to budge. "Okay, sweetie. It's up to you."

"You're going to miss out on pestering Melanie about Mike," Maggie teased.

"Oh, I think you guys can handle that without me," Jo said. "Have fun. Bring home dessert. Something decadent."

She headed for the house before they could take one last shot at arguing with her.

"Any idea what that was about?" Ashley asked, staring after her worriedly.

"None," Melanie said.

"Oh, well, Maggie and I can gang up on her on the way home," Ashley said. "Let's concentrate on you for now. Organizing one sister's life at a time is all I can handle."

"And we thought you prided yourself on multitasking," Maggie commented.

"A law practice is not nearly as complicated as Melanie's life," Ashley explained breezily.

"Let's leave my life alone, too," Melanie retorted. "Or I'll be staying here with Jo."

Her sisters determinedly linked arms with her.

"Not a chance," Maggie said.

Ashley grinned at her. "It'll be painless. We promise."

Judging from the glint in her eyes, she was lying through her teeth. She was actually eager to put Melanie through the wringer.

Melanie was jumpy as a June bug. She'd been skittish ever since Mike had arrived with a load of topsoil first thing Monday morning. If he didn't know better, he'd actually think she was scared of him. What the hell had her sisters asked about him after he'd left on Saturday?

"Have a good visit with your sisters?" he asked, eyeing her curiously.

"Great."

"They go back home?"

"Last night," she confirmed.

"You sleep okay?"

She frowned at him. "I slept just fine. Why do you ask?"

"You look the way you did that first morning I showed up here, edgy and out of sorts. The only thing missing is the lamp."

She stared at him blankly.

He chuckled. "You're not clutching it so you can crack my skull open with it, but you do look as if you don't quite trust me."

"Oh."

"Don't want to talk about it," he concluded.

"About what?"

"Whatever has you so edgy."

"Not really."

"Okay." He dumped a wheelbarrow filled with rich topsoil in a cleared spot in the backyard, then headed back to his truck for more.

Melanie trailed after him, silent and clearly troubled. Eventually she sighed heavily.

Mike stopped shoveling dirt into the wheelbarrow and stared at her. "Okay, that's it. Something is obviously on your mind. Spill."

"It's nuts."

"Maybe so, but it's bugging you, so ask."

"My sisters think I should ask if you're still carrying the torch for your ex-wife," she said, color flooding her cheeks.

Mike's pulse throbbed dully. "Who actually wants to know? You or them?"

"All of us, I guess."

"No," he said succinctly, hoping that would put an end to it.

"Is Jessie your only child?"

He regarded her incredulously. Where the hell had they come up with that one? "Yes," he said tightly. "Did you think I kept two or three more stuffed in a closet somewhere? Or that I'd left them with a woman who's addicted to drugs?"

She flushed at that. "No, of course not. I just had to be sure."

He couldn't help wondering if this had something to do with whoever had sent her scurrying away from Boston. What the hell had that guy—and he was assuming a man was at the root of her flight—done to her?

He gave her a quizzical look. "Anything else?"

"And you have full custody of Jessie?"

"Yes."

"I see."

He glanced over at her. "What is it you think you see?"

"Nothing. I just meant… Oh, hell, I don't know what I meant."

"If you're out of questions and you're not going to help me spread this topsoil, go find something else to do," he suggested curtly. "Or at least drop the inquisition. Something tells me it has less to do with me than it does with that past you refuse to discuss."

A wounded expression in her eyes quickly turned to wariness. She whirled away and headed toward the house. "I'll be inside if you need me."

After she'd gone, Mike sighed. He'd made a mess of that. She'd only been asking perfectly reasonable questions. Well, except for that one about him having more kids. That one was out of left field. Still, it wasn't her fault that the whole subject of his marriage and divorce was so damn touchy. He thought he'd already made that clear to her, but obviously her sisters had filled her head with a lot of doubts and nonsense about him. He could hardly blame them for wanting to look out for her, especially when it was so plain that someone had hurt her recently, but that didn't make it any easier to be asked about all that stuff he preferred to block out of his mind.

Hell, *he* should have been the one asking questions. He should have pushed harder to find out who'd hurt her and how. Maybe then he'd know just how fragile Melanie was and whether he was destined to do the same thing to her.

The questions would have to wait for another day, though. Or at least until he worked off this ridiculous

desire to go inside and kiss her senseless. If things between them were confusing now, that would pretty much
send the complication meter into the stratosphere.

Melanie stood by the window and tried not to stare.
Mike's shirt was stretched taut over flexing muscles as he
shoveled the topsoil from his truck onto a growing mound
in the area he'd designated for a perennial garden. She'd
made an absolute mess of things just now. She knew what
a private man he was, at least when it came to his marriage. Why on earth had she allowed her sisters to prod
her into poking around in his personal business?

Of course, the answer was obvious. She wanted to
know. She'd been burned all too recently by a man who'd
kept silent about the important relationships in his life.
She'd learned from bitter experience that she was inca-
pable of telling when a man was lying to her.

Not that it mattered in Mike's case, of course. It wasn't
like she was getting involved with him. Her emotions
weren't on the line. Her future wasn't at stake. What did it
really matter if he still had feelings for Jessie's mother?

She glanced outside, saw that he'd stripped off his
shirt, and sighed. She was lying through her teeth. She
wanted him, all right. Her sisters had seen that immediately. That's why they'd spent the entire weekend poking
and prodding and asking all those unanswerable questions
about Mike. They'd obviously seen her all but drooling
over him. They'd definitely seen the way he kissed her.
And they knew her well enough to understand that as
clever and sneaky as Mike might be, that kiss would never
have happened if Melanie hadn't wanted it to. She could
duck an unwanted advance with the best of them.

She ought to go out there right now and apologize for
poking into things that were none of her concern, but

the truth was, she did need to know the answers to those questions. She did need to protect herself before this thing with Mike, whatever it was, went one step further.

Of course, he would only say he'd already answered her. Unfortunately, his curt, one-word replies had only stirred more questions.

It took a while, but she finally gathered her courage and went back outside. He glanced up, nodded, then went right on raking the topsoil over the ground.

"I'm sorry," she said.

He stopped then and leaned on the rake. "Really?"

She flinched under his steady, disbelieving gaze. "Okay, I'm not sorry for asking, only for making you uncomfortable."

"Thought so."

"They're reasonable questions, Mike."

"Yes," he agreed. "But I don't have any other answers."

"You could elaborate."

"Have you elaborated on why you came up here looking like a wounded soul?"

"It's not the same thing."

"Isn't it? How do you figure that?"

"What happened to me is over."

"My marriage is over."

"Not as long as you have Jessie," she pointed out. "Jessie ties you to her mother forever. Linda could be in rehab right now trying to get her act together to come back to you."

"I hope she is in rehab," Mike said. "But she won't be coming back to me. That door is closed."

He sounded so sure of that. Melanie wanted desperately to believe him. Some crazy part of her wanted to take a risk and get closer to him, even if it was only for

a few short weeks. But despite the finite end to their relationship that was in the cards, there were far too many
emotional perils to be weighed.

He stepped across the freshly raked dirt and stood directly in front of her, tipping her chin up until she couldn't
avoid his gaze.

"Linda is not an issue," he repeated softly. "This is
between you and me."

Before she could question his declaration, before she
could say that old baggage couldn't simply be dismissed,
his mouth covered hers and her senses went haywire,
just as they had on the previous occasions when they'd
kissed.

She couldn't think, couldn't remember even one of the
questions she'd meant to ask. All she could do was feel
the way his lips caressed hers, the way his heat and scent
surrounded her, the way his body fit hers, the play of his
muscles under her fingers when her hands drifted to his
sun-warmed shoulders to cling to him.

It seemed like an eternity passed—or maybe only a
split second—before he released her and went back to
raking as if nothing the least bit monumental or life-
altering had just occurred.

How the heck could he be so cool not ten seconds after
sending her up in flames? she wondered irritably.

If she hadn't already had her sisters' warnings screaming in her head, that kiss would have been a wake-up call.
She was up to her eyebrows, not in topsoil but in quick-
sand…and she was sinking fast.

8

He had to stop kissing her, Mike thought as he concentrated on getting that topsoil spread out just so, mainly to avoid meeting Melanie's eyes. She was watching him warily. He could almost feel her gaze boring into him. He could practically hear the endless list of questions on the tip of her tongue.

Like what the hell was he thinking? He didn't have an answer to that one.

Or what did he want from her? He didn't have an answer to that one, either, at least not one that wouldn't get him slapped silly. Oh, yes, he wanted to haul her into bed, but that was not exactly what she was itching to hear right now. And since he wasn't going to let it happen, anyway, it was a moot point.

There were probably a whole litany of questions he hadn't even thought of. Heck, there were probably a few that hadn't even occurred to her sisters, and they were the grand masters of asking the unanswerable.

"We need to talk," she finally said, sounding as edgy as she had when he'd first arrived.

His gaze narrowed. The very last thing on his mind was talking. What was it with women that they wanted

Sherryl Woods

to talk about everything? The only woman in his life who'd ever kept silent was Linda, only because she'd had so blasted many secrets she wanted to keep from him.

"About?" he asked cautiously.

"I can't talk to you when you're only half-dre..." She blushed furiously. "When half your attention is on that dirt. Put on your shirt and come inside. I just made some iced tea."

Inside? Mike stared at her. Inside was a very bad idea. Inside was where her bed was. Inside was where no casual passerby could happen to see whatever they were up to. Inside was damned dangerous.

"I'm filthy," he protested, grabbing at the most obvious and convenient straw. "Why don't you bring the tea out here? We can sit on the swing." The chance of a passing boater intruding on their privacy was slim, but it might be enough to keep his hands where they belonged...away from her.

"I'm not worried about you tracking a little dirt through the house," she said impatiently. "Besides, it's hot out here. I've turned on the air-conditioning. The kitchen will be cool."

Not as cool as the ice-cold shower he needed at the moment, Mike thought desperately. "Give me a minute," he said, hoping to buy himself enough time to talk himself out of the insane desire he had to just go with the flow and haul her straight upstairs to her bed. "Go on in. I'll be there."

She regarded him skeptically, as if she didn't entirely trust him not to take off, which, come to think of it, wasn't a bad idea. Cowardly, but not a bad idea under the circumstances.

"Go," he repeated. "I won't be long."

She nodded and walked toward the house, her hips

swaying provocatively in what was more than likely a totally instinctive and unintended turn-on. He was such a jerk. Women walked past him all the time with the deliberate intention of trying to snag his attention. Brenda put more sway into her caboose when she sashayed past his table at the café than any woman he'd ever seen. It never did a thing for him. Melanie walked away, all innocence and hurt feelings, and he wanted to jump her bones. Ridiculous. He really had been celibate way too long.

He yanked on his shirt and buttoned it all the way to his neck as if that might prevent her from getting any wild ideas about dragging it right back off him. Then he spent another ten minutes getting his hormones and his wayward thoughts under control before he followed.

En route to the house, he gave himself a very stern lecture on what was *not* going to happen. Whatever Melanie's agenda, he was going to sit across from her at the kitchen table and keep his damn hands to himself. He was going to listen politely, nod when it was called for, then hightail it out of there at the first opportunity.

Inside, he found her pacing. She frowned at him as if he were unexpected and as if he'd caught her doing something vaguely compromising.

"Sit down," she said at last.

She took her own place at the table. Ignoring the full glass of iced tea in front of her, she folded her hands primly on top of the scarred table, her expression troubled. His tea was waiting for him in front of the seat next to her.

Mike snagged the glass and moved to the opposite end of the table, grateful that it was one of those oval things with a leaf inserted. That ought to be sufficient distance to keep him on his best behavior.

Her brow rose at his actions, but she didn't comment.

Instead, she met his gaze and asked, "What are we going to do about this?"

Mike tried to pretend he didn't have a clue what she meant. "This?"

"Us. The kissing."

Curiosity and that flustered expression on her face got the better of him. "What do you want to do about it?"

"It needs to stop," she said at once.

"Which isn't exactly an answer to the question I asked, is it? Do you want it to stop?"

Temper flashed in her eyes. "What am I supposed to say to that? If I say yes, you'll call me a liar, since it's obvious I'm as much into it as you are. If I say no, then I'm opening myself up to something I don't want to happen."

He gave her a quizzical look. "In other words, the kissing is okay, but what you really want to stop is anything more? Am I interpreting what you said accurately?" He really needed to be very clear, because one tiny miscue and they'd both wind up in bed…in flames.

"Why are you making this so difficult?" she asked with a trace of annoyance. "We're adults. We should be able to decide in a perfectly rational way to quit playing dangerous games. We both know this can't go anywhere. You have your reasons. I have mine. They're all valid. Let's stop tempting fate."

Mike couldn't help it, he had to ask. He was a man, after all. "Then you are tempted?"

"Oh, don't be an idiot," she snapped. "You know I am, or we wouldn't be having this conversation."

"What would we be doing?" Mike asked. He was fascinated with the way her mind worked. She'd obviously given this a lot of thought since coming inside. He wondered if her thoughts had paralleled his own. He wondered if she was having half as much difficulty as he was listening to her head, rather than her hormones.

"I'd have slapped you out there and put an end to any more wild ideas about you kissing me," she insisted, though not very forcefully. She didn't sound as if she believed it for a minute.

"So, instead you're going to talk it to death," he concluded. "Maybe get a written agreement, spelling out the parameters for all future contact?"

She sighed, her cheeks flushed. "When you say it like that, it sounds absurd."

"It *is* absurd. I think we can control ourselves. I think we can prevent anything from happening that we don't want to have happen."

"In a perfect world, yes, we could," she agreed.

Mike finally caught on to what was really worrying her. "But you're just a little bit afraid that this isn't a perfect world," he suggested. "You're worried that one of these days one of us will snap and lose our heads, and all these good intentions will go flying out the window."

"Exactly."

"That could happen even if we put the rules in writing and have them notarized," he informed her. "You know what they say about the road to hell."

"Yeah, that it's paved with good intentions. Okay, bottom line, I don't want this to get any more complicated than it already is." She leveled a look straight into his eyes. "I'm trusting you to see that it doesn't."

Mike stared at her. Well, hell. His intentions were every bit as solid as hers, but that didn't mean he was a saint. "You probably shouldn't do that."

"Well, I do," she insisted, looking pleased with herself. "Let's get back to work."

She was up and out the door before Mike could gather

his composure, much less his thoughts. The naive woman had just dumped all responsibility for whatever happened between them from here on out on his shoulders. She'd planted a virtual No Trespassing sign in front of her and expected him to honor it. If she'd wanted to fill his head with nonstop schemes for getting around such a thing, she couldn't have done a more effective job. Getting her into bed was just about the only thought dancing around in his brain. It was crowding out all the sane, rational reasons for keeping his distance. It was nudging aside all of *his* rules for keeping his life uncomplicated.

Oh, he was going to sleep with her. No question about it.

And then he was going to hate himself for letting it happen.

Melanie was rather proud of herself. For once she'd taken the initiative, laid all her cards on the table and told a man exactly what she wanted—or in this case, what she didn't want. Mike had seemed a little startled by her honesty, but in the end he was bound to admire a woman who knew her own mind. And of course he was bound to be grateful that she'd set ground rules that would keep things from getting complicated for either one of them.

Of course, that analysis didn't explain why he was watching her as warily as someone keeping a close eye on a snake that was coiled to strike. In fact, he seemed downright edgy, when the exact opposite should have been the case. He should be relieved.

"Is something wrong?" she asked eventually, poised at the edge of the pile of topsoil, rake in hand.

"Nothing," he said grimly.

"Then why do you keep looking at me like that?"

"Like what?"

"As if I'm some strange species you've never encountered before."

He chuckled. "You're a female. That's strange enough. Men far wiser than I have spent entire lifetimes trying to figure you out."

"There's no need to be insulting."

"Actually I find the way your mind works rather intriguing."

"Oh? In what way?"

He shook his head. "You really don't have a clue, do you?"

"About what?"

"That now that you've declared yourself off-limits, all I can think about is how to get around that."

She swallowed hard and stared at him. That was definitely not what she'd intended. Or was it? "Are you serious?"

"Very."

"But we just agreed—"

"Not exactly, darlin'. You reached a conclusion, put me in charge of following the rules, than sashayed away as if there was nothing more to worry about."

"Because I trust you."

"You shouldn't. I told you that inside."

"But you don't want to get involved with someone who's leaving town soon, do you?"

"No."

"And I don't want to get mixed up in something that could get complicated and messy."

"So you say."

"Do you doubt me?"

"Intellectually, I think you believe that."

"I *do* believe it," she said emphatically.

"Then you obviously have no idea how men's minds

work. Tell us to stay away and all we want is the opposite."

She regarded him incredulously. "But that's just perverse," she said.

"True, but it's a fact of life."

"So now you want to have sex, even though we both know it's a terrible idea?"

He grinned. "Pretty much."

"It's not going to happen," she declared.

His grin spread. "Is that a challenge? Oh, boy, now you're really making it interesting."

Melanie stared at him, trying to fight the sudden desire to take her rake to him. "You're just tormenting me," she accused, aware that now the idea of sex was firmly planted in her head, too. "You're getting some kind of kick out of watching me squirm."

"I think you've got that backward. You're the one doing the tormenting. This is verbal foreplay, darlin'."

Shocked that he could have leaped to such a conclusion, she snapped, "Don't you foreplay me, Mr. Mikelewski. Right this second I wouldn't get anywhere near you if you were the last man on the planet."

He laughed. "Uh-oh, now you've done it. You've questioned my ability to change your mind." He took a step toward her. "Want me to see how quickly I can prove you wrong?"

Melanie backed up, her pulse humming with something that felt a lot more like anticipation than anxiety. Was this the outcome she'd subconsciously been after? Surely not.

"No, I most certainly do not." *Liar, liar, liar.* The voice in her head was raising quite a din.

His gaze never left her face. "You sure?"

"Very sure," she declared, though some traitorous part of her was all but shouting that the opposite was true.

Mike laid down his rake, his expression suddenly sober. "Think about it, Melanie. Because the next time I come by, we won't just be talking about this. We'll be testing all those rules of yours."

When he walked right on past her without so much as a casual touch, she stood there trembling, maybe with outrage, more likely with need. Damn, he was right. All this talk had obviously made both of them want the exact opposite of what they knew was sensible.

"You're spending a lot of time at the Lindsey cottage lately," Jeff observed when he and Mike took a break on a job a few days later.

Since Mike was still wrestling with his conscience over the game he and Melanie were playing, he was in no mood to get drawn into this particular discussion with his best friend. Jeff tended to cut through the crap, and Mike was trying very hard not to be totally honest with himself. He feared if he admitted the truth, he'd be over at that cottage like a shot.

"The garden's almost finished," he said tersely.

"As if you being there has anything to do with the garden," Jeff commented dryly.

"That is my *only* reason for being there," Mike insisted.

"Maybe it started out that way, but something tells me things have changed. What would be so wrong about you getting together with Melanie D'Angelo?"

"If she were the type to have a casual fling, nothing. But she's not."

"Then have a serious fling with her," Jeff said reasonably. "You're long overdue for one. You're single. She's single. Maybe it'll develop into something amazing."

"I can't take that chance," Mike replied. "I have a daughter to consider, and Melanie's made it clear she's going back to Boston."

"Change her mind. I notice she hasn't left yet. Something around here must be interesting enough to keep her right where she is."

"She's on an extended vacation, that's all."

"People fall in love with this area all the time. Her grandmother did. You did. Maybe she will. Give her a reason to stay."

"Maybe's not good enough, not for Jessie," Mike said, sticking to his guns. "She wants a mom. I don't want her to get attached to Melanie and have that rug yanked out from under her."

"I suppose you have a point," Jeff conceded. "You do have to consider Jessie." He gave Mike a sideways glance. "Seems a shame, though. I haven't seen you this happy since you moved here."

"Maybe I'm happy because you actually turned up today with some decent-looking plants," Mike teased, hoping to divert Jeff's attention.

"And maybe pigs fly," Jeff retorted. "My plants are always excellent, and you know it. Your good mood doesn't have a damn thing to do with me. It's all tied up with that woman you claim you're not the least bit interested in."

"I never said I wasn't interested," Mike grumbled. "Only that it's not going to go anywhere."

"Seems like a waste not to give it a chance," Jeff repeated. "Pam says—"

"Heaven protect me from whatever your wife has to say about my love life."

"She says you're just scared," Jeff continued doggedly. "I can't blame you, but you're letting life pass you by."

Mike sighed heavily. "Yeah, it seems that way to me, too."

He didn't realize he'd muttered the wistful words aloud until he heard Jeff's hoot and saw the grin spreading across his face.

"Told you so," Jeff gloated.

"Go to hell."

"No way, pal. I'm sticking around to watch this one play itself out. It's the most entertainment I've had in years."

"Then you must be leading a very dull life."

"Not half as dull as yours before you met Melanie," Jeff reminded him. "Something you ought to consider when Jessie's in bed tonight and you're staring at the TV with nothing but a beer for company."

Unfortunately, Mike had spent several nights just like that lately. Jeff was right. His life was boring. Melanie D'Angelo could change that. He just had to figure out if it was worth the risk.

He thought of the way she'd felt when she was in his arms, of the need that thundered through him. It was pretty damn irresistible, all right.

If only he understood what was holding Melanie back, if only she would open up to him about her past, maybe then he'd know if the pleasures outweighed the risks. Until that time, he needed to proceed with caution.

9

Melanie stared at the tuna on rye on her plate, trying to figure out how anyone could manage to screw up such a basic sandwich. It had so much mayo and sweet relish in it, it was virtually impossible to taste the tuna. She couldn't help but wonder if this was yet another of Brenda's attempts to discourage her from coming into the café, or even from staying in town.

She was trying to work up some enthusiasm for finishing the tasteless sandwich when an unfamiliar man slid into the booth opposite her.

"Hey," he said with an engaging grin. "You're Melanie D'Angelo, right?"

She was still getting used to the fact that no one in this small town thought twice about approaching a stranger. If this man hadn't been wearing a wedding ring in plain sight, she would have worried he was hitting on her, but there was nothing but simple friendliness in his demeanor. She nodded.

"Thought so. I'm Jeff Clayborne, a friend of Mike's. I've heard a lot about you."

Clayborne? That was the name of the nursery they'd

gone to. And this was Mike's friend. She couldn't help wondering how Mike had explained their relationship.

"Oh? What exactly does Mike say about me?" she said just to see what sort of response it would elicit.

He grinned, evidently responding to the edginess she hadn't been able to disguise. "No need to panic. It's all been good. That's why it's been so intriguing."

She wasn't sure what to say to that.

Jeff wasn't the least bit put off by her silence. He gave her an intense look. "So, I was wondering if you'd like to come to dinner at our house one night. My wife's dying to meet you."

She stared at him blankly. "Why?"

"Because you're the first woman Mike's ever shown the slightest interest in," he said candidly.

"So she wants to check me out," Melanie concluded. "Why don't you just tell her she has nothing to worry about? Nothing's going on between Mike and me."

Jeff regarded her with barely suppressed amusement.

Melanie frowned at his blatantly skeptical reaction. "Why is that funny?"

"Because you're both in denial."

"I'm not denying anything," Melanie responded half-heartedly. "Mike took an interest in my grandmother's garden. That's it."

"Really?" Jeff said, still not bothering to hide his skepticism.

"Yes, really," she replied.

"Mike's been driving past that house every day since he moved to town. If he was so fascinated by the garden, why didn't he do something about it before?" Jeff challenged.

"Oh, I don't know. Maybe he has a thing about trespassing," she suggested sarcastically.

He laughed again. "That's one possibility. Personally, I think my explanation makes more sense."

A shadow fell over the table. "What explanation is that?" Mike inquired, his voice chilly.

Melanie's gaze snapped up to meet his. She glanced toward Jeff. She noticed that there wasn't the slightest hint of guilt in his expression at having been caught meddling in his friend's personal life.

Mike slid into the booth next to her and scowled at Jeff. "Well?"

"I was just inviting Melanie to dinner at the house one night," Jeff said easily, ignoring Mike's question.

"Really? Did she accept?"

"Nope. As a matter of fact, she turned me down."

Mike nodded approvingly. "Smart woman."

"Well, I guess I'll leave you two alone," Jeff said. He winked at Melanie. "If you change your mind about dinner—or about anything else—let us know."

"I won't change my mind," Melanie said with less confidence than she might have if Mike's thigh hadn't been pressed to hers. It was just about all she could think about.

When Jeff was gone, Mike scooted away from her as if the contact was too much for him, too. "I'm sorry if he made you uncomfortable. He and Pam have become good friends since I moved here. They think that gives them the right to poke around in my personal life."

"It was no big deal," she said.

He studied her intently. "You sure about that?"

"Absolutely."

"Okay, then. How've you been?"

"Fine. You?"

"Fine."

They fell into an awkward silence. Melanie desperately wanted to break it but couldn't think of a single thing to say. The only thing she really wanted to know was where he'd been and why he hadn't come by the house for days. She already knew the answer, though. Mike was avoiding her. She could hardly blame him.

"Sorry I haven't been by lately," he said as if he'd read her mind. "I've had a big job to complete before the owners get down here next week. They want the landscaping finished before their housewarming party."

Something that felt a lot like relief washed over her. "Will you make it?"

"If Jeff stops meddling in my personal life and gets all the plants over there," Mike said.

"I suppose he meant well."

"The same way your sisters meant well," he replied. He met her gaze and held it for what seemed like an eternity. He seemed to be debating with himself about something. "Do you want to go out with me?" he asked eventually.

She swallowed hard under the intensity of his gaze. "On a date?"

"Call it whatever you want to." He shrugged. "It's just dinner."

"I don't know." She managed to get the lukewarm response out, even though her libido was screaming an emphatic *yes*.

"It wouldn't have to be a big deal. And it definitely wouldn't involve Jeff and Pam putting us under a microscope to dissect our every move."

But it would be a big deal, whether Jeff and Pam were there or not, she thought desperately. It would be a very big deal. Because if she went out with Mike, if he so much as touched her, there would be no turning back.

* * *

Mike wasn't sure what had possessed him to ask Melanie out, not after everything they'd both done to see that their hormones didn't get the best of them. Maybe it was the vulnerability he'd seen in her eyes when he'd offered an explanation for why he'd stayed away. He'd realized then that his absence had actually mattered to her. He'd suddenly wanted to prove that he hadn't been avoiding her, that he wasn't some macho jerk who teased a woman, planted all sorts of ideas in her head, then never followed through.

Maybe he also wanted to prove the same thing to himself. Maybe he wanted to make a liar out of Jeff with his smug declaration that Mike was in denial about his feelings.

Maybe he just wanted another chance to kiss Melanie and make mincemeat out of all those rules she'd established. That was probably the one, he admitted to himself. He'd thought about little else since the last time he'd set eyes on her. All those rules and challenges were practically irresistible.

"Tonight," he pressed when Melanie had been silent way too long. "Jessie can spend a couple of extra hours with the sitter." He liked that. Knowing that Jessie couldn't be left with anyone for too long would keep the evening short. There would be no danger of anything getting out of hand. Yep, that was a great plan.

Melanie nodded slowly, as if she got the implied message. There would be no hanky-panky, no dangerous lingering under the stars, lips locked, hands roaming.

"Okay, then," she said at last. "Just dinner."

Mike bit back a smile. She sounded so emphatic. "I'll pick you up at six."

"And have me home by eight," she added.

"Or thereabouts," he agreed. After all, even he wasn't delusional enough not to leave himself *some* wiggle room. Just in case, he'd leave things a little loose with the sitter.

He glanced into Melanie's eyes and felt his pulse scramble.

Maybe, just in case, he'd see if the sitter could spend the night.

Dinner was lovely. They were able to sit on the restaurant's deck and linger over coffee.

True to his word, Mike had Melanie back at the cottage by eight, but then he suggested a stroll down to the river. She couldn't seem to deny herself that much.

The moon shimmered on the surface of the water. A soft breeze stirred the balmy air.

"It's beautiful," Melanie murmured, caught up in the tranquility of the night.

"Beautiful," Mike echoed, his voice sounding oddly choked.

Melanie turned and saw that his gaze was on her. Her own breath caught in her throat.

"Mike," she whispered.

"Don't talk," he said, leaning down until his mouth hovered over hers. "Don't say another word."

And then he apparently forgot all about the rules and kissed her as if there was no tomorrow. Melanie thought she was going to go up in flames just from the simple touch of his lips on hers. It was as if she'd been waiting her whole life for this man. Doubts fled as passion stirred.

"I want you so much," Mike whispered, his breath ragged. "I know it's a lousy idea. I know we swore we weren't going to let this happen, but I'm not sure I can go another minute without making love to you." His gaze searched hers. "How do you feel about that? Say the word and we'll pretend this never happened."

Pretend it had never happened? That would be next to impossible, Melanie thought as her blood hummed. The memory of his mouth on hers, of his hands skimming over her breasts, was forever seared on her brain. She'd known what it was like to want a man, but not to crave him, not like this. There was no way in hell she could go back fifteen minutes and pretend nothing had ever happened.

"Don't stop," she whispered at last. "Please don't stop."

He scooped her into his arms, and before she knew it, they were in her room, in her bed, and nothing else mattered. Not her own lousy choices in the past, not whatever secrets Mike might still be keeping from her. All that mattered were his tenderness and undisguised need for her.

It scared her how much she'd come to need Mike in such a brief time, but she had no idea how to fight the feelings. They simply were.

Someday she would need answers, but not tonight. Tonight all she needed was Mike.

His rough hands were gentle on her skin, the callused fingers wickedly clever as they manipulated the delicate buttons on her blouse until it fell away, exposing her lacy bra and bare flesh. His eyes turned dark with passion as he took his time surveying her before a deft flick of his fingers had her bra undone and she was entirely naked from the waist up.

His mouth captured the tip of her breast, his tongue circling the nipple until it was a tight, hard bud capable of sending shock waves straight to her toes.

He groaned and fell back on the bed. "It's been too long. I'm never going to last unless we slow things down."

Melanie reached for the hem of his T-shirt, sliding her fingers along the hard flesh of his abdomen before she lifted the shirt free of his jeans, then tugged it over his head. "I don't want to go slow," she said. "I want everything now."

He grinned. "Impatient, huh?"

"Maybe it's a female thing. Once we know what we want, we don't like waiting for it."

He cupped her cheeks. "And you know what you want where I'm concerned?"

"I want this," she said at once.

"And nothing more?" he asked, his expression solemn. "There can't be anything more."

"I know that," she said. "I'm leaving, anyway. All any of us has is the here and now."

He regarded her skeptically. "That's very philosophical, but is it the way you really feel?"

Melanie sat back, vaguely irritated by the string of questions. "Do you think I don't know my own mind?"

"No, of course not, but I saw the way you were with your family. I know closeness must be what you want for yourself, and I can't be anything more than an interlude."

"You don't have the right to assume you know what I want out of life," she retorted, realizing even as she spoke that the argument was rapidly escalating out of control.

"Then tell me what you want."

The request deflated her anger. Instead, an exasperated laugh escaped. "You want to have that conversation *now?*"

He tucked his hands behind his head and leaned back

against the pillows, looking relaxed and sexy as sin. "Yes, I think I do."

"Are you crazy?"

He laughed. "More than likely. Heaven knows, I'll probably be convinced of that in the morning." He winked. "Then again, maybe you can convince me that you really do want a fling and we'll both leave this bed satisfied."

"You're impossible." She studied his expression. "But you're not giving in on this, are you?"

"No."

"What about getting home early?"

"Jessie's fine. Tell me what you want, Melanie."

She sighed heavily and fell back against the pillows next to him. "I wanted to make love to you. I wanted to know what it would be like to have you inside me, filling me up, making me scream."

Mike swallowed hard next to her. Good. He deserved to be squirming about now.

"And long-term?" he asked, his voice ragged. "What do you want for the long haul?"

"I have no idea," she said honestly. "I've been trying very hard lately not to think too far into the future. I've been discovering that there are advantages to living in the moment, to not having too many unrealistic expectations."

Frustrated as she was, she found herself glancing at him. "What about you? What do you want long-term?"

"To make a decent home for my daughter," he said without hesitation. "To do work I enjoy."

"What about having someone to share it with?" she asked, voicing the one longing she hadn't been able to push out of her own heart no matter how hard she'd tried.

"An unrealistic expectation," he said tightly.

"Because you won't let yourself trust another woman?"

He nodded. "I can't. If it were only me, maybe I could take that chance, but I won't put Jessie through losing someone else, just because I'd like to have someone to come home to at night."

She propped herself up on her elbow and leveled a look straight into his eyes. "You know what I think? I think it doesn't have anything at all to do with Jessie. I think you're scared of getting your heart broken again. I think you're the one who hasn't recovered from not being important enough to your ex-wife for her to do anything necessary to get off the drugs and save your marriage."

Mike's gaze never wavered. He never even flinched under the harsh accusation.

"You're probably right," he said at last. "If I hold on to the anger, if I remember every minute of the day and night what it was like to watch Linda self-destruct and abandon Jessie and me, even when she was still right there in the same room, then I won't ever make that mistake again."

"That's sad," Melanie said.

"Are you any better?" he challenged her. "Are you ready to plunge right in and take another chance on love?"

"I'm here, aren't I?"

"Sure," he agreed. "Because I'm a safe bet. I've made it plain I'm not looking for anything more than right here and right now and, for tonight, anyway, that suits you. You're as much of a coward as I am, Melanie." He gave her a sad look. "Worse, you won't even talk about why."

She shivered as the truth hit home. "Because I'm ashamed of what happened," she suddenly told him. "The man I was involved with, the man I thought I knew so well, the man I loved, turned out to be married with two kids."

Mike stared at her incredulously. "Turned out to be? You didn't know?"

"I had no idea," she admitted. "There were probably a million signs, but I either didn't recognize them or ignored them because I didn't want to know the truth. So now you know. I'm an idiot."

He touched her cheek. "You trusted him and he lied to you. *He's* the idiot."

"At least now you know why my sisters were so determined to ask all those questions when they found out about you. They didn't trust me to get it right this time, either."

"I've been honest with you from the beginning," he said. "I might not elaborate too much, but I've told you the basics."

"So, what now?" she asked. "Are we just using each other for sex?"

"Nobody's using anybody," Mike said fiercely. "We're just clearing up the ground rules, deciding if we want to go on."

"If we have to think this much, maybe it's the wrong thing to do," she admitted reluctantly, then moaned. "I can't believe I'm in bed, half-naked with a gorgeous man, and suggesting that we call the whole thing off."

"Frankly, that goes double for me." He glanced sideways at her. "Now that everything's crystal clear, we could pick up where we left off."

Melanie poked him in the ribs. "Not a chance. Honesty has thoroughly spoiled the mood."

He leaned over her, his mouth just above hers. "Bet we could recapture it in a heartbeat."

Her heart skipped a beat, and renewed heat spread through her. "Think so?"

"I know so," he said, right before he claimed her mouth and kissed her until she was writhing beneath him.

"Hmm," she murmured, when she finally caught her breath. "I guess I was wrong."

"Wrong about what?"

"Honesty's one heck of a turn-on, after all." She had no idea why she'd waited so long to tell Mike the truth. Now there were no secrets left to bite either of them in the butt.

When morning came, Mike rolled out of bed, grabbed his pants and headed for the shower. He hadn't felt this alive in a long, long time. There was something about energetic sex that set the blood to humming in a way that nothing else on earth could do.

When he emerged from the bathroom, Melanie was sprawled across the whole bed, the sheet twisted around her in a way that revealed far more than it concealed. His body responded at once, and his plan to get to work early and pretend this was just an ordinary day promptly fell by the wayside.

He sat down on the edge of the bed and smoothed his hand over her rounded backside. The little whimpering sound that emerged from low in her throat reminded him of all the other sexy little moans she'd uttered when they'd made love.

"Wake up, darlin'," he murmured, pressing a kiss to the hollow at the base of her spine.

"Is it morning?" she asked sleepily.

"It is by my standards."

"You leaving?"

"That was the plan," he said.

She rolled over and squinted at him. "Was?" she echoed, sounding intrigued by the possibilities.

"Unless you're interested in having me stay," he said.

"For breakfast?" she taunted.

"Maybe later."

"Ah." She reached up and touched the damp curls on his chest. "You've already taken a shower."

"True."

"And you're half-dressed."

"Only half," he emphasized.

"So it wouldn't take much to persuade you to get undressed?" she concluded, clearly amused.

"Not much at all," he agreed. "Maybe a kiss."

"I can do that," she said, reaching for him and giving him a chaste peck on the cheek.

Mike laughed. "You'll have to do better than that. Think you're up to it?"

She wound her fingers through his hair and kissed him thoroughly until there was no question at all of leaving. The only question was how fast he could get out of his jeans and back inside her.

She was ready for him, her hips arching to meet him, her body already straining toward yet another hard, fast climax that sent shudders sweeping through her right before they triggered his own explosion.

Sweet heaven, he thought, collapsing. How had he missed the fact that urgent, demanding sex could be just as rewarding as long, lingering caresses and a slow buildup of anticipation? The night had been filled with the full range of experiences, each one more satisfying than the one before.

And still it hadn't been enough. He would want Melanie again in an hour or a day or a month. The realization slammed into him like a freight train. Panic followed, clawing at him, churning up a fight-or-flight reaction that made him want to leap from the bed and head for the door. Only an awareness that Melanie didn't deserve that kind of cowardly escape kept him where he was, silent and withdrawn, but at least present. She'd trusted him with her deepest secret last night, told him about the man who'd lied to her and betrayed her. He couldn't prove that he was just as much of a lowlife in his own way by running out on her now.

Next to him she sighed. "You can go," she said softly. "I know you want to."

"No, I…" he began, but the protest died in his throat when he saw the knowing amusement lurking in the depths of her eyes.

"It's okay, really. Go pick up Jessie. I'll be fine. No expectations, Mike. That was our agreement."

"It doesn't feel right to take off on you like that," he said.

"I'm not responsible for your conscience," she told him. "You do have my permission to go, though."

Because he did need to pick up Jessie and get her to school, because he was terrified of what he was feeling for Melanie right this instant, he crawled from the bed and pulled on his clothes.

"I'll call you later or stop by," he said, looking down at her. "Maybe the three of us can do something tonight."

Melanie shook her head. "Not tonight."

"Why? Do you have other plans?"

"No. I just think we both need to take a step back and remember what we talked about here last night, not just how it felt to be together. The sex was fabulous, but the words were just as important, Mike. We can't let ourselves forget them, not for a minute."

Mike bit back a sigh. She was right. "I will call you later today, though."

Her smile didn't quite reach her eyes. "That would be nice."

He turned and left the room, her words echoing in his ears. *Nice.* Wasn't that just *special,* he thought derisively. They were reducing something incredible to nothing, minimizing it so they could both live with it. What the hell were they thinking?

10

There was a wicked gleam in Pam's eye when she cornered Mike in the supermarket. Since he was well aware that Jeff's wife had a tendency to meddle, it was worrisome. So far he'd evaded all of her clever machinations to fix him up, but there was always a first time for her to sneak in under his radar with one of her perfect-for-you dates.

"Well, hello there," Pam greeted him. "You're just the man I've been looking for."

Mike regarded her with amusement. "You must not have been looking too hard. I've been around, mostly with your husband. You do still keep track of him, don't you?"

She made a face. "Unfortunately, Jeff has forbidden me to come by the job sites."

Mike quirked an eyebrow. "He forbade you? That must have gone over well."

"He said I distract him. That made up for it." She shrugged. "Besides, I let him give orders from time to time, when it's not worth arguing over. It's good for the marriage."

Mike grinned. "I'll keep that little pearl of wisdom in mind, should the occasion ever arise."

"You should. It's very sound advice. Now, let's talk about when you're going to bring Melanie to dinner. I know Jeff invited her."

He should have guessed Pam was behind that invitation, even though Jeff had given the impression it was his own idea. In fact, since Jeff's wife had seen him with Melanie weeks ago at the nursery, he was a little surprised it had taken her so long.

"And she said no," he told her flatly. "I think we'll leave it like that."

"Why?"

"Because you'll make too much of it."

"I promise I'll be on my best behavior."

Mike chuckled. "Darlin', I've seen your best behavior. You could give Mike Wallace a run for his money when it comes to asking tough questions."

"Do the two of you have something to hide?" she inquired, her expression innocent.

"Nothing," Mike assured her.

"Then I don't see the problem. Besides, if you want Melanie to stay here, she needs to make friends. Jeff and I are eager to do our part to make her feel welcome, so she won't be quite so anxious to get back to Boston. She is still planning to go back, isn't she?" Pam asked sweetly. "How does that make you feel?"

Obviously she'd done her homework. Mike wondered how much information Jeff had passed on to his wife and how much she'd gleaned on her own. Pam had sources all over town.

"I am not having this conversation with you," he said tightly.

"I just want to help."

"How gracious and utterly unselfish of you," he said dryly.

She gave him a bland look. "We're your friends. It's the least we can do," she said magnanimously.

"I'm still not bringing Melanie over."

"How about if I invite her? Will you come, too?"

Mike saw the trap for what it was. "If she says yes, you bet I'll be there, but only to make sure you don't pester her to death."

Pam grinned, a satisfied glint in her eyes. "I'll call you with the details."

"She won't say yes."

She gave him a pitying look. "Wanna bet?"

"Twenty bucks."

"And you throw in the steaks," she challenged. "Thick New York strip steaks for four."

"Deal."

Mike stood there as Pam walked away, her expression triumphant. What had he been thinking? He knew precisely how sneaky and persuasive Pam could be. He might as well buy the blasted steaks now.

"Do you know some pint-size steamroller named Pam?" Melanie asked when Mike called that evening. She was still reeling from her encounter with the stranger who'd appeared on her doorstep earlier and wouldn't take no for an answer. While Jeff Clayborne had been friendly and persistent, his wife had taken persistence to an art form.

Mike groaned. "I was just calling to warn you she might call."

"Well, she didn't call. She came by."

"And?"

"We're having dinner there tomorrow night."

"How did that happen? I thought you were made of sterner stuff."

"Apparently," she said, her tone wry. "I heard about the bet. That pretty much clinched it."

"You wanted her to win?" he asked incredulously.

"No, I wanted to get to know the woman who could get you to agree to something so ridiculous. I think she might have some maneuvers I should know about."

"You don't really have to go," he told her.

Melanie laughed at the hopeful note in his voice. "Nice try, but it's too late. We're going. Jessie's invited, too, by the way."

"Pam doesn't miss a trick, does she?" he muttered.

"You should have known that. She's your friend, after all."

"I might have to reconsider that. What time?"

"Six. She said with the kids there, it would be better to make it an early night."

"I'll pick you up at quarter to six," he said, sounding resigned.

"*You* could stay home," Melanie said. "I actually only committed for myself. It's up to you if you want to honor your bet."

"Fat chance," Mike responded.

She laughed. "That's what Pam said you'd say."

"Damn straight. I'm not leaving you alone with that woman for a minute. If she's going to pry all your deep, dark secrets out of you, I want to be there."

For the first time since she'd agreed to dinner, Melanie had serious second thoughts. She hadn't been considering Pam's actual mission when she'd caved in under pressure and accepted the woman's invitation. She'd merely been curious to see the interaction between Mike and this woman who seemed to know him so well. Besides, once again, days had passed since he'd been by to see her.

To her regret, she'd missed him. Seeing him with other people around seemed like a safe way to satisfy her longing for a glimpse of him.

"You, Jessie and I could go out for pizza instead," she said wistfully. "In fact, I've been craving pizza for days now. One of those great big ones with everything on it."

"Sounds great, but I'm not sure you're prepared to have Pam hunt us down," Mike replied. "It wouldn't be pretty. Buck up, Melanie. I'm sure she'll make the inquisition as painless as possible."

"Maybe Jessie will be having a bad day tomorrow," Melanie suggested, only partially in jest.

"You would use a little girl to wriggle off the hook?" he asked, feigning shock.

"Yes," she answered without hesitation. "Yes, I would." And she wouldn't suffer a moment's guilty conscience.

"So would I," he admitted. "But my daughter loves going over there. Being around the Claybornes' daughter, Lyssa, is good for Jessie. I won't deny her that because the two of us are cowards."

Melanie heaved a resigned sigh. "Okay, then, I'll see you at five forty-five."

She was about to hang up when Mike said, "Hey, Melanie, one more thing you should probably keep in mind."

"What?"

"No touching. No kissing."

She laughed. That was a given, especially if they intended to at least maintain the illusion in public that there was absolutely nothing between them. "I don't think that will be a problem."

"Wanna bet?"

She sobered at once at the mischievous tone in his voice. "I think you've done enough betting for one day, Mike, don't you? How's that working for you?"

* * *

How had he let himself get drawn into spending an entire evening with Melanie under the watchful gaze of his two best friends? Mike wondered. All too recently he'd crawled out of her bed and vowed once more to steer clear of her entirely because the complications were getting to be too much for him.

Worse, he'd agreed to bring Jessie along tonight, and his daughter was currently chattering like a little magpie, telling Melanie all about her best friend at school and the accident she'd had with a pot of paste that had necessitated getting her hair cut very, very short.

"I'm glad that didn't happen to me," Jessie said. "I'm never getting my hair cut."

Melanie laughed. "You might reconsider that when it gets so long you're sitting on it and it takes hours and hours to dry."

Jessie fell silent, her expression thoughtful as she studied Melanie. "Your hair's long."

"Not that long," Melanie said. "Just long enough for me to braid it or pull it into a ponytail when I don't have time to do anything else with it."

"Daddy puts my hair into a ponytail sometimes, but it's usually crooked," Jessie said, sounding forlorn. "I never had a braid."

Melanie chuckled. "Well, fixing hair requires a talent some men don't have. That's why they wear theirs so short."

"Hey," Mike protested. "I can do anything you can do."

Melanie regarded him with amusement. "Is that one of those challenges you're so fond of?"

The memory of another challenge, one she'd issued very recently, slammed into him and made the temperature in the car climb by several degrees. And he'd foolishly trumped her just last night with that no-kissing, no-touching nonsense. It promised to be a very long evening and with Jessie along, there would be no relief at the end of it.

"I think maybe we ought to call it quits when it comes to making challenges," he said in a choked voice.

"What's a challenge?" Jessie asked.

"It's like a dare," Melanie told her.

Jessie's expression brightened. "Like when Kevin Reed dared me to climb to the top of the jungle gym?"

Mike felt his heart drop. "Please tell me you didn't do it?"

Jessie gave him an unconcerned look. "Kevin's dumb. I wouldn't do anything he said."

"Thank God," Mike murmured fervently. "Maybe we should change the subject."

Melanie regarded him knowingly. "Any particular topic you'd find a bit safer?"

"Yeah. Let's decide how we're going to get away from here tonight before dessert."

"Daddy!" Jessie protested. "We have to stay for dessert. It's the best part."

"It certainly is," Melanie agreed.

"But it's usually accompanied by lots of questions everyone's been too polite to ask up until then," Mike reminded her.

Melanie frowned. "You have a point. However, it would be rude to try to duck out. We'll just have to be evasive."

"You did say you'd met Pam the steamroller, right?" he inquired.

"I can handle Pam, now that I've seen her in action," Melanie foolishly insisted. "I'm prepared."

"Ha!"

She gave him one of those superior female looks designed to make men feel like idiots. "Watch and learn."

Mike barely contained a groan. This was one time he really didn't want to be right, but he knew Pam. If she was tricky on her own, she was the queen of sneakiness when she had Jeff around for backup. He and Melanie were doomed, no question about it.

The front yard of the Clayborne house was littered with toys. Melanie had to weave her way through bicycles, wagons and an obviously pricey miniature convertible—to say nothing of basketballs and beachballs—to get to the front door, which was already standing open. Pam was waiting on the front steps.

"Sorry about the chaos," she said, coming forward to give Melanie a hug as if they were old friends. To Mike, Pam offered a smug, told-you-so grin and a peck on the cheek. "The kids aren't required to put everything away till they come in for the night and, believe me, they always wait till the very last minute." She leaned down to scoop up Jessie. "How's my girl?"

"I'm fine," Jessie said, clinging to Pam's neck. "Where's Lyssa?"

"She's in her room, expecting you. Wait till you see her new dollhouse. Go on up," Pam said, setting her down at the foot of the stairs. "I'll call you when the pizza gets here."

"The kids are having pizza?" Melanie said wistfully.

"It'll keep 'em out of our hair," Pam said. "We can get to know each other."

She grabbed Melanie's hand as if she feared Melanie might bolt. "You can come in the kitchen and talk to me while I finish the salad. And Mike, Jeff's out back waiting for those steaks."

Mike nodded, then leaned down to whisper in Melanie's ear as he passed. "Divide and conquer. Told you she was sneaky."

"I heard that," Pam said.

"I meant for you to," he responded happily. "I want you to know we're on to you."

Melanie reluctantly followed Pam into a large, bright combination kitchen and family room with a huge island in the middle and windows all around. It was obvious that the family spent a lot of time here. There was a cozy built-in breakfast nook that was big enough for six, and at the opposite end a comfortable sofa sat in front of a fireplace. A giant-screen TV was angled toward the sofa, but could be seen from the kitchen, as well. It was a great setup for having the guys over for football. In the kitchen itself, there were professional-grade stainless-steel appliances that Melanie's sister would envy.

"You must like to cook," she said to Pam.

"Actually I hate it," Pam responded. "But with five of us, I have to do it, so I figured I might as well create a space I'd enjoy."

"You help Jeff with the nursery?"

Pam's expression immediately brightened. "That's how we met. I love plants. When I first came to town—right after I got out of college with a degree in horticulture—his dad hired me."

"And it was love at first sight?" Melanie asked.

Pam laughed at her assessment. "Hardly. With my fancy degree, Jeff thought I was a know-it-all. He used to tell me book learning wasn't nearly as important as practical experience. He'd grown up in the business and thought he'd seen just about everything. Then one very expensive garden died just days after he'd put it in, and he had no idea why."

"Let me guess. You told him why."

"Of course not," Pam said airily. "I let him sweat. He worried and fretted and flatly refused to ask for my help, so I just kept on doing my job and keeping my mouth shut. After about a week the customer came in and started raising a ruckus about throwing all that money down the tubes. She threatened to go to another nursery if we didn't fix the problem pronto. Jeff was about to offer her a refund, when I took pity on him and stepped in."

"What did you say?"

"That she'd be making a huge mistake going to anyone else, because she'd just have the same problem all over again. I'm not sure who was more surprised, the customer or Jeff, but he caught on right away."

"Did he know what you'd figured out?"

"Of course not," Pam said with a grin. "But he told her that I was their resident expert, and I knew how to solve the problem."

"Which you did and saved the day," Melanie concluded.

"Pretty much. I'd seen some of the plants Jeff had dug out of the ground. Their root systems were being destroyed. We got rid of the little underground critters that were dining on them, and the next plants we put in thrived. That night Jeff asked to borrow a couple of my textbooks. We started having study dates and eventually concluded we made a pretty good team."

She beamed at Melanie. "And here we are ten years later, happy as can be."

"Sounds like a match made in heaven," Melanie said, unable to keep the wistful note out of her voice.

"It is," Pam agreed, then seized on the opening Melanie

had inadvertently given her. "So what about you and Mike?"

"What about us?" Melanie responded evasively.

"What kind of match are you?"

"The impossible kind," Melanie said at once.

"I know he has all sorts of baggage where his ex-wife is concerned," Pam said, "but what about you?"

When Melanie said nothing, Pam added, "Am I being too personal?"

"Pretty much," Melanie told her, hoping that would put an end to the subject.

"Sorry," Pam apologized, though she didn't sound particularly sincere. "How serious is this baggage of yours? An ex-husband?"

Melanie chuckled despite herself. Pam obviously wasn't a quitter. "No," she told her. "No ex-husband."

"Ex-boyfriend, then?"

"Something like that."

Pam's eyes widened. "Ex-*girlfriend?*"

"Heavens no!"

"Then what *did* you mean?"

Melanie thought about responding honestly but finally decided she didn't know Pam well enough for that sort of personal exchange of information. "It's not worth talking about," she said eventually, and for the first time realized it really wasn't. Jeremy was the one with the problem. That didn't mean her issues would vanish overnight, but she was gaining some perspective, realizing the whole experience had taught her some home truths about her judgment skills.

Pam regarded her sympathetically. "I know I'm prying, but it's only because I care about Mike."

"So do I," Melanie admitted softly. It was the first

time she'd allowed herself to say even that much about her feelings for Mike.

"Then I don't see the problem," Pam said. "There's obviously a powerful attraction at work here. Why not play it out?"

"Too much baggage on both sides," Melanie said succinctly. Mike's had made him reticent and gun-shy. Hers had made her aware of her own shortcomings. In such an environment it would be all but impossible for trust to flourish. It was not, she cautioned herself, a combination destined for happily-ever-after.

"But that's old news," Pam insisted. "You can both make a fresh start."

"Maybe neither of us wants to," Melanie responded.

"You'd rather wallow in your misery the way Mike has been doing ever since he and his wife split up?"

"I don't want to wallow in it," Melanie insisted. "But I do hope to learn something from it."

"How will you know if you've learned anything if you don't put yourself back into the game?" Pam demanded.

"I honestly don't know," Melanie admitted.

"I think what you both need is a little nudge from some good friends," Pam concluded just as the men came in with the steaks.

"Give it a rest, Pam," Mike said tersely, his worried gaze on Melanie.

Melanie forced a smile. "We're just indulging in a little girl talk."

"Ha!" Jeff muttered, giving his wife an affectionate peck on the cheek. "Pam's on a mission. Mike's been her personal project since the day he hit town. How many women have you tried to fix him up with, sweetheart?"

"*Tried* being the operative word," Mike said. "I've never said yes."

"Not even once," Pam confirmed, looking disgusted. "He's ruining my track record. I did very well with some of Jeff's other bachelor friends."

"What have I always told you?" Mike asked.

"That you'd find someone on your own when you were ready," she said. Her gaze narrowed as she looked speculatively from him to Melanie and back again. "Have you?"

Mike laughed, even as Melanie's heart did a little flip-flop.

"Nice try, darlin'," he said. "Now let's eat before the steaks get cold."

He snagged Melanie's hand and rubbed his thumb reassuringly across her knuckles as he led the way to the table. "Sit next to me," he requested, pulling out a chair. "That way I can protect you when Pam gets another bee in her bonnet about our relationship."

"I think Pam's done for the night," Jeff said, giving his wife a pointed look.

"Hardly," she retorted. "But I will give it a rest until dessert. I made a triple-threat chocolate cake. It's been known to make grown women weep and even a few men. It's also a great incentive for getting people to talk."

"I hate chocolate," Mike declared.

"Liar," Pam accused with a grin. "Last time I made it, you told me all sorts of secrets just to get a second slice."

Melanie chuckled at Mike's stunned expression.

"You used that cake to wheedle information out of me?" he asked incredulously.

"Of course," Pam confessed.

Mike turned to Melanie. "Told you we needed to get out of here before dessert."

"For a triple-threat chocolate cake, I think I'll take my chances," Melanie said.

"Your funeral," he muttered darkly.

More than likely, Melanie thought. But she didn't have to reveal anything she didn't want these three people to know. She could have her cake and keep her secrets, too.

But gazing into Mike's eyes, feeling the faint beginnings of the same heat he'd stirred in her a few nights ago, she was beginning to wonder why she felt it necessary.

11

Mike couldn't recall the last time he'd felt so relaxed or spent such an enjoyable evening with friends. Even Pam's persistent questions hadn't fazed him after a while, probably because Melanie had taken them in stride and fended them off with considerable aplomb. She'd gotten through a huge piece of Pam's triple-threat chocolate cake without revealing a single secret. Since he'd hoped for a few more insights into her relationship with the married man who'd betrayed her, he'd found that a little frustrating, but he had to admire her clever avoidance tactics.

Carrying a sleeping Jessie out to the car at midnight, he was struck by how right it all felt. He couldn't think of a single time during his tumultuous marriage that he'd experienced such a sense of contentment. After the first months of their marriage, Linda had flatly refused to socialize with their old friends, no doubt because she preferred doing drugs in private. It had isolated them, making it that much harder for him to adjust once the breakup happened.

Knowing—from bitter past experience and from Melanie's own commitment to leaving—that the contented feeling wouldn't last made him suddenly edgy and silent.

"What's wrong?" Melanie asked eventually as they neared her cottage.

"Nothing."

She regarded him with obvious impatience. "Come on, Mike. You had a smile on your face not fifteen minutes ago, when we left Jeff and Pam's. Now you look as if you've just received the worst possible news."

"In a way, that's exactly what happened," he admitted. "I realized that this entire evening was phony."

She stared at him incredulously. "What on earth is that supposed to mean?"

He struggled to put his emotions into words, something he usually avoided at all costs. "There we were," he began, "pretending not to be a couple."

Melanie nodded. "Which we aren't."

He regarded her bleakly. "Yet everything felt as if we were. Jeff and Pam could see it, too. They won't let me hear the end of it. Pam's going to want us to announce a wedding date soon. It's just the way she is. She's happy, and she wants everyone around her to be happy, too. She's convinced marriage is the key."

Melanie's expression faltered. "Oh, Mike, I'm sorry. I hadn't thought of it that way, but you're right. I should never have agreed to go to dinner. It just added fuel to her already overactive imagination, didn't it?"

"Yes, but that's not the worst of it," he admitted.

"Then what is?"

He wasn't sure he wanted to lay his own emotions so bare, so he settled for asking her, "You enjoyed it, didn't you?"

"Except for dodging some of Pam's questions, yes," she admitted candidly.

"It felt right?" he prodded. "Comfortable?"

"Yes, it did."

He pulled into her driveway, cut the engine and turned to face her. "Does that make as little sense to you as it does to me?"

"Which part? That we enjoyed ourselves or that we're fighting it?"

"Either one."

Melanie stared straight ahead for so long, Mike was sure she didn't intend to answer, but she finally turned and met his gaze.

"It's where we are," she said quietly. "We can't change that. We're both trying to be as honest as we know how to be."

"Maybe we should try to change where we are," he persisted. It was something he'd never thought he would say. He'd never imagined that he would reach a point when he might be willing to risk his heart again, but to have the feelings he'd experienced tonight last forever, maybe it would be worth it. Melanie wasn't Linda. Far from it. She was strong. Maybe this time things wouldn't fall apart, if they recognized what they had and fought like hell to keep it.

"Can you do that?" she asked doubtfully. "Can you put aside the past and move forward?"

He wasn't sure. He wanted to, but he was as terrified as she obviously was. "Frankly, I've never tried before, but I'd like to," he admitted. "You?"

"I don't know if I can, Mike," she whispered. "I just don't know. It's not just you I'm not sure about. In fact, it really has nothing to do with you. It's my own judgment I don't trust."

"Aren't you even willing to try?" he asked. "What we have is too precious, too rare, to turn our backs on it, just because we're scared. You were with that married man for how long?"

"Six months."

"I was with Linda for a couple of years. I'd vowed to stick by her in sickness and in health, for better or for worse. For nearly a year of that the marriage was a disaster. It was the worst. If I can try to put that behind me, surely you can move beyond a few months with a guy you obviously never knew very well."

"You make it sound so easy, as if we can just snap our fingers and all those pesky hurts and bad choices will disappear."

"I know they won't disappear," he said impatiently. "But maybe it's possible to put them in perspective, to leave them in the past." He gave her a penetrating look. "Or are you still hung up on the guy? Is that what's really going on?"

"Absolutely not," she said so fiercely he had to believe her.

"Then why are you hesitating? I'm not suggesting we run off and get married tomorrow, just that we work on what we have, see where it could take us."

"I still have to go back to Boston," she said with a trace of stubbornness, ignoring the rest. "That hasn't changed."

Mike wanted to pound his fist on the steering wheel in frustration, but he didn't. He merely asked, "Why? What's holding you there?"

She hesitated, as if she weren't quite certain herself, then said, "My family. My roots."

"You have roots here, too," he reminded her.

"I have memories," she corrected. "It's not the same thing."

Mike stared at her silently, aware that he'd lost.

Whatever she'd left behind in Boston—and he didn't believe for a minute it was as simple as family or roots—was more important than what she'd found here. And he couldn't continue pushing, couldn't continue fighting a losing battle, not with Jessie's heart to consider along with his own.

"I guess that says it all, then," he said finally. "Come on. I'll walk you to your door."

She looked almost as miserable as he felt. "You don't need to do that," she said stiffly.

"I'll walk you to the door," he repeated, climbing from the car and going around to yank open the passenger door with considerably more force than necessary.

Only when Melanie was standing next to him, with the moon casting light on her cheeks, did he notice the tears. He brushed them away with the pad of his thumb and felt his heart wrench.

"This is wrong," he murmured, right before bending down to kiss her. Even as he spoke, he wasn't entirely certain what he meant...the kiss, the unnecessary parting, any of it.

Because he wasn't sure, he didn't let himself sink into the kiss the way he wanted to, didn't taste her greedily or linger long enough to make her moan. It was enough just to feel her respond, to feel her sway instinctively toward him, to feel her heat. All of that felt every bit as right as the rest of the evening had. How could she turn her back on that? How could *he?*

He sighed at the mess they'd gotten themselves into. It was wrong to want her so badly, knowing that it couldn't be.

But, damn, no matter what she said, no matter what his head told him, it felt right.

* * *

Melanie was still shaking long after Mike returned to his car and his daughter and drove away. She put her fingers to her lips, which continued to tingle from that last, lingering, unexpected kiss.

There had been so much sorrow in his voice, so much pain in his eyes, and she was responsible for that. She'd only been honest, only told him what they both already knew, that whatever this was they were feeling couldn't last. Even so, she felt as if she'd ripped out his heart.

And her own.

Why else would she feel so miserable if she hadn't fallen just a little bit in love with him?

"That can't be," she said fiercely, denying the feelings that bubbled up inside of her every time she thought of him.

There was no one around to challenge the claim, so she accepted it, just as she'd used it to keep a firm distance between them. Refusing to acknowledge her feelings was enough for now. If she pretended hard enough that Mike didn't matter, then she'd be able to leave when the time came.

And it had to be soon, she warned herself. She couldn't let this situation drag out forever, for his sake and her own. If she'd made up her mind to go, then she needed to do it.

She'd barely closed the front door behind her when the phone rang. Grateful for anything that might take her mind off Mike, she grabbed it.

But when she heard her big sister's voice, she burst into tears.

"Mel, what's going on? Melanie, talk to me right this second," Ashley ordered when Melanie's sobs went on and on. "Dammit, do I have to get in the car and drive down there?"

That prospect dried the tears as nothing else could have. "No," Melanie whispered hoarsely.

"That's better," Ashley soothed. "Now tell me what happened."

"I think I'm falling in love with Mike," she blurted, mostly to hear the words aloud, to see how true they rang. Unfortunately, they sounded dead-on accurate.

"Well, hallelujah!" her sister said.

"But I can't be in love with him," Melanie protested. "It's absurd. I hardly know him. Besides, I don't live here. I live in Boston."

"Not at the moment," Ashley reminded her, obviously trying to suppress a chuckle. "As for it being too soon, sometimes it doesn't take all that long. Not when it's right."

"The last time I fell in love, it was all wrong."

"I'll say," Ashley said lightly. "But you're a smart woman. You learned your lesson."

"Did I? How can you tell? I can't."

"Are there things Mike's keeping from you?"

"Yes," she said automatically, seizing on the excuse.

"What?"

Pressed, Melanie wasn't entirely sure she knew why she was so uneasy about his lack of openness. "He won't talk about his marriage, not in any kind of detail. He's only told me it's over, that his ex-wife was into drugs, so he divorced her and got full custody of Jessie."

"That sounds like a lot of information to me," Ashley commented. "Did you believe him?"

"Yes."

"Well then, what's the problem?"

"What if I'm wrong? What if there's more to it? What

if he'd take her back in a heartbeat if she got her life straightened out?"

"And what if you're right to trust what he's telling you?" Ashley demanded. "What if it's all over and it's you he wants?"

"I thought you guys didn't trust him," Melanie reminded her, irritated that her big sister was defending Mike now.

"No, we just told you to be sure you'd gotten all the facts about his past up-front. Look, sweetie, we can't make this decision for you. You're the only one who can decide if you love him and if he's worth the changes you'll need to make to keep him in your life."

"He might be." Melanie thought of the way she'd felt when they'd made love. It hadn't been just about sex. He'd made her feel…cherished.

And tonight? Tonight he'd opened a part of his life to her by sharing an evening with his friends. That was something Jeremy the jerk had never done, because he couldn't, because she was nothing but a dirty little secret in his life.

There was Jessie, too. Despite his concerns, Mike was permitting Melanie to get to know his daughter, the most precious person in his life. She knew him well enough by now to realize that he would never have allowed that to happen if he hadn't trusted Melanie not to break his little girl's heart.

He was letting her, slowly but surely, into his life, but she couldn't say the same. She'd kept her secrets, tried to keep Mike away from her sisters, pushed him away when he'd tried to ask for anything more than the most superficial relationship. She was doing a damn fine job of trying to protect herself, but what had it gotten her?

She'd fallen for him anyway. She could walk away, but her heart would still be broken.

"I'm an idiot," she said eventually.

"Never," Ashley said loyally.

"Mike wouldn't agree with you."

"Then he's the idiot."

"No, he's not," she said adamantly.

Ashley laughed. "If you're that quick to jump to his defense, I think you have your answer, baby sister. Now what are you going to do about it?"

Melanie leaned against the wall and slid down until she was sitting on the floor. "I wish to hell I knew."

"You'll figure it out," Ashley said with confidence. "If you need any help, all you have to do is call. We'll come down there and cut through all the nonsense until the answer's plain as day."

Melanie smiled. "I think I'll try to get this one on my own."

"You know we love you."

"That goes both ways," she told her sister.

"And something tells me you'll find room in your heart for Mike and Jessie, too."

Melanie was beginning to believe that herself. She just had to pray that it wasn't too late.

"When can we see Melanie again?" Jessie asked for the thousandth time over breakfast. It had been a week since Mike had left her at her door, tears on her cheeks, his own heart heavy. "I thought she was our friend."

"She is," Mike replied grumpily. He'd been having a lot of sleepless nights, thanks to Melanie and her stubborn refusal to give the two of them half a chance. He wasn't inclined to cut her much slack this morning. He'd honestly thought she might call him by now, that she'd reconsider.

"Then why can't we see her?" Jessie persisted.

"What's this sudden fascination with Melanie?" he asked, although he already knew the answer. Melanie had captivated both of them. As for him, he'd been in a lousy mood ever since he'd made love to her, ever since he'd discovered he was half in love with her and then realized she was going to walk out of his life all the same.

"She's nice," Jessie explained, as if that was more than enough to inspire her undying loyalty. "And she's a girl. She knows stuff you don't."

"Such as?"

"She can braid my hair."

Mike stared at his daughter, bemused. "I didn't know you wanted your hair braided."

"Well, I do."

"How do you know Melanie can do it?"

"She told me," Jessie explained patiently. "In the car. Weren't you listening?"

He'd heard something about his crooked ponytails and long hair, but he'd obviously missed the implications.

"And she said we could paint my fingernails," Jessie added excitedly.

"You most certainly cannot!" Mike said, appalled. He hated seeing kids running around trying to look like grown-ups. Adulthood and responsibilities came soon enough. He wanted his daughter to be a child as long as possible.

Jessie's eyes promptly filled with tears. "Why not?"

"You're six years old!"

"It's just for fun," she wailed.

Mike stared at her helplessly. Braids? Painted fingernails? If he was this far out of his element when Jessie was only six, how the devil was he going to cope with the teenage years?

He'd sworn that, for his own protection, he wasn't going to go near Melanie again. But it was a measure of his devotion to his daughter that he was actually considering breaking that vow just so Jessie could have her hair fixed the way she wanted it and get her nails painted.

Ha! he thought sarcastically. He'd been looking for the perfect excuse for days now. Jessie had just handed it to him, all wrapped up in little girlie bows.

"I'll talk to Melanie after I drop you off at school this morning," he promised with a good show of reluctance. "If Melanie says it's okay, we'll stop by later. You two can play beauty shop to your heart's content."

Jessie beamed, her tears forgotten. "Thank you, Daddy."

If only he could end all her tantrums so easily, Mike thought wistfully. If only the path to his own happiness were so obvious.

Instead lately he'd felt as if the ground were shifting beneath him, turning all of his determined resolutions about avoiding relationships into chaos. He'd actually begun wondering if maybe he should consider trying just a little harder to convince Melanie to stick around. Maybe her first response had been a knee-jerk reaction. Goodness knows, he'd had a few of those himself since he'd met her.

That was why he'd made it a point to avoid her in recent days. He'd been afraid he'd utter the words, beg her to stay and then decide ten minutes later that he wanted to take the plea back. Better to steer clear of her until he knew his own mind. Better to avoid a rejection that would remind him all too painfully of the way he'd felt when

Jessie's mother had turned to drugs, rather than to him or their daughter.

In the meantime, though, dropping off Jessie shouldn't be a problem. If Melanie agreed to the visit, he'd never have to set foot inside the house. And with Jessie underfoot, he wouldn't act on any wild urges to drag Melanie into his arms and kiss her until she relented and agreed to stay in Virginia with him.

He could do this, he concluded. It was just a matter of concentration and keeping his hands to himself.

Mike's plan pretty much went up in flames the instant he set eyes on Melanie right after he dropped Jessie at school. There were dark circles under her eyes, as if she'd gotten no more sleep lately than he had. Her lush mouth curved into a cautious smile that all but begged him to kiss her.

"I was thinking about calling you," she said.

The words sounded forced. She'd uttered them only after they'd stood and stared at each other for so long, Mike had begun to feel awkward.

"Oh?" he said, not sure what to do with that bit of information.

"I'm sorry about the way things ended the other night."

"Oh?" He felt he was beginning to sound like an idiot, but she seemed to be on a roll. He might as well let her take the lead here. Maybe it would save his pride.

"I shouldn't have pushed you away," she said, "not when what I really wanted was for you to stay and talk things out."

He shook his head in confusion. "You didn't push me away."

Melanie laughed. "Not literally, no—but the outcome

was the same as if I had. You haven't been near Rose Cottage since then."

Pride be damned! "To be honest, I was thinking of calling you, maybe suggesting you put some nasturtiums in the garden. Did you know you can eat them?"

She grinned. "Actually I did. My sister Maggie is a magazine food editor. She passes along all sorts of little oddities like that. Maggie might like it if I planted nasturtiums."

"I'll see about getting some, then," he said, the awkwardness suddenly back.

"Did you come by for some other reason, or was this just about the nasturtiums?"

He shook off the daze he'd been in since setting eyes on her. "It's about Jessie, actually."

"Is she okay?"

"I suppose that depends on how important hairstyles are to you girls."

She regarded him blankly. "What?"

"She wants braids. She says you can do them."

"Sure."

"And painted fingernails," he added.

"I can do those, too," she said.

"Would this afternoon work for you? You know how kids are when they get an idea. They'll nag you to death until you give 'em what they want. Jessie's worse than most."

"This afternoon would be fine." She studied him curiously. "Do you intend to stick around for this makeover?"

"Lord, no," he said, appalled. "Unless you need me to. Normally I wouldn't leave Jessie, but she's eager to come, so I don't think it will upset her if I take off."

Melanie laughed. "I think we can manage without having you underfoot. I have to admit, though, that I'm a little surprised. I thought you didn't want me getting too involved in Jessie's life, especially after what I said the other night."

He studied her intently while debating how to reply. He opted for the truth. "It's too late for that. She likes you. This was her idea."

Surprisingly, delight lit her eyes. "I'm glad. I like her, too."

"Be careful, okay? Kids get attached real easily."

"Adults, too, sometimes," she said in a tone that caught him off guard.

He searched her face but couldn't read anything in her expression. "What are you saying?" he asked cautiously.

"I'm still working that out," she told him.

A tiny spark of hope flared to life inside Mike, but he knew better than to fan it into a full-fledged blaze. "Let me know when you figure it out, darlin'."

"Believe me, you'll be the first to know."

He met her gaze and saw the longing there. Eventually he nodded. "See you later, then."

She smiled slowly. "See you later."

"About three-thirty."

"That'll be good."

He couldn't seem to get his feet to move, couldn't seem to tear his gaze away.

"Is there something else?" Melanie asked, amusement lurking in her eyes.

"Nothing." He forced himself to turn away.

He was pitiful, he chided himself. Pathetic. He was acting like a lovesick kid who was scared to make a pass.

Then again, so was she. The realization made him grin. By the time he reached his truck, Mike was laughing. Maybe coming here hadn't been such an idiotic move after all.

12

After a trip to the drugstore for a selection of nail polish, Melanie sang along at top volume with an oldies radio station as she gathered the rest of the essentials for Jessie's makeover. It was the first time in practically forever that she'd felt completely carefree. Maybe this beauty day for Jessie was just what Melanie herself had been needing, too—a chance to focus on someone else's needs for a change. She remembered how much fun she and her sisters had had when they were Jessie's age, playing dress-up and using their mom's makeup. It had been their favorite rainy-day activity.

Melanie was still singing, making up words when she didn't know them, when the phone rang. She cut the blasting sound on the radio as she picked up the receiver.

"Hello."

"Is this Melanie D'Angelo?" an unfamiliar voice asked.

"Yes."

"This is Adele Sinclair, the principal at the elementary school. I'm really sorry to bother you, but this is a bit of an emergency. It involves Jessica Mikelewski."

Melanie's heart began to pound. An emergency? Involving Jessie? Why on earth would the school be calling her? "What's wrong? Is Jessie okay? Have you contacted her father?"

"She's had one of her incidents," the principal said, her tone dire. She seemed to expect Melanie to understand the implications.

"Incidents?" Melanie asked. "What does that mean?"

"In a nutshell, something upset her and she threw a tantrum. We can't get her to settle down."

Even as Ms. Sinclair spoke, Melanie could hear a child's pitiful wails in the background. Even though Mike had told her about Jessie's behavior problems, even though she'd witnessed a couple of the little girl's tantrums first-hand, it had been weeks since there had been any such incidents, at least none that Melanie was aware of. Maybe Mike hadn't mentioned them because he'd come to take them in stride.

"I've tried to reach her father," the principal continued, "but his cell phone is apparently out of range. Jessie's been crying for you. Normally we wouldn't contact someone we don't know, especially since you're not on the emergency list Mr. Mikelewski gave us, but Pam Clayborne, who is on the list, said she thought it would be okay for me to call you. I can't release Jessie to you, but could you please come over here and see her? It might help to calm her. Otherwise, Mrs. Clayborne said she'd come."

"I'll be there in five minutes," Melanie promised, even though there were a million and one questions on the tip of her tongue. She could ask them once she'd seen for herself how distraught Jessie was, and after she'd done what she could to soothe her.

The weather had turned cloudy and chilly, so she grabbed her sweater, along with her purse and car keys, as she ran out the door.

The school was less than a mile away. She knew the location thankfully, because she and her sisters had loved going to the playground there as children. Her grandmother had taken them often. The big, old-fashioned three-story brick building was as solid today as it had been when it was built at least a half century earlier. There were new swings and other colorful equipment for the kids now, but at the moment no one was using any of it.

As soon as Melanie reached the main entrance, she could hear the same choking sobs that had echoed on the phone. She followed the sound to the principal's office.

The instant she opened the door, Jessie's small body hurtled into her. Melanie knelt down and held the little girl, murmuring soothing words even as she gazed up at a distraught woman who was undoubtedly Ms. Sinclair. She gave Melanie a sympathetic look.

"I'll give you some time alone with her," the principal murmured, obviously relieved. She retreated toward her office. "Meantime, I'll try again to reach Mr. Mikelewski."

Melanie nodded.

Jessie's arms clung to her neck, and her body quivered with sobs.

"Shh," Melanie soothed. "It's okay, sweetheart. I'm here now. Can you tell me what happened?"

Jessie shook her head.

"Why don't we sit on this bench over here?"

"No," Jessie wailed. "I want to go home."

"Baby, I can't take you home."

"Why not?" Jessie murmured into her neck.

"Because the school can't let you leave with me. They don't know me."

Jessie stared at her with tear-filled eyes and damp,

blotchy cheeks. "But I do," she protested. "I told 'em you were my friend."

"I'm afraid that's not good enough. We need to wait for your dad. In the meantime, if you'll tell me what upset you, maybe I can help." Without asking again, Melanie scooped Jessie up and settled on the bench with the child in her lap. Slowly Jessie's tense little body began to relax against Melanie, but she still refused to say a word.

"Did something happen in class?" Melanie prodded, wanting to get to the bottom of whatever had set Jessie off.

"No," the child whispered.

"On the playground?"

Jessie's head bobbed, but she didn't look at Melanie.

"Did you have a fight with one of your classmates?"

Again, a faint nod.

Melanie took a wild stab in the dark. "Kevin Reed?"

Jessie pulled back, her eyes widened in shock. "How come you knew that?"

"It doesn't matter. Did he do something to you?"

Jessie sniffed. "He said I was a baby."

"Why on earth would he say something like that?"

"'Cause my daddy brings me to school and waits for me after. I *like* it that Daddy comes with me. It doesn't make me a baby, does it?"

"Oh, honey, there's nothing wrong with that at all. I'm sure lots of moms and dads bring their kids to school. Kevin's just being mean." Melanie couldn't help thinking that there was more to this than a bit of name-calling. "Did something else happen?"

"Uh-huh," Jessie admitted.

"What?"

"Kevin's dad doesn't bring him to school. That's why he was being mean to me," Jessie said knowingly. "He doesn't even have a dad. I said that, and then he hit me, and he said I didn't have a mom and that was worse."

Oh, boy, Melanie thought.

Jessie gave her a pleading look. "Can you be my mom? Please?"

"Sweetie, I wish I could be. You're a wonderful girl, and anyone would be lucky to be your mom…."

"Then how come my real mom left us?" Jessie asked plaintively.

"I don't think it was something she wanted to do," Melanie replied, feeling her way through the minefield. "I'm sure it made her very sad."

"Then why didn't she stay?"

"Because she couldn't," Melanie said, though she couldn't imagine such a thing herself. She tried to explain anyway, hoping she could find words that would reassure Jessie and wouldn't be too far from the truth or at least whatever version of the truth Mike had shared with Jessie. "Sometimes adults have to do things that are very painful, but they don't see any other choice. That doesn't mean your mom didn't love you. I'll bet your dad's told you that."

"I suppose," Jessie conceded grudgingly.

"If he said it, you can believe it."

"My real mom's never even come to see me. I'd rather have you as my mom," Jessie said fiercely.

The ache in Melanie's heart nearly overwhelmed her. She was completely out of her depth. It didn't help that she knew she, too, was going to abandon this precious little girl.

"It's just not that simple," she said eventually.

"How come?"

"Because it's up to the grown-ups to decide if they want to get married."

"Don't you like my dad?"

"Your dad's terrific," Melanie said honestly.

"I know he likes you," Jessie said with confidence. "I think you should decide to get married, so you can be my mom."

Melanie was impressed with Jessie's persistence, even as she tried to think of some way to deflect it. "I hear you want me to fix your hair and paint your fingernails."

Jessie's expression immediately brightened. "Did Daddy ask you if I could come over today?"

"He did."

"Is it okay?"

Melanie nodded, though she wasn't sure how Mike was going to feel about it once he learned of Jessie's fight at school. There needed to be some consequence for her misbehavior, as understandable as it might be.

"Then let's *go*," Jessie said urgently. "I want to go now!"

"I'm not allowed to take you," Melanie explained again, but her words fell on deaf ears. Jessie's face clouded over and the tears began to fall again.

She was working up to another full-fledged tantrum when Ms. Sinclair emerged from her office. "I reached Mr. Mikelewski," she said. "He's on his way."

Thank God, Melanie thought. She was doing the best she could, but it was obvious that it wasn't enough. Jessie needed her father. The little girl was once again clinging to her and sobbing as if her heart would break. Melanie rubbed her back and murmured nonsense words until at last Jessie closed her eyes and fell asleep, obviously exhausted by her outburst.

Melanie continued to hold and rock her gently. Eventually she heard footsteps running through the school corridor and knew instinctively that it was Mike. He came charging through the door and skidded to a stop, his expression frantic. When he spotted them, a sigh seemed to shudder through him.

"Is she okay?" he asked, hunkering down to brush a curl from Jessie's tear-streaked face.

"She wore herself out crying," Melanie said just as they were joined by the principal.

Mike stood and glowered at Ms. Sinclair. "What the hell happened?"

"I'm not entirely sure," the principal admitted. "She and Kevin Reed got into some sort of argument that erupted into a shoving match. I don't know any more than that."

"Where was the teacher?"

"On the other side of the playground. She got to them in seconds. Neither of them was physically hurt, but Jessie was far too distraught to go back to class."

Mike turned to Melanie. "Did she say anything to you about what happened?"

Melanie nodded. "I think we should talk about it somewhere else, though."

Mike looked as if he wanted to argue or maybe punch his fist through a wall, but he fought for control. "Okay, then, let's get out of here."

"Wait just a minute," Ms. Sinclair commanded. "As you know, this isn't the first time Jessie has had one of these episodes, Mr. Mikelewski. It's possible that she needs more attention than we can give her here."

Mike looked shattered. "What are you saying?"

"That I can't have her disrupting class again. If it continues to happen, other arrangements will have to be made."

"You're kicking her out of school?" he demanded, his

expression incredulous. "She's six. She's not some teen-age delinquent."

"A disruptive child is a problem no matter what the age," Ms. Sinclair said. "I'm not asking you to remove Jessie just yet, but I am warning you that it's a possibility."

"But she's been so much better," he said. "I don't understand this."

"I think I do," Melanie said, giving his hand a squeeze. "Let's go."

He nodded slowly, then reached for Jessie, cradling her against his chest with heartbreaking tenderness. When his tortured gaze finally lifted to meet Melanie's, he said, "I'll meet you at my place."

Melanie nodded, her heart aching for him. "I'll be right behind you."

Mike kept glancing back at his sleeping child on the way home. Jessie looked so sweetly innocent now, but he knew all too well what she was like when she was out of control. He'd been deluding himself that the worst was behind them. How could he even consider a future with Melanie, when Jessie required every bit of love and attention he had to give? Even Melanie would have to see that after today. Hell, maybe that was even the real reason she'd been hesitating and she'd just been too kind to say so.

He carried Jessie inside, took her to her room and put her in bed. She barely whimpered as he removed her shoes and tucked a blanket around her. As worn-out as she was, she would sleep for at least another hour or two. That would give him and Melanie a chance to talk. There was a lot of ground to cover.

When he went back downstairs, he found Melanie in the kitchen brewing a pot of tea.

"I hope you don't mind," she said. "I thought we could both use it."

"It's fine," he said, raking his hand through his hair. "Now what the hell happened back there, and how did you get involved?"

As Melanie described the incident on the playground, Mike fought off the desire to go and pummel little Kevin Reed himself. Obviously, though, the kid had just been lashing back. He couldn't have known how devastating his words would be to Jessie. Nor, likely, had she grasped how hurtful she was being when she'd reminded Kevin he didn't have a dad.

"Kids that age have no idea how powerful words can be. They're unintentionally cruel to each other sometimes," Melanie said, echoing his thoughts.

"It's my fault," Mike said.

"How on earth can you believe that? You weren't even there!"

"Not today. I meant I should have done something to force Linda to face facts and get herself straightened out. Then Jessie would have her mom in her life. Dammit, I should have done something," he repeated.

"Such as?" Melanie asked, her skepticism plain. "What could you possibly have done that you didn't do?"

He sank onto a chair and regarded her with bewilderment. "I have no idea."

"You couldn't make her better if she didn't want to get better," Melanie reminded him.

How many times had he heard the same words from the counselor he'd seen at the time, from his attorney, even from Linda's parents? He knew they were all right, but he couldn't help thinking that there must have been something he could have done or said to get through to her.

"Maybe if I went to her now," he said, beginning to formulate a plan even he could see was desperate and doomed to failure. "Maybe she'd be ready to listen."

Melanie looked stunned. "Is that what you want, to get your wife back?"

"No, of course not," he said without hesitation. "I swear to you, that's the last thing I want. But I want Jessie to have her mom back. I want her to be the happy-go-lucky, carefree kid she deserves to be."

"She will be," Melanie assured him. "It will just take time and patience."

"You heard Ms. Sinclair. We're running out of time."

"Talk to the teacher. Explain the situation. Talk to Kevin's mother. Since she's a single mom, surely she'll understand and help to stop Kevin from tormenting Jessie about not having a mom. And if you can explain to Jessie how badly Kevin must feel about not having a dad, maybe you can avert another incident like this one."

"But if it's not this, it will be something else. And if it's not Kevin, it will be some other kid," Mike said. "Jessie doesn't cope well with disappointment. Anything can set her off. Not getting the color crayon she wants, not getting the teacher's attention the instant she wants it, not getting to go to a party. Everyday life is filled with endless possibilities for disaster." He lifted his gaze to Melanie's and saw that her eyes were filled with sympathy.

"I'm sorry," she said. "It must be so difficult for both of you."

"I'm just sorry you got dragged into it. You never did say how that happened."

"Jessie asked for me," Melanie said.

"Really?" Mike wasn't sure how to interpret that. Jessie trusted very few people. Her attachment to Melanie was obviously stronger than he'd realized, maybe too strong.

"When Ms. Sinclair couldn't reach you, she called Pam, and Pam said she thought you wouldn't mind if I at least came to the school to try to calm Jessie down." Melanie studied him. "Was that okay? Did I overstep?"

"Of course not. Thank you for doing that. I try never to be out of cell phone range when Jessie's at school, but sometimes I can't help it. Things have been going so well lately that I didn't think it would be a problem if I rode out to a new job site for a couple of hours."

Melanie regarded him sympathetically. "Mike, there's not a parent on earth who could be more caring and attentive than you are. Don't beat yourself up over this. Sometimes things just happen. I'm glad I was around and could help."

"At least you see now why I've shied away from relationships. I can't drag someone else into this situation. It's too unpredictable. Jessie's too volatile for me to expect someone else to take her on. Forget all that stuff I said to you the other night. You were smart to turn me down flat."

Melanie gave him an incredulous look. "You think you and Jessie are too much trouble? Is that what you're saying? Do you honestly think that had anything at all to do with why I said no?"

"Isn't it obvious?"

"Not to me. Jessie has some problems, sure, but she's a wonderful, smart, funny little girl. Any woman would be lucky to have the two of you."

"How can you say that after what happened today?"

"Because it's true," she said fiercely. "Good grief, Mike, no one's perfect. No relationship is smooth every second. There are bound to be bumps and heartaches and problems of one sort or another. As for kids, sooner or later they're going to stir up trouble, whether it's the terrible twos or the traumatic teens or sometime in between, it's a guarantee they're going to make parents want to tear their hair out. Getting through all that just makes the relationship stronger."

He knew she was trying to be kind and reassuring, but he didn't buy it. People bolted when the going got tough. That was what Linda had done. She'd chosen drugs, convinced that they would give her the pleasure that her marriage didn't. He'd taken off with Jessie rather than fighting to keep their marriage afloat.

Maybe Melanie was made of sterner stuff. Maybe she would stick it out the first few times Jessie caused problems, but over the long haul? He doubted it. He sure as hell couldn't risk it. Besides, if he cared about Melanie at all, why would he put her through that?

"Look, Jessie will be waking up soon. Maybe you should go," he said stiffly.

Melanie looked for a moment as if she might argue, but then she stood up and started for the door, her expression sad.

Mike thought he was going to get her out of there before she saw that his heart was breaking, but she turned back, then crossed the room and leaned down to press her lips to his. She didn't linger, but his pulse raced just the same.

"I'll be expecting Jessie after school tomorrow," she said quietly but emphatically.

He stared at her. "What?"

"She and I have a date for a makeover. Obviously today's a bad day. Even if she were up to it, she shouldn't be rewarded for bad behavior, so I'm changing the date till tomorrow. Bottom line, I'm not breaking that promise." She gave him a warning look. "And neither are you."

"Come on, Melanie," he protested. "You can't want to do that after all this."

"Yes, I can," she said. "In fact, I want to do it more than ever. Three-thirty, Mike. Don't stand me up." She gave him another hard look and added, "Don't disappoint your daughter."

Now there was the clincher, he thought, staring at her. She knew he wouldn't be able to disappoint Jessie, not ever. When had Melanie learned to push his buttons so cleverly?

"We'll be there," he conceded reluctantly.

She beamed at him. "I knew you'd see it my way."

And then she was gone, leaving him filled with the oddest sense that maybe, just maybe, he'd gotten it all wrong. Maybe, rather than scaring her off, today's mess had almost convinced her to stay.

He smiled despite everything. Wouldn't that be just about the closest thing to a miracle he'd ever had any reason to hope for?

13

Melanie was mad as spit by the time she got home from Mike's. The idea that Mike and Jessie were too much trouble, too undeserving of love, was ludicrous. The man was an idiot! A loving, doting father, but an idiot nonetheless! How could he even think that was the reason she didn't want to be with him? How shallow did he think she was?

She was muttering under her breath about his stupidity when she got out of her car and realized that Pam was sitting on the porch steps watching her with undisguised amusement.

"Something—or someone—upset you?" Pam inquired.

Melanie considered being discreet but chucked the idea. Maybe Pam could help her make sense of what had just happened. After all, she and Jeff were Mike's best friends. They'd known him and Jessie for years.

"Mike," Melanie said succinctly. "Who else?"

"He is a stubborn one, all right. What did he do now?"

"Did you know that he's convinced himself that he and Jessie are too much for any woman to take on? That's why he doesn't get involved with anyone."

Pam nodded slowly. "I'd guessed as much, though he's never actually admitted it to me. I suppose it makes sense, given what he's been through, first with Linda and now with Jessie's behavior problems."

"Why the dickens haven't you told him he's crazy?" Melanie demanded. "Someone needs to get through that thick skull of his before he ruins his life."

Pam chuckled. "I don't think hearing it from me is going to convince him. He thinks I'll say anything to get him to date again. He's going to need proof from a woman who's brave enough to ignore all of his No Trespassing signs." She regarded Melanie speculatively. "Are you that woman? Or has he already scared you off?"

Melanie sank down on the step beside her. That was the issue, wasn't it? Was she playing a game here or, after everything she'd told Mike about going, was she really willing to put her heart on the line? Her ambivalence had nothing to do with Mike and Jessie being too much trouble. They were wonderful. It was her own self-doubt that was keeping her from getting in any deeper.

"I honestly don't know," she finally admitted.

"Then don't get his hopes up," Pam advised. "If you do and then change your mind, it will destroy any chance he ever has of believing in love."

Melanie scowled at Pam. "Gee, pile on the pressure, why don't you?"

Pam regarded her with absolutely no evidence of pity or contrition. "There's something you need to understand, Melanie. I like you. I'd like to be your friend, but right now Mike's my first priority. He and Jessie have been through enough. Jessie's a thousand percent better than she was when they first got here, but as you saw today, she still has her moments. Another upheaval in her life could destroy whatever fragile progress she's made. The same goes for Mike. Can you imagine what it must have been like for him to have this darling little child depending on him and to have his wife say—through her actions, anyway—that they weren't enough?"

"No, I can't," Melanie said with a sigh. She knew all too well how badly rejection and betrayal stung.

An uncomfortable silence fell between them. The sun had finally broken through the clouds, providing a faint warmth against the earlier chill, but even so, Melanie shivered.

Pam turned to her. "So, what's holding you back? Why won't you let yourself get serious about Mike?"

"Long story."

"I've got time."

Melanie shook her head. "I really don't want to talk about it."

"Was it that awful? Are you still in love with someone else?"

"Hardly," she said with undisguised bitterness. "I just don't want you to know what an idiot I was."

Pam regarded her intently, then chuckled. "A really, really bad choice, huh?"

"You have no idea."

"Does Mike know?"

Melanie nodded.

"That's good. Can I say one more thing before I go?"

Melanie doubted if she could stop her. "Sure."

"Mike could never be a bad choice. He's one of the best guys around, along with Jeff, of course."

Melanie grinned. "Of course."

"You'd be a fool to let him get away," Pam persisted.

It wouldn't be the first time in her life Melanie had

been a fool where love was concerned. But there was no comparing Mike with Jeremy. Even she could see that.

Still…stay here? Because that was what loving Mike would mean. Was she ready to make such a drastic change in her life? Was she ready to trust—especially after only a few brief weeks—that this time she'd finally gotten it right? Six long months hadn't been enough for her to figure out that Jeremy was lying to her and cheating on his wife. She'd had to be slapped in the face with that one.

"Think about it. That's all I'm asking," Pam said. "Now I'd better get out of here before Jeff comes looking for me. He wouldn't be happy if he knew I was over here meddling again."

Melanie grinned. "I'm glad you came, though. After this afternoon, it was good to come home to a friendly face."

"If you ever need someone to listen, give me a call. I'm known for my excellent, if slightly biased, advice."

"I may take you up on that," Melanie told her.

In fact, before all was said and done, she had a hunch she was going to need all the advice she could get. She might even be forced to call in her sisters, though only as a last resort. When it came to love, they rarely agreed on anything. In fact, the only time they were all in complete agreement was when one of their own needed moral support. Then they banded together like a bunch of protective mother hens. It was a reassuring unity, but Melanie knew that in the end this decision had to be completely and totally her own.

"Heard Jessie had a rough day yesterday," Jeff commented when he and Mike took a break from planting shrubs around a new home.

"Pam, I suppose," Mike said. There were times—like now—when he regretted making hers the first name after his own on his emergency contact list at Jessie's school. At the time he'd filled out that form, though, she'd seemed like a godsend.

"Of course," Jeff confirmed. "She told me the school had called her, and then she stopped by to see Melanie on her way home."

Mike frowned at that. "Oh?"

Jeff gave him an apologetic look. "I know. I told her she needed to stay out of it, but you know Pam. She cares about you guys. She thinks she's looking out for your interests."

"I'm sure she does," Mike said dryly. Pam had a reputation for good intentions. Unfortunately, they sometimes went awry, like the time she'd fixed up a friend with one of the nursery's customers, only to discover afterward that the man was already involved with the woman's best friend. Needless to say there had been three people very unhappy with her over that one.

"Is Jessie okay today?" Jeff asked, wisely changing the subject.

"She seemed fine when I dropped her off at school." He still wasn't sure how to take the fact that she'd insisted he drop her off a block away, rather than in front of the door. Had she taken his advice to heart about being more considerate of Kevin's feelings or was she merely trying to prove that she wasn't a baby? He suspected the latter.

Still it had given him an odd feeling to sit in the car down the street and watch her walk that final block all by herself. Only when she was safely inside had he finally driven off, aware that they'd reached a milestone. Jessie was growing up, whether he liked it or not.

It was going to be even stranger to take her over to

Melanie's this afternoon and leave her there for whatever pint-size spa day Melanie had in mind. Her cries for Melanie during the incident at school yesterday had shaken him. She'd never called out for anyone other than him before. Was that yet another sign that her world was growing or was it a warning that her attachment to Melanie was becoming too deep? He had no idea how to interpret it.

"Hey," Jeff said. "Where'd you go? Is there something you're not telling me?"

"Jessie's spending the afternoon with Melanie," he said.

"Is that some sort of a problem?" Jeff asked.

"I wish to hell I knew."

"You want those two to get along, don't you?"

"Of course."

Understanding finally dawned on Jeff's face. "But you're terrified Melanie will leave and break Jessie's heart?"

"Something like that."

"And yours?" Jeff guessed.

"Jessie's my only concern," Mike insisted.

"Liar. Who're you trying to convince? Me or yourself?"

Mike gave him a rueful look. "That one's gotten a little muddy."

"For what it's worth, I think you could do a lot worse than inviting Melanie D'Angelo into your life."

"That's the problem," Mike said wearily. "I've already done worse. I'm not sure I could go through that kind of emotional chaos again. And Melanie's not exactly jumping for joy at the prospect, so maybe it would be smarter not to pursue it."

"What if you don't have to go through any sort of

chaos?" Jeff asked philosophically. "What if Melanie's as perfect as you think she is, and the future's filled with unparalleled happiness? Are you willing to miss out on all that because you're scared of history repeating itself?"

Unfortunately, Mike had lived with the kind of fear Jeff was describing for a lot of years now. He'd been acting on it, keeping away from the dangers of another failed relationship. Old habits were tough to break... even when the potential rewards were extraordinary.

"I guess I'll figure that out when the time comes," he told Jeff.

"Don't look now, pal, but the time has come."

Mike sighed heavily. Yeah, he'd heard the clock ticking himself.

Mike dropped Jessie off at Melanie's at three-thirty with a promise to be back after all the girlie stuff was over. Jessie had already raced to the bathroom to see the selection of nail polish and hair ribbons Melanie had set out. Mike, however, hadn't budged from just inside the door. His troubled gaze kept drifting down the hall as if he wanted to follow his daughter and make sure she was okay.

"You can stay, if you'd like," Melanie offered, her sympathy stirring for him. It was plain as day that he was having trouble letting go.

"No way," he said, then drew himself up. "I'm sure she'll be fine."

"She will be," Melanie assured him. "And I have your cell phone number. I'll call if anything comes up that I can't handle."

He nodded. "When I come back, I'll bring that pizza you were talking about the other day, one loaded with everything," he promised. "Thanks for doing this for her."

"No problem," Melanie insisted. "It will be fun."

He finally made a move toward the door, then hesitated, obviously reluctant to leave. "Sometimes she needs a lot of patience, especially when she gets tired."

Melanie saw the genuine anxiety in his eyes and fell just a little bit more in love with him at that moment. At this rate, there was going to be no turning back, probably way before she was ready for any commitment.

She put her hand on his arm, felt the muscle tense, then relax. "We'll be fine," she assured him, echoing his words. "I won't lose patience with her."

"I know that. It's just that I don't leave her with strangers much."

"I'm hardly a stranger."

"I know and she wanted to do this. She was really excited when I told her it was still on. She was afraid you wouldn't want her after what happened yesterday."

"Mike, stop fretting. It's only going to be a couple of hours," she said. "We're going to be so busy the time will fly by."

"Two hours," he said as if he were clinging to the thought. "Make sure she knows I'll be back in two hours. I told her, but she may need to hear it again."

"I'll tell her."

He still looked uneasy. "Maybe I should stay, after all," he said. "I could work in the yard. She wouldn't even have to know I'm here unless something happens."

Melanie realized then that his concern ran much deeper than some sort of father-daughter separation anxiety. He'd spent six years devoting himself to Jessie and her behavior problems. Letting go was going to be as difficult for him as it was for her.

"If you want to do that, it's okay with me," Melanie told him. "But something tells me you need this break as much as Jessie does."

He rocked back on his heels, considering her words. "Yeah, I guess I do," he admitted.

He gave her a plaintive look that made her heart twist.

"She's growing up, isn't she?" he asked, his tone oddly sad.

Melanie bit back a grin. "She is, but she has a long way to go. She'll still be your little girl for a while yet."

He gave her a resigned smile. "I guess I'd better get used to this, though."

"Today's a good time to start," she told him. "I'll take good care of her. I promise."

Only after she'd watched him walk to his car and take one last glance back at the house did she fully realize the magnitude of what had just transpired. Mike Mikelewski had entrusted her with the most precious thing in his life.

Whatever doubts she'd been harboring about him or about her own judgment vanished. Seeing his heart in his eyes like that was all she needed. The last bit of protective wall around Melanie's heart crumbled. She was in love with him, and she'd been right…there was no turning back.

Mike couldn't figure out what to do with himself. He had two hours to kill, time he normally would have spent with his daughter.

He was barely out of Melanie's driveway when he was tempted to pick up his cell phone and call to see how the two of them were doing. He resisted the temptation, because he didn't want to look like more of an overprotective idiot than he had earlier.

He jumped when the cell phone rang. Heart thudding, he grabbed it, sure that calamity had struck already. Jessie had probably painted the bathroom with nail polish while he and Melanie were talking. Or she'd gotten hold of the scissors and chopped off her own hair. His imagination ran wild, until he realized the voice on the other end of the line wasn't Melanie's.

"Meet me at the Graingers," Jeff said without preamble.

"Now?" Mike asked, his heartbeat slowing to normal. "I just left there an hour ago."

"What's wrong with now? Jessie's with Melanie, right?"

"Yes."

"Then get over here."

Jeff hung up before Mike could ask what was so important that it couldn't wait till morning.

He made the twenty-minute drive to the Graingers, muttering to himself about his friend's call. When he'd left earlier, everything had been fine. There'd been no potential landscaping disasters on the horizon. When he arrived to find Jeff sitting on a log, gazing at the river, his curses escalated.

"What the hell's the big emergency?" he demanded.

"No emergency," Jeff said, regarding him serenely.

Mike stared at him. "Then what am I doing here?"

"Having a beer," Jeff said, holding one out for him.

Mike ignored it. "Explain," he said tightly.

"I figured you'd be a little antsy by now, so I'm providing a diversion. I would have met you at a bar, but I figured you'd never agree to it."

"Are you nuts?"

"I don't think so. I'm in a tranquil setting, taking a break, having a cold one. What's crazy about that?"

Mike could have listed half a dozen things, but instead he sank down beside Jeff and accepted the beer. He might as well. He did have two hours to kill and absolutely nothing better to do with them besides worry.

"How did you know I'd be going out of my mind about now?" he asked.

"Intuition. That and the fact that you were all but twitching with dread when you told me you were leaving Jessie at Melanie's this afternoon. Man, you have got to chill about stuff like this. Do you want Jessie underfoot for the rest of your life?"

"She still needs me," Mike insisted. "She's only six."

"She needs to figure out she can do okay with somebody other than her dad, too," Jeff said.

Mike frowned. "I know that. I leave her with you guys sometimes."

"Long enough to run to the store. That's about it," Jeff said. "Lyssa's been begging for Jessie to spend the night, but you've refused to let her."

"She's too young for a sleepover," Mike replied. "Besides, those two get along great for a couple of hours and then they're at war. I don't want you all to have to deal with that."

"They fight. They get over it. It's what kids do. Haven't you been around when my three start picking on each other?"

"That's different."

Jeff stared at him over his bottle of beer. "This I've got to hear. How is that any different?"

"They're siblings."

"And that makes the fighting easier to take?"

"No, but they're your kids," he said, knowing he wasn't

making a lot of sense. If Jeff and Pam could handle it when their three were on a tear, then adding Jessie to the mix wouldn't faze them. Rationally he knew that. In his gut, it was harder to accept. Jessie was his responsibility, not theirs.

"We consider Jessie one of the family," Jeff reminded him. "We're perfectly comfortable putting her in a time-out if she misbehaves."

Mike held up his hands. "Okay. Okay. She can spend the night some weekend."

"This Friday," Jeff said, seizing the opening. "You can take Melanie out and have the whole night to yourselves." He winked. "You can have your own sleepover."

It was definitely an intriguing possibility, but Mike wasn't sure how he felt about all of these people ganging up on him to get some distance between him and Jessie. Or to close the distance between him and Melanie. It was all moving just a little too fast.

"Don't even try to tell me that you're not going to take advantage of this opportunity I'm giving you," Jeff said. "You, Melanie, alone all night long." He dangled the prospect like a very tempting carrot.

Visions of making love to Melanie slammed through Mike. Jeff was right again. Mike could hardly turn that down.

"I'll talk to her about it when I get back over there. She may be convinced by then that the Mikelewskis are a bad bet."

Jeff rolled his eyes. "You're not giving Jessie nearly enough credit. Most of the time these days, she's a good kid. You've done a great job of getting her to this point. And, frankly, to everyone else it's obvious that Melanie is charmed by her."

"If you say so," Mike responded, though he still harbored his own doubts.

He glanced at his watch and was surprised to see that with the drive back to town and the pizza to pick up, he was actually going to be a little later than he'd intended. He waited for the anxiety to rush over him, for the desire to grab his phone to call and alert Melanie that he was going to be maybe ten minutes behind schedule. Nothing happened. No gut churning. No desperation. Just the comforting realization that Jessie was in good hands.

He grinned at Jeff. "I owe you."

Jeff nodded. "You do, indeed."

"I'm not talking about this weekend. I'm talking about making me see that I don't have to hover over Jessie every single instant."

"Then my work here is done," Jeff said, standing up. "Pam will be proud."

Mike stared at him. "This was her idea?"

"Of course. You sure as hell don't think I'm this sensitive, do you?"

Mike laughed, feeling more relaxed than he had in a very long time. "Come to think of it, no."

14

"I can't choose," Jessie said, her brow puckered in a frown.

She studied the row of bottles of pink, mauve, beige and red nail polish Melanie had accumulated. In addition to those she'd purchased the day before, there was quite a collection left from when Melanie and her sisters had visited as teenagers. Some were all dried up by now, but there had been a half dozen that were still usable. Some shades were brilliant and clear, some frosted. Melanie could understand why Jessie was having such a tough time deciding. She had a hunch, though, that it wasn't just the variety that was holding things up. It was evident that Jessie didn't want the afternoon to end. She'd hugged Melanie a zillion times and said she was having the "bestest time ever."

"I like 'em all," Jessie added, her expression wistful as she studied the nail polish.

Melanie grinned. "Well, I can't very well paint every nail a different color. You have to choose, and soon, too, or your dad will be back."

"What color do you like?"

Melanie held out her hands. Her nails were cut short

and buffed but unpainted. "I'm not the best person to ask," she told the little girl. "I never get around to painting mine."

Jessie's eyes lit up. "We can do yours, too. I'll help."

Now there was a frightening idea, Melanie thought. She'd already noted that Jessie had more enthusiasm than finesse with a hairbrush and the lipstick she'd convinced Melanie to let her try. Who knew what she'd do with a bottle of nail polish?

"This is your day," she told Jessie quickly. "Besides, I've been working in the garden. My nails would get all messed up."

"Not if you wore gloves," Jessie said reasonably. "Pam has really pretty ones at the nursery. They have little flowers on 'em. I like 'em a lot, but she doesn't have 'em in my size."

"I'll give that some thought," Melanie promised. "But we're running out of time now. Your dad will be back soon, so you'd better choose a color, so your nails will be beautiful when he gets here."

Jessie crawled into her lap and gave the bottles lined up on the edge of the sink a closer inspection. "This one," she said at last, choosing a hot pink. "Pink's my very favorite color in the whole world."

No one would have known that given the way she'd lingered over choosing. The chili-pepper red had been in the lead for a while, Melanie thought with amusement. Melanie was considering that one for her own toes one of these nights when she had time for a pedicure.

"Then pink it is," she said as she gave the bottle a few quick shakes. "Now give me your hand."

Only when Jessie's little hand was tucked in hers did Melanie realize that Jessie had bitten her nails to the quick. Trying not to wince at the sight, she said mildly,

"You know, your nails would be much prettier if you didn't bite them."

Jessie frowned. "I can't help it."

She would have jerked them away in obvious embarrassment, but Melanie wouldn't allow her to. "Sure you can," Melanie said easily. "I used to bite mine. You know what got me to stop?"

"What?"

"I kept thinking how pretty they were going to be when they grew out. Every time I started to bite a nail, I thought about that, and soon they were growing. That's when my mom let me use nail polish for the first time."

Jessie finally relaxed again and regarded her with curiosity. "How old were you?"

"Way older than you. Twelve, I think."

Jessie looked incredulous. "And you still bit your nails?"

Melanie nodded. "Whenever I got scared."

Jessie watched her painting each tiny nail and seemed to be considering what Melanie had just told her. "Didn't you ever get scared again?" she asked at last.

"Sure," Melanie told her, starting on the other hand. "Lots of times."

"What did you do if you couldn't bite your nails anymore?"

"I drew in a great big breath, like this," she said, demonstrating until Jessie giggled. "And then I told myself I could do anything. I could get up in front of the class if I had to or I could climb the rope in the gym or I could ace my math test. Pretty soon I began to believe in myself, and I never even thought about biting my nails again."

Jessie nodded, her expression solemn. "I can do that. I can even beat up Kevin Reed, if he picks on me again."

Melanie smothered a laugh. "No, you cannot beat up

Kevin Reed," she said emphatically. "It will only get you into trouble, just like yesterday."

Jessie sighed heavily. "Sometimes Kevin needs to get beat up."

"Was he mean to you today?"

Jessie shook her head. "He found somebody else to pick on."

"I see."

"Janice won't hit back." She gave Melanie a hopeful look. "Shouldn't I hit him for her?"

"Absolutely not. Let the teacher handle Kevin."

Jessie looked disappointed. Then she held out her hands to admire her new pink nails. "They look beautiful," she said excitedly. "I can't wait for Daddy to get back. Let me see in the mirror again. Is my hair still okay?"

"Your hair is perfect," Melanie assured her, lifting her up so she could see for herself. The lipstick was another matter, but Jessie seemed happy enough with it. Mike was probably going to have a cow.

Obviously satisfied with her own reflection, Jessie threw her arms around Melanie's neck. "I love you."

Tears immediately stung Melanie's eyes. "Oh, baby," she whispered, hugging Jessie tightly and breathing in the little-girl scent of strawberry soap and shampoo. "I love you, too."

For the first time in her life, Melanie felt needed. How was she going to give this feeling up when the time came? She'd had no idea that all these maternal instincts had been lurking deep inside her, just waiting for a chance to emerge.

Why did she have to give up anything? The thought came from out of nowhere to plant itself in her head. Once there, she couldn't seem to make it go away. Of course, loving Jessie was one thing. Committing herself to a relationship with Jessie's daddy was something else entirely. And for all the warm and fuzzy feelings she was having right this second, she still wasn't sure if she was ready to take that next step.

Even if she were, Mike might have other ideas about what the future held. There was no point in deluding herself that she was any match at all for the fears and doubts he had about his and Jessie's worth to another person. Those doubts had driven his life for years now.

She was still holding Jessie, lost in all these mixed emotions, when the doorbell rang.

"Daddy!" Jessie shouted, squirming to get down. "I'll get it. Where's my feathers and shoes?"

Melanie handed her the boa she'd found in her grandmother's closet. It was shocking pink and Jessie had fallen in love with it on sight. She'd also claimed an old pair of red high heels from the closet.

"Remember, you have to walk slow in those shoes," Melanie reminded her.

"I will," Jessie promised.

Jessie tottered from the bathroom and left Melanie to wipe away any trace of tears from her cheeks before she went out to face the two people who could change her life forever.

Mike knew he was a goner when he came back to Melanie's at five-twenty with a large, deep-dish, everything-on-it pizza and found his giggling, bright-eyed daughter with her hair in an elaborate braid of some kind and bright-pink polish on her tiny nails. He could have lived without the lipstick, but gathered that was a necessary part of playing grown-up. She had some sort of feather thing wound around her neck and dragging on the floor behind her. She was wobbling in a pair of high-heeled shoes that were much too large for her. It was the most normal moment he could ever recall, and it made his heart ache that Melanie had been the one to share it with her and not him. But how could he regret anything that had made his baby girl so happy?

He looked at Melanie and mouthed a silent thank-you before scooping Jessie up in his arms and tickling her.

"You've gone and turned into a gorgeous grown-up lady on me," he said. "Where's my little girl?" He glanced at Melanie and asked with feigned ferocity. "What have you done with her?"

"No little girls here," Melanie teased. "Right, Jessie?"

"Just me, Daddy. But this is for when I'm at Melanie's," she recited dutifully, then gazed at him hopefully. "Can we come here all the time?"

Mike looked at Melanie and came to the conclusion he should have reached way before this. "That's something Melanie and I will have to discuss one of these days."

"Ask her now," Jessie prodded.

"No," he said firmly. "Now we have to eat pizza before it gets cold."

"But—"

"No arguments," he said firmly. "Or I'll have to call Lyssa and tell her you won't be able to have a sleepover at her house tomorrow night, after all."

Jessie looked awestruck. "I can spend the whole night at Lyssa's?"

"You can," he said, glad that Jeff had backed him into that particular corner. It was obviously something Jessie had wanted and had never dreamed he would allow.

"How come?" she asked.

"I think you're old enough now, don't you?"

She bobbed her head enthusiastically, but then worry creased her brow. "Won't you be lonely, Daddy?"

Mike met Melanie's gaze and held it until her cheeks turned pink. "I don't think so," he said quietly.

"I got an idea," Jessie said excitedly. "Why don't you have a sleepover with Melanie?"

Mike bit back a groan. Out of the mouths of babes. "Don't worry about me," he told Jessie. "I can make my own plans for the evening."

"But—"

He gave her a warning look. "Jessie!"

She sighed. "I just want Melanie to be my mommy," she said wearily. "I wish you'd hurry up and ask her."

Mike glanced at Melanie and saw the bright-red patches on her cheeks and something that looked like panic in her eyes. She definitely wasn't ready to hear that he was beginning to think a lot like his daughter. He was ready to give Jessie the new mommy she'd been dreaming of.

She should never have agreed to go out with Mike tonight, Melanie thought, her pulse scrambling frantically and her stomach knotting. She was not ready to have the kind of discussion he clearly had in mind, especially when she was almost a hundred percent certain that his motives had nothing to do with love and everything to do with Jessie. He was going to dangle everything she'd ever wanted in front of her—a home, a family—and she was going to say no because he wasn't offering the most important thing of all, his love.

But maybe she was getting ahead of herself. Besides, it would be cowardly to back out. Maybe she'd gotten the signals all wrong anyway. Maybe he was really interested in nothing more than an entire evening for just the two of them. Maybe that glint in his eye had been about sex, not marriage.

She had almost convinced herself that it was as simple as that when he announced they were going to spend the evening at his place.

"I've got chicken slow-roasting in the oven," he told her, his gaze locked with hers. "I hope that's okay."

"It sounds perfect," she answered honestly. "I hope it's roasting *very* slowly."

He grinned. "I can always turn the heat down when we get there."

"And I can turn it up," she countered, enjoying the flare of desire in his eyes and relieved that there'd been no hints about serious talk for the evening's agenda.

They made the drive to his house in silence, but rather than feeling uncomfortable, Melanie was filled with anticipation that seemed to grow with each mile that passed. She'd missed being close to Mike, feeling his touch.

"Is Jessie settled for the night at Lyssa's?" she asked eventually.

"I hope so," he said, suddenly looking worried. "This is a big step for her."

"And for you," Melanie guessed.

He shook his head. "I know it's ridiculous, but she's been my responsibility for so long, it's hard to stop worrying about her."

"From what I hear about parents and kids, you'll never stop worrying about her," Melanie told him. "But you will learn to cope with it and keep it in perspective." She grinned. "I'll do my best to provide a distraction tonight."

"I don't think there's any question that you'll do an excellent job," he said, putting his hands on her waist and lifting her from the truck.

He looked into her eyes, then slowly lowered his mouth to take hers in a long, greedy kiss.

Melanie felt as if she were floating, which she was, she realized eventually when she could think straight again. Mike was still holding her off the ground, her body molded to his.

"Maybe you ought to put me down," she suggested lightly.

"I don't want to."

"We'll get inside faster if you do."

He laughed. "You do know how to create a powerful incentive, don't you? But I don't have to put you down to get inside."

Before she realized his intention, he'd put an arm under her knees and rearranged her against his chest. He set off toward the house in long, determined strides.

"Are you suddenly in a hurry?"

"Darlin', I've been in a hurry for this since the last time we made love."

She studied him curiously. "Why haven't you done anything about it?"

"Too many complications."

"And now?"

"I think we're getting them untangled."

Melanie wished she were half as sure of that as he seemed to be. But before she could express her concerns, they were inside, in his room and Mike was lowering her to his bed. The heat in his eyes was enough to melt away whatever crazy ideas she'd had about talking.

"Do you know how incredible it is that we have the whole night ahead of us?" he murmured. "I want to take this slow. I want to get to know every inch of your body. I want to watch you come apart in my arms time and again."

Melanie trembled at his words, at the gentle touch of his hands as he worked the buttons on her blouse until they were free and he could shove the material away. Then he skimmed his fingers over her lace-covered breasts until the peaks were tight, aching buds.

"You are so amazing," he whispered, his voice husky. "Amazing."

Melanie tried to find the words to respond, but her breath caught in her throat when he covered her breast with his mouth and sucked. Her hips rose off the bed in response to that incredible sensation.

"Forget slow," she said in a choked voice, writhing beneath him. "Slow's for next time or the time after that. I want you now, Mike. Please."

A smile spread across his face. "Well, when you ask so sweetly, how can I possibly say no?"

He stripped away her panties, pushed down his own pants and entered her in one hard thrust that filled her and took the last of her breath away.

Then he began to move, teasing her, tormenting her until the sensations were too much, too raw and needy. Her body felt as if it were on fire, as if it were one exquisite nerve that was wound so tightly it was destined to snap with one more stroke, one more caress, one more flick of his tongue across her feverish skin.

In the end that was exactly what sent her flying over the edge, his tongue on her nipple sending a shock wave through her that reached her toes. She screamed, but he caught the sound by covering her mouth with his own.

And as their breath mingled and their bodies came apart in perfect harmony, Melanie was filled with a joy so pure it uncomplicated everything. There was only this man, this moment and the waves of love washing through her.

It seemed like an eternity before Mike could move again. Melanie had worn him out in the most pleasurable way possible. He didn't care if he never budged from his bed again.

He felt an elbow prod his ribs and moaned. "Again?"

She laughed. "No, you idiot. Even I know my limits. What I'm after is food. That chicken ought to be way past done by now."

"It's probably so dried out, it's chicken jerky," he said.

"I'm not sure I care at this point."

He grinned at her. "You really are hungry, aren't you?"

"Starving. Mind-boggling sex will do that."

"Ah, flattery. You definitely know how to motivate a man," he said, reaching for her.

"I'm not trying to motivate you to make love again," she said impatiently, giving him a gentle shove. "I'm trying to get you out of this bed and into the kitchen."

"Then you used the wrong tactic."

She eyed him curiously. "What will work?"

"Mention the triple-threat chocolate cake that Pam sent over for us."

"Oh, my God!" Melanie said, scrambling past him to grab his shirt from the floor.

Mike watched her unabashed eagerness and laughed. "Since you're up, you can bring a tray in here."

"Dream on. That cake is mine," she said as she bolted from the room.

Laughing, Mike dragged on his pants and followed. By the time he reached the kitchen, she had her first forkful of cake.

"For me?" he inquired.

"I don't think so," she said, biting into it, then groaning with obvious ecstasy.

"Careful, or I'm going to think you like that better than sex," he scolded.

"It's a toss-up," she retorted.

"You're going to spoil dinner."

"I don't think so. I took a look at that chicken. It's a goner."

"Then I'll nuke a frozen homemade lasagna. How does that sound?"

"Great, but I'm not waiting for it," she said, pulling a chair out from the table and sitting down. His shirt rode so far up her thighs, Mike could hardly think straight. He simply stood and stared. She chuckled. "The lasagna?"

"What?"

"In the freezer," she prodded.

He sighed and turned to the refrigerator. A few minutes later, the meal—one of many prepared and provided by Pam—was heating. He put the salad he'd tossed earlier on the table, then took the fork and cake away from Melanie. She didn't protest. She just closed her eyes and sighed with pure bliss.

"I really need that recipe. I have to pass it along to Maggie, so she can use it in the magazine. She'll be worshiped by women everywhere as a chocolate goddess."

Mike chuckled. "Is that a goal of your sister's?"

"Not really, but a little adoration is always good for the soul."

"Do you want to be adored?"

"Not by hordes and hordes of people," she said thoughtfully. "Maybe by one person."

Mike wondered if now was the time to ask the question that had been spinning around in his head ever since he'd seen her with Jessie yesterday afternoon. It was as good a time as any, he finally concluded, searching for the right words.

"Jessie obviously adores you," he began.

Her head shot up and her gaze met his. "She's a great kid," she said, an unmistakable note of caution in her voice.

Mike plunged ahead. "I'm glad you can see past the problems and recognize that. Does that mean you'd consider something a little more permanent?"

Alarm flared in her eyes. "Such as?" she asked, her tone wary.

"Don't look so terrified. I'm not going to ask if you'd like to be her nanny," he said. "I was thinking more along the lines of her mom. Would you consider marrying us?"

She studied him for what seemed like an eternity. "Because it's what Jessie wants?" she asked eventually.

"No, because it's what I want, because I think you'd be happy here. I think I could make you happy here."

"You haven't said anything about love."

Mike hesitated. He knew women wanted the pretty words, but he didn't believe in love, even now. It hadn't done anything but cause misery in his life. His continued silence apparently spoke volumes, because Melanie shook her head and stood up.

"I need to go," she said, looking unbearably sad.

"Now?" he asked incredulously. "You want to leave now? Why?"

"Because this is never going to work. I see that now."

"What's not going to work? We've been making love for hours. I just asked you to marry me," he all but shouted.

"For Jessie," she reminded him. "Not for you or even for me. That's not good enough. I want more, Mike. I want it all. I didn't think I did. When I came here, I was just like you. I was sure love didn't exist, not the way it's portrayed in novels. Now I have this tiny glimmer of what it can be like, and I'm starting to believe."

He wished he shared her conviction. "I can't give you what you want," he said, his heart heavy.

But even as he said the words, even as he saw her slipping away, he saw what she'd seen…a future that was bright because they were together. He wanted to grab it. He wanted desperately to believe that everything was possible.

But Melanie was already running from the room, leaving him behind. It wasn't the first time a woman had left him, but this time it hurt even more.

For the first time ever, he knew the real meaning of despair and loneliness.

15

Mike knew he had to go over to Pam's to pick up Jessie, but he was dreading it. He knew there would be a thousand questions on the tip of her tongue, questions he flatly refused to answer. He wasn't sure he could bear to see the sympathy that was bound to fill her eyes when she figured out that Melanie had turned his proposal down flat.

Or maybe what really worried him was the possibility that she would laugh herself silly and call him an idiot when she realized he'd done it all for Jessie and offered nothing of himself to Melanie. He still wasn't sure what had kept him from laying his heart on the line. Fear, more than likely. It was the ever-present fear that had kept him from reaching out to anyone for a long time now.

Oddly, keeping the proposal all about Jessie didn't seem to be making the sting of Melanie's rejection one bit easier to take. That rejection was all about him and his inadequacies, just as Linda's abandonment had been. He wasn't enough for either one of them.

Even as he thought that, though, he knew how ridiculous it was. Linda hadn't left because he was inadequate. She'd left because the drugs were powerful and addictive. Period. As for Melanie, hadn't she really said that he *was* enough for her? He was the one who'd been unwilling to offer his heart.

Walking up to the Claybornes' front door, he drew in a deep breath and braced himself. Thankfully, it was Jeff who answered the door.

"You look exhausted. I'll take that as a good sign," Jeff said, putting a typical male spin on things.

"You shouldn't," Mike growled. "Where's Jessie?"

Jeff's gaze narrowed speculatively. "She's out back with Lyssa. They're swimming. It's a gorgeous day, in case you haven't noticed. I can loan you a bathing suit if you'd like to join us. Pam and I are about to have breakfast out there. There's more than enough for you, too."

"No, thanks," he said curtly. "I'll just find Jessie and get out of your hair. I'm sure you've had enough of her by now."

"Actually she's been a little angel," Jeff said, continuing to study him with a frown. "You're the one I'm worried about. What's up with the attitude? Didn't things go well with Melanie?"

Mike scowled right back at him. "Look, you did the sensitive thing once. That's enough. You're not that great at it."

They'd known each other long enough that Jeff didn't take offense. He merely shook his head. "Now I really am worried. Should I get Pam?"

"God, no!" Mike said. "Please be a pal—get Jessie and don't let on that anything's wrong."

"One look at your face will be all it takes for Pam to see that something's very wrong," Jeff warned. "Maybe you should go away and work things out with Melanie, then come back later."

"Not going to happen," Mike said. "Will you get Jessie or do I have to do it?"

Jeff looked as if he might poke and prod some more, but he finally shook his head. "Whatever you want, man."

Mike heard Jessie's screams of protest a minute later and sighed. He should have known it would be impossible to do this the easy way.

Before he could take a step in the direction of the backyard, Pam came through the house like a whirlwind.

"Why are you insisting on dragging Jessie off when she's having such a good time?" she demanded. "And what's with standing out here on the front stoop instead of coming around back and getting her yourself?"

Mike ignored the second question, because he figured Pam wouldn't like hearing that he'd been avoiding her. "I came to get my daughter because it's time for her to go home," he said tightly.

Pam studied him as intently as Jeff had. "Not when you're in such an obviously lousy mood," she said emphatically. "I'll go tell Jessie she can stay, then you and I are talking."

"No, we're not," Mike said just as emphatically. He relented on one point but not the other. "Jessie can stay, but you and I are definitely not talking."

Pam scowled at him. "Stay here," she ordered, then went to give Jessie the good news.

Mike stared after her, muttered a curse and turned on his heel. Jessie was in good hands, and Pam was right about one thing. He was in a lousy mood. He needed to do something physical outdoors and work off some of his frustration.

Instinctively he headed for Melanie's, just as he had on so many other Saturday mornings lately. He didn't have to see her. Hell, he didn't *want* to see her. He could rip out a few more weeds, check on the progress of the plants he'd put in last week, spread around a little fertilizer, then hightail it out of there. With any luck Melanie wouldn't even be home.

But, of course, she was. He could feel her gaze on him, but she didn't come out of the house. When he couldn't stand the tension a moment longer, he sighed heavily, put his gear back into his truck and left.

Instead of soothing him, for the first time in his life the work had left him edgy and more miserable than ever. But he knew from bitter experience that when his heart was aching, the only answer was work.

Just because Melanie was abandoning him didn't mean he had to abandon their project. He would be back next week and the week after that, no matter how painful it was, because he'd made a promise to her and to her grandmother's memory. He didn't make a lot of promises these days, but the ones he made, he kept.

Melanie swiped angrily at the tears running down her cheeks. Why had Mike shown up here today? Was he deliberately trying to make her even more miserable than he had the night before? And where was Jessie? Melanie had grown used to having the two of them out there together, kneeling on the ground, heads bent close as Mike taught Jessie how to settle a young plant in the rich, dark earth. Jessie's bright-as-sunshine laughter had always had a knack for making Melanie's heart lighter. She could have used a little of that today.

But, of course, he wouldn't bring Jessie with him. His daughter would have too many questions about why her father and Melanie weren't even looking at each other, much less talking. That would have made an already tense situation unbearable.

So today he'd been all alone, working at a feverish

clip as if he were trying to forget something. She sure as heck knew what he was trying to forget, the same thing that was tormenting her. Damn the man and his stubborn refusal to see what was right under his nose. She loved him. She'd done everything but spell it out to him, and he'd sat there insisting that his proposal was only about providing a mother for Jessie. Well, he could just take that notion and shove it.

When the phone rang, she snatched it up. "What?"

"You sound cheery," Maggie murmured. "Maybe I'd better call back when you're in a better mood."

"That could take weeks," Melanie told her sister.

"Uh-oh. What happened?"

"Nothing I want to talk about."

"Does that mean things aren't going so well with the sexy gardener?"

"He's not a gardener. He's a landscape designer."

"Whatever."

"Why are you calling? Is it just to annoy me?"

"Actually I was calling to let you know that there's a job opening here at the magazine. It's in marketing."

Melanie sank onto a kitchen chair. "You're kidding!" She wasn't sure which stunned her more, that Maggie had found the ideal job for her on a well-respected regional magazine or the fact that it would mean they'd be working together. Maggie liked having her own niche in the world. Of all of them, she'd always been the least likely to share. But she loved her sisters, and they'd always known that in a crunch she would do what she could for any one of them. This offer was proof of that.

"Not something I'd kid about," Maggie assured her briskly.

"Are you sure you'd be comfortable having me around?" Melanie asked.

"As long as you don't try to tell me how to run the food pages, we'll get along just fine," Maggie said in a dry tone that wasn't entirely meant in jest. "Come on, sis. This is perfect for you. It's one step above entry level, the number two spot in the department. Of course, there are only three people in the department, but that's even better. You'll get experience in every aspect of the marketing process. If you're interested, I can set up an appointment first thing Monday morning. If you drove back tomorrow, you'd have plenty of time for me to brief you about the magazine. I've already told the marketing director all about you. She can't wait to meet you."

"Does this mean I'd finally get a glimpse of that sexy photographer you've been going on and on about?" Melanie teased.

"Let's leave Rick out of this," Maggie said tartly.

Melanie tried to read her tone and couldn't. She'd thought Maggie was merely in lust with the photographer, but maybe there was more to the story than she knew. Whatever it was, she wasn't going to get it out of her tight-lipped sister.

But thinking of the reportedly hunky photographer made Melanie glance outside. Mike was gone. She barely contained a sigh. It was over between them, so why was she even hesitating? This was just the shove she needed to head back to Boston.

Still, she couldn't seem to make herself say yes to Maggie's offer. "I really appreciate this, but can I think about it, at least overnight? I'll call you first thing tomorrow morning. You can't do anything before Monday anyway, right?"

"Why aren't you jumping at this?" Maggie asked, obviously irritated that Melanie wasn't reacting with more enthusiasm. "Is it Mike?"

"Mike and I are over," Melanie insisted.

"Then I really don't see the problem," her sister said. "Are you worried about working with me? I'm telling you, it will be okay."

"I'll call you in the morning," Melanie said without offering the explanation Maggie so obviously wanted. Maybe she kept silent because she didn't have one, at least none that made a lick of sense.

She was still pondering the reason for her lack of enthusiasm at daybreak on Sunday. She was no closer to making a decision than she had been the day before, and maybe that was answer enough.

Fortunately, when she called home, Maggie was out. Melanie left her sister a message saying thanks but no thanks, then hung up before she could change her mind.

After that she sat staring at the phone for an eternity, wondering what on earth she'd just done. She'd turned down the chance to interview for her dream job. For what? A man who couldn't see what was right in front of his face? Staying on in a little town where job opportunities like this one might never come along?

Apparently so. She sighed. All she knew for certain was that she needed time—time to know her own mind, time for Mike to figure out his.

Then, if there was obviously no hope at all, she'd go back to Boston. This job might be gone, but there would be others. Much as she hated admitting it, given how furious she was with him, Melanie knew in her heart that finding another man like Mike wouldn't be nearly as easy.

Mike was beginning to question his own sanity. He couldn't seem to stay away from Melanie's. He was back in the garden every Saturday waiting for who knew what to happen. Maybe he was hoping that eventually she would get his unspoken message that he wasn't going anywhere.

He was actually surprised that she hadn't left by now, fled to Boston just to avoid the pain of seeing him, just as she'd fled here in the first place. There was obviously nothing holding her here.

Or was there? Had she started to see through his muddled proposal to what was in his heart? Had she figured out yet that he was too terrified, too vulnerable, to put himself on the line the way she expected, the way she deserved? He was obviously waiting for a miracle that might never come.

Jeff and Pam had been badgering him for weeks now to talk to Melanie and straighten things out. They still didn't know the whole story, only that whatever had happened had been his fault. He'd admitted that much.

Jessie was retreating into sullen silences more and more each time he refused to arrange a visit to see Melanie. Things had never been more tense between him and his daughter.

Why not just talk to Melanie and lay everything on the line? Mike asked himself. Surely he couldn't be any more miserable than he was now.

He woke on Saturday morning to brilliant blue skies with not a cloud in them. The temperature was already in the mid-seventies by the time he dropped Jessie off at Lyssa's and got to Melanie's. His mind was made up. He was going to settle things once and for all today. It helped that all the plants were in the ground and flourishing. After today he'd have no more excuses for hanging around if she turned him down a second time. He'd even driven to Richmond the day before and picked out a ring. Surely that would show Melanie how serious he was.

Of course, planning the whole thing out and actually working up the courage to knock on the door were two entirely different things. The backyard might as well have been a million miles wide. Add in a moat and that was the width of the divide between them.

He remembered something his mother had once told him years ago when he'd been scared to try out for his high school baseball team. "Nothing beats a try but a failure." It had been her favorite saying, a message that sometimes people defeat themselves and that he should never allow himself to fall into that trap.

He knelt down to loosen the soil around the rosebushes, put a few stakes in the hollyhock garden, then tended to the foxglove and snapdragons. None of it was necessary, but it gave him time to gather his courage, all the while aware that Melanie was standing at the kitchen window, watching him.

"It's now or never," he told himself, but before he could move, he looked up and, like the miracle he'd been waiting for, she was there.

Melanie hadn't been able to bear it another moment. Every Saturday for weeks now, Mike had worked in the garden. He'd never brought Jessie again and he never announced his arrival. She would just look outside suddenly and see him there, the sun glinting off the threads of gold in his hair, his muscles straining as he worked.

If he chanced to look up and spot her, he waved, but that was all. He never smiled or beckoned.

Nor did Melanie seek him out. It hurt too much simply to see him, his big hands so gentle with the fragile plants he was tending. It hurt to know that those hands would never touch her with such tenderness again.

Today she had watched from the cottage's kitchen window and imagined his work-roughened hands on her skin, remembered the tenderness with which he'd coaxed responses from her body.

Maybe it was need or yearning, but suddenly, with a flash of insight, she knew exactly what love was. It was a man who didn't believe in it risking his heart by asking her to marry him. It was a man who couldn't find the words showing her over and over again with his steadfastness and tenderness that he loved her. It was a man who hadn't gone away because she'd said no, but instead had stayed, proving his love with his presence and commitment. It was a man who trusted her enough to ask her to become the mother of the daughter he adored.

Hands shaking and heart pounding, she walked outside and knelt in the dirt beside him. He glanced at her, his eyes filled with desire and shadowed by questions.

"Yes," she said quietly, praying that single word would be enough. Like him, she wasn't sure she knew what else to say to make things right, to grab forever.

He gave her a puzzled look. "Yes?"

Her lips curved. "Have you forgotten the question?"

After an eternity, hope suddenly shone in his eyes. "How could I?" he asked simply. "It's the most important one I've ever asked." He searched her face. "Are you sure?"

"That I love you? Yes. Without question."

"Enough to stay here?"

"Yes."

"What about the rest?" he asked. "Do you know how I feel?"

Even now he was leaving it to her to figure things

out, but she no longer minded. The truth was in his eyes. "About you loving me? I know that, too. Someday you'll see the feelings for what they are, and then you'll say the words. I can wait. I just can't wait alone."

He nodded slowly. "I was thinking a summer wedding," he said, reaching into his pocket.

His tone was nonchalant, but Melanie could see the vulnerability in his eyes. He still wasn't sure of her, wasn't sure of any of this, but he was taking a gigantic leap of faith for her, for both of them.

"The garden should be in shape by then," he continued as he withdrew a velvet jeweler's box and held it out. "What do you think?"

Melanie took the box with shaking hands and opened it. The diamond inside sparkled like the sun. She grinned. "Is that why you've been working so hard out here?"

He gave her a chagrined look. "I guess subconsciously I was hoping you'd change your mind."

"And if I hadn't?"

"Then I would have found the words," he said confidently. "They're in my heart, Melanie." He pressed her hand to his chest. "Can you feel them with each beat?"

She smiled at him. "Steady and enduring," she said at once. "They're good words, Mike."

"And love?" he asked quietly. "You didn't feel that?"

She lifted her gaze to his. "It's in your eyes," she told him. "In your touch. In everything you do."

He sighed. "As long as you know," he said.

He took the ring and slipped it on her finger. It was a perfect fit. *They* were a perfect fit.

"I'm sorry I ever doubted it," she said.

"Maybe we both have to learn to have more faith," he said quietly. "We've been given a gift. We simply have to nurture it."

Her eyes stinging with tears, Melanie glanced around at the profusion of flowers that had come from this man's nurturing touch. Love was blooming everywhere. "I think you're just the man to show me the way."

Epilogue

Colleen D'Angelo stood at the back door of Rose Cottage, staring out at the garden, tears in her eyes. Melanie regarded her mother worriedly.

"Mom, are you okay?"

"I'm speechless," she said, her voice barely above a whisper. "It's beautiful, just the way it was when your grandmother was alive. How on earth did you remember it so clearly? I'd forgotten."

"I didn't," Melanie admitted. "I showed Mike a picture, and he knew exactly what to do. It's almost as if he felt some sort of connection with Grandmother. He fussed and badgered until I agreed to let him put the garden back the way it had been."

"He's a wonderful man, this Mike of yours," her mother said, smiling at her. "He's making you happy?"

"Of course," Melanie said, laughing. "We're getting married in an hour."

"That's more than enough time to change your mind," her mother informed her. "I can't believe you want to move here. You've always been such a city girl."

"Mike's here," Melanie said simply. "And when we get back from our honeymoon, I'm going to open my own marketing firm. Mike will be my first client. Not that I want him working any harder than he already does, but he won't be nearly as demanding as other clients might be. He'll forgive my mistakes while I'm learning the ropes. And Jeff and Pam want me to put together a marketing proposal for the nursery. Starting out with two clients isn't bad."

Her mother gave her a fierce hug. "I'm so happy for you. Your father's fit to be tied that you're not coming home. Don't be surprised if he punches Mike in the nose for taking you away from us, instead of giving the bride away the way he's supposed to."

Melanie stared at her with alarm. "Dad wouldn't really do that, would he?" She asked because it wasn't beyond the realm of possibility. He was a very protective dad, and he'd been regarding Mike with suspicion ever since they'd arrived for the wedding.

"Not as long as Mike keeps you smiling," her mother assured her.

"That won't be a problem," Melanie said, just as her sisters burst into the kitchen.

"Hey, why are you two standing down here in your robes crying? We have a wedding in less than an hour," Ashley announced.

"I think they're having the *S-E-X* talk," Jo teased.

"Ah, that must be it," Maggie chimed in. "See how flushed Melanie's cheeks are."

"Stop it, girls," their mother ordered in the no-nonsense tone they'd learned early to obey.

"Yes, ma'am," they chorused, then burst into giggles.

Melanie grinned at them. They'd laughed more in the past twenty-four hours than they had in years. She was going to miss them desperately.

Maybe she'd just have to figure out some way to lure

them to Virginia. Surely the magic of Rose Cottage hadn't been used up on her and Mike.

"Daddy, stop wiggling," Jessie said, her expression solemn as she surveyed him. "You look gorgeous." She twirled around. "How do I look?"

"Like a fairy princess," Mike said, his heart in his throat. Melanie's insistence that Jessie give him away, rather than taking the more traditional flower-girl role, had been just right. Jessie was taking her responsibility very seriously. Jeff had hardly anything left to do in his capacity as best man.

"I'm feeling extraneous," he grumbled, running a finger under the collar of his shirt. "Tell me again why I'm wearing a tux, when I could have been sitting in the crowd in a suit?"

"You're the best man," Jessie told him. "But I'm more important."

Jeff laughed as Mike scooped Jessie into his arms. "You are indeed, short stuff. Now let's get this show on the road."

The three of them took their places in the garden as the organ music began. Mike's gaze locked on the back door of the house, where first one D'Angelo sister emerged and then the next. They were all beautiful in their rose-colored gowns, but there was only one sister he was desperate to see.

Then Melanie emerged in a slim gown of white silk and lace, a bouquet of white roses and lily of the valley from the garden in her hands. Her gaze locked with his, and a radiant smile blossomed on her face. It was a stark contrast to the glower on her father's features. Max D'Angelo didn't scare Mike. He knew the man wanted only the best for his daughter, and Mike intended to exceed his expectations. He had a hunch he'd be just as fiercely protective when Jessie found the man of her dreams—say, thirty years from now.

When Melanie reached Mike's side, the minister asked, "Who gives this couple to be wed?"

Max D'Angelo glanced down at Jessie standing solemnly by his side and tucked her tiny hand in his. "We do," they said together.

"My love for you will be eternal," Mike said when the time came, clearly taking Melanie by surprise with vows he'd labored to write himself. "Like this garden, it will have cycles, but it will always bloom and thrive. It will weather every storm and reach for the sunlight. If we nurture it, our joy will be bountiful."

"Oh, Mike," she whispered, looking as if she might weep.

"Don't you dare cry," he said. "Or I'll never say anything romantic again."

She laughed at that, and the world righted itself. He sighed, gazing into her sparkling eyes. This was it, he thought. This was love—looking into Melanie's eyes and finding that his world was complete.

"I thought I was the one who had all the words," Melanie said slowly. "But you've left me speechless, Mike. 'I love you' doesn't seem to be nearly enough, and yet it's everything. I love you and your daughter. I love the family we will become, the children we will have somewhere along the way. I love that you've taken me into your heart, and I promise you will always be in mine."

Mike grinned at her. "Not so speechless, after all."

The minister cleared his throat. "My turn?" he inquired.

"Absolutely," they both said.

"Then I now pronounce you husband and wife." He

gazed out at the crowd. "Ladies and gentlemen, I present Mr. and Mrs. Mikelewski."

Jessie tugged on the minister's clerical robe. "What about me?" she asked, drawing laughter.

"And daughter," the minister said.

Mike was about to reach for Jessie, but Melanie was there first, scooping her new daughter up in her arms, then reaching for Mike's hand. Together the three of them walked down the aisle.

A family, he thought happily. The way it should be. The way it would *always* be.

* * * * *

What's Cooking?

Prologue

She was apparently addicted to sex. That was the only conclusion Margaret D'Angelo could come up with to explain this ridiculous habit she had of convincing herself she was wildly in love with a man she barely knew. She'd made way too many bad choices in her twenty-seven years based on letting her hormones overrule her head. She was not about to make another one.

And when it came to photographer Rick Flannery, he all but had the phrase "bad choice" tattooed on his forehead. It didn't take a genius to figure that one out. The man was a talented, world-renowned fashion photographer. That Maggie had even met him was such a fluke, she could still hardly believe it. Under normal circumstances, their paths would never cross. She set up photo shoots of *food,* for goodness' sakes! The most glamorous things on her magazine's pages wore decadent icing, not makeup.

Rick had merely stepped in at the last minute to do a favor for a friend. She figured that was about the most luck she could count on where he was concerned.

To add to her conviction that any relationship was doomed, she recognized that he was surrounded daily by some of the most gorgeous women in the world. The tabloids carried a picture of him almost every week with yet another model on his arm. Society columns linked his name with women from around the globe. Rarely was it the same name twice. That did not bode well for her own relationship with him.

Yes, indeed, for once in her life Maggie actually got it *before* she made the kind of mistake she'd live to regret, *before* she confused passionate sex with eternal love. Just this once she was going to sever all ties with a man before he could break her heart. This sane, rational thought might not have come to her in time to keep her from sleeping with Rick, but it sure as hell was in time to keep her from falling for him.

Proud of herself for making such a calm, intelligent decision for once and backing it up with a plan of action, she marched into her big sister's law office in a prestigious Boston skyscraper and held out her hand. "Give me the key," she demanded grimly.

Ashley's head snapped up from the stack of paperwork on her cluttered desk. She stared at Maggie blankly. Clearly her mind was still on whatever high-profile case she was preparing to take to court.

"What key?" Ashley asked, sounding surprisingly less quick-witted than she did when she was defending one of her clients against an aggressive prosecutor.

"To Rose Cottage, dammit!" Their grandmother's cottage was far away from Boston. Rick knew absolutely nothing about it. Maggie figured she could hide out there until this attraction or addiction or whatever it was cooled down, until it became nothing more than a distant memory. Down there in the boonies, she might not even have to see his picture in some tabloid with whatever model du jour was taking her place. That was definitely an added bonus.

"Why?" Ashley asked.

"I'm taking a vacation, that's why," Maggie retorted.

Ashley looked even more surprised. Maggie was no more in the habit of taking time off than Ashley was. She might not maintain Ashley's workaholic pace, but she didn't like being too far from the office and the whirlwind that publishing a monthly magazine entailed.

"Sit," Ashley commanded, waiting patiently until Maggie relented and complied. "What's going on, Maggie?"

"Rick Flannery is going on," Maggie responded, blurting out the words without thinking of the consequences. Ashley went into full protective big-sister mode. It was an awesome, sometimes intimidating transformation, especially for the person on the receiving end of her wrath.

"The photographer?" Ashley asked, getting a better grip on her pen and looking as if she might start taking notes and readying some sort of suit against the man at any second if she didn't find Maggie's answers satisfactory. "The one you've been raving about ever since he stepped in at the last minute to do the photo shoot for the July issue of your magazine? The one who could make the most ordinary mac and cheese look like gourmet fare, even though he normally takes pretty pictures of gorgeous women? The man who has eyes as crystal-blue as a lake and a tight little butt? *That* Rick Flannery?"

"Yes, that Rick Flannery," Maggie snapped. As if there could possibly be another one, she thought irritably. Wasn't it bad enough that there was one of them? And did her sister have to remember every blasted thing she'd ever said about the man?

To Maggie's shock, Ashley leaned back and grinned. "The man's got your hormones all stirred up, hasn't he? Why didn't I see that the first time you mentioned his name? When you started waxing eloquent about his body, it should have been a dead giveaway."

Maggie remained stubbornly silent.

"So?" Ashley prodded. "Does he make your heart pound and then some?"

"So what if he does? Nothing's going to come of it." Actually quite a lot had come of it, several glorious days and nights of unbridled passion, in fact. That was the problem, but Ashley didn't need to know it. Nor was Maggie about to add that he'd failed to call for six endless days now, pretty much proving her impression of a hit-and-run kind of a guy.

"Why not? Is there some reason the two of you can't be together?" Ashley persisted.

"Because he's Rick Flannery, dammit! There are a hundred—no, maybe a thousand—absolutely gorgeous, willowy women who drool over him on a regular basis. I am not about to set myself up to compete with that." What they had might be very hot right now, but it wouldn't last, not with that kind of competition underfoot day in and day out. Maggie hadn't been able to sustain a relationship yet, not once the sex cooled down. And Rick, according to all sorts of tabloid accounts, was not known for ignoring temptation.

"You've already slept with him, haven't you?" Ashley inquired knowingly. "And it was fabulous. Otherwise you wouldn't be this scared."

Leave it to Ashley to see straight through her, Maggie thought with disgust. She'd hoped to get through this conversation with one tiny shred of dignity intact. Apparently that wasn't to be.

"Will you just give me the stupid key?" she grumbled.

"So you can hide out in grandmother's cottage until the attraction wears off?" Ashley surmised.

"Exactly."

"You do recall what happened when Melanie went there a few months ago, don't you? She was just as determined to avoid men as you are. One popped up anyway and she's now married." There was a gloating note in Ashley's voice.

"A fluke. Lightning can't possibly strike twice," Maggie insisted. "That town is only so big. How many men can there possibly be like Melanie's Mike?"

Ashley chuckled. "It only takes one, sweetie." But even as she said it, she dug in her purse and retrieved the old-fashioned key that she kept there as some sort of bizarre talisman. She claimed it was a reminder to her that there was life outside the office. She held it out to Maggie. "Go. Enjoy."

"Thank you," Maggie said, grabbing the key and heading for the door.

"You're welcome. But when temptation comes calling, don't say I didn't warn you."

Maggie glared at her. "Bite your tongue."

Wasn't that the whole point of going into exile, after all? Temptation was going to be hundreds of miles away.

1

Rick emerged from his darkroom at 3:00 a.m., exhausted but pleased with his day's work. The photos for Boston's *Cityside* magazine were spectacular. Maggie was going to be over the moon when she saw them. If it wasn't so late, he'd call her and take them over to her apartment right now, just so she could see for herself how she'd inspired him, how well they'd collaborated together on his first photo shoot that didn't involve live models. He was as proud of these pictures as he'd been of some of his award-winning fashion layouts. It had been fun trying something new. It had been even more fun getting to know Maggie D'Angelo.

He loved that cozy little nest she'd made for herself in a loft space with its soaring ceiling. She'd filled it with sumptuous overstuffed furniture and sensuous fabrics that suited her passionate personality. They'd made some pretty spectacular fireworks in the huge bed with its satin sheets and down pillows. He got hard just thinking about it.

Not tonight, genius, he told himself. He doubted he could muster the energy to drive across town, much less act on the steamy thoughts racing through his head.

Tomorrow would be soon enough to get his fix of the woman who'd taken him to wild new places in bed, then followed up by cooking him a meal that he'd never forget. Maggie was one food writer who definitely knew her way around a test kitchen.

She also had a mouth on her that could drive a man insane. No, not like *that*. The woman had an opinion about everything. Sometimes Rick agreed with her. Often he didn't, which made for some fairly lively pillow talk. He'd never before realized what an aphrodisiac stimulating conversation could be. It lent a lot more credence to the concept that great sex began in the head, rather than other regions of the male anatomy.

He grinned as he thought of the last heated discussion they'd had. It had led to some even more heated activity.

Damn. It had been nearly a week since he'd seen her, and his body had apparently been keeping track of every minute. He needed to get his head off Maggie and concentrate on something soothing, or he'd never get a wink of sleep tonight.

The one good thing about leading the kind of demanding life he led was that he'd trained himself to sleep anytime, anyplace. As he had for the past five nights, Rick dragged himself over to the cot he kept in the back room at his photography studio for late nights just like this and collapsed, asleep in seconds.

Unfortunately Maggie followed him straight into his dreams, which made for a restless night. As a result Rick was even more irritable when he walked into her office first thing in the morning, a large cup of her favorite latte in hand, only to discover that she'd taken off for parts unknown.

"But *I'm* here," Veronica offered a little too generously,

batting eyelashes that had about four coats of mascara too many. "Maybe I can help you."

The last was laced with unmistakable innuendo. Rick dodged the offer. "Is it like Maggie to just disappear like this?" he asked her assistant.

"No," Veronica admitted grudgingly. She was evidently offended that her overtures weren't going to lead anywhere.

"Where'd she go?"

"I don't know."

"When will she be back?"

Veronica shrugged. "No idea."

Rick fought to keep impatience out of his voice. "You didn't speak to her?"

"She left a note. She said she'd be checking in and to contact her by email if anything urgent came up. That's all I know."

Since it was evident that Veronica was tapped out in the information department, Rick left the photos for the food layout with her, then went downstairs to an over-priced coffee shop for the breakfast he'd been hoping to share with Maggie.

Something about this whole vanishing act of Maggie's struck him as totally out of character. Not that he was an expert on Maggie D'Angelo, but he'd hoped to be, and he'd already picked up quite a few clues about her way of handling things.

For one thing, she met most crises head-on. He'd reached that conclusion when she'd seized on his offer to fill in on one of her photo shoots for a friend who'd had to leave town for an emergency. He'd made his reputation as a fashion photographer, so lighting and shooting food was hardly his area of expertise, but Maggie hadn't hesitated.

Nor had she wasted time berating his friend who'd left her in the lurch. Apparently she'd figured if Rick could click the shutter, he would do. She'd been surprisingly unimpressed with his résumé.

In fact, he recalled with amusement, she hadn't trusted him one damn bit. She'd all but crawled all over him to get a peek through the lens to assure herself he had exactly the shot she wanted. Normally Rick would have been offended by the interference, but he'd enjoyed the close contact a little too much to object too strenuously.

So, what would make a strong, opinionated woman suddenly vanish into thin air? Fear, he concluded. He'd beat a few hasty exits himself when a relationship had gotten too hot, so he recognized the symptoms. Heaven knew, their relationship had gotten hot fast, but for once he didn't seem to be the least bit inclined to run. That made it all the more annoying that Maggie had.

Come to think of it, though, he should have anticipated this. He'd detected hints of vulnerability in her eyes from time to time while they were together, but had never called her on them. Obviously he should have.

What the hell, he concluded as he finished his coffee. It wasn't too late. He had a few days to kill before his next assignment, and there was nothing he liked more than the thrill of the chase. Wherever Maggie had gone, he'd find her.

Maybe this thing of theirs would burn itself out like every other relationship in his life, but a tiny part of him seemed to be clinging to the surprising hope that it wouldn't.

Maggie sat in the backyard swing at Rose Cottage with a glass of the finest Merlot and waited for serenity to steal over her. The Chesapeake Bay was calm, the evening balmy. She'd been here for an entire two hours and she was ready for some inner peace, dammit!

Unfortunately an image of Rick Flannery kept sneaking into her head. He had wickedly clever hands, and she could all but feel them on her skin. Despite the perfectly comfortable summer temperature, she shivered.

This simply had to stop. She was not going to become another one of Rick's conquests. Okay, it was a little late for that. But she absolutely was not going to be one of those foolish women who thought their amazing encounters amounted to anything more than fabulous sex. She was not going to get involved with him. She was not going to get her heart broken. The tabloids were littered with the names of women he'd left behind. She had too much pride to join that list.

Normally when she had something on her mind, she retreated to the kitchen and cooked, but she couldn't seem to summon up the energy to bother. Besides, the cottage's air-conditioning barely stirred the air, much less cooled it. When she'd called to announce her impending arrival, Melanie had warned her that it needed to be replaced, but Maggie had waved off her concern.

"I'm used to test kitchens with a couple of ovens going full blast. I'm not worried about the heat," she'd said. "If it gets too oppressive, I'll check on putting in central air."

"Really? How long are you planning on staying?" Melanie had asked cautiously.

"As long as it takes," Maggie had replied grimly.

Unfortunately, based on the way she was feeling after just a few brief hours, she had a hunch she could be here weeks, maybe months. Inner peace seemed a long way off.

She sighed and took another sip of the excellent wine,

then glared at the Chesapeake Bay as if it were somehow responsible for not doing more to soothe her.

The sound of a car's engine caught her ear, but she didn't bother to move. Nor did she budge when two car doors slammed. It was bound to be Melanie and Mike and his daughter, the irrepressible Jessie. Maggie had known perfectly well that she wouldn't be able to hide out from them.

Fortunately Melanie was the least likely of all of her sisters to pester her with intrusive questions. And Mike was a man of few words. With any luck, the only one doing much talking would be the little six-year-old chatterbox, who'd wormed her way into Maggie's heart when Maggie had come down for the wedding just a few weeks ago.

Sure enough, it was Jessie who rounded the corner of the house first, coming at full throttle in Maggie's direction.

"Aunt Maggie," she hollered excitedly. "I didn't know you was coming." She crawled up on the swing and flung her arms around Maggie's neck. "Did you bring me a present?"

Maggie laughed. "Of course I did. How could I possibly come to see my very favorite new niece without a present?"

"Where is it?" Jessie asked.

"Still in my suitcase, but we'll go in and get it in a minute."

Jessie beamed at her. "I missed you," she said, snuggling closer. "I'm glad I got a mommy with lots and lots of sisters to be my aunts."

Maggie sighed at the feel of the warm little body next to hers. Her sister was so damn lucky to have found a man like Mike who came with a ready-made family. There was nothing Maggie wanted more, which probably explained her tendency to fall head over heels in love in a heartbeat. She was desperate for that elusive happy ending, but she always managed to choose precisely the wrong men to provide it. Besides, desperation was never a good way to start off a relationship. That was another tendency she needed to tame.

"So, has she wheedled a present out of you yet?" Melanie called out as she and Mike strolled in their direction.

Judging from the blush on Melanie's cheeks, they'd stopped for a few kisses en route. After all, this place was where they'd fallen in love. They were bound to get a little nostalgic, especially in the garden that had brought them together and where they'd been married.

"I told her we'd go inside and get it in a little while," Maggie said, giving her sister an amused grin. "Don't pout. I brought something for you guys, too."

"A cake?" Mike asked, his expression hopeful.

Maggie laughed, despite the sour mood she'd been in before their arrival. "Doesn't your wife ever bake for you?"

"No, thank goodness," he said fervently.

Jessie sat up. "She does, too," she protested loyally. "She bakes us cookies."

Melanie scooped Jessie up and gave her a squeeze. "Thank you, my precious angel. I haven't burned a batch in ages and ages, have I?"

"Just the edges," Jessie said, drawing a resigned, I-told-you-so look from her father and a protest from Melanie.

Maggie grinned. "The truth at last." She regarded her brother-in-law with amusement. "What's it worth to you to have me bake you a cake?"

"Depends on what kind and how good it is," he replied. "Let's negotiate."

"Sour-cream cake, fudge frosting," Maggie offered.

"I'll stop by and water the lawn."

Maggie shook her head. "Not good enough."

"Neither was the cake."

She knew what he was angling for. "If you want that triple chocolate threat cake, why don't you go see your friend Pam?"

"She says now that I'm married, she's not baking for me anymore," Mike said. "Those cakes were all bribes to try to get me to date her friends."

Melanie tucked her arm through his. "Want to go back to being single?" she inquired sweetly.

He gazed at her, his lips curving into a slow smile. "Not a chance."

Maggie gave him a thumbs-up. "For that, you get a triple chocolate cake that will be more decadent than anything Pam ever made you."

"I suppose you still want something in return," he said suspiciously.

"The name of an air-conditioning contractor."

"Deal."

Jessie, who'd been silent for an astonishingly long time, piped up, "I want my present now, please."

Maggie stood up and held out her hand. "Since you asked so sweetly, let's go get it." She glanced at her sister. "You two coming, or do you want to wait here?"

"We'll wait here," Melanie said, her gaze on her husband's face as if she still couldn't quite believe how lucky she was.

"Shall I bring you both a glass of wine? Or would you rather I stayed inside for, say, an hour?"

Melanie regarded her with a frown. "Forget it. I know

what you're up to. Bring the wine," she said. "Then Mike can take Jessie down by the water, and you and I can have a nice long talk."

"Now there's something to look forward to," Maggie muttered sourly.

Inside, she popped open her suitcase and retrieved a brightly wrapped package. "For you," she said, handing it to Jessie.

Her niece promptly sat on the floor and started tearing off the paper. When she saw the pink makeup case inside, she gasped. "How did you know this was what I wanted more than anything in the whole wide world?" she asked, gazing with awe at the pastel lipsticks, bottles of matching nail polish and lighted mirror.

"A little bird told me," Maggie said. "Now, remember, it's just for when you play dress-up."

"I know," Jessie said with exaggerated patience. "I can't go out of the house looking like I'm all growed up. Daddy won't let me."

"Your dad just doesn't want you to grow up too fast," Maggie told her. "And he's right. Life gets complicated soon enough as it is."

Jessie regarded her with confusion. "Huh?"

"Never mind, sweet pea. Take that out and show your mom and dad. I'll be right along with the wine."

After Jessie had gone, though, Maggie leaned against the counter and took a deep breath. She was in no hurry to go back outside and face her sister's questions. She doubted Ashley had filled Melanie in about Rick. Ashley would never betray a confidence, but she would rally the troops to make sure that Melanie was looking after Maggie and providing a shoulder to cry on if Maggie decided she needed it.

In addition, her presence here alone was probably

enough to alert Melanie that something wasn't right. Maggie was a city girl through and through, and lovely as the scenery was around this part of Virginia, there was nothing close by that fit Maggie's definition of civilization.

She poured the wine for her sister and her brother-in-law, then poured another full-to-the-brim glass for herself. She found the bag she'd brought from home with a few of Melanie's favorite Boston treats and hauled everything outside, hoping the gifts would distract her sister for a while.

The tactic worked, too, for about five minutes. Then Melanie shot a pointed glance at Mike, who immediately took the hint and led Jessie a discreet distance away.

"Okay, talk," Melanie ordered.

"About?"

"Why you're here. What are you running away from? Or should I ask whom?"

"Maybe I was just overdue for a vacation," Maggie retorted evasively.

"When you take a vacation, which you rarely do, you go to cooking school in Tuscany, you don't come down here."

"You did," Maggie replied testily.

"*I* was running away," Melanie reminded her. "Which is why I recognize the symptoms."

"Oh, for pity's sake, isn't it possible to have any secrets in this family?"

"No."

Maggie laughed, but even she could hear the edge of hysteria in her voice.

"Talk to me," Melanie repeated. Her patient expression suggested they would be here a very long time if Maggie didn't open up.

"I thought for sure you were the one sister who wouldn't pester me for details."

"You must have me confused with someone who wasn't born a D'Angelo," Melanie retorted. "Talk."

"Okay, here's the condensed version, and it's all you're getting. I met a man," Maggie revealed finally. "The wrong man, but at least this time I recognized it and got the hell out of Dodge."

Melanie regarded her with amusement. "So, how's running away working for you?"

"I've only been here a few hours. It hasn't had time to work."

"Want to tell me about him?"

"No," Maggie said flatly. Talking about Rick would only keep him front and center in her mind. She needed to bury all thoughts of him.

Melanie looked disappointed. "Not even a little hint?"

"Nothing," Maggie insisted.

"Want Mike to go beat him up?"

Maggie bit back a grin. "If I'd wanted someone to beat him up, I'd have told Dad. Besides, he didn't do anything wrong. This is about me, about the way I turn everything into some major big deal, even when it's evident that it's nothing more than a fling."

"Who said that's all it was? You or him?"

"Nobody had to say it," Maggie replied. "It was obvious."

"Really? How is it obvious if nobody says it?"

"It just is," Maggie said stubbornly.

Melanie rolled her eyes. "You know what they say about making assumptions about what somebody else is thinking, don't you?"

Maggie frowned. "That only applies if the evidence isn't plain as day."

"Really? What evidence is that?"

"Past history."

"Whose?"

"His. Mine."

"Maybe one or both of you have learned from your mistakes," Melanie suggested.

Maggie wanted to believe that she had. That's why she was here and not in Rick's bed with his hands all over her.

As for Rick, why would he have learned anything? She doubted he considered his past behavior to be a mistake. He was probably perfectly content with the revolving door his love life had become.

"Look, the point is that it's my decision to cut my losses. I don't need you to question it," Maggie told her sister irritably. "Not when you don't know what you're talking about."

"Because you won't tell me," Melanie countered. "I give really good advice when I know what I'm dealing with."

"I'm telling you this is the way it has to be. End of story. I don't want or need your advice. I just need your company from time to time to keep from going stir-crazy."

Melanie looked as if she might argue, but instead she cupped her hand under Maggie's chin and looked into her eyes. "I'm here if you need me, okay?"

Tears stung Maggie's eyes. "Thanks, sis."

"That's what the D'Angelo sisters do," Melanie reminded her. "We stick together."

"Through thick and thin," Maggie agreed. She slid a sly glance toward her sister and asked the one question bound to get Melanie off on a safer tangent. "How's married life treating you?"

A dreamy expression immediately crossed Melanie's face, and her gaze sought out her husband. She sighed in obvious contentment. "Better than I expected."

"And Jessie? I know you've both had your share of problems with keeping her behavior in check."

"It's like she's a different little girl," Melanie said. "Not that she's perfect, far from it, but she hasn't been out of control in weeks and weeks now."

"Must be your mellowing influence," Maggie teased, nudging her sister in the ribs. They both knew Melanie had a temper of her own, though she kept it in check ninety percent of the time.

"I think it's just knowing that I'm not going anywhere," Melanie corrected. "I think Mike's finally gotten that through his thick head, too."

"I hope so. He married you, after all."

"But I think he still had doubts. You should have seen the way he watched me the first time we had a huge argument. I think he was convinced I'd take off."

"But you stayed."

"I love him. Of course I stayed." It was Melanie's turn to give her sister a sly look. "Unlike some people I know, who run at the first sign of trouble."

Maggie groaned. "I thought we'd stopped talking about me."

Melanie laughed. "Nope. Just took a break."

Maggie stood up. "I'm tired. I'm going to bed."

"It's not even eight o'clock."

"I had an exhausting day. It's a long drive from Boston."

"And you're a night owl. Maybe I'll send Mike and

Jessie home, and you and I can have an old-fashioned slumber party. We can talk about men."

"I've done *all* the talking about men I intend to do," Maggie said emphatically. "Change the subject or go home."

"Ungrateful wretch."

"Nosy witch."

They laughed at the familiar bickering.

"I've missed this," Melanie said. "I hope you stay a long, long time."

"It's just a vacation," Maggie warned her.

Melanie's smile spread. "Yeah, that's what I said when I came down here last March."

"It's a vacation," Maggie repeated.

She had a hunch she was going to need to keep reminding herself—reminding both of them—of that. That was the trouble with running away from home. Sometimes it was very hard not to let pride and fear stand in the way of going back. That was especially true since the man she was running from was likely to be right there when she got back…maybe not waiting for her, but still too damn close for comfort.

2

On Melanie's recommendation, Maggie found the café in Irvington that served a decent latte and settled at one of the outdoor tables with a stack of regional magazines. Studying the competition always provided a great distraction. She usually knew what to expect from the publications she saw regularly, but she'd found some new ones this morning. With any luck those would be intriguing enough to keep her mind off Rick. Of course, there was no denying that was a tall order.

In fact, she'd deliberately left her cell phone back at the cottage, since the blasted thing had been ringing every five minutes all morning long. She'd finally shut it off, but since she didn't entirely trust herself not to check for messages, she'd decided to put some distance between herself and that possible link to the man she was so determined to avoid.

Did Rick know by now that she was gone? Did he even care? Veronica had sent an email earlier to let Maggie know that his photos were in and that they were spectacular. The email hadn't mentioned whether Rick had asked about Maggie or even whether he'd come by personally or sent the pictures by courier. Maggie hadn't wanted to ask. If the photos had come by courier, it would suggest that Rick, too, was taking extra measures to avoid any more contact between them.

"Want me to scan the pictures in so you can see them?" her assistant asked.

Control freak that she was, Maggie had replied at once, then waited and checked to see if the files had come through. As soon as she'd seen the photos, her heart beat a little harder. Rick had done an amazing job. He was every bit as talented as his reputation implied, even if he had been shooting pictures of summer squash and corn instead of willowy blondes. Maggie had immediately wanted to pick up the phone and call to congratulate him.

That was what had finally driven her out of the house. She was perfectly capable of making her own coffee, but the prospect of sitting outside, thumbing through unfamiliar magazines to look for some ideas that would be fresh to her readers, promised to be almost enticing enough to keep her mind off Rick for an hour or two.

Unfortunately as she studied some of the region's best photography, she realized none of it held a candle to what Rick had been able to do on short notice. When she realized she was sitting there making comparisons to his work, rather than forgetting about him, she tossed the magazines back into her canvas tote bag and headed home. If she was going to obsess about the man, she might as well be in her own surroundings.

As soon as she stepped inside, she spotted her cell phone on the kitchen table where she'd left it. She told herself that anything work related would be communicated by email. She reminded herself that her family would simply call the cottage. Only Rick was likely to leave a message on her cell-phone voice mail. There was no reason on earth to pick up that phone and check messages, but naturally she did.

To her regret—or was it relief?—there were precisely fourteen messages on her voice mail, thirteen of them from Rick. Apparently there was going to be no escaping the man, after all, unless she gathered the courage to toss the phone into the bay. And since she seemed to get a little thrill just from hearing the increasing frustration in his low, sexy voice, she doubted the phone was going anywhere.

The last message, which had been left only minutes earlier, was from Ashley, and she sounded odd, a little less confident than usual.

Other than acknowledging that annoying little stutter-step of her heart at the sound of Rick's voice, Maggie ignored his messages and called her sister on her private line. Ashley picked up at once.

"Hey, Ash, what's up?"

"Well, hello there," Ashley said a little too brightly. "Thanks for calling me back so quickly. I wasn't sure you'd be checking your cell phone for messages, since you're on vacation."

Maggie groaned and sank down on the sofa. She knew what that odd tone and the cryptic remark about her vacation meant. "He's there, isn't he? Rick is in your office."

"That's correct. Today's the day for surprises, all right."

"Send him away," Maggie told her urgently. "Whatever you do, Ashley, do not tell him where I am. Do not tell him I'm on the phone."

"Yes, I'm doing my best to do exactly that," Ashley agreed cheerfully.

Ashley mumbled something Maggie couldn't understand. "What did you say?" Maggie asked her sister.

"She said I'm being too damn persistent," Rick replied tersely.

There went that stutter-step of her heart again. "Oh," Maggie said weakly. This was it. Her worst nightmare. Unless she found some way to toughen her resolve immediately, Rick was going charm her whereabouts out of her. Then he was going to track her down, and every one of her noble intentions about ending their doomed affair was going to go up in smoke. She had absolutely no willpower where he was concerned. He was more addictive than chocolate, and in her life that was saying something.

"Where are you, Maggie?" he asked, sounding as if his patience had already been tested beyond its limits. "Why did you take off?"

She ignored the questions and asked one of her own. "How did you find my sister?"

"You mentioned her a couple of times. She works for a high-profile law firm. It wasn't all that tricky," he said, a familiar wry amusement threading through his voice. He was clearly awfully damn proud of himself.

"I meant, *why* did you go looking for her?" Maggie revised. "You know how to reach me if you're that anxious to talk to me."

"I know your number," he corrected. "I can't speak to you, though, unless you pick up. After leaving a dozen messages—"

"Thirteen," she corrected, without thinking of the implication.

He chuckled. "Then you did get them."

"Yes, I got them, but only a few minutes ago. Ashley's seemed more urgent."

"Then you did intend to call me back?" he asked skeptically.

"Eventually."

"That's what I figured. It wasn't nearly soon enough to suit me. I decided I needed to be more proactive, so I came looking for your sister."

"I'll ask again—why?"

"To find out where you ran off to and why you left without a word to me."

"I did not run off. I'm on vacation," she said, sticking to her story.

"Do you usually take totally unscheduled vacations?"

"What makes you think this was unscheduled? I could have been planning it for months."

"Were you?"

"No," she admitted, "but you didn't know that."

"Actually I did. Veronica told me. She said this was highly unusual."

"My assistant doesn't know everything," Maggie said defensively, because the truth was, she was not normally an impulsive person, except when it came to love. And that was a habit she was trying very hard to break. "Why does any of this matter to you?"

"Because something tells me that this sudden vacation has something to do with me."

"Your ego needs a reality check."

"Does it really? Okay, then, since you didn't run off to avoid me, you won't mind telling me where you are, so I can join you. I have a few days off."

"As a matter of fact, I *do* mind," she said emphatically, ignoring the fact that her blood had suddenly started humming with anticipation.

"Because you're with another man?"

Maggie sighed. They both knew she wasn't. She'd made the mistake of telling Rick it had been months since she'd dated anyone else. That stretch of celibacy had been her last drastic attempt to keep from making another mistake in the romance department. Sleeping with Rick had ruined a six-month track record she'd been very proud of.

"That's not the issue," she said. "I don't want to see you."

Rick chuckled. It was the laugh of a man who knew better. "Give me a couple of hours. I'll bet I can make you change your mind. If I can't, I'll leave."

It wouldn't take him ten minutes, Maggie thought with self-derision. She had to keep him far, far away from Rose Cottage.

"Sorry," she said. "I'll call you when I get back. Maybe we can go out for drinks and catch up."

She hung up before he could try to convince her to change her mind. She'd simply have to have faith that Ashley wouldn't fall victim to Rick's charm and draw him a blasted map.

It was dusk when a car pulled to a stop in the driveway at Rose Cottage. Filled with a sense of dread—and okay, maybe just a tiny little, traitorous *zing* of anticipation—Maggie peered out the window. Sure enough, Rick emerged from his low-slung Jaguar. Maggie's pulse zipped straight into overdrive. Apparently her body hadn't gotten the message that this man was bad for her. She couldn't seem to drag herself away from the window. It had barely been a week since she'd last seen Rick, and she was drinking in the sight as if it had been months.

The man was seriously gorgeous. He moved like a sexy, predatory cat, radiating confidence and danger.

He was also the kind of low-key man who could carry off jeans and a T-shirt with a wrinkled dress jacket and move from work to a cocktail party and never appear out of place. Maybe it was because the faded jeans fit in a way that kept all eyes on his trim butt and excellent thighs. No one—no sane woman, at least—ever gave two figs what he was wearing. Not that he didn't look fantastic in a tux, as well. He did. He'd accompanied Maggie to a black-tie event one night, and it had required all of her willpower not to attack him in the back of the limo he'd rented for the evening. She also happened to know for a fact that he looked pretty spectacular in nothing at all.

His brown, sun-streaked hair was a little too long and his jaw unshaven, but the careless look, too, suited him. The impression he exuded was one of total self-confidence, which, of course, he had. In spades, as a matter of fact. Who else would show up where he'd been told only a few hours ago that he was most definitely unwanted?

Resigned to dealing with him, Maggie opened the door and waited on the threshold. Rick grinned when he saw her.

"Hi, honey, I'm home."

"I'm not your honey and this is absolutely not your home," she said, blocking the way when he would have walked right in. She was trying really, really hard to muster the strength and indignation necessary to keep him on the other side of this door. Once he crossed the threshold, she could no longer be held accountable for her actions.

His grin never faltered. "Not happy to see me?"

"No."

"Not even a tiny bit?"

"Absolutely not."

He chuckled. "Liar."

"I am not lying. How many ways do I have to say it?"

"Until you can do it without those telltale patches of red in your cheeks."

"If my cheeks are red…" She could tell they were. Her skin was burning, in fact. "If they are, it's because I find you infuriating. It takes a lot of nerve to come here after I told you not to."

"Bravery should be rewarded, don't you think?"

She had to fight to keep from smiling. The man was impossible, to say nothing of impossibly sexy.

"Go away, Rick. Please."

His expression turned serious. "Only if you tell me why you're so anxious to have me gone. Make me understand and I'll go."

She studied him skeptically. "Seriously? You'll really go if I just tell you why I don't want you here?"

"Promise," he said solemnly. He even sketched a little cross over his heart.

Maggie regarded him with undisguised suspicion, but decided to take a chance that he would honor his promise. "Okay, then," she said. "I don't want you here because I don't want to see you anymore."

He nodded slowly. "In other words, it was great while it lasted, but it's over, Rick."

"Exactly," she said, relieved that he'd caught on so quickly. "That was the rule from the very beginning, wasn't it? Either of us could walk away at any time?"

He looked perplexed. "Did we discuss that?"

She thought back to the first night they'd tumbled into bed. There hadn't been a lot of conversation, much less any outlining of the rules of engagement. "It was understood," she asserted loftily.

He shook his head. "I guess I missed that. Besides, I'm not buying your act," he said. "You may not want me here, but it's because you're running scared, not because you don't feel any desire for me."

Of all the times in the world for a man to suddenly develop insight, it had to be now, Maggie thought, beginning to feel trapped and desperate. She had to make him leave before she did something totally insane and jumped right back into bed with him. Her hormones were all but pleading with her to cave now and damn the consequences.

"You said you'd take my word for it," she protested. "You promised to go. I expect you to honor that."

He shrugged. "I lied. Well, I didn't exactly lie."

"Yes, unless you turn around and walk away right this second, then you lied," she corrected.

"No," he insisted. "I just wasn't clear enough. I want more than a two-second explanation. I want the truth, the whole unvarnished truth. You say it's over, I'll take your word for it."

"Thank you." She started to shut the door.

"Not so fast," he said. "I still want to know *why* it's over."

"I doubt your ego can take it," she said, seizing on an explanation that was likely to rattle him. "Are you sure you want to hear my reason?"

To her chagrin, he didn't back down. If anything, he actually looked amused. "Try me."

She searched for a delicate but unmistakable way to put it that would be guaranteed to take the wind out of his sails.

"You don't do anything for me," she said finally, managing to get the words out without tripping over the blatant lie.

Rather than looking insulted or even angry, he actually laughed. "Really?"

"Nothing," she insisted. "No zip, no zing, nothing."

"And it took how many times in my bed and yours for you to figure that out?"

"I was giving you the benefit of the doubt."

"I see. Let me make sure I understand this. You're not attracted to me, so you took off from Boston just to get away from me? That's what you're saying?"

She didn't trust herself to speak, so she nodded.

Rick chuckled. "Sweetheart, I may be a totally clueless, dense male, but even I can see the contradiction in that."

So could Maggie, but she refused to back down. She just dug the hole a little deeper. "I was hoping to spare your feelings. I was hoping to avoid an awkward, uncomfortable scene exactly like this. I figured by the time I got back, you would have moved on."

"To what?"

"Some other conquest."

He stared at her for what seemed like an eternity, clearly mulling that over with more attention than he'd given her earlier claim. "*That's* what you're scared about, isn't it?" he said slowly, as if understanding were finally dawning. "You think I'll find someone else, so you're ending things before I can. And you're here because you didn't trust yourself to stick to your guns if you saw me long enough to tell me face-to-face."

"Don't be absurd," she said, but without much gumption. It was hard to argue with the truth. She gave him what she hoped was a quelling look. "I'm not going to stand here and argue with you all night long. I gave you my answer. Now go."

He leveled her a long, steady, disbelieving look at her, then finally nodded. "Okay, I'll go," he said at last.

Just when Maggie was about to breathe a sigh of relief, though, he winked at her.

"See you first thing in the morning," he said.

"What?"

"You've had your say," he explained patiently. "In the morning, I'll have mine."

Even as Maggie was plotting how far away she could be by dawn, he added, "And don't even think about taking off again. I think it's evident that if I could find you here, I can find you anywhere, unless you cut all ties with your family."

So Ashley had blabbed, after all. Maggie had guessed as much the instant Rick appeared. "Maybe I won't tell Ashley where I've gone next time," she muttered with new resolve. "She seems to be unreliable."

"Don't be too hard on her. She has your best interests at heart," Rick said.

"Yours maybe. Not mine," she said sourly.

He grinned. "I'm beginning to think they could be the same thing."

He was gone before she could come up with any sort of quick rebuttal to that. Maggie stared after him as he drove away. Well, hell.

As soon as he was out of sight, she marched inside and called her big sister.

"You traitor!" she blurted as soon as Ashley picked up.

"What did I do?"

"As if you didn't know."

"I don't know," Ashley said, sounding amazingly sincere.

"Rick just left here," Maggie told her. "Do you get it now?"

Ashley gasped. "How on earth did he find you?"

"Only one way I can think of," Maggie said.

"I swear I didn't tell him where you were," Ashley insisted.

Maggie's irritation began to fade. Ashley would never lie so blatantly. "You didn't just happen to leave a little note on your desk where he could see it?"

"No," her sister said flatly. "It's interesting, though."

"What is?"

"That he was determined enough to find you that he didn't stop looking after he ran into a dead end with me."

"That's not interesting. It's annoying," Maggie retorted. He had all but said Ashley had blabbed, hadn't he? Was that another lie? She went over his words carefully and realized that he'd talked about cutting ties with her family, not just her sister.

"How do you suppose he found you?" Ashley asked, her tone thoughtful. "I suppose if he tracked me down, he could have found Jo."

She'd obviously seized on the same possibility that had just occurred to Maggie.

"Jo doesn't even know I'm down here," Maggie said, then sighed. "Or does she?"

"Of course she does. She's your sister."

"And Mom and Pop?"

"I had to tell them something," Ashley said defensively. "They would have worried."

"I don't suppose you published a notice in the Boston papers, did you?"

"That's insulting. I'm hanging up now," Ashley replied.

"Sure. Hang up when the heat's getting a little too hot for you," Maggie said bitterly.

"Do you really want to belabor the whole issue of who told what to whom?" Ashley asked. "Shouldn't you be concentrating on figuring out what to do now that Rick has found you?"

"Aside from taking off for parts unknown, I don't have a clue," Maggie admitted. "Any ideas?"

"Stay put and let this play itself out," her sister suggested. "The man did go to an awful lot of trouble to find you. That must mean something."

"He likes a challenge," Maggie guessed.

"What if it's more than that?"

"It isn't."

"How can you know that?" Ashley asked reasonably. "Take a chance. That's my advice."

"As if I'd take relationship advice from a workaholic who hasn't had a date in two years."

"I date," Ashley replied indignantly.

"No, you have meetings with other lawyers who happen to be men. It's not the same thing."

"I'm saying goodbye now."

Maggie chuckled. "Goodbye. Love you."

"You, too, brat."

After she'd hung up, Maggie stared at the phone and debated calling her folks or her youngest sister to see who was responsible for Rick turning up here. Why bother, though? That particular horse was out of the barn. Rick was here, and now she needed to spend all of her energy devising some scheme to keep him out of her bed.

And judging from the way her pulse had been scrambling and her willpower had been weakening, it had better be one heck of a scheme.

3

On some level Rick knew he probably should have turned around and driven straight back to Boston. In fact, his well-honed instincts for self-preservation were all but screaming for him to do precisely that. In Boston there were plenty of women who would be eager for his company, rather than one prickly woman who claimed to want nothing to do with him.

But he didn't want those other women. It seemed he wanted Maggie D'Angelo, in all probability simply because he couldn't have her. That had to be it, he concluded. Every guy wanted what he couldn't have. He was no different from any other man on that score. He loved a challenge, and too few women over the years had offered him one.

Lying in an antique brass bed on a feather mattress in a waterfront Victorian-style bed-and-breakfast later that night, he indulged in a rare bit of introspection, contemplating the perversity of his decision to stay here and convince Maggie that she wanted him.

What happened when he pulled it off? And he *would* pull it off. It wasn't as if he wanted anything permanent. He never had before, and he couldn't think of anything that had changed. He still liked answering to no one. He liked his space. And he really, really liked the fact that no woman ever got close enough to break his heart.

Did that mean this was nothing more than a game with him? The proverbial thrill of the chase? A tiny little flicker of conscience warned Rick that he shouldn't be playing this game, not with Maggie, not unless he intended to follow through.

But follow through to what? A rollicking affair? It was pretty clear she didn't want that. Otherwise she would have welcomed him with open arms and one of her mind-blowing kisses back there at her front door. A rollicking affair was precisely what she'd run away from.

That brought him to marriage. Not that Maggie had ever made any noises around him about wanting marriage, but she was the kind of woman who would eventually want happily-ever-after. He'd gotten that early on. She came from a large and loving family. He'd only met Ashley and spoken to their mother on the phone, but Maggie talked about all of them, probably even more than she realized. She seemed to take particular delight in her parents' long and loving marriage and her sister Melanie's recent whirlwind courtship and wedding. It would be perfectly natural for her to want the same thing for herself one day. Maybe that was why she'd kicked him out. Maybe she'd recognized that he was a bad bet for that kind of permanent relationship.

He tried to imagine himself in the role of devoted husband, tried to envision being tied down to one woman, to having kids underfoot. He'd been footloose for a long time. His folks had been divorced when he was only ten, and after that, his dad was gone and his mom had lost interest in parenting, turning to booze to drown her sorrows. Rick had pretty much raised himself. He knew a whole lot about growing up independent, but he didn't know beans about what it took to keep a family happy, except maybe sticking around. He wasn't sure that was a gene he possessed.

The Flannery men apparently had a long history of being rogues and scoundrels, going all the way back to Ireland. Rick's mother had drunkenly recited all the tales to him on numerous occasions to explain why his father was no longer around. She'd said it was history repeating itself.

Given all that, his decision to stay put and pursue Maggie made no sense. But after listening all night to his conscience asking the hard questions—and even when he couldn't come up with any credible answers—Rick found himself picking up a couple of lattes first thing in the morning. Filled with a familiar anticipation, he headed for that quaint little cottage on the bay for another encounter with the stubborn, sexy woman who seemed dead set on tying him into knots.

He told himself he didn't need to have a long-range plan. Living in the moment had served him well enough for years. One step at a time, that was the key.

Today his goal was merely to get inside the door. Maybe by tomorrow he'd start worrying about pinning down why Maggie was really running so scared around him and what she really expected from him. Then, if he didn't like *those* answers, he could head for the hills.

She was going to go to bed with him. Maggie knew it the instant Rick showed up looking all rumpled and sexy with two lattes in hand. She'd spent the whole night telling herself she was right to send him away, that they couldn't possibly have any sort of future because she wasn't cut out to compete with women who made her feel like a whale, even if she was a perfectly respectable size ten instead of a two. She was not that masochistic. She reminded herself that she wanted a whole lot more from a relationship than explosive passion.

But even as she'd been congratulating herself on her good sense, a part of her had been yearning for the man's touch. Another part—her libido, no doubt—had been bargaining with her brain, telling it that if Rick actually came back again, all bets were off. Explosive passion didn't come along all that often. A woman would have to be an idiot to turn her back on it, at least while she was off on vacation. Back in Boston, she'd have to face facts, not now.

After all, she justified, Rick would only be here a few days at most. How much more complicated could things get in a few days?

She tried to keep all of that off her face when she accepted the cup of coffee with a perfectly uncomplicated, "Thanks."

"Expecting me?" Rick asked.

"Not really. I thought you'd wake up and think twice about what you're doing here."

"I did."

"And?"

"I came down here to see you."

"No, you came to annoy me," she insisted. "If I'd asked you to go away with me, you would have turned me down flat, trumping up some excuse or another. Face it, Flannery, you came because I told you not to."

"No, I came in spite of that," he corrected. "You should know by now that I'm not that easy to shake."

"Neither is a stalker. It's not a recommendation."

He looked momentarily nonplussed. "Please tell me you don't think that's what I'm doing," he said.

She sighed. "No, of course not." After all, who would be obsessed with her? Men were infatuated with her. Then they weren't. That was the cycle she expected. She met Rick's gaze. "But I honestly don't get why you came all this way when I'd made it clear on the phone that I didn't want you to. Is it some sort of macho pride thing?"

"Do we have to discuss this right here on the front porch?" Rick asked.

"It's not as if there are a lot of passersby to overhear," she told him.

He held up the bag. "But I brought lattes and freshly baked bear claws. I thought we could sit down and have a civilized chat."

"You really just want to talk?" she asked skeptically. That would be a first. They'd done precious little talking, at least not about anything meaningful, during their whirlwind romance.

"For now," he admitted with one of the lopsided grins that never failed to charm her.

Maggie debated with herself, then stepped past him. "We'll go out back. It's pleasant down by the water this time of day. That's where I always have my morning coffee."

His grin spread, and there was no mistaking the smug ego behind it.

"What?" she demanded, determinedly leading the way to the backyard swing…and at least the illusion of safety.

"Still scared that if you let me inside, you won't want me to leave?" Rick asked.

She returned his gaze. "Yes," she admitted candidly.

He nodded. "The truth at last."

"You only recognize it as truth because it flatters you."

"None of this is about ego, Maggie."

"Then what is it about?" she asked, as she sat on the double swing and curled one leg under her, leaving plenty of room for Rick beside her. The sun glistened on the Chesapeake Bay, which was already alive with watermen pulling in crab pots and reeling in rockfish. There was a tangy scent of salt in the air, mingling with the sweet fragrance of her grandmother's roses, now back in bloom after years of neglect.

"It's about meeting someone who fascinates me and wanting to spend more time with her," he said simply. "I thought we'd gotten my motives out of the way a couple of weeks ago. I was candid with you from that first night."

All Maggie remembered from that night was the unexpected shock of Rick's mouth on hers, the unexpected surge of need that had swept over her when he'd touched her. If they'd talked at all, it had gotten lost in a haze of heat and passion.

"So you explained the rules and gave yourself an out, in case I got any ideas," she surmised. "Bully for you."

"It wasn't an out," he corrected. "I was being honest."

"And then you disappeared," she reminded him, thinking about how much it had hurt when the phone hadn't rung and how furious she'd been with herself that she'd cared. He'd told her exactly who he was. She hadn't wanted to believe it.

He stared at her, obviously stunned. "Disappeared? I didn't go anywhere."

"I didn't mean it literally. You stopped calling."

"Is *that* what has you all worked up?" he asked incredulously. "I didn't call for a few days, so you think I went off with some other woman?"

Maggie ignored the indignation in his voice. She leveled a look straight into his eyes. The truth would be there, if not in his words. "Did you?"

"No, dammit! I spent six solid days and nights in my studio, finishing up photo shoots and working in the dark-room, so I could get ahead and have some free time to spend with you. You told me you'd have a break once the August issue was wrapped up, so I wanted to be free when you were."

Maggie was beginning to feel foolish. "You couldn't call and explain that?" she muttered defensively. Would it really have mattered if he had? Wasn't her decision the right one, no matter what?

Rick tensed. "I'm not used to having to call and ex-plain myself to anyone," he said. "Besides, I thought you wanted to keep things casual. That is what you told me, isn't it? You said you have a habit of getting in over your head too quickly and then realizing you'd made a mistake. You said you didn't want anything too heavy, right?"

"Yes." It was her first line of defense against the inevi-table. She'd wanted to be the one to set the tone for their fling. If she implied from the outset it was meaningless, then he couldn't possibly leave her heart or her pride in tatters. Or at least he'd never know it. She'd pretty much ruined that illusion in the past few minutes.

"What changed?" he asked, giving her a searching look.

What had changed? She'd meant those words when she'd said them, but it wasn't all that difficult to figure out. They'd slept together, and she'd liked it entirely too much. Ashley had picked up on that right off, so it was hardly mysterious. Her sister had guessed that Maggie had suddenly wanted more. In fact, she'd wanted things she'd sworn never to want again, all in the blink of an eye, because the man excelled in bed. To be perfectly honest with herself, she had no idea how compatible they were out of it, which meant that all this angst, all this irrational fleeing, was totally absurd. Flings had their parameters, and a fling—albeit a grand and glorious one—was definitely all they'd had.

She met his gaze. "I lost my mind," she suggested lightly. "Sorry."

His gaze held steady with hers. "Maybe we both did," he said quietly. "I wanted more, too, Maggie, and damned if I have any explanation for it, either."

She heard the sincerity and bewilderment in his voice, and it reassured her. Maybe she didn't have to plunge off the deep end. Maybe they could start over and take things slowly, get to know each other a bit before the fireworks got out of hand. That would be something new for her. Perhaps for Rick, too.

He tucked a finger under her chin and gazed into her eyes. Her entire body trembled. Okay, maybe they couldn't take things too slowly.

"What are you thinking?" he asked.

"With my brain?" she responded wryly.

He laughed. "For starters."

"That we could start over, take things a little slower this time. Get to know each other." She regarded him with a sideways glance, trying to gauge his reaction. She couldn't.

"And with whatever other part is chiming in?" he asked, amusement dancing in his eyes. "What's it telling you?"

"That we should go inside and make love right this second and to hell with everything else."

Heat glittered in the depths of his eyes. "How about we listen to that part first, then give your brain its say a little later?"

She wanted to say no. She really did. But her hand was in his and they were heading inside before one single coherent sentence could cross her lips. When it did, it wasn't "Forget about it" or even a simple "No." Instead, she said, "The bedroom's this way."

Rick wasn't entirely sure what had gotten Maggie to change her mind. He doubted it was anything he'd said. Reason and sanity didn't seem to be what they were about. No, if anything, they were all about passion and hunger.

They'd barely crossed the threshold to Maggie's bedroom when their clothes went flying. From the first they'd had no inhibitions, no false modesty. Maggie had been as eager as he'd been. Today was no different. Now that the decision had been made, she was coming to him with no apparent hesitation or regret.

He crushed her lush mouth under his, tasted her even as she fit her body to his, hip to hip, thigh to thigh. His hands were busy with buttons and snaps and zippers, seeking hot skin and her moist core. Hers were just as frantic, tugging aside his shirt, diving below the waistband of his jeans. When she found him, he was already hard and aching.

Rick couldn't wait, not this time. There was barely time to slip on a condom before he took her hard and fast, clothes tangled around their feet. Maggie was backed up against a wall, her legs around his waist. Her nails dug into his shoulders as she took him in, sheathing him in slick heat.

Rick paused, tried to catch his breath, tried to make it last, but the sensations were too sweet, too intense, too commanding.

In mere seconds, Maggie convulsed around him until he exploded inside her with the kind of heart-pounding, mind-blowing orgasm he'd experienced few times in his life, all of them with this woman.

Her breath came in ragged gasps. His kept the same rhythm, as he stilled, letting peace steal through him bit by bit. Even then he didn't let her go, didn't move to separate their slick bodies. There was something powerful about staying like this, intimately and literally connected. He barely noticed that she was growing heavy, not when holding her close was so wickedly wonderful.

"Don't you think you should put me down?" she finally asked.

"Not really."

"Why not?"

"Because as long as we're together like this, I doubt you'll be thinking."

She laughed. "Definitely not thinking," she agreed.

She gave a little wiggle that made him hard all over again.

"Oh, my," she said when he began to stir inside her.

"Oh, my, indeed," he said. "See the advantages of staying like this now?"

"Maybe you should explain them," she teased.

He gazed into her eyes, saw the quick flare of heat once more, felt her body already starting to shudder. "Why, darlin', it's obvious. Without moving a muscle, we're already halfway there."

"Where?"

"Heaven."

"Rick, what do you know about me?" Maggie asked hours later. They were in bed now, but she was still wrapped in his arms. They'd barely left the room all day long.

"I know that you're amazing in bed."

Even though she knew he'd meant it as the highest compliment, tears stung her eyes. It was what she'd asked for, wasn't it? Wasn't she the one who'd let him think that was enough? Even so, she asked wistfully, "Is that all that matters to you?"

"Of course not, though it was damn important about five minutes ago."

Irrationally angry, she crawled over him, dragging the sheet with her. She could feel his gaze burning into her, but she couldn't seem to halt the hasty exit. She had to get away from this, away from him. She'd done it again, done exactly what she'd sworn not to. She'd let passion trump any emotional connection.

"What did I say?" he asked, his voice tense. "Obviously you're offended."

"Not offended," she insisted. "What woman would be offended at being told she's great at sex?"

He snagged her hand, pulled her back to the bed. "Then talk to me. Tell me what's going on here. I can't read your mind, Maggie."

Maggie sat on the edge of the bed, trying to ignore the fact that Rick's hand was on her thigh. She struggled to find the right words. She had to make them good ones, words powerful enough to match the passion that tended to rule the two of them.

"It's like I told you before, we rushed into this without knowing anything about each other," she began. "Compatibility in bed isn't enough."

"Which is why I'm here right now, to spend time getting to know you better."

"In bed," she retorted.

He sighed. "Not just in bed."

"Then why haven't we spent time anywhere else, not today, not in Boston, aside from that one event we went

to. I had to do a lot of fast talking to get you to agree to
that. You would have turned the limo around halfway
there and gone straight back to your place," she reminded
him.

"But we did go to the party," he said. "And there was
the photo shoot. That lasted a whole day."

She smiled despite her exasperation. "We'd just met.
And practically the minute everyone else left your studio,
we were on that cot in your back room," she countered.

He shrugged. "Just proves how powerful the chemistry
between us is."

"Chemistry doesn't last," she said flatly.

Rick studied her for what seemed like an eternity. "And
that's the real problem, isn't it? You figure it'll burn itself
out."

"It will," she said with conviction.

"Probably."

"Then why bother?"

"What's wrong with living in the moment?" he countered. "I'd rather be a thousand percent alive some of the
time than bored to death all the time."

"You don't think there's a middle ground?"

"Haven't found it yet," he said. "Have you?"

"No," she told him honestly. But that's what she wanted.
She knew it existed because her parents had it. Melanie
had found it with Mike. Maggie had already had enough
of these whirlwind relationships to realize that she wanted
more than this.

"What's the bottom line here, Maggie? Do you want
me to take off?"

The sensible answer, of course, was yes. She couldn't
seem to get the word out. As unrealistic as it might be, it
seemed she wanted more with Rick, a man who obviously

had no experience with making anything last longer than a few days or, at most, a few weeks.

"I can't think on an empty stomach," she said instead, keeping her tone determinedly breezy. "That bear claw wore off a long time ago. I'll go fix something."

His gaze held hers. "And then?"

"We'll discuss it some more."

His lips twitched. "Till you talk it to death?"

"Maybe," she said defensively. "A little talking will be good for a change. It's not as if we've ever done much of it."

He laughed at that. "Okay, then, Miss Maggie, we will talk to your heart's content, as long as you don't mind if I do what I do best."

"What's that?"

"Try to convince you to shut up and come back to bed."

To her sincere regret, she shivered with anticipation. "You can try."

"Thank you," he said solemnly. "I promise you, I will give it my absolutely best shot."

She frowned at him. "Arrogance is not appealing."

"Then I'll be sure to let my actions speak for themselves," he said agreeably.

Maggie sighed. That was exactly what she was afraid of. When his actions challenged her willpower, it was no contest.

4

To Rick's surprise after the intensity of the conversation they'd had upstairs, dinner was actually more fun than he'd ever had with a woman outside of bed. Maggie ran her kitchen like a drill sergeant, issuing commands and organizing ingredients with an impressive level of efficiency. He went along with it and found himself enjoying her bossiness, mainly because it was so much fun to tease her about it.

"You ever think about joining the military?" he inquired when he'd lined up a row of requested spices precisely according to her specifications.

She shot a daunting look at him. "Why on earth would you ask that?"

"It boggles the mind to imagine how many potatoes you could have peeled while on kitchen duty."

"Very funny."

He gestured toward the row of spices, apparently intended for spaghetti sauce. "Wouldn't it be easier just to buy the sauce in a jar?" he asked, knowing she would consider the question to be bordering on blasphemy.

"If that's what your palate's used to, then prepare to be awed," she retorted. "Trust me, there's no comparison."

"If you say so," he said, hiding a grin at the indignation in her voice and the patches of red on her cheeks. He'd discovered a whole new way to stir Maggie up that was almost as enjoyable as sex.

She frowned at him. "Why are you standing there? Aren't you supposed to be crushing those tomatoes?"

"Am I?"

"You said you wanted to help," she reminded him. "If you can't keep up with the instructions, maybe you should stand back and let me do this."

"No way. I said I'd help and I will." He eyed the bowl of canned tomatoes with exaggerated wariness. "You want me to stick my hands in there?"

"Yes."

"Why not throw 'em in a food processor?"

"There's none here."

"A blender?"

"Sorry. And even if we had one, in my family we do this the old-fashioned way. My father's Italian. He's taught us all how it was done in the old country. We try to follow tradition. Of course, if you're afraid to get your hands dirty…" She let the unspoken challenge trail off.

"I am not afraid of anything," he said, sticking his hands in and squishing the tomatoes. He hadn't done anything this disgusting since he'd made mud pies when he was a toddler. "Like this?"

She watched him for a moment, shook her head, then stepped up and gingerly took his hands in hers and showed him what she wanted him to do. His body promptly stilled, even as his pulse took off like a jet seeking altitude. His response was poking her in the hip. There was no mistaking the moment she became aware of his arousal. She shuddered, then stepped carefully away, clearly trying to pretend she hadn't noticed.

"I think you have it now," she said, her voice shaky.

"I definitely have something," he responded, keeping his expression innocent.

"Rick!"

"Yes, Maggie?"

She gave him an impatient look, then muttered, "Never mind." She turned her back on him.

Rick regarded her with amusement. She was trying so blasted hard to keep things cool. She didn't seem to get the fact that heat was what life was about. All the rest was marking time.

"Okay, the tomatoes are properly squished," he said at last. "Now what?"

"Now you go for a walk or something and stay out of my way," she replied.

"Afraid I'll steal your trade secrets?"

"Hardly. I think we can both agree that you're no gourmet chef."

Rick had to bite back a laugh. "Oh, really?"

"It's obvious."

"Just because I asked you to show me how to squeeze a few canned tomatoes?"

"That was definitely one clue. Then there was the comment about getting spaghetti sauce from a jar."

"I said it would be easier, didn't I? Did I say anything about better?"

She regarded him with a quizzical expression. "What are you getting at? Do you actually cook?"

"A few things," he said modestly. He'd been a bachelor for too long, and somewhere along the way he'd developed a cultivated palate. He knew his way around the kitchen. In fact, he suspected he was a more than even match for her, when he chose to be.

"You want to make the sauce?" she inquired in a way

that implied she was throwing the suggestion out as a challenge she was confident he wouldn't accept.

"Sure."

Looking startled, she stood back and made a dramatic sweep of her hand. "Be my guest."

"Are you sure?"

"Why not? I have a cast-iron stomach."

"There's no need to be insulting." And just for that remark, he intended to test her mettle. He'd make an arrabiata sauce that could match the fires of hell.

With practiced movements, he tossed the ingredients into the saucepan, then began deftly adding spices. Next thing he knew, Maggie was at his shoulder, peering into the pot.

"Something wrong?" he asked.

"What did you get out of the cabinet?"

"Another spice or two."

"Which ones?"

"I think I'll wait till you taste it and see if you can guess."

She reached for the spoon, but he held it away. "Not now. It has to simmer for a bit."

"There's nothing worse than a testy, controlling cook," she muttered, retreating to her place at the table.

"Something for you to keep in mind," he said. "Any wine in the house? You could pour us a glass." One was usually his limit, but tonight he might make an exception.

"Oh, goody. An assignment for the little lady," she mocked.

"Pouring the wine is a macho thing, a very big responsibility, in fact. I didn't ask you to set the table, did I?"

"Good thing," she muttered.

Rick laughed.

Twenty minutes later dinner was on the table. The fragrance of the sauce was rife with garlic, oregano and other spices. When Maggie had been getting the wine, he'd switched the angel-hair pasta for a denser penne that would hold up to the chunky, flavorful sauce. It was a lesson he'd learned from a famous Tuscan chef. Not all pastas were created equal, and the selection could make all the difference in the success of a meal.

Maggie eyed the bowl in front of her with surprise as Rick grated fresh parmesan cheese over the top. He couldn't fault the quality of the ingredients in her pantry. Even though she'd just arrived a few days ago, she'd brought in only the best.

"This looks fabulous," she admitted. "Smells good, too."

"You sound shocked. It's just pasta."

She laughed. "There's no such thing as *just* pasta to an Italian. This is the food of the gods."

"The Italian bit slipped my mind for a minute," he said. "I was more panicked about performing to the high standards of the food editor."

She tasted her first bite, then sighed. "Not to worry. You passed with flying colors for both the Italian *and* the food editor. Even my father would be impressed, and he's a tough critic. He doesn't think anyone on earth cooks Italian the way his mama did, though it never stopped him from trying to teach all of us. To his regret, Ashley showed absolutely no interest. Melanie can barely boil water, and Jo likes to take shortcuts that make him insane. I'm the only one who took what he said to heart."

"I'll have to cook for him sometime, then."

"Sure you won't suffer from performance anxiety?" she teased.

"Performing for you is the only thing that ever makes

me anxious," he responded. He gazed into her eyes. "I want to get it right, Maggie. I really do."

She swallowed hard, her gaze locked with his. "Are we still talking about cooking?"

He shook his head. "Not entirely."

A surprising hint of a smile tugged at her lips. "You brought sex up first," she gloated. "And after accusing me of wanting to talk things to death."

Rick sighed. "My mistake. Let's discuss what we're going to do tomorrow."

Maggie looked far more shaken than the suggestion warranted.

"Something wrong with that?" he asked.

"You're not leaving?"

"No, not as long as you're here."

"You said you'd only be here a few days," she said, sounding a little panicky.

He shrugged. "I assumed you'd only be here a few days."

"Well, I'm not. I'm here indefinitely," she said with a note of belligerence.

"Then I guess I am, too," Rick replied. That was the blessing of a career in which he made his own schedule. He might have to call his agent eventually and shuffle a few assignments, but he could manage to stay for however long Maggie did.

"Why?"

"I think we've established that," he reminded her. "I intend to get to know you."

"Outside of bed?" she asked skeptically.

He laughed, even though he could see that to her it wasn't a joking matter. "And in."

Unfortunately, there was no spark of amusement in

Maggie's eyes. Obviously she was in no mood to be taunted.

"Okay," he relented. "It's more than that, but I'm not sure I can explain it, Maggie. I have no idea what you expect me to say."

"To be honest, I don't know what I want you to say, either," she admitted, gazing at him plaintively. "Do you think we could spend an entire week together here without sex?"

He gave her a horrified look. "Why would we want to?"

"Because sex is not the only thing that counts in a relationship. People have to be able to communicate in other ways, too. They have to have things in common, enjoy spending time together."

He could see she was totally serious. When he recalled what she'd told him at the beginning, that she'd taken a break from all relationships, it finally dawned on him why she was so gun-shy about the way things were between them. "Is that what happened to your other relationships, Maggie? They cooled down and then they died? Did that convince you that the only thing you were any good at was sex?"

She seemed startled by the question. "Where did you come up with that idea?" she asked defensively.

"Added up a few comments," he said. "Am I right?"

"As a matter of fact, yes," she admitted with obvious reluctance. "I seem to have this part down really, really well. The rest is usually a disaster. I'm not even sure I can carry on an intelligent, stimulating conversation with a man anymore."

Rick laughed until he realized that she was serious. He sobered at once. "Trust me, sweetheart, you can. In fact, that was one of the first things that attracted me to you.

You came into that photo shoot knowing exactly what you wanted, and you didn't hesitate to tell me."

"Well, of course, I did," she said, dismissing it as if it were nothing. "That's my job."

He grinned at her confidence. "True, but a lot of people tend to be intimidated when they deal with me for the first time. Some expect me to be temperamental, so they tiptoe around me. Others simply let me call the shots, because they figure that's why they're paying me the big bucks."

"Because you're the internationally famous photographer?" she asked, her expression thoughtful. "Yes, I can see how that might intimidate some people."

"More than a few."

"But they're the client," she protested. "Besides, you mostly do fashion work. I knew we got you at the last second to do this food layout only because you owed a favor to a friend. I figured you'd welcome some pointers."

He laughed. "You gave more than a few pointers, Maggie," he said, his expression wry. "You never shut up. Most clients don't have a clue what they're talking about. You did. I liked that. You challenged me every step of the way, and I liked that, too. We made a good team. The proof of that is in those pictures."

"I was fairly certain at the time that you thought I was being a pain in the butt," she admitted.

"I did, but a fascinating pain, just the same. Why did you think we wound up in bed that night?"

"Chemistry," she said simply. "That and the fact that it's what you do. You meet a woman you're attracted to, and you get involved for a bit."

"That's fairly insulting," he pointed out, then sighed. "But unfortunately, true. This time is different."

She looked doubtful. "How?"

"I don't know, but I can tell you that you are the first woman I've chased to the middle of nowhere."

"This is not the middle of nowhere," she retorted, even though that was hardly the point. "You found a café that serves lattes, didn't you? Isn't that civilized enough for you?"

"The only thing that kept me here, I assure you," he said, enjoying the quick flags of color that burned in her cheeks. "Well…and you, of course."

"Of course."

He met her gaze. "Do I get to stay?"

She looked surprised by the question. "Is it actually up to me?"

He made up his mind that this would never work if she was having second thoughts. He met her gaze and took a chance. "I want to stay, but if you still want me to go, then I will. So, yes, it's up to you."

She hesitated for what seemed like an eternity, then said firmly, "You can't stay *here*. That would pretty much destroy the whole starting-over-slowly thing."

"Deal," he said, relieved. He could play by those rules, for a while at least.

"And when you're bored out of your mind in the middle of nowhere and with me, you'll just say so, right? You won't feel compelled to stay or take off without a word?"

"Not going to happen, but okay."

"Then you can stay," she relented.

Something told him, though, that she wasn't entirely happy about it. He had a hunch it was the sex thing, that she didn't trust herself—or him—not to fall back into that old, apparently self-destructive pattern of hers. Maybe a week would give him enough time to convince her that what they had was unique…in bed and out.

* * *

Even though Rick had agreed to her ground rules, even though he was staying out of her path as they cleared up the dinner dishes, there wasn't an instant when Maggie wasn't fully aware that he was close by. The hairs on her arms all but stood up and did a little dance each time they brushed by each other, no matter how innocently.

She had to get him out of here soon, before she weakened and broke one of those vows she'd made him agree to respect not ten minutes earlier. How pitiful would that make her look?

When the doorbell rang, she raced to answer it, then realized she should have ignored it when she found Melanie and Mike on the doorstep. She had a hunch their arrival while Rick was here wasn't strictly happenstance.

"Go away," she told her sister.

Melanie simply laughed. "Don't want me to meet your company?"

"No, and how do you know he's here, anyway?"

"Mike heard it from a friend, who heard it when he went to pick up coffee this morning. I believe Rick was buying lattes and bear claws for two. I called Ashley, who knows everything going on in this family, and picked up a few more tidbits about the intriguing Mr. Flannery."

Maggie groaned. "Is there any little detail you've missed?"

"I don't think so, but I definitely feel out of the loop, since I haven't even gotten a peek at this hunk who chased you all the way from Boston. I am your sister, after all."

Maggie turned a beseeching look on Mike. "Can't you take her home? Isn't it time to pick up Jessie or something?"

"Jessie's over at Pam and Jeff's, playing with Lyssa," Melanie retorted. "She'll be fine for another hour or so."

"You're going to stay, aren't you?" Maggie muttered with a sigh of resignation.

Mike gave her a sympathetic look. "Was there ever any doubt?"

Melanie pushed past her. "Where is he? Hidden away in your bedroom?"

Maggie flushed to the roots of her hair. "Mel!"

Her sister grinned. "Ah, I hear the rattling of pans in the kitchen. Don't tell me you have a man who does dishes. Marry him now."

"I don't think marriage is on the table," Maggie said. "Come on, let's get this over with. Say hello, get a good long look at him and then go."

Melanie breezed by her and headed for the kitchen. "Oh, it smells wonderful in here. What did you make for dinner, Mags?"

"Rick cooked," Maggie said tightly. "Rick, this is my sister Melanie and her husband, Mike Mikelewski. They won't be staying."

Rick's expression went from dismay to relief in a heartbeat. Maggie could relate.

"Would you like some wine?" he asked.

Maggie groaned as Melanie immediately brightened.

"Sure. I'd love a glass," she said at once, pulling out a chair and settling at the kitchen table. Mike shrugged, then straddled the chair next to her.

Maggie remained standing. As Rick poured the wine, she gave him a surreptitious what-were-you-thinking look. He ignored her and sat down with the others.

"I didn't know Maggie had a sister living in the area," he said.

"Actually I lived in this house when I first came down from Boston in March," Melanie said. "Then I met Mike, and we got married a few weeks ago."

Rick's eyes widened. "Really? That fast? Maggie'd mentioned a whirlwind courtship, but that's faster than I'd realized."

Melanie nodded happily. "I think it had something to do with this cottage. When we were girls and our grandmother lived here, we always thought it was magical. It certainly seemed to work that way for me. I came here miserable and, voilà, I met Mike and his little girl, and now we're deliriously happy."

Maggie kept her gaze on Rick's face as Melanie related the story. She was pretty sure he turned a little pale at the implication that Rose Cottage was somehow responsible for Melanie's marriage.

"I see," he said, then looked to Maggie for an instant, his expression quizzical. "Do you think this place has magical properties?"

"Actually, I think my sister is a bit of a romantic with an overly active imagination," she said flatly.

Melanie laughed. "Wait and see."

Maggie gave her a daunting look. "Do you honestly think Rick will stick around now that you've all but warned him that he's doomed to marry me if he spends another minute in this house?"

"You could always make it a dare," Mike suggested. "Men can't resist a dare."

Rick shot him a disbelieving look. "Hey, man, whose side are you on?"

Mike chuckled. "Melanie's, of course. I have to go home with her."

"And the sooner the better," Maggie snapped.

Her sister beamed at Mike. "I think our work here is done," she said cheerfully. "We've checked out the situation, planted a few seeds, now we can wait to see how they grow." She winked at Rick. "That's what landscape designers like my husband do, you know. That way it escapes being labeled 'meddling.'"

"I doubt Rick's mind is fertile enough for an idea like that to grow on him," Maggie said dryly. "You're wasting your time."

"It's never a waste of time to look out for one of my sisters," Melanie insisted.

Maggie scowled at her. "I imagine you'll be reporting in to Ashley tonight, too."

"Of course."

"Why wasn't I cursed with brothers, instead of sisters?" Maggie inquired of no one in particular. "Surely they wouldn't meddle—or whatever it is you're calling this untimely visit."

"No, a brother would just bust in here and demand to know Rick's intentions toward his sister," Melanie said. "Be grateful for what you have. I haven't asked him a single question."

"Why is that?" Maggie asked.

Melanie grinned. "Because the answer's already written all over his face. The man is smitten. That'll do for now."

Before Maggie could rally, her sister and Mike were gone, leaving her to face Rick.

"I am so sorry," she said, mortified. "Melanie may have expectations, but I assure you I don't."

"It's not a problem," he assured her, even though he looked a little shell-shocked. "I think I'd better take off, though."

"Probably a good idea," Maggie concurred. "For all I know, she's out there peeking in the windows and taking notes so she can report back to everyone in Boston."

She walked Rick to the door, feeling oddly out of sorts and fearful. Had Melanie's frank analysis scared Rick silly? It had certainly terrified her. She wouldn't blame him if he headed to Boston—or maybe Timbuktu—first thing in the morning.

When they reached the door, Rick tucked his hand under her chin and tilted her face up till their eyes met. "See you tomorrow."

"Really?" There was an annoying hint of relief in her voice.

"You don't think a five-minute visit with your sister is going to scare me off, do you? We have a deal."

"You made it before you realized what you were going to be up against. I wouldn't blame you for taking off."

"Not going to happen."

"Why?" she asked, honestly bewildered.

His lips curved slightly. "Haven't you heard? I'm smitten."

She watched as he strolled away, her heart in her throat. Oh, boy, she thought a little desperately. That little revelation was far more dangerous than he realized, because she was apparently more than a little smitten herself.

5

Rick cursed himself for being far too eager to see Maggie the next morning. Then again, with any luck, maybe he could convince her to postpone the start of the ground rules for another day. He'd spent a very long night missing the feel of her in his arms.

As soon as the scheme entered his mind, he told himself to forget about it. He'd made a promise and if Maggie really was hung up on the shallowness of her past relationships, having him turn up first thing today trying to get her into bed would only add to her conviction that it was all she had to offer. He needed to spend a couple of hours otherwise occupied before he saw her. Maybe that would take the edge off his desire.

Though the bed-and-breakfast where he was staying offered a morning meal, he was feeling too uptight to stick around and wait for it. Besides, he wanted something more substantial than the continental spread they put out. He'd seen a diner in town the day before that looked promising.

When he walked in, he immediately spotted Maggie's brother-in-law and another man in a booth. Mike saw him and waved him over. Despite the potential minefield joining Maggie's brother-in-law presented, Rick knew there was no choice. He crossed the room and dragged a chair over to sit at the end of the table.

"Jeff, Rick Flannery," Mike said. "Rick, this is Jeff, who owns the nursery in town."

Rick gave Jeff another look. After years in photography, he had an eye for faces. He recognized this one. "You're the blabbermouth," he said at last, more amusement than condemnation in his voice. "You were in the café when I was getting coffee yesterday."

Jeff grinned. "Guilty," he admitted.

"Uh-oh," Mike said. "Should I get out of the way before fists start flying?"

Jeff gave him a quizzical look. "Why would we fight?"

"Because I passed along what you told me. Melanie called Ashley for information, then dragged me over to Maggie's so she could get a firsthand look at Rick. Poor guy was squirming by the time we left." He turned to Rick. "Frankly, I'm a little surprised you're still in town."

"I don't scare off that easily," Rick said, though there had certainly been times in his life when last night's interference by a protective sister would have been more than enough to send him away.

Mike chuckled. "Brave words. You should be terrified. Remember, I've gone up against the D'Angelo sisters. Look at me now."

"Don't pay any attention to him," Jeff said. "He's as happy as a bull in clover. Melanie's the best thing that ever happened to him."

"True," Mike said complacently. "But Rick might not be as eager to settle down as I was."

Jeff hooted. "Eager? You? Please. Don't pay any

attention to him, Rick. He was as gun-shy as a man can be." He grinned. "Sort of like you, I imagine, if you've been able to resist all those gorgeous models this whole time."

Rick grinned at him, not surprised that even here in a tiny town in Virginia's Northern Neck his reputation had gotten around. He'd been on the pages of some of those supermarket tabloids and appeared on TV entertainment shows often enough to become a celebrity in his own right. And he'd discovered that a lot of men envied his proximity to some of the world's most gorgeous women.

"Who says I resisted?" he asked Jeff, in part because it was the kind of comment most men expected of him.

"Oh, please tell me I did not hear that," Mike said with a groan.

"Jealous?" Jeff asked. "Can't say I blame you."

"No, I am not jealous," Mike said. "I'm just trying to figure out how Melanie's going to react if she thinks her sister is involved with a guy who's worked his way through the fashion world with more than his camera lens."

"I can't speak for your wife, of course," Rick told him. "But Maggie knows all about my past history. She's okay with it."

Both men stared at him incredulously. "Really?" Mike said. "You sure about that?"

They looked so skeptical, Rick was forced to reconsider. Wasn't the truth a little murkier than that? Maggie knew about his past, but wasn't that one of the very reasons she didn't trust their relationship to last? Well, hell.

Acceptance of something that couldn't be changed was one thing. Obviously, though, it wasn't going to be quite so easy for her to pretend it had never happened, that it hadn't shaped who he was, or that it wouldn't affect his relationship with her. His love 'em-and-leave-'em reputation would hardly bolster her confidence that he was a good bet for her own transformation into a woman who was looking for stability and steadfastness from a man.

"Okay," he admitted at last. "She's probably not happy about it."

"There you go," Mike said. "A reality check. Women love it when we recognize those. Makes 'em think we're sensitive."

Jeff nodded. "And speaking of reality checks, you and I need to get over to the Winstons and get those shrubs in the ground. I told her we'd be there by eight."

Rick glanced at the clock and noted they were already twenty minutes late. "Sorry I kept you."

"Not to worry," Mike said. "We're talking Northern Neck time here. The world's a little more laid-back than what you're probably used to." He gave Rick's shoulder a squeeze. "See you around. Try not to tick off Maggie. It'll have a ripple effect and land on me."

Rick chuckled, but Mike's expression remained somber.

"Not joking, pal. Trust me on this. The D'Angelo sisters stick together. It can be a bit daunting."

"I'll keep that in mind," Rick promised.

"By the way," Mike added, "next time you come in here, you might prefer to avoid me if you're actually interested in eating. The owner—Brenda Chatham—has never quite forgiven me for marrying Melanie, so the service I get usually sucks."

Sure enough, as soon as he and Jeff were gone, the elusive Brenda finally appeared. By then, though, his conversation with Mike and Jeff had cost Rick his appetite. He ordered coffee.

She regarded him with disappointment. "Sure I can't get you anything else? The waffles are the best around."

He shook his head. "I don't think so. And, come to think of it, make the coffee to go."

He needed to hit the road and clear his head. The few minutes he'd spent with Mike and Jeff had been entirely too disconcerting. Rick had the uneasy feeling he'd just stumbled into a gigantic spider's web, and it was already tightening around him.

Maggie was getting antsy. It was close to noon, and there had been no sign of Rick yet. She was doing precisely what she'd vowed not to do. She was obsessing over the man.

To avoid falling into that trap, she grabbed her purse and headed for the door, only to run smack into her sister.

"Going someplace?" Melanie asked. She seemed disgustingly cheerful this morning.

"Out," Maggie said tightly. She was in no mood for a continuance of last night's cross-examination.

"Where? If you're going to lunch, I'll join you."

"I'm not going to lunch," Maggie said.

Melanie gave her a sharp look. "Maybe you should. Your blood sugar seems to be a little low. You're cranky."

"Thanks for the observation, but my blood sugar's just fine."

Her sister chuckled. "Then it must be Rick. Has he done something to upset you?"

"Of course not."

"Oh, I thought maybe you were starting to worry that he'd taken off," Melanie said mildly. "And if that was worrying you, I could put your mind at ease."

Maggie scowled at her. "Oh?" she asked as if it didn't matter.

"Mike saw him this morning."

"Where?" she asked a little too eagerly, spoiling the whole indifferent effect she'd been going for.

Melanie's expression turned triumphant. "Then it *is* Rick that has you in such a foul mood," she concluded. "Mike saw him at the diner. Rick joined him and Jeff for a bit."

"What time was that?"

"Seven-thirty or eight, I imagine. I didn't ask for a timetable."

That was hours ago, Maggie realized. It didn't tell her a blessed thing about where Rick was now. It shouldn't matter, dammit, but apparently it did.

"Where the hell is he now?" She didn't realize she'd spoken aloud until she saw the worried expression on Melanie's face. "Pretend you didn't hear me say that," she pleaded.

"Did the two of you have plans this morning?" Melanie asked, sounding as if she would willingly gear up for battle if Maggie had been stood up.

"No, not exactly," Maggie moaned. "I'm being absurd, aren't I? This is precisely why I can't get involved with Rick Flannery. I start to fall for a man, and the next thing you know, he's all I think about. I obsess and ruin everything."

"Then every time you start to obsess, do something else," her sister advised. "Rick's not going anywhere, Maggie. I meant what I said last night. It's obvious he's fascinated by you. Ashley thought the same thing. Otherwise I'd be over here helping you try to run him off."

As much as she wanted to believe her sisters, Maggie wasn't so sure. She fully expected Rick to tire of her, to

tire of the rules she'd laid down. He'd tired of more so-
phisticated women. Maybe with her it had just happened
sooner than she'd anticipated.

Before she could say any of that, though, Rick's sleek
little sports car turned off the road and came to a stop
beside Melanie's dusty SUV. Rick emerged, looking
windblown and sexy as hell.

"Ladies," he said, coming over to drop a casual peck
on Maggie's cheek. "Am I interrupting?"

"Nope, I'd say your timing is perfect," Melanie replied,
giving Maggie an I-told-you-so look. "I'm on my way.
Take her to lunch. She's getting cranky."

Maggie shot an appalled look at her sister. "I am not."

Despite the denial, though, she had to fight to keep a
sharp note out of her voice when she turned to Rick and
asked, "What have you been up to this morning?" She
hoped she sounded casual and interested, not possessive
and panicky.

"Miss me?" he asked.

"Hardly. I've been busy around here," she fibbed. "You
still haven't answered my question. Did you have a good
morning?"

"Sure."

She had a weird feeling he was being deliberately evasive. It made her more determined than ever to get to the
bottom of his absence. "Doing what?"

He gave her a quizzical look. "I went for a drive, took
a few pictures, nothing much," he said with a shrug. "Am
I missing something, Maggie? Are you upset that I wasn't
here sooner?"

"No, of course not. We didn't have plans."

"And I thought we'd agreed that you wanted some space,
that you didn't want me underfoot every second."

She sighed. "Yes, we did agree to that."

"But you started feeling insecure, didn't you?"

She felt ridiculous that he could see through her so easily. "I thought maybe you'd changed your mind and left. I wouldn't have blamed you, after all the pressure you got from Melanie last night."

"Your sister doesn't worry me. You do. You have to trust me when I tell you that I won't leave without saying goodbye. And if you want something from me that I'm not giving you, you have to tell me that. I can't read your mind." He tilted her chin up and looked into her eyes. "Deal?"

Duly chastened, she nodded. "Deal, and you're absolutely right," she said. "So here's the plan."

He shook his head, obviously amused. "More rules?"

"More rules," she agreed. "Your mornings are your own. I'll do my thing around here, catch up on work, whatever. I won't even look for you till lunchtime unless we make plans ahead of time. If something comes up for either of us, we'll call."

"Sounds very fair," he said, obviously biting back a grin. "Let me clarify one thing, though. Do I need to schedule when I'm going to kiss you?"

She swallowed hard at the glint in his eyes. "No. I think that can be perfectly spontaneous."

"Good," he murmured just before he closed his mouth over hers.

Heat slammed through Maggie, wiping out thoughts and worries and any remaining self-consciousness about her pathetic little performance a few minutes earlier. Obviously her idiotic behavior hadn't turned him off completely. Quite the opposite, in fact. They were both breathless and gasping when he finally released her.

"Come on, darlin'," he said, grabbing her hand. "Let's go to lunch."

"I could fix something here," she offered.

"Bad idea."

"You don't trust my cooking," she asked incredulously.

"Your cooking's spectacular. What I'm afraid of is the kitchen getting a little too hot and chasing us straight up to the bedroom. I know that's a violation of one of those rules of yours." He gave her a hopeful look. "Of course, if you want to rescind that particular rule, I won't hold it against you. In fact, I'll applaud your generous spirit."

For the first time all day, Maggie laughed. "You wish. Let's go, Flannery."

"Where?"

"It hardly matters, as long as there's not a bed in sight."

He winked at her. "Who needs a bed when there are all these fields and secluded beaches close by?"

Maggie groaned. Now *that* image was going to be in her head all afternoon. They weren't going to pass a cornfield without her imagining the two of them hidden away from view, their hands all over each other.

"You are a cruel man," she murmured as she stepped into Rick's car.

"Just wanted to even things up. You've been tormenting me ever since I got here."

She smiled. "Good to know." Maybe if he said it often enough, she'd finally start to believe he really meant it.

After several days of fighting to keep his hands to himself, Rick recognized the absolute necessity of finding a lot of distractions. Otherwise he'd spend every minute trying to convince Maggie to jump into bed with him.

Of course, he argued, if he were around all the time,

she might start to believe that he wasn't going to run out on her at the first opportunity. Better, though, that she learned that lesson during his absences.

Besides, as they'd discussed when she'd laid out more of those absurd ground rules of hers, she'd come here because she needed space away from him to think. They'd agreed very sensibly that she could hardly do that if he was underfoot every second. He wasn't convinced that thinking was the answer, but she was, so for now he'd let her have her way.

But all that thoughtfulness and consideration was leaving him at loose ends most mornings. Usually having so much time on his hands would wear thin after a day or two, but he'd started packing up his camera, climbing into his car and exploring the region, heading off in a new direction every day.

After the first day, he was forced to admit that it was no longer just an exercise. It was, in fact, oddly exhilarating to be taking pictures for the sheer pleasure of it, rather than for an assignment.

Nature was turning out to be an even more fascinating subject than the gorgeous women he usually shot. Models had their idiosyncrasies, most of which he'd seen by this time, but nature's lighting, the capriciousness of the birds, the ever changing swells on the Chesapeake, were just as challenging. He'd spent one entire morning taking pictures of the centuries old Christ Church as the light filtered through the surrounding trees. As a result, his excursions were taking longer and longer, but he always called to let Maggie know he was running late. It was a concession he wouldn't have made for most women, but it was such a small courtesy that it seemed absurd to balk at it or to view it as some sort of attempt on her part to put him on a short leash.

On his wanderings he'd found plenty of out-of-the-way restaurants with home cooking and no pretensions. There was always a local around who was eager to strike up a conversation, if Rick was so inclined. He'd picked up bits of history and plenty of gossip, all of which he shared with Maggie when he got to her place each afternoon.

Not five minutes ago he'd heard that Cornelia Lindsey's granddaughter—Maggie, in fact—was staying at Rose Cottage. "Has a beau there, too. Followed her all the way from Boston," the waitress said, her expression dreamy. "Isn't that romantic? Maybe she'll wind up getting married in her grandmother's garden, the way her sister did."

Rick choked on his soup at that. The girl slapped him on the back and studied him worriedly.

"You okay?" Willa-Dean asked. "Don't know why I'm telling you all this. You probably didn't even know Mrs. Lindsey, since you're not from around here."

"No, I didn't know her," Rick admitted.

"Where'd you say you were from?"

"Boston, actually."

The waitress stared at him, the coffeepot in her hand suddenly bobbing so erratically that Rick felt compelled to take it from her.

"You're the one," she said, blushing all the way to the roots of her bleached hair. "You're with Maggie."

He nodded, since there seemed to be little point in denying it. He did feel compelled to correct one thing, though. "I'm not staying at the house," he told Willa-Dean.

"Why on earth not? It's plenty big enough," she said, then blushed furiously again. "Sorry. It's none of my business."

She didn't seem to see the irony in worrying about that

now, after spending ten minutes dispensing every tidbit she knew about Maggie's anonymous suitor.

"No problem, but maybe you should bring me that pie now," he suggested gently.

Willa-Dean looked completely rattled. "The pie, of course. I'm so sorry. I'd stuff some in my mouth, but there's no room with my foot in there."

He laughed. How could you be mad at someone who was as bouncy and friendly as a puppy? Maggie, however, was not going to be overjoyed to learn that her love life was the hottest topic in the local gossip mill. Maybe he wouldn't share this tidbit with her.

Willa-Dean brought his warm apple pie with a scoop of vanilla ice cream melting on top. "It's on the house," she said. "Consider it an apology."

"You don't owe me an apology," he insisted, then took a bite of the pie. The distinctive combination of tart and sweet flavors burst in his mouth. The crust practically melted on his tongue. As soon as he'd swallowed, he said, "Willa-Dean, will you marry me?"

She stared at him, clearly shocked. "What?"

"This pie is amazing," he explained. "Please tell me you'll marry me."

She laughed. "You wouldn't be getting what you're bargaining for," she said. "I didn't bake it. We buy 'em from a lady over toward Reedville."

"Then I'll marry her."

"She's eighty."

"I don't care."

He was barely exaggerating. Apple pie was a dessert staple and one of his favorites, but this woman had raised it to an art form. If he could have this pie every day, he could live here and be content.

"Does she bring in pies every day?" he asked. "I'd like to meet her."

"Actually, she's never here. She sends the pies over on Tuesdays and Fridays. Her husband brings them."

"Then consider me a new Tuesday and Friday regular," he told Willa-Dean. "Can I buy a whole pie to take home? Maggie has to taste this."

"Sure you can. I'll get one for you." When she returned with the pie in a box, she asked, "So, since you're going to become a regular in here, does that mean you and Mrs. Lindsey's granddaughter are staying here for good?" She was clearly eager to have a fresh tidbit for the gossip mill.

Since his plans with Maggie seemed to change on a day-by-day basis, Rick opted for an evasive reply that covered what he knew at this moment. "For the foreseeable future," he told her.

No need to explain that he couldn't predict a future with Maggie much beyond tonight. Usually that wouldn't have bothered him one bit, but for some reason he left the restaurant feeling oddly restless and uneasy. Not even the prospect of sharing the incredible pie with Maggie cheered him.

Rick sighed heavily. When in the heck had the promise of an evening with an incredible woman ceased to be enough? When had he started wanting more?

6

"You're doing what?" Ashley asked, her tone incredulous.

"Playing Monopoly," Maggie said, her gaze never leaving Rick. She had to watch the man like a hawk. "And unless you called for something specific, sis, I need to get back to it. Rick cheats."

"I do not," he protested indignantly, even as Maggie caught him trying to unobtrusively slide a hotel onto one of his properties.

Maggie snatched the hotel out of his hand. "Stop that," she commanded, then tried to focus on her sister. "Ashley, did you want something?"

"I just called to check on you, but I don't even have to ask how you are. I think it's obvious you've lost your mind," Ashley muttered.

"How is that obvious?"

"You are tucked away in a cozy seaside cottage with a man most women would kill to spend time with, and you're playing board games with him. I'm no shrink, but I'm pretty sure that translates into insanity."

Keeping her gaze fixed on the game board and Rick's sneaky hands, Maggie tried to come up with a response that would satisfy her sister. "Games are fun. You should try them sometime, Ms. Workaholic."

"Look who's talking," Ashley retorted. "You weren't exactly a slouch in the work department before you ran away. And speaking of that, how's the magazine getting along without you?"

"The magazine is doing just fine. I'm able to do most things by email anyway." She gave Rick a daunting look when he tried to slip a couple of houses off one of her properties. He grinned, clearly not the least bit contrite. "Ashley, I really do have to go. I have a lot riding on the outcome of this game."

"Oh?"

"If I win, we go out for ice cream."

"Ah, I think I'm beginning to see what you're up to. And what happens if Rick wins?"

"I have to fix him Dad's famous lasagna for dinner tomorrow." She tried really hard to inject a self-pitying note into her voice for Rick's benefit. He was very proud of himself for coming up with such an extreme and demanding penalty.

"You do know there's a frozen lasagna in the fridge, don't you?" Ashley asked. "We brought it down for Melanie before the wedding."

"I know that," Maggie said cheerfully. "Rick doesn't."

"Ah," Ashley murmured knowingly. "He'll be impressed and you'll barely have to lift a finger."

"Exactly."

"Very clever," Ashley said with approval. "But tell me again, why are you trying so hard to impress him if you think there's no future in the relationship?"

"I'm not trying to impress anyone," Maggie insisted. "I'm trying to keep him entertained. He is a guest, after all."

"I'm sure there are other forms of entertainment Rick would find more to his liking than Monopoly."

Maggie laughed. "I'm sure you're absolutely right, but most of those are absolutely off-limits. This is tonight's diversion."

"And tomorrow's?"

Maggie wasn't sure she had an adequate answer to that one. She'd been scrambling for safe diversions from the moment Rick arrived. It was not a topic she intended to discuss with Ashley while Rick was blatantly eavesdropping on every word.

"Got to go," she said instead, and hung up before Ashley could ask any more uncomfortable questions.

She frowned at Rick as she sat back down. "Did you cheat?"

"How could I? You were watching me every second," he grumbled. "Want some more wine?"

She'd noticed that he hadn't touched the wine tonight. She had to wonder if that was part of his plan. "You just want me to have another glass so my defenses will be weakened and you can sneak something past me," she accused. "Forget about it." She rolled the dice and moved her token to a pricey piece of property. She bought it without comment.

Rick laughed. "You really don't trust me at all, do you?" he asked as he took his turn.

"Not when it comes to Monopoly," she confirmed. "Or any other game, for that matter. I know you did something behind my back to win at Scrabble last night."

He tried very hard to look offended, but he couldn't quite pull it off. "How does anybody cheat at Scrabble?" he demanded.

"That's what I'd like to know, but I guarantee you I'm

not even leaving the room to go to the bathroom next time we play."

"I think this distrust of yours is symptomatic of a bigger issue," he said. "I think you have deep, psychological scars going back to childhood, probably when one of your sisters consistently beat you at games. My money's on Ashley."

"Ashley never had time for games," she said, putting a hotel on another property. "And I don't have any scars from childhood except the one on my knee from when Jo pushed me down in the gravel so she could get to the ice-cream truck first."

A mischievous spark lit his eyes. "I've seen that scar," he recalled. "Kissed it, too."

A little shiver washed over her. He had, indeed. It was just one of the wicked kisses that had turned her into putty the first night they were together. "Let's not go there," she said hurriedly. Too much talk of kissing was almost as bad as having his lips locked with hers. It was fascinating how that worked. Since Rick, too, seemed to be distracted, she claimed another piece of property. Pretty soon he wasn't going to be able to make a move without going into serious debt.

"Why don't you want to talk about it?" he asked, his expression innocent. "Does thinking about me kissing your knee make you all hot and bothered?"

"Absolutely not," she insisted, but her cheeks burned at the lie. As observant as he was, it was probably a dead giveaway. He seemed to enjoy taunting her for precisely that reason.

"Want to talk about something else?" he asked, his gaze focused on her and not on the board, which she was about to control.

"Please." Although all this talk of kissing was working

nicely to her advantage at the moment, maybe she should ignore her own discomfort and keep his mind on something besides Monopoly.

"Let's talk about that fabulous dinner you're going to make for me when I win this game," Rick suggested before Maggie could return to the topic of kissing. "I'm thinking the lasagna alone won't be enough. We should have garlic bread, maybe a key lime soufflé drizzled with raspberry sauce. What do you think?"

He turned the recitation into something so seductive, Maggie almost dived across the table to smother his face with kisses. He knew the effect he was having, too. She could see it in his eyes.

"How did I miss the fact that you have this diabolical streak?" she asked.

"Me?"

"Yes, you. You turn everything into a seduction."

He laughed. "What can I say? It's a talent."

"It's annoying," she corrected.

"Then you're not even remotely tempted to toss aside this Monopoly board, forget all those ridiculous rules of yours and make wild, passionate love to me right here, right now?"

She scowled at him. "Not at all," she lied flatly. "And my rules are not ridiculous."

"Amazing," he said. "You said all that with a straight face."

"Because it's the truth."

"Really? Maybe I'm having a hard time buying it, because being wickedly impulsive is all I want to do."

"Too bad," she retorted, refusing to give him the satisfaction of admitting that she was as turned-on as he was. She gestured toward the board. "And you just landed on one of my very high-priced properties. Pay up, Flannery. I think that should pretty well bankrupt you."

He stared at the board, then at her. "How the hell did you do that?"

She grinned, filled with an amazing sense of triumph even though it was only a game. At least this was one she was apparently good at playing. "I'm not so bad at distraction myself," she told him. "And I am very hungry for a double-dip cone of mint chocolate chip ice cream."

"On one condition," he said.

"No conditions," she protested. "I won fair and square."

"One condition," he repeated, his gaze locked on her mouth.

Maggie swallowed hard. "Which is?"

"Just this," he murmured as he leaned across the table, scattering hotels, houses and pretend cash in every direction. He claimed her mouth.

Maggie sighed against him, welcoming the kiss with an enthusiasm that was dangerous. Who needed ice cream when this was the alternative?

Rick couldn't figure out when a game of Monopoly or Scrabble had become almost as enticing as sex. He couldn't recall a single time in his life, in fact, when there had even been time for games. His mom was rarely sober enough, and there hadn't been anyone else around. The guys he knew were more into hard-driving games of basketball or football than they were into quiet evenings at home. He'd had no idea how relaxing and ultimately stimulating such an evening could be.

Or maybe it was Maggie who provided the stimulation. She played to win and didn't seem the least bit inclined to let him get away with anything less than real competition,

either. He loved trying to slip something past her watchful gaze, just to see the sparks of indignation flare in her
eyes.

He was lying in bed—alone—remembering the Monopoly outcome and the amazingly steamy kiss that had
followed, when his cell phone rang. It was so rare to get
halfway decent reception that it startled him.

"Yes?"

"Flannery, where the hell are you? I've been leaving
messages for you for twenty-four hours now," his agent
groused.

"I'm on vacation," Rick said complacently.

"You don't take vacations," Frank Nichols replied with
the confidence of experience. He'd been managing Rick's
career for a very long time.

"I'm turning over a new leaf. I called your office and
told Lacey I'd be in touch when I'm ready for a new assignment. Didn't she pass along the message?"

"Of course she did. I didn't believe her. Besides, you
won't want to turn your back on this offer that came in
yesterday."

"I'm on vacation," Rick repeated. "Don't even tell me
about it. I'm not taking it."

"I'll back off when you tell me you have no interest in
going to the Greek Isles," Frank said. "Can you do that?"
he asked, his voice laced with skepticism. "Isn't that the
one place you've always wanted to go?"

It was, and for an instant Rick suffered a little twinge
of regret. But as he compared that prospect with a few
more days or weeks with Maggie, to his amazement, he
really wasn't even tempted to say yes.

"Not unless we're talking a month from now," he told
Frank.

"This is next week."

"Too bad. They should have thought of me sooner. Obviously they had someone else lined up who bailed. I'm nobody's second choice."

"Come on. This is a great opportunity. Actually, they did ask for you first, but you were booked. When they changed the schedule, they called me first."

"Then I'm flattered, but I'm busy, Frank. I'll be in touch when I'm ready to go back to work."

"Rick!"

"Bye." He hung up before his agent could dangle any more tantalizing offers in front of him.

Since he was giving up this dream assignment for her, he rolled over, grabbed his cell phone and dialed Maggie's number. He needed to hear the sound of her voice. He needed to make sure that little kick to his gut was still there. He'd hate to have turned down Greece, then realize that the attraction had faded, literally overnight. After all, that sort of thing had happened before.

"Hello," Maggie said, sounding breathless.

There it was, the groundswell of anticipation. Rick leaned back in bed with a contented sigh. "Good morning."

"You're up early," Maggie said.

"I had a call from my agent."

"Oh?"

There was no mistaking the disappointment in her tone, Rick concluded happily. "He had an assignment for me next week."

"Really?"

"In Greece."

There was a long pause. Rick waited it out.

"Greece," she repeated with obviously forced enthusiasm. "How fabulous! When will you have to leave?"

If he hadn't believed he'd made the right decision

before, he did now. He was making progress with Maggie. Leaving now for any reason would have destroyed the fragile inroads he was making.

"I turned him down," he said at last.

"Why on earth would you do that?" she asked, sounding genuinely shocked.

"Because I'm on vacation with you," he said simply. "We have a deal."

"But I would never hold you to it, if it means missing out on a chance like this."

"There will be plenty of other chances," he told her. "But I might have only this one chance with you. I'm not blowing it, Maggie. It's too important."

This time the silence went on so long, Rick began to worry. "Maggie, you okay?"

She sniffed. "Fine," she said, her voice oddly choked.

"Are you crying?" he asked, stunned.

"Just a little."

"Why?"

"Because it's so damn hard to keep you at arm's length when you say such sweet things."

He bit back a chuckle. "You don't have to keep me at arm's length, you know."

"Yes, I do."

"It's not like we haven't slept together before," he reminded her.

"Believe me, I know."

"Well, then?"

"I want to get it right this time, Rick."

If anyone else had said that, if Maggie herself had said it a few weeks ago, Rick would have been on the first plane to anywhere in a heartbeat. Now, instead, he felt like dancing a little jig.

"So do I, darlin'. So do I."

* * *

It had been ten days, and to Maggie's amazement Rick didn't appear to be bored yet, not even after he'd sacrificed a trip to Greece to stay here with her. Even after their conversation the morning his agent had called, she still wasn't convinced his attentiveness would last indefinitely without sex being thrown into the equation, but so far he'd seemed reasonably content to live within the ground rules.

Not that he hadn't continued to test her resolve from time to time with some kisses that curled her toes, but he hadn't pushed for anything more than she was prepared to offer.

She wasn't sure what she'd expected to feel during the same self-imposed period of celibacy, but it wasn't this amazing sense of having finally found someone who was on the same wavelength about so many other things. Maybe the real test here hadn't been for Rick at all, but for her. She was beginning to discover that there was more to her—more to the way she could relate to a man—than being clever in bed.

She was enjoying the routine they'd worked out. While Rick spent the mornings roaming the area, camera in hand, taking photographs of the region, she puttered around the kitchen trying out new recipes, which he was more than happy to taste when he got back from his wanderings.

When they weren't playing one of the games she'd found tucked in a box upstairs, they talked about their days like an old married couple.

When she'd asked what he intended to do with all the pictures he was taking, he'd told her he planned to convince some splashy magazine to combine the shots with a travel article he'd been urging her to write.

"Trying to draw more people to the middle of no-where?" she inquired, lips quirking.

"Something like that, at least in small numbers. Have you seen the osprey around here? They're amazing. There's so much undisturbed land. It needs to be protected. The bay's already in trouble. I read a report this morning on the impact pollution is having on the fish, the crabs and, worst of all, on the oyster harvest."

She laughed at his indignation, not because she didn't agree with it, but because even away from work, he'd found something to become passionate about, a cause she shared, as a matter of fact. Only since coming back to her grandmother's cottage had she rediscovered the magical beauty of this place, and she didn't want thoughtless people destroying it for generations to come. Maybe she would write that travel article and make it a plea for preserving some of the pristine land that remained and saving the bay for the watermen who worked it for a living.

In the meantime, though, she was trying to plan the food pages for the magazine's September issue. Just because she was on vacation didn't mean she could delay her deadline. Her editor was sending almost daily emails begging for some clue about what she had in mind.

Back-to-school lunches had been done to death. What was wrong with peanut-butter-and-jelly sandwiches, anyway? Nor could she get excited about doing yet another spread on football tailgate menus. September was too late to focus on summer vegetables and too early to write about soups. She needed a fresh angle, something entirely new, at least for *Cityside* readers, and it wasn't coming to her.

Thoroughly frustrated by the lack of ideas, she waited

anxiously for Rick to arrive. Maybe he could inspire her. He usually did, though his form of inspiration had less to do with food than it did with other passions she was trying to resist.

When he walked in the door, he crossed the room, dropped a kiss on her forehead and sat down on the sofa beside her. Before he could even say hello, she said, "Picture this. It's a cool September evening and you've just come home from a long day at work. What's on your mind?"

He gave her a long, lingering look that set off sparks and spoke volumes.

"Not that," she said impatiently. "I mean for dinner. What do you want? What food says fall to you?"

He stared at her blankly. "Huh?"

"Oh, come on," she said, nudging him in the ribs. "You know what I mean. In summer we wait for the first tomato off the vine or the first watermelon or the first peach pie. At Christmas we can't wait to start baking cookies. See what I mean?"

He nodded, his expression turning thoughtful. "Apples," he said at last. "Apples for school lunch boxes. Apple cobbler. Bobbing for apples. Sweet apples. Tart apples."

"Bingo." Maggie grinned as the spread began to take shape in her mind. "I knew we'd make a great team. Want an assignment?"

"Doing what?"

"Pictures of apples for the September issue of the magazine. I'm not asking for a freebie. I can call your agent tomorrow."

"Don't worry about Frank. What kind of pictures did you have in mind?"

"Maybe you can find some orchards around here someplace. That would provide a great backdrop for the pictures. We could do a red-checked tablecloth on the ground with apple pies and cobblers. I'll start looking for recipes tonight."

"Hold on a minute," he said, his expression thoughtful. "Forget all those cookbooks of yours. I know the perfect recipe for you to use."

"You do? How?"

"Remember that pie I brought home a while back? I told you about the restaurant where I got it."

Maggie recalled that pie. It had been heavenly. "Is it baked there?"

"No, it's baked by an eighty-year-old woman who lives over toward Reedville. Seems to me she could be at the heart of your story."

Maggie considered the idea. "Does she have an orchard?" she wondered aloud.

"I never asked. I only know she bakes like a dream."

"Can you find out?"

"Sure."

She beamed at him. "This is perfect. It's probably some old family recipe that she used to make for her children and grandchildren, then the neighbors. Now it's a community favorite. It'll give new meaning to the idea of the apple pie as an all-American dessert. Do you think the restaurant is open now? Can you call and get this woman's name?"

"Not until we do this," he said, drawing her into his arms. "All that talk of food has made me hungry."

She gazed into his eyes and saw the unmistakable heat. Unless she was very much mistaken, it wasn't food he was hungry for.

"Rick?"

"Sssh," he said. "Don't talk. Just let me taste you." His

mouth covered hers. His hands began to roam, following the curve of her hip, the gentle swell of her breast.

She was breathless by the time he released her. Regret washed over her. Why had he quit? she wondered, but it wasn't what she asked. Instead, trying to keep her voice steady, she asked, "What was that for? You've been following the ground rules so carefully. What happened tonight?"

He grinned. "You're so sexy when you talk about work and food. You get all passionate and excited. It makes me want to be part of it."

She laughed, though there was a nervous edge to it. The temperature in the room had escalated by a good ten degrees. She'd been in saunas that were cooler. Her willpower, so carefully nurtured up till now, was withering faster than a daisy out of water.

"That must mean you're starving," she said, making one last desperate attempt to pretend that she didn't know that the rules between them had suddenly changed. "Can I assume you want dinner? Here or out?"

"Out's safer," he said, his expression solemn.

It was, but Maggie was suddenly feeling reckless. Impulsiveness had always gotten her into trouble, so she made one last attempt to tamp it down.

"Probably wise," she said, but without much conviction.

"Are you feeling particularly wise?" Rick asked quietly, watching her intently.

"Not really," she admitted. In fact, wisdom had pretty much flown out the window about ten minutes ago. She gave herself a minute to see if it would come surging back, but it didn't.

"In fact," she said eventually, "let's eat in." She bounced

up to get started before wisdom could kick in, but Rick caught her hand.

"Are you sure?" he asked. "We had a deal. I need to be perfectly clear here. This is about more than dinner, Maggie. I want you."

She nodded slowly. It was time to be honest. It was time to trust the feelings that hadn't gone away, feelings that had only gotten stronger.

"And I want you," she admitted. "I think we've both been patient long enough."

He stroked a finger along the curve of her jaw. Her pulse jumped, then skittered crazily. She was making the right decision. She had to be.

"Be certain, Maggie," Rick begged. "I'd rather be patient days or even weeks longer, if it means you won't wake up in the morning with regrets."

"No regrets," she promised. Whatever happened, she wouldn't regret it. Not this time.

And morning would be soon enough to worry about whether or not her impulsiveness was going to set the experiment back. Or whether it even mattered anymore.

7

Rick fought off the sense of urgency that had his blood pumping hard through his veins. He intended to take it slow and easy with Maggie tonight, to savor every moment of anticipation. Now that she'd agreed to sleep with him again, he planned to let the evening unfold at its own pace.

The risk, of course, was that she'd change her mind, but it was a risk worth taking to savor this sweet anticipation. Watching the color rise in her cheeks each time their hands brushed, feeling the leap of her pulse when he skimmed a finger along her wrist, made every second of the delay worthwhile.

He stepped up behind her as she rinsed lettuce in the sink and trapped her there with his body, his arms linked loosely around her waist.

"What are you up to?" she asked, a breathless hitch in her voice.

"Helping," he said, all innocence.

"Really?"

"Sure. I'll wash the vegetables for the salad for you," he offered.

"Then I can get the chicken ready to go in the oven," she said, though she didn't try to move away.

"Why would you want to do that when this teamwork is going so well?" he asked, picking up the vegetables she'd dropped and holding them under the running water. To do it, he had to press his body even more tightly to hers.

She laughed. "Is that what you call this? Teamwork? Now that you've got the lettuce, peppers and tomatoes under the faucet, I'm just standing here. That's not much of a contribution."

"Sure, it is. You're providing inspiration."

"I suspect what I'm really providing is a cheap thrill," she taunted, deliberately wriggling her hips in a move designed to drive him mad.

Rick's breath caught as every bit of blood rushed south. "Bad move, darlin', at least if you hope to have dinner anytime soon."

"Thought so," she taunted triumphantly. "Let me go so I can fix the chicken."

"I'm not stopping you," he insisted.

"You're not getting out of my way, either."

Rick chuckled at her firm refusal to try to wriggle free on her own. He finally stepped aside. "Bet you don't have this much fun in that test kitchen at work."

"I don't know," she said, her expression thoughtful. "Mordecai is pretty sexy."

He stared at her. "Who the hell is Mordecai?"

"My assistant."

Rick didn't recall any sexy males around the *Cityside* test kitchen. "Really? Was he at the photo shoot?"

"No."

"Why not?"

"He's shy."

"You have an assistant who's sexy and shy?" Rick asked, unable to hide his skepticism.

"Very sexy, very shy," Maggie confirmed.

Rick studied her with a narrowed gaze. "You're pulling my leg, aren't you? There is no Mordecai."

"Of course there is. I would never lie to you."

"But…?"

"There's no but," she insisted.

His suspicions were not allayed. Nor was this unexpected and totally unfamiliar streak of jealousy. "Well, there's definitely something you're not telling me," he groused.

She laughed then. "You are so hysterical. You're practically turning split-pea-green right in front of me."

"If you're suggesting that I'm jealous, you're nuts," he retorted, though the truth was he wanted to find this Mordecai person and remind him very forcefully that Maggie was officially off-limits. Come to think of it, maybe he should punch the guy for good measure.

"Then you don't care if I spend a lot of late nights with Mordecai?" she asked, looking innocent as a lamb.

He studied her with a narrowed gaze and concluded she was having way too much fun at his expense. He knew precisely how to put a stop to that.

"No more than you care if I spend a lot of late nights with the *Sports Illustrated* swimsuit models," he retorted just as innocently.

As Rick had expected, her amusement instantly vanished. "Mordecai is very sweet and very sexy," she repeated, then added, "for a seventy-year-old man."

Rick felt as if a huge weight had been lifted off his chest. "Ah, I see."

She gave him a hard look. "Now's the part where you

tell me you're only doing landscape photography for the rest of your life."

He had a hunch she wasn't entirely joking. "I can't do that, Maggie."

She sighed with undisguised disappointment. "No, I suppose not."

"My work isn't really going to be a problem, is it?"

"I wish I could say it won't be, but I honestly don't know," she admitted. "It's not very enlightened of me, is it? I'm sorry."

"Forget about being enlightened," Rick said with a trace of impatience. "Tell me what I have to do to prove to you that you have nothing to worry about."

"I don't think you can prove it," Maggie told him. "I think this is something I have to work out for myself. It won't happen overnight, either. It'll take time."

Rick had no idea where this low self-esteem of hers came from. From the instant they'd met, he would have bet money that Maggie had more confidence than any ten women, but maybe that was just in the professional arena. He studied her intently.

"Would it help if I hauled you up to bed right this instant and showed you just how much you excite me?"

She frowned at him. "You are such a guy," she accused. "You think everything can be solved with sex. I *know* we're fantastic together in bed."

Rick bit back a sigh. He'd gotten it exactly wrong, after all. "Maggie, you're going to have to help me out here. I *am* a guy. And you're sending out a million signals, but they're getting garbled."

She whirled on him, looking as if she might explode, but then all the steam went out of her. "You're right," she said at last.

She looked so forlorn, he couldn't help reaching for her.

She resisted at first, her body still and filled with tension. "Come on, sweetheart. I'm not hitting on you, at least not right this second. I just want to hold you. I want you to talk to me," he urged. "Tell me what you want, what kind of reassurance you need for this to work."

"I need to know this thing between us is about more than sex," she said simply.

"Of course, it is," Rick said, then realized there was no *of course* about it. He tried to find the right words to reassure her. "When I agreed to stay here and keep my hands to myself, it was because you matter to me. *You,* Maggie, not just your body. Otherwise I would have hit the road. I'm not sure where this is going or why it's so important to me that we give it a try. I just know that I couldn't walk away from you the way I have every other woman I've been with." He searched her face. "Is that enough for you for now?"

To his astonishment, tears were welling up in her eyes. She nodded. "More than enough."

Because he didn't want to make another mistake, he asked, "Does that mean I can forget about sleeping here tonight?"

Even as the tears spilled down her cheeks, she laughed. "No, you're staying, Flannery. I'm getting tired of going to bed all alone when you're right across town. And every time you touch me, I'm reminded of how much I've been missing by being so stubborn."

"Really?" She sounded so eager, he risked pushing for more. "Does that mean I can pack up and move over here?"

For an instant he thought she was going to say yes, but he could see the internal war she was waging over the question. Before she could reply, he touched a finger to her lips. "Never mind," he said, hoping that the short-term sacrifice he was making would pay off in the long run. "Let's concentrate on tonight. We'll worry about tomorrow another time."

It wasn't enough that Rick could make the very air around her sizzle, now the man had to go and get all sensitive and intuitive on her. Maggie was pretty sure she was going to be head over heels in love with him before too much longer if he kept this up.

"That can't happen," she told herself sternly. She didn't realize she'd spoken aloud until she saw the quizzical expression on Rick's face as he sat across from her at the kitchen table.

"It was nothing," she assured him. "Just talking to myself."

"Anything you'd like to share?"

"Nope. Are you ready for dessert?"

"Only if we can eat it in bed," he said, his gaze locked with hers.

Maggie shivered with anticipation. "Dessert can wait."

Rick grinned. "Good answer," he said, scooping her up from her chair and cradling her against his chest. "What about the dishes?"

Maggie felt a little twinge of conscience about leaving them where they sat on the table, but one look in Rick's eyes pretty much dispelled that. "They'll be here in the morning."

His smile spread. "That's my girl, throwing caution to the wind."

Little did he know that she usually did. She fought off the mental reminder that she'd been trying to change that. "Kiss me," she pleaded.

"Upstairs," Rick promised.

"No, now."

"We might not get upstairs," he warned. "I'm just about clean out of self-control."

She grinned. "Good. Me, too."

This time the trail of clothes led only as far as the living room. With Rick's hands all over her body, caressing and coaxing, Maggie wondered why she'd ever held out. Wicked sensations, heart-stopping anticipation, the lick of fire through her veins, these were the most basic of life forces. Why should she deny herself this, especially with a man who excelled at it?

She was already on the edge, every nerve raw, every muscle tensed, when Rick finally entered her and sent her reeling. He waited for her delicious spasms to end and then started to move, his gaze on her face.

It was only as she looked into his eyes that she got the difference between this man and every other man she'd ever been with. Rick was looking back at her, reading her, intent on pleasing her. This wasn't just about his pleasure, or even hers. It was about theirs. It was about the two of them, united for this moment, body and perhaps even soul.

Suddenly, for the first time ever, she truly understood what all those storybook romances were talking about. And even as she came undone, even as waves of pleasure crashed over her, somewhere deep inside, the magical intensity of it scared her to death.

Rick reluctantly crawled out of Maggie's bed at dawn, gave her a lingering kiss goodbye, then went back to his place to shower and change and make arrangements for the photo shoot she wanted him to do. More than that, though, he needed a little time on his own to think about what had changed between them the night before.

Something had, there was no question about that. He'd seen it in her eyes, a sudden spark of awareness, a sudden look of shock, to be honest. He'd tried to interpret it, but he couldn't. Maybe it was another one of those inexplicable female things that a mere man would never get. For an instant, he'd even wondered if it was the difference he'd always heard about between having sex and making love. Did that awareness come crashing over a person in a heartbeat?

He groaned at himself. When had he ever given a damn about putting a label on what happened with a woman in bed? He wasn't going to figure it out on his own, and it was hardly something he intended to discuss with the guys. Maggie had clearly gotten some crazy notion that he was sensitive, but he wasn't *that* sensitive. This was beyond him, which meant he'd just have to backburner it for another time.

Instead, as soon as he'd had his second cup of coffee, he called Mike to check into the orchard situation around the region. Surely a landscape designer who did jobs all over would be able to point him in the right direction.

"You're up awfully early," Mike said, then added a little too cheerfully, "Having trouble sleeping these days?"

Rick glanced at the clock and realized it wasn't even seven yet. "Geez, man, I'm sorry. Did I wake you?"

"Hardly. I have to hit the road any minute now. I'm meeting Jeff for breakfast. Want to join us?"

The prospect of having those two cross-examine him held no appeal. "Not today. I called to see if you know of any apple orchards around the region."

"I don't, but Jeff would. Give him a call. He'll be up," Mike said. "It's a little soon in the season to go picking apples, though."

"I'm not interested in picking them. Maggie wants

pictures for the magazine. And I'm hoping she can snag this incredible recipe for apple pie while she's at it."

"Are you telling me that a woman who writes about gourmet food can't bake an apple pie?" Mike asked.

"I don't think anyone bakes a pie quite like the one I've been getting at a little country restaurant over by Callao. Do you know the place?"

"Afraid not."

"You should try it. The pie alone is worth the drive. If you're free for lunch, you could come with me. I need to get information about the woman who bakes them. Willa-Dean, she's the waitress, says the woman lives somewhere near Reedville."

"Wait a minute, that must be Mrs. Keller," Mike said. "Her pies are always the hottest baked goods at the church bazaar. I'll bet Jeff can tell you how to find her. If he's not around when you call the nursery, ask Pam. She's as knowledgeable about the area as he is, and she usually works on the bazaar, so she's bound to know Mrs. Keller."

"Thanks, pal."

"So," Mike ventured casually, "everything okay with you and Maggie?"

Rick laughed at the sudden switch in topic, to say nothing of Mike's lousy attempt at subtlety. "Are you asking for yourself or gathering information for your wife?"

Mike chuckled. "Both. She's hanging over my shoulder right now."

"Then Maggie and I are doing just fine," Rick assured them both. "That's the official statement."

"No details?"

"Not a one."

"Ah, well, at least Melanie knows I tried."

"Think that will satisfy her?" Rick asked curiously.

"Not a chance," Melanie chimed in. "I guess I'll just have to go over to the house and pester my sister."

"Sorry," Rick said, not feeling the first hint of guilt over the lie he was about to tell. He would just work hard to make sure it turned into the truth before Melanie could get over there. "She won't be home today."

"Oh?"

"We're working," he said, seizing on the most obvious solution.

"Nice try, pal. If you think that's going to put Melanie off for long, you're crazy," Mike said. "Quick, call Jeff before my wife starts in on you again with the third degree about what work the two of you could possibly have planned when you're both supposedly on vacation."

"Thanks. I appreciate the backup and the information," Rick told him.

Five minutes later he was able to track Jeff down on his cell phone. Jeff was already in his truck en route to meet Mike. Rick explained what he was after. "Any idea how I can find this Mrs. Keller?" he asked. "Is it too much to hope that a woman who bakes apple pies happens to own an orchard?"

"As a matter of fact, the Kellers have an apple orchard about fifteen miles outside of town," Jeff told him. "They're getting on in years, so they don't harvest the crop themselves anymore. Their kids weren't interested in running the orchard, so now they just open it up to families or local businesses to come in and pick their own apples. They make enough to supplement their Social Security, I guess."

"And those pies of hers must bring in a tidy sum," Rick surmised.

"I imagine they do. Everybody around here drives clear over to Callao to get them," Jeff said. "She refuses to sell to any other restaurant. Says the owner there was loyal to her from the start, so she's going to return the favor."

"Do you think the Kellers would be agreeable to letting me do a photo shoot at their place?" he asked Jeff.

"I can't imagine them turning down a chance to be famous. They love company. I'll give 'em a call and set things up. If they balk for any reason, you can always go to the Westmoreland Berry Farm. They have plenty of apple trees there. It's a little early in the season, though. The apples aren't ready for picking yet," Jeff said, echoing Mike's warning.

"Doesn't matter. Maggie's looking for a backdrop, not ripe apples."

"Then let's see what I can set up with the Kellers. I was over there not long ago checking on a blight affecting one of their maple trees. It's a great setting for what you're talking about. When do you want to go?"

"This morning, if it suits them," Rick said eagerly. "I won't be taking pictures today, but I'd like to look things over and make sure it will work."

"I'll call and get right back to you," Jeff promised. "Is Maggie going with you?"

Rick chuckled. "When it comes to her magazine, Maggie's a control freak. What do you think?"

"I'll tell the Kellers to expect both of you. They knew Cornelia Lindsey, so I doubt it will be a problem."

While he was waiting for Jeff to get back to him, Rick called Maggie. "Hey, gorgeous."

"Don't call me that," she said testily.

It wasn't the first time she'd reacted irritably to any suggestion that she was beautiful, but each time it threw Rick. Surely she knew how lovely she was. Hadn't he spent half the night proving to her how enchanted he was with her body?

"Why not?" he asked, taking a stab at getting to the bottom of it. Knowing Maggie, though, she'd probably stonewall him.

"Because you know what real beauty is," she snapped, surprising him. "Don't insult me by pretending that I'm in the same league."

"Are you crazy?" he asked, unable to keep an incredulous note out of his voice. "If you're referring to the models I photograph, they can't hold a candle to you. Their figures are perfect for the camera, but yours is perfect for real life."

She sighed heavily at that. "Nice try," she said softly.

"I'm not trying to placate you, Maggie. That's honestly how I see you."

"Why did you call?" she asked, clearly not buying a word he said.

Rick wanted to push harder and get to the bottom of her lousy body image, but this wasn't the time. Her defenses were already firmly in place. He thought they'd made huge strides in their relationship the night before, but apparently not.

"I've found an orchard. Jeff's making arrangements for me to take a look around. Want to come?" he asked, managing to keep his tone light. He refused to let a ridiculous argument over whether or not he really thought she was gorgeous spoil the morning.

"Absolutely," she said, her mood abruptly shifting. She hesitated, then asked, "Is that why you took off so early?"

Ah, so that was what was really bugging her, he deduced. She thought he'd slipped away to avoid some sort of awkward morning-after scenario.

"You gave me an assignment. Of course I wanted to get started on it."

"I know I have a reputation as a slave driver, but you could have waited till daybreak."

He laughed. "Actually the sun was already up when I left. I thought you were awake for that kiss."

"Then it wasn't a dream."

"Oh, no, darlin', it was real. You try remembering that, and I'll be there as soon as I hear back from Jeff."

"I'll be ready."

The Kellers looked like a couple of those apple dolls Maggie had seen in a country craft shop years ago. Their wizened, nut-brown faces spoke of years in the summer sun. And like so many people who'd been married for more than fifty years, they'd started to look a bit alike with their wiry bodies and white hair cropped in similar short styles. Hers had a bit more curl than his. Both of them had bright blue eyes that sparkled with interest when they opened the door to Maggie and Rick.

"Come in, come in," Matthew Keller said, his hearty voice a surprise. "Sally's been baking apple pies this morning, if you'd like some before we go down to the orchard."

Maggie glanced at Rick and was surprised that there was no trace of impatience in his eyes.

"I'd love some pie," he said easily. "And we'd both enjoy hearing about the orchard before we take a look around."

The old man's eyes lit up. "Not many young folks want to listen to me go on and on about growing apples. Used to take some school kids down there in the fall, but all they wanted to do was run around and enjoy a day of freedom from classes. I suppose one apple tree looks pretty much like another unless you take the time to study them."

As they sat down in the Kellers' sunny kitchen, Sally

put huge servings of pie in front of them. Rick took a bite
and sighed with pleasure. He beamed at Sally.

"No question about it, you are the culinary genius
who bakes the pie they serve at the café in Callao, aren't
you?"

A huge smile spread across the woman's face. "How
on earth did you figure that out from just one bite?"

"Pie this good is not something a man forgets." He
turned to Maggie. "This pie is the reason the whole apple
idea popped into my head last night. Have you ever tasted
anything like it?"

Maggie had been so busy taking notes on what Matthew had been telling them that she hadn't tried a bite of
the pie. She put a forkful in her mouth and tasted the tart
burst of apple, the hint of sugar and cinnamon, but it was
the melt-in-the-mouth crust with its own hint of cinnamon
that made her sigh as heartfelt as Rick's had been.

"The crust," she murmured around a second mouthful.
"How do you get it to turn out like this, Mrs. Keller?"

"Please, call me Sally. As for the crust, I could show
you," the elderly woman offered, then waved off the idea.
"What am I thinking? You said you write about food.
You probably have one of those fancy, state-of-the-art
test kitchens. I imagine you bake better than I do."

"I can't make a pie like this," Maggie told her honestly.
"I'd be honored if you'd tell me your secret and let me
publish the recipe for my readers. Was this recipe handed
down to you, or is it something you came up with on your
own?"

Sally Keller's expression grew thoughtful. "I don't
know if I could give away the recipe. See, folks around
here think there's something a little extra in my pie. I'd
hate to ruin it for 'em. Besides, how many slices would

the restaurant sell if everybody around these parts started baking it at home?"

Matthew Keller turned to Maggie. "Where'd you say that magazine is published?"

"Boston. Most of the circulation is in Massachusetts."

"See there, Sally, it won't be a bit of a problem. We don't know a soul in Boston."

His wife gave him a chiding look. "Folks around here do travel, Matthew. And isn't that boy of Lila Wilson's somewhere up north?"

"He's in New York," Matthew retorted. "Now stop your fussing, Sally, and give Cornelia's granddaughter the recipe. No sense keeping it to yourself till you go to your grave. Then no one will be able to enjoy it."

"Haven't you passed it along to your children?" Maggie asked her.

"Heavens, no," Sally said with a sad shake of her head. "The boys aren't interested in cooking, and their wives are too busy to worry with baking anything from scratch. I tried to teach my daughter, Ellen, when she was growing up, the way my mama taught me, but she didn't have the patience for it. Said there were too many calories anyway."

"I don't care how many calories it has," Rick told her, "it's worth every one of them. Best apple pie I ever had. You ask Willa-Dean—since I've been in town, I've been to the restaurant every day the pies are due in."

Sally beamed at the praise. "Have another piece, why don't you? You'll burn off all those calories once Matthew takes you out for a look around. He'll talk your ear off, too. Don't be afraid to tell him to hush up when you've heard enough."

Rick dived right into the second piece of pie, then sat back with a contented sigh. "Matthew, you have to save me. Let's go see the orchard. Maggie, are you coming?"

"I think I'll stay and talk to Sally about the recipe. You can show me around later."

When the men were gone, Sally gave her a knowing look. "Handsome fellow, that one. Your grandmother would approve."

Maggie regarded her with surprise. "You think so?"

"Heavens, yes. She had an eye for a good-looking man. Loved your grandfather till the day he died, but that didn't keep her from appreciating a fine specimen when she ran across one. Me, either, if the truth be told. Even at my age, it doesn't hurt to look."

Maggie laughed at the unmistakable sparkle in the woman's eyes. "Something tells me you've given your husband fits, Sally."

The older woman chuckled. "Indeed I did and I'm proud of it, too. Keeping things lively is what keeps a marriage going as long as ours has been."

"And how long is that?" Maggie asked.

"It'll be sixty-two years next month. I was only eighteen when we got married and I'm closing in on eighty now. I'd known Matthew from the time we were toddlers causing havoc during church services." She grinned at Maggie and confided, "To tell you the truth, I never thought much of him till I turned sixteen and spotted the twinkle in his eyes when he saw me coming. There's a lot to be said for a twinkle like that. Your young man gets it when he looks at you."

Maggie was intrigued by the observation. "Really?"

"My goodness, yes. You haven't seen it?"

Maggie thought about the way Rick looked at her and realized that Sally was right. There *was* a twinkle in his eye. She'd just never realized before that it was important.

She'd been too busy worrying that it meant there was nothing more between them, rather than realizing it was the spark that lit everything else.

She reached over and gave Sally's hand a grateful squeeze. "Thank you."

"What on earth for?"

"For making me see something that's been right in front of my eyes all along."

"Honey, if you haven't seen that man's attributes before now, you need more than a wake-up call. You need glasses."

Maggie was still laughing over that one when Rick and Matthew Keller came back. Rick gave her a curious look.

"Did you get what you came for?" he asked.

"And more," Maggie told him. She turned to Sally. "May we come back again? Rick will need to take pictures, and I'd like to watch while you do your baking."

"Baking days are Monday and Thursday, but you're welcome anytime," Sally assured her, then glanced pointedly at Rick before giving Maggie a wink. "We're way past overdue for some excitement around here."

8

"So, what did you think?" Rick asked as he and Maggie drove back to her place.

"They're remarkable people," she replied enthusiastically. "Can you imagine being married for over sixty years? I am so impressed."

Rick was startled that Maggie had picked up on the Kellers' personal history, rather than the orchard setting. Usually she was totally focused on work. He had to readjust, then give her question some thought. To be truthful, he had never imagined being married at all. He'd always assumed he'd be lousy at staying put, much less staying committed to one woman. Over the last couple of weeks, he'd begun to wonder about that.

"Honestly, I never gave marriage or its duration much thought," he replied.

"Why?"

"I never pictured myself married," he admitted.

She regarded him with more curiosity than disappointment. "Really? Too many temptations?"

"Something like that," he said evasively.

Rather than daunting her, his reply apparently sparked even more curiosity. She studied him intently. "What

about your own parents? Didn't they set a good example
for you?"

Rick didn't talk about his family. In fact, in relationships as fleeting as most of his had been, he'd never talked
much about anything important. The shallow women with
whom he'd been involved were more than content to discuss the celebrity world in which he traveled.

"Tell me about *your* parents," he suggested, hoping to
buy himself some time.

He glanced over and saw at once that Maggie wasn't
fooled a bit by the tactic, but she answered anyway.

"I think my folks will eventually be just like the
Kellers, still madly in love when they're eighty," she said.
"Back at the beginning, though, I suspect most people
thought they'd never last a year. My mom's the epitome
of the Southern steel magnolia. She has a sweet demeanor
and a backbone that doesn't bend. My dad's this boisterous Italian guy from Boston. They're both so strong
willed, you'd think they'd clash over everything."

She grinned. "And sometimes they do. My father
shouts. My mother replies in icy tones."

"Who usually wins?" Rick asked.

"Eventually they compromise. And when it comes to
anything that really matters, they may fight about it in
private, but publicly they present a united front."

"And they taught you and your sisters to do the same
thing, didn't they?" Rick asked, trying to imagine what
it would have been like to have family that stuck together
through thick and thin. His hadn't stuck together at all.
He and his mom had occupied the same space, but they'd
hardly been united.

"Absolutely," Maggie said. "Melanie, Ashley, Jo and I
have very different personalities, but give us a common

enemy and we band together." She gave him a sideways glance. "I gather your family wasn't like that."

"What makes you say that?" Rick asked testily, irritated that she'd apparently seen right through him.

"Because you avoided my question so neatly. People who come from happy homes tend to brag about them."

"I suppose."

"Tell me about your dad."

"There's nothing to tell," he said tersely.

Maggie clearly didn't buy it. "There's always something to tell," she chided.

Rick frowned at her. "Okay, fine. He left when I was very young. End of story, at least as I know it. I never saw him again."

Maggie regarded him with a shocked expression. "Oh, Rick, I'm so sorry. You must have missed him."

"You can't miss what you never really had." He risked a glance and spotted the sympathy welling up in her eyes. It made him want to curse. This was exactly why he never talked about his past. He didn't want anyone feeling sorry for him. His life had been what it was. He'd survived it. He was probably stronger because of it. That was all that really mattered.

"And your mother?" Maggie asked more gently.

"Got lost in a bottle," Rick said succinctly.

"Which is why you barely drink at all," Maggie guessed.

"I suppose. I know alcoholism is a disease, but I don't know if it's inherited. I always figured why take chances," he said. "Now let's talk about something else. Did you look around at all while we were at the Kellers'? Any idea what pictures you want? I have some thoughts, but I'd like to hear yours first."

Maggie looked as if she might insist on poking and

prodding into his personal life some more, but instead she merely sighed. "No. You're the one with the eye for this sort of thing. Tell me your thoughts."

Rick seized the chance to move on to neutral turf. "The orchard would be fantastic, if that's the way you want to go. The trees are loaded with apples, and the light filtering through the leaves on a sunny day will be amazing."

"But?" Maggie prodded.

He wasn't surprised she'd recognized his unspoken message. "But I think you should use shots taken in the kitchen."

She gave him a startled look. "Why?"

He tried to put his gut instinct into words that wouldn't sound absurd. "A couple of reasons, actually. People are always more interesting than scenery. And because Mrs. Keller's hands tell a story," he said, hoping Maggie would understand. One glance at her, though, and it was obvious that she didn't.

"They do?" she said, evidently bewildered. "In what way?"

Rick bit back a sigh. Maybe it was something only a photographer would notice. "They're weathered and gnarled," he explained. "Those hands have lived, yet I imagine when she works the dough for her piecrusts, they have the gentle touch of a mother. I think the whole spread ought to be shot indoors. The house is a wonderful, turn-of-the-century farmhouse and the setting is tranquil, but the kitchen's what it's all about. It's not some sterile test kitchen. It's homey and filled with light. One look at that kitchen and you can practically smell the aroma of the pies as they come out of the oven. And once readers get a look at Sally Keller, they'll want to know her. You'll have a feature that's about more than food."

When he finally wound down, he caught Maggie's amused expression. "What?" he demanded.

"I never thought I'd hear you going on and on so eloquently about a kitchen," she teased. "Or about a woman who's not in a fashion spread."

He grinned. "Hey, the bedroom's not the only important room in a house. I get that."

"Apparently so."

"Well? What do you think? You're the client."

"I think you're remarkable," she said softly, her eyes shining with excitement.

Rick's gaze shifted from the road to her and back again. "There's nothing remarkable about me, aside from an eye for a pretty picture."

"Don't do what you're always accusing me of doing," she scolded. "Don't sell yourself short."

Uncomfortable with the topic yet again, Rick was relieved to see Melanie pulling into the driveway at Rose Cottage just ahead of them. "Uh-oh," he said. "Company."

Maggie took one look at her sister and groaned. "You know this isn't good, don't you?"

Rick laughed. "It may not be good for you, but it's great for me. I can drop you off and hightail it out of here before the awkward questions start rolling off the tip of your sister's tongue."

"Coward," Maggie accused.

"Damn straight. Besides, I had to answer quite a few of her questions first thing this morning."

She regarded him with surprise. "You did? Why?"

"She interrupted my conversation with Mike to see what she could find out about how we're getting along."

"Oh, no," Maggie said with a groan. "I am so sorry."

"That's okay. It could be worse."

"How?"

"It could have been Ashley," he reminded her. "She's the one with courtroom cross-examination experience, and something tells me she'd come after me like I'm a hostile witness."

"More than likely," Maggie agreed. She gave him a wistful look. "You're really going to run off and leave me here to face this alone?"

"Yep, and I'm doing it without so much as a twinge of guilt," he said. "I have things to do."

"Such as?"

"I need to get on the computer and order film. I have enough to get started, but I'll need more. And I need to call my agent and tell him to agree to whatever terms you offer when you call him."

"Wow! Whatever terms I offer?" she asked, clearly delighted.

"Don't get carried away. I never work for peanuts."

"How about apple pie? Will you work for all the apple pie you can eat?"

"You'll have to do better than that. Mrs. Keller likes me," he said confidently. "She'll give me as much pie as I want. And there's always that café in Callao. Willa-Dean saves pie for me."

Maggie frowned at him. "Not every woman in the world falls for your charm, Flannery."

"Maybe not," he agreed. "But Mrs. Keller and Willa-Dean did." He winked at her. "And so did you. What more do I need?"

Maggie shot him a disgusted look as she climbed out of the car. "Fine. Run away. Will you be back later?"

"Call me when your sister's gone."

Melanie strolled over just in time to hear his comment. "Don't tell me you're taking off?"

"You bet I am."

"But I have so many questions for you," Melanie said.

"Exactly," he retorted. "Like I told you this morning, ask your sister. I don't kiss and tell."

"Then there has been kissing?" Melanie asked, her expression triumphant. She linked an arm through Maggie's. "We definitely have a lot to talk about."

Rick chuckled at the scowl Maggie shot in his direction. Better her than him, he thought as he headed for the safety of his room at the bed-and-breakfast. He'd already answered way too many tough questions for one morning.

"My, my, looks to me like things are heating up between you and the hunky photographer," Melanie commented as she made herself a cup of tea, then sat at the kitchen table, clearly prepared for a long visit.

"Make yourself at home, why don't you?" Maggie grumbled, wondering why anyone had ever thought Rose Cottage was serene. Her life had been in upheaval ever since she got here.

"This was my home, at least for a while," Melanie replied, obviously undaunted by Maggie's sour mood. "And technically, I suppose it's Mom's, now that Grandmother's gone."

"Whatever."

Melanie gave her a knowing look. "Is Rose Cottage working its magic on you, too? Is love in the air?"

"You are so annoying," Maggie retorted, sidestepping the question. "What on earth does Mike see in you?"

"I don't annoy him," Melanie replied easily. "I save my best pestering for my sisters."

"How unfortunate for me."

"Don't complain. You were right in the thick of all the pestering that went on here when I was first seeing Mike. It's my turn now. Come on, Margaret, talk. If you don't spill all your secrets to me, I can have Ashley and Jo here this weekend."

Heaven forbid! Maggie thought. She frowned at her sister. "What do you want to know?" she asked cautiously. She wasn't about to divulge more than she absolutely had to.

"I want to know what's going on with you and Rick, of course. In detail. For a man you claim to have run away to avoid, he seems to be around a lot."

"Typical man. He doesn't know when he's not welcome," Maggie claimed.

"Or he's determined to change your mind," Melanie suggested. "Is that it? Is he wooing you?"

"Wooing me?" Maggie echoed incredulously. "Where do you get this stuff?"

"We were raised by a Southern belle. In Mama's world, men wooed women."

Maggie laughed. "Yes, I suppose they did. Can you imagine Dad doing all that wooing?"

"Actually, I can," Melanie said, her expression thoughtful. "Have you ever heard how passionate he gets over the freshness of the ingredients for one of his famous Italian dinners?"

"And you think that translates to other passions?"

"Of course."

Maggie thought of Rick's passion for photography, of his growing passion for the Northern Neck of Virginia. She supposed there were some parallels to his passion for her.

Melanie eyed her curiously. "Is Rick as passionate

for you as he is for the perfect shot of some model in a bikini?"

Maggie blushed even as she gave a shrug. "Maybe."

Her sister's gaze narrowed. "Why don't you look happier about that?"

"It's not the passion that worries me," she told Melanie. "It's all the rest. What if there isn't anything more?"

"Have you ever spent one dull moment with him?"

"No," Maggie admitted.

"Then I don't think that's something you need to worry about."

"But we haven't known each other that long. We could still run out of shared interests."

"You don't have to marry the man right this second," Melanie reminded her.

"I know that," Maggie snapped. Marriage wasn't the issue. The problem was that she was likely to fall in love with him way before she knew if they had anything besides sex in common. "How did you know Mike was really the one? You didn't know each other that long before you got married."

Melanie's expression turned nostalgic. "I was looking out this very kitchen window one day and I just knew. He'd taken every miserable thing I'd dished out and he'd kept coming back. He couldn't say the words, but he showed me every day that he was steadfast and that he loved me."

Maggie snapped her fingers. "Just like that?" she asked skeptically.

"Pretty much. It was as if everything suddenly fell into place. Stop worrying, Maggie. You'll know it, too. It'll be one of those lightning bolts Mama used to tell us about."

"Really? Then explain all the other times I thought I was in love. Those turned out to be disasters."

Melanie gave her a sympathetic look. "I had one of those, too, if you'll recall. Believe me, in the end there was no comparison. Trust me, Maggie. When it happens, you'll recognize the difference."

"I hope so." Maggie gave her sister a wistful look. "I want Rick to be the one."

"Maybe he is."

Maggie forced herself to ask the question that had been tormenting her from the beginning. "What if I think he is, but he doesn't get it?"

"Then you'll survive," Melanie said confidently. "But I don't think it's something you need to worry about. I've seen the way he looks at you, remember?"

"Sally Keller said he gets a twinkle in his eye when he sees me."

"Oh, yeah," Melanie agreed. "And then some."

If both her sister and a woman as wise as Mrs. Keller could see it, maybe one of these days Maggie would be able to believe in it, too.

"Is it safe?" Rick asked, doing an overly dramatic survey of the kitchen before setting foot inside.

"That depends," Maggie said. "Are you more scared of my sister or of me?"

He crossed the kitchen and dropped a kiss on her delectable mouth. "You don't scare me," he said.

"Really? What if I said I thought we ought to run off and get married?"

His heart plummeted till he got a good look at the spark of amusement in her eyes. "I'd say you'd lost your mind and work on getting your sisters to commit you."

She poked him hard in the ribs with her elbow. "Nice."

"Hey, it's not something you joke around about," he retorted. "Marriage is serious stuff."

"And you don't do serious, do you, Rick?"

Something in her tone suggested that the joking was over. "No," he said quietly. "Not that kind of serious, anyway."

"Because of your folks," she suggested.

"No, because of me. I have a short attention span. You've seen the tabloids."

"I'm beginning to think they've gotten it all wrong," she told him.

"Wishful thinking," he said dismissively.

"I don't think so."

"What brought this on, Maggie? What ideas was Melanie putting in your head this afternoon?"

"Don't panic. She didn't leave a list of places where we could go for a marriage license."

"Thank goodness for that." He tucked a hand under her chin and searched her face. She looked serene, which was a relief. He'd hate to think her sister had gotten her all stirred up about the future, when he was trying desperately to take one day at a time, waiting every second for the usual panic to set in. That it hadn't so far was something of a miracle, but he knew from experience that could change in a heartbeat.

"I talked to your agent," Maggie said, slipping away from him and giving him some much-needed space. "He thinks you're crazy as a loon for agreeing to do this shoot, especially after you turned down Greece."

Rick grinned. "Obviously he's not aware of all the perks."

"Well, I didn't tell him about those, that's for sure,"

she said. "He might get some crazy idea to work them into all your contracts."

Rick laughed. "I doubt that will ever be an issue, darlin'. Frank is always lecturing me about taking my work home with me, so to speak. The tabloid stories make him cringe."

"Good for Frank," she said enthusiastically. "At any rate, everything's cleared. When do you want to get started?"

"I called the Kellers this afternoon. They're expecting us back in the morning. It's baking day."

"Which means?" Maggie asked.

"That Sally gets an early start. She wants us there by seven."

"Seven o'clock? In the morning?" Maggie repeated. "That's not vacation. That's torture."

Rick grinned. "We're not on vacation anymore, sweetheart. This is work, remember?"

Maggie shook her head. "Actually it's all getting a little muddy," she told him.

Rick agreed. The lines between work and play had never been blurred before he got mixed up with Maggie. All the playing he'd done in the past had been after hours, and he'd managed to keep it cleanly compartmentalized, despite what his agent and the tabloids thought.

He tugged Maggie into his lap. He was beginning to like this murkier arrangement better. "So, what are we going to do tonight?" he asked. "Another hot Monopoly game? Scrabble? Cards?"

"I found this round puzzle in the attic. It's a picture of nothing but marbles. There must be thousands of them. Want to tackle that?"

Rick studied her totally serious expression. "You really want to spend the evening doing a jigsaw puzzle?"

"Or you could seduce me," she suggested casually. "Is that more appealing?"

"Much more appealing," he confirmed, covering her mouth with his own.

When he finally released her, she stared up at him with dazed eyes. "Dinner?" she asked weakly.

"Later."

As it turned out, they didn't make it back downstairs till breakfast.

"This has to stop," Maggie said, her head down on the kitchen table while Rick made coffee.

"Lord, I hope not," he commented.

"If it doesn't, we're either going to die of exhaustion or starvation."

"No chance of either one," he insisted. "Human survival instincts are very strong. That's why we're down here at dawn. Hunger pangs."

"Speak for yourself. I'm down here for coffee. I want at least one brain cell alert when we go to see the Kellers this morning. Otherwise they'll guess what we were doing all night."

Rick chuckled. "I'm pretty sure they know. Matthew told me I had a live one."

Maggie stared at him. "He what? You two talked about me?"

"Oh, as if you and Sally didn't talk about me," Rick chided. "I saw that look she gave me before we left."

"Okay, okay, she thinks you have a fascinating twinkle in your eyes. She says it reminds her of Mr. Keller."

Rick looked surprisingly pleased. "Really?"

"Sweet heaven, do you really have to have an eighty-year-old woman falling all over you, too?" she asked indignantly.

He leaned down and kissed her. "No, you're all the woman I want," he assured her.

She shoved him away. "Stop that. There's no time."

"Sure there is," Rick insisted.

"You're the one who scheduled this appointment for practically the middle of the night," she reminded him. "Live with the consequences. I'm going to take a shower."

"I'll join you. It'll save time."

Maggie laughed. "Nice try, Flannery. Go back to your own shower. You have less than twenty minutes before we need to be out this door and on our way. I wouldn't waste a second of it if I were you."

"I don't need to go to my place. I have everything I need in the car."

"Oh?"

"Camera, film, a change of clothes."

She should have been annoyed by his confidence that he'd still be here this morning, but at the moment, she was impressed by his foresight.

She grinned at him and reached for his hand. "Then why are we wasting time down here, when we could be upstairs in that shower?"

Fifteen minutes later, they were soaking wet and untangling themselves from the damp sheets. Maggie scrambled for her clothes, but Rick wasn't moving.

"Hurry up, Flannery."

"Can't," he said.

"Why not?"

"My clean clothes are still in the car." He gave her an innocent look. "I could go out like this and get them."

"I don't think so. I'll get 'em for you as soon as I get buttoned up and run a comb through my hair." She looked over her shoulder and noted that he was sprawled against the pillows looking entirely too comfortable and way too sexy. There was nothing like staring at a naked man in her bed to ruin her concentration.

"Umm, Maggie, don't you think you ought to get a move on?" he teased.

"What?" She blinked and shook her head. "Right. Your clothes." She tore down the steps and ran to his car, only to run smack into Ashley.

"You!" she said, dismayed.

"Hello to you, too."

Her gaze narrowed. "Did Melanie call you?"

Ashley looked perplexed. "No. Why? And why are you running around outside looking as if you're barely out of the shower?"

"Because I am barely out of the shower."

Her sister glanced pointedly at the sports car. "And Rick? Where is he?"

Maggie bit back a groan. There was no way around this one. "Upstairs," she admitted.

"In the shower?"

She shook her head. "Not exactly."

Ashley's eyes widened. "In your bed?"

Maggie grimaced. "Pretty much. And we're running very late. I need to get his clothes up to him."

"Did you hide them in his car, so you could hold him hostage?"

"No, these are clean clothes. I really don't have time to discuss this. Could you maybe go away and come back later? Pretend this never happened?"

Ashley's grin spread. "I don't think so," she said, trailing Maggie inside. She poured herself a cup of coffee and sat down. "Tell Rick I'm looking forward to seeing him again."

"Yeah, sure," Maggie said. She'd tell him exactly that and then pray that he didn't dive straight out of the upstairs window.

9

Rick took one look at Maggie's flushed face and panic-stricken eyes and knew something was wrong. Had there been an intruder? Had she gone downstairs to find the place ransacked? What other possibilities were there? The phone hadn't rung. Nor had he heard the doorbell. She'd been gone a lot longer than the few minutes he'd expected, and that stunned look on her face was not the cheery expression of the woman who'd left this room a short time ago.

"What took so long? Did something happen while you were downstairs?" he asked, already reaching for the clothes she was clutching to her chest.

"You could say that," she muttered, giving the clothes up reluctantly. It was as if they were providing some sort of weird security, like a toddler's well-worn blanket.

"Maggie, talk to me," he urged.

She met his gaze with unmistakable reluctance. "We have company," she said with obviously forced cheer.

"Oh?" he said, keeping his tone deliberately neutral. This was apparently not a good thing. In his mind, her parents would be the worst-case scenario, but she might have other ideas. "Who?"

"Ashley's arrived." Her tone was still way too bright, bordering on hysteria.

"Uh-oh." He touched her cheek. "And she caught you getting my clothes out of my car. That must have gone over well. Are you okay?"

She jerked away from him. "Do I look okay? You said it yourself. Ashley is a dangerous woman when she has questions and, trust me, after finding me gathering your clothes from your car when it's plain I just stepped out of a shower five minutes ago, she has lots and lots of questions."

"Too bad we have no time to answer them," he reminded her. "All those pesky questions will have to wait."

"She'll be here when we get back," Maggie pointed out, looking resigned to the inevitable. "In fact, I wouldn't be too sure we'll get away from here without her being hot on our trail."

"We'll manage," he said with feigned confidence. "And maybe by the time we see her again, we'll have answers for her." Now he was the one faking good cheer. "Stop worrying. You're a grown woman. She's your sister, not your mother."

Maggie shuddered. "Yes, that would be worse. My mother would tell my father and then you'd be chopped into itty-bitty pieces all over the kitchen floor. It wouldn't be pretty. But keep in mind, if Ashley's not satisfied with our answers, all of that could still happen. She learned a lot about being protective from our father."

Rick shuddered. "Let's deal with one crisis at a time, shall we?"

"Right." She visibly drew in a deep breath. "Okay, Flannery, do your charm thing and get us out of here."

"Forget the charm. I say we just make a run for it," he

said, but Maggie was clearly not amused. "Okay, okay."
He plastered a smile on his face and grabbed her hand.
"Let's do it."

They strolled into the kitchen and found Ashley at the
table sipping coffee. Compared to the polished, sophis-
ticated woman he'd met a few weeks earlier, she looked
like something the cat had dragged in. Some of that could
be attributed to the long, all-night drive from Boston, but
he was pretty sure there had to be more to it. He forgot
all about the quick-exit strategy and gave her a worried
look.

"Are you okay?" he asked.

Both women seemed startled by the question. Maggie
took a long, hard look at her sister.

"I'm fine," Ashley said tersely.

"No, you're not," Maggie said at once, dropping
down beside her. "Why didn't I see it before? You look
awful."

"Thanks so much," Ashley said. "And I imagine you
didn't notice before because you were too busy panick-
ing that I was about to walk in and discover Rick in your
bed." She gave him a fierce look that was more in character. "What's up with that, by the way?"

Maggie was on her feet at once. "Never mind. You're
obviously not that upset if you're ready to interrogate
Rick. We have an appointment. Help yourself to whatever you want to eat. Take a nap. Call Melanie. Whatever.
We'll see you later."

"I won't forget that I have questions," Ashley called
after them as they bolted from the kitchen.

"She won't, either," Maggie told him as they got into
his car.

"It's not a big deal," Rick said, mostly to reassure
Maggie.

"Tell me that tonight after she's zeroed in on all your secrets and weak spots."

He chuckled. "I have no secrets or weak spots."

"Ha!"

"Okay, maybe a few, but I don't have to answer anything I don't want to. Let me handle your sister."

"How?"

"By turning the tables on her. You saw for yourself that she's all messed up about something. We'll just concentrate on getting to the bottom of that. She'll be eager enough to go off and hide in her room."

Maggie actually laughed at that. "You don't know Ashley, but it sure is going to be fun watching the two of you get acquainted."

Something in her delighted tone suggested to Rick that he wasn't going to have half as much fun as she was.

Maggie forgot all about her sister and the questions that would be waiting for her and Rick at home as she watched the way Rick interacted with Sally Keller.

It was amazing to watch him work with her. He had an endless amount of patience. He teased and flattered her and treated her as if she were delicate bone china, all the while snapping pictures that Maggie knew from experience would be incredible. He made it look so easy, even when he'd turned the woman's kitchen into a stage of sorts.

"Just pretend I'm not here," he told Sally.

She laughed at that. "How am I supposed to do that when you've got all these lights blinding me and you're underfoot every time I turn around?" she retorted. "I expect I'll trip over something before the morning's over."

Rick winked at her. "I'll catch you," he promised.

"Now that's an incentive to risk a broken hip," she replied, her eyes sparkling.

"Don't be talking about breaking a hip," Matthew grumbled from his place beside Maggie. "That's the last thing you need."

"Well, I won't be doing it on purpose," Sally told her husband. "Stop fussing. This is the most fun I've had in ages."

Matthew gave Maggie a helpless look. "Don't know why I encouraged her to do this. I had no idea she'd turn out to be such a ham."

Maggie chuckled. "Are you sure you're not jealous? Don't worry. Your turn is coming."

"I'm not getting my face in some northern magazine," Matthew insisted. "Sally's the photogenic one."

"But you're the one who puts the sparkle in her eyes," Maggie told him. "How can we let Rick miss a shot like that?"

Matthew patted her hand. "You're a good girl. Don't pay any attention to all my grumbling. It's good to have some commotion in this house again. When our kids were young, there was something going on every minute. Lately it's gotten way too quiet around here."

"Where are your children living now?" Maggie asked him.

"One boy's down in Richmond. Another one's in Charlottesville. Our daughter's in Atlanta."

"Do they get home often?"

"Not nearly often enough to make Sally happy. We've been talking about selling this place and moving to be closer to at least one of them, but neither of us can bear to let go. This is home, if you know what I mean."

Maggie knew. It was the way she'd always felt about Boston, but lately the city didn't seem to have the same pull it had once had. She'd found an unexpected sense of contentment right here. Melanie had been surprised to discover the same thing.

Maybe it was because Rose Cottage was home in its own way. She and her sisters had spent many summers and holidays there with their grandmother. It had always seemed magical.

After their grandmother's death, though, the place had been neglected. None of them had wanted to visit without Cornelia Lindsey there to welcome them. Maggie saw now what a shame that was, when all this time they could have been surrounded by her spirit. It was something they all felt, especially in the garden that Mike had re-created for them.

"You know that expression about home being where your heart is?" she asked Matthew. "It's true. Wherever you and Sally wind up, you'll make it into a home."

Matthew gave her a surprised look. "That's a real wise observation, young lady. Sounds like something Sally would say. She has a thousand of 'em for every occasion. They're all little nuggets of truth, if you listen close enough."

She gave Matthew's strong, weathered hand a squeeze. She had a hunch he needed a distraction, and Rick probably would like them to get out from underfoot, though he hadn't said a word about their presence.

"Would you mind showing me around a little?" she asked Matthew. "I didn't get to see much when we were here yesterday."

The old man beamed at her. "I'd be pleased to," he said.

Rick glanced away from his camera as they passed. "Where are you two off to?"

"The nickel tour," Matthew told him. "Don't worry. I'm not out to steal your girl."

Rick grinned. "As if you could, old man."

"Now don't be uttering dares," Matthew scolded. "There's some fire left in me yet."

Maggie laughed. "Okay, you two. I'm the one who gets to choose. You keep bickering and you'll both be out of the running."

Sally laughed. "Good for you."

Outside, Matthew walked her around to the front of the white clapboard house with its neat black trim. "If you take a good look at that part in the middle, it was built by my granddaddy around 1870, right after he got married. Not much more than a box, but it's stood the test of time. My daddy's the one who added on just after the turn of the century. Put that wing over there so the house would accommodate me and my brothers and sisters. There were eight of us in all. Only two of us left now. I was the youngest. My sister Jane is still living over in Reedville. She's eighty-five and feisty as the dickens. She can't get around the way she used to, but her mind's sharp as a tack. We keep trying to get her to come live with us now that she's a widow, but she likes her little home over there. Says she wants to die in her own bed."

"I suppose a person can't ask for a more peaceful passing than that," Maggie said.

Matthew gave her an approving look. "True enough, but I'm beginning to think Sally and I have a few adventures left in us. We stayed put all these years. Between the kids and all the work there is to do around here, there was no time for anything else. I'd like to see some more of the world, maybe live where we can have some grandkids underfoot. This place is getting to be too much for us."

"Have you thought of selling it?"

He nodded. "Sally's the one who balks. She says I'll regret it. She could be right. There's nothing easy about turning your back on your own history." His expression brightened. "But there's a lot to be said for change, too. Keeps the blood flowing, don't you think?"

Maggie thought of how her blood had been flowing—practically sizzling, in fact—since she'd come to Rose Cottage. "I think you're a very smart man, Mr. Keller."

"Call me Matthew. We don't hold much with formality around here."

"I'd be honored," Maggie said.

Matthew linked her arm through his and led her around back. "Now you take a look out there," he encouraged, gesturing with a sweep of his arm. "Apple trees as far as the eye can see. It's a picture in the spring, I'll tell you that. And the air is filled with the scent of all those blossoms. Sweetest smell in the world. I used to lie awake nights when I was a kid and listen to the crickets and the hum of the bees. That scent would drift in my bedroom window. Folks these days turn on an air conditioner and miss all that." He shook his head sadly. "Seems like a damn shame to me."

It did to Maggie, too, though she tended to be the queen of air-conditioning back home.

Matthew gave her shoulder a pat. "I've bored you long enough," he said. "Let's go see what those two are up to inside." He glanced at his watch. "The first of the pies ought to be coming out of the oven about now. If I know that man of yours, he'll be wanting to take a break so he can have the first slice."

Maggie chuckled. She was pretty sure Matthew had it exactly right. "Then let's go beat him to it."

* * *

Maggie hadn't said much since they'd left the orchard. In fact she hadn't said much after she and Matthew had gone off on that mysterious tour of theirs. Rick studied her out of the corner of his eye. He thought she looked a little sad.

"Something wrong?" he asked eventually.

"Do you know they're thinking of selling?" she asked him.

Rick wasn't surprised. Matthew had said as much to him the day before. "It's a lot for them to keep up with," he told her.

"I know, but it seems so sad. They've spent their whole marriage there. Matthew grew up there."

"Isn't he the one who wants to move?" Rick asked. "He hinted at it yesterday."

Maggie nodded. "I still think it's sad that none of their kids have stuck around."

"This area is beautiful, but it probably has limited opportunities for young people," Rick said pragmatically.

"That orchard's an opportunity," Maggie retorted. "Sally and Matthew have made a livelihood from it. Even now, they've found a way to keep it going without having to do more work than they can handle."

He gave her a curious look. "You almost sound as if it's something you'd like to do."

"Don't be ridiculous," she said derisively. "What would I do with an orchard?"

"Good question."

"It's just sad, that's all." She forced an obviously feigned smile. It was no more believable than those she'd tried out earlier to convince him she was thrilled about her sister's arrival. "Let's not talk about that anymore. We have more pressing fish to fry."

"Your sister and her questions," Rick guessed.

"Exactly. Maybe we should consider staying out really, really late and avoiding the whole inquisition," she suggested.

"Or you could sneak into my room at the B and B," Rick said. "That could be fun."

To his disappointment, Maggie shook her head. "Too obvious. She'll think to look there."

He laughed. "Where would you suggest we hide?"

"Richmond, maybe." Her expression turned wistful. "Alaska."

He chuckled, even though it was plain she wasn't entirely joking. "What are you really worried about, Maggie? That she'll ask a question we can't answer or that I'll get tired of all the questions and take off?"

She gave him a surprised look, as if she hadn't expected him to be so intuitive. "A little of both, I suppose."

"Then you're forgetting something. I'm a pretty jaded guy. I've been interrogated by tougher people than your sister. She doesn't scare me. And you and I have a deal. I'm not going anywhere."

"You could change your mind."

"Not because of Ashley," he reassured her. "You're the only one who could get me to leave and only if you kick me to the curb and mean it. I'm not running just because things get a little sticky."

His claim seemed to startle her. "Why not? Isn't that what you do?"

The accusation stung, despite its accuracy. "Yes," he admitted.

"Then what's different now?"

"You," he said simply. "You make the difference."

She looked perplexed, rather than pleased. "How?"

Because she was so obviously struggling to believe him, Rick tried to find an answer that she would understand.

"For one thing, I have had more stimulating conversations with you than I've had with all those other women combined. Then there's the work we're doing right now. I'm enjoying that."

"So am I, but it won't last forever."

"Okay, but there's more. We have fun together, Maggie. And for another thing, being with you is easy." He grinned. "At least when I'm not having to fend off your fiercely protective sisters."

"But that's precisely my point—" she began.

Rick cut her off. "Do I need to go on with all the other things that are keeping me here? Trust me, the list far outweighs the inconvenience of having to deal with Melanie and Ashley." He studied her intently. "Are you really worried about me not being able to come up with the answers to pacify Ashley, or are you worried that you don't have the right answers?"

"Me?"

He nodded. "I'm not the only one on the hot seat, you know. She's bound to ask you if you've thought this through, if you've weighed the risks of getting involved with a guy with my reputation. Heck, she knows that's why you took off in the first place."

"I didn't take off because of your reputation, at least not exactly," she retorted. "I ran because of my own track record."

"Which is?"

"I've told you," she said impatiently. "I fall too hard, too fast. I can't sustain a relationship. Add *that* to your track record, and it's pretty much a sure bet that we're headed for disaster."

Rick nodded slowly. "Could be," he admitted and saw

the instant hurt in her eyes. He took her hand and gave it a squeeze. "It hasn't happened so far, though. Would you rather not have any of this just to prevent some possible heartache in the future?"

She sighed at that. "I honestly don't know."

Rick felt his stomach clench. "If you're not sure, then maybe we should forget about this. I'm a live-in-the-moment kind of a man, Maggie. It's the way I grew up, the way I had to be to survive. I can't promise you anything beyond right here, right now. If you don't think that's going to be enough to appease your sister, if it's not enough for you, then I'll finish this photo shoot tomorrow and take off."

Alarm flared in her eyes. "No," she said at once.

The quick and heartfelt response wasn't enough to reassure him. "Are you sure?" he persisted.

"Yes," she said, then shook her head. "No. It's gotten very confusing."

Rick had a feeling he should stop tormenting her and take the decision out of her hands, but he couldn't seem to make himself do it. He had an undeniable weakness for Maggie that he didn't understand and couldn't explain. Every time he kissed her, every time he touched her, the need for her grew stronger. He knew that for as long as she was willing to have him underfoot, there was no place else on earth he'd rather be.

That could change tomorrow or the day after that, but for now this little nowhere town on the Chesapeake Bay was where he needed to be as long as Maggie D'Angelo was here, as well.

10

As soon as Maggie and Rick walked back into Rose Cottage, Maggie could feel the decided chill in the air, and it wasn't due to the new central air-conditioning she'd purchased running on high. Ashley was waiting for them, her expression hard and unyielding, the way it was in the courtroom whenever she faced down a prosecutor. Maggie shivered, even though it was her own sister. She knew what Ashley could be like when she was in this mood. Something told her Ashley was disturbed about a whole lot more than discovering Rick in Maggie's bed when she'd arrived that morning.

"Did you get any rest?" Maggie asked her sister.

"No."

"Maybe I should send Rick home so you and I can have a long talk. Obviously there's something serious going on with you."

"Forget about me," Ashley said. Her gaze shifted to Rick. "I think you should hang around for this."

"Sure," Rick said easily, sprawling in a chair opposite her as if that hard glint in Ashley's eyes wasn't the least bit worrisome.

"I'll make some tea," Maggie said. "Rick, maybe you should help me."

Her sister's lips quirked at the ploy. "Don't even think about trying to hustle him out the back door. Let's just get this out of the way."

Rick leveled a calm look at her. "What's on your mind? Is this about finding me here earlier?"

"No, that's a whole other topic. Since then, you've had a phone call," Ashley said.

Rick looked puzzled. "No one I know has this number."

"Actually it was on your cell phone, which you'd apparently tossed aside at some point last night." She paused as if to allow the significance of that to sink in, then added, "I picked it up by mistake, thinking it was mine."

He shrugged. "Obviously, I forgot all about it this morning. I've gotten out of the habit of checking to make sure I have it since the reception's so lousy."

Ashley gave him a wry look. "It wasn't lousy this morning. In fact the call came in quite clearly."

Rick finally frowned at her. "So, you intercepted a call of mine by mistake and something about it has you all worked up. Am I with you so far?"

"You're very astute," Ashley confirmed. It didn't sound like a compliment.

"Are you sure you weren't deliberately spying on me?" Rick asked mildly.

He was one step ahead of Maggie. She'd been about to utter the same question. She didn't like the way this conversation was going. She'd kept her mouth shut till now, but enough was enough.

"Back off, Ashley," she ordered. "Rick's phone calls are none of your business."

"Sorry. I can't pretend I didn't take this one." She gave

Maggie a commiserating look. "Are you aware that this man is supposed to be in Greece right now?"

Rick chuckled. "Actually, I'm not. I turned the assignment down. Is that what this is about? Did my agent call and go on and on about how your sister is interfering in my career?"

Ashley looked startled. "No, but that's an interesting take on things. Actually this was your very good *friend,* Laurina. If she has a last name, she didn't mention it. She seemed to think Laurina would be sufficient."

Maggie knew the name even if her sister didn't. Laurina was one of the top international models whose face Rick had immortalized on more than one fashion magazine cover. They'd definitely been an item a few months back. Just hearing the name was enough to send a chill down Maggie's spine. She should have guessed the women from his past wouldn't all be content to remain in the background. If she'd concluded he was worth fighting for, some of the other women might have, as well.

Rick didn't seem to be rising to Ashley's bait, though. He merely shrugged. "So? We *are* friends. We do talk from time to time."

"Apparently you've done quite a bit more than talking," Ashley said coldly. "She's apparently expecting a little bambino. She thought you should know."

Maggie felt sick to her stomach, but before she could bolt from the room, Rick laughed.

"You think this is funny?" Maggie demanded incredulously, waving off whatever comment was on the tip of her sister's tongue. She could handle this part. "This woman is having your baby and you're laughing about it?"

Rick returned her heated gaze without so much as a flicker of an eyelash. "If she's having my baby, then it must be by artificial insemination," he declared calmly. He almost sounded believable.

"You expect us to buy that?" Ashley demanded, obviously unable to keep quiet despite Maggie's warning look.

"I don't expect you to do anything, except maybe to listen to both sides of the story rather than jumping to all sorts of wild conclusions," Rick said mildly. "Shouldn't an attorney, of all people, understand the concept of innocent until proven guilty?"

Before Ashley could respond, Maggie stepped in again. If she and Rick were ever to have a chance, she had to deal with this herself. Ashley would never be able to sit silently by while she tried, so she turned to her sister and said, "Ashley, I think you should go and pay Melanie a visit. I'm sure she's anxious to see you."

"But—"

"Go," Maggie repeated. "I can handle this."

"You can't simply believe whatever story he decides to tell you," Ashley warned. "I talked to this woman. She was very convincing."

"About the fact that she was pregnant or about the baby being mine?" Rick asked.

Maggie waited as anxiously for the response as Rick did. Maybe even more so. For an instant, her big sister looked thoroughly flustered. Maggie seized on that. "You didn't really ask, did you? You jumped to a conclusion." The same way she had, in fact. "Let me deal with this, Ashley."

Her sister nodded finally, then looked at Rick. "I'm very sorry if I got it all wrong, but if I find out later that I didn't, there will be hell to pay."

"Fair enough. You did get it wrong, but I can understand you wanting to look out for Maggie. Trust me when

I tell you that there is nothing remotely like this that's going to come along to hurt her."

"I hope not," Ashley said, then left.

Maggie closed her eyes and took a deep breath, then faced Rick.

"You are telling me the truth, aren't you? Laurina's baby isn't yours?"

"There's not a chance of that," he insisted.

"But you were together," she stated flatly.

"We were *seen* together," he corrected. "Often, in fact. Laurina's been wildly in love with a man in Italy for a very long time. He's very publicity shy. He wouldn't commit to marriage to someone who's always being trailed by the paparazzi, so she used me to make him jealous. We purposely got our picture taken all over the place for a few weeks. The tactic worked. He realized a few unwanted snapshots weren't important enough to cost him the woman he loved. They were married, very quietly, two months ago. There wasn't a paparazzo in sight." He grinned. "And now she's pregnant. I'm thrilled for her, for both of them."

It all sounded so plausible, but could she believe him? Maggie wished she could be sure. She'd seen those pictures, too. They'd been very convincing.

Rick held out his cell phone. "Call her, if that's what it will take to convince you," he offered. "She won't mind. I had to do my share of fast-talking to get her off the hook with Antonio. He wanted to carve me up when Laurina insisted I come to the wedding."

"Did you go?"

"Yes."

And he'd survived this Antonio's scrutiny. That had to mean something. Maggie made a decision. If they were ever to have a real chance, trust had to begin sometime.

It might as well be now. "No. I don't need to call her. I trust you."

Rick regarded her with approval. "You can, you know. I won't ever lie to you and I won't sugarcoat the truth. Not every time I've been seen with a woman was as innocent as the times I was spotted with Laurina. We all have a romantic history of one sort or another, Maggie."

She thought of her own less-than-stellar past. Her relationships might not have been as well documented as some of Rick's, but that didn't mean they hadn't happened. He wasn't cross-examining her about those.

She recalled what he'd said earlier about living in the moment. It had always gotten her in trouble before, but there really wasn't any other way to live life. If she filled her head with regrets about the past or worries about the future, she would have nothing in the present.

"Let's go to Melanie's," she said, standing up and reaching for his hand.

Rick looked momentarily alarmed. "You want to face both of your sisters down?"

She nodded. "We have nothing to hide, nothing to be ashamed of."

He laughed. "All right, Maggie!" he enthused.

She frowned at him. "Knock it off. This isn't going to be a picnic, Flannery. Ashley may have been thrown off stride by discovering she might be wrong about Laurina, but she's still not through with you."

"Duly noted."

"Why aren't you quaking in your boots?"

"Because I think you're tough enough to defend me."

Maggie regarded him with surprise and the slow dawning of pleasure. She was tough, she realized. And getting tougher by the minute. The past had done that for her. It gave her a whole new perspective on all that heartache.

Maybe it hadn't been such a bad thing, after all, if it had made her ready for a man as complicated as Rick Flannery.

"You're still in one piece, I see," Mike commented when Rick joined him outside at the backyard grill on which several steaks were cooking.

"Fancy footwork and the truth," Rick commented dryly. "I imagine Ashley filled you in."

"Actually, she didn't. She muttered something about possibly having gone a little overboard. Closest I've ever heard the woman come to admitting she might be wrong."

Rick glanced into the house and saw Ashley sitting quietly, while Melanie and Maggie laughed as they worked to get dinner on the table.

"I only met her once before she turned up here, so you know her better than I do," Rick said, watching her thoughtfully. "Does Ashley seem okay to you?"

Mike stared in the direction of his sister-in-law. "She's quieter than usual. Why? You think she's here for some reason besides grilling you?"

Rick shrugged. "I would have bet on it this morning. Maggie picked up on it, too. I think she got temporarily sidetracked by a phone call of mine she intercepted, but look at her now. She's way too quiet in there with those two."

Mike studied her, then nodded. "You could be right, but thankfully, we can leave it to her sisters to wheedle the truth out of her eventually. We're just men. They don't expect us to be intuitive about this sort of stuff."

Rick laughed. "That is a blessing, isn't it?" Even so, he couldn't quite shake the sense that Maggie's sister was bottling up something serious enough to require the support of everyone around her.

"Daddy," six-year-old Jessie said impatiently, arriving with her hands on her hips and a pouting expression, "are we ever going to eat?"

Mike scooped her up and tickled her until she giggled. "Ten more minutes, kiddo. Your aunt Ashley is the only one around here who likes her meat raw. The rest of us have to wait till it's cooked medium rare."

Rick wished he had his camera with him. The look of adoration in Mike's eyes as he gazed at his daughter was priceless. It was the epitome of what the love between a parent and a child ought to be. Too bad it was so rare in the world, he thought cynically.

He took another look at the happy scene inside and saw that her sisters had finally managed to draw Ashley into the conversation. Maybe close-knit families weren't as unusual as he'd imagined. Maybe it was simply his own dysfunctional family that had colored his view.

"Mike, you've been around all of the D'Angelos. What's that like?"

Mike regarded him curiously, but before he could reply, Jessie piped up, "They're the bestest family in the whole world. I'm glad they married us."

Mike chuckled. "There you have it, a thoroughly un-biased report. She's right, though. They're remarkable." He gave Jessie a squeeze. "I'm glad they married us, too, short stuff."

Something that might have been longing filled Rick's chest at the testimonials. For the first time in his life being part of a remarkable family was within his grasp, if only he had the courage to reach for it.

He could choose to do that, just as Maggie had chosen to trust him earlier. He could step out of his comfort zone and take a chance that something better was right around the corner. Or he could retreat and protect his heart the way he always did.

He bit back a sigh as an all-too-familiar panic crept through him. He didn't have to decide tonight or even tomorrow, but the day would come. Maggie would lose patience with having nothing more than today. She would want a future. She'd been surrounded by people who believed that love could endure. Right now, this second, Rick wanted to believe that, too. Like capturing that image of the adoration in Mike's eyes as he gazed at his daughter, having such strong faith in love would be priceless.

Ashley was tipsy. Maggie kept staring at her strong, invincible sister, trying to make sense of it. Ashley was never out of control. In fact, she rarely had more than a glass of wine with dinner. Tonight she'd had two glasses, maybe three, which was apparently more than enough to loosen her tongue and make her giggle at the slightest provocation.

"You're riding home with us," Maggie told her, steering her toward Rick's car. There was no backseat to speak of, but she could manage in the cramped space for the few minutes it would take to get to Rose Cottage.

"I'm fine," Ashley said, balking.

"You haven't been fine since you got here," Maggie retorted. "And now you're drunk."

"Uh-oh," Rick muttered, apparently guessing that the accusation wouldn't sit well with the always-in-control Ashley.

Maggie scowled at him. "Well, she is."

"I am not," Ashley said haughtily. "I am totally sober." She proved it by tripping over nothing more than a loose piece of gravel and almost falling facedown on the ground.

"Yes, I can see how totally sober you are," Maggie commented.

Ashley tried to jerk away. She dangled her car keys under Maggie's nose, even as she sank into the passenger seat of Rick's car. "I have my car here."

Maggie snatched the keys and tossed them to Rick. "Will you drive her car home? I'll take yours, since I've gotten her this far."

He cast a worried look at them. "You sure? We could come back for her car in the morning."

"No, this is better," Maggie said. "And there's no need to panic. I promise not to wreck your precious car."

He grinned. "I wasn't worried for a minute."

"Ha!"

Only after he'd gone did Maggie gingerly get behind the wheel of the sports car. She had a hunch if Rick knew she'd never driven a straight shift before, he'd be having heart failure about now. How hard could it be, though? She just had to back up a few feet, get onto the highway and drive a couple of miles. No big deal.

The grinding sound that immediately filled the air when she put her foot on the gas suggested she'd missed some important step.

Beside her Ashley groaned. "The clutch, Maggie," she muttered. "You have to use the clutch."

Now was a fine time for her sister to collect her thoughts. "Where the hell is it?" Maggie asked.

Ashley cast a disbelieving look in her direction, then began to giggle. Maggie stared back at her, then began to laugh with her. They were howling and holding their sides when Melanie came out of the house.

"What on earth is going on?" Melanie asked, studying

them worriedly. "Where's Rick? I can't believe he let you behind the wheel of his car."

"To be honest, neither can I," Maggie admitted. "He drove Ashley's car home."

"What the hell was he thinking?" Melanie asked.

"He doesn't know I've never driven a straight shift before," Maggie admitted meekly. "I thought it would be easy."

Melanie shook her head. "Sit tight. I'll get my car and drive you both home. I don't know what's going on around here tonight. I've got one sister who's smashed and one who's lost her mind."

When Melanie pulled alongside with her SUV a few minutes later, Maggie and Ashley climbed in, both of them duly chastened. Maggie hated to think what Rick was going to have to say when they arrived home without his car.

Fortunately, she noted when they turned into the driveway at Rose Cottage, he was inside. Unfortunately, he appeared in the doorway before Melanie could drive away.

"What the devil?" he said, sounding more than a little unnerved. "Where's my car?"

"Still at Melanie's," Maggie soothed. "It's fine."

"Then why didn't you drive it home?"

Ashley paused in her unsteady walk toward the house to announce, "Because Maggie couldn't find the clutch." She patted Rick's cheek. "And you thought I was the one who shouldn't be on the road."

She wobbled on past him and went inside. Rick stared at Maggie. "You can't drive a straight shift?"

"Apparently not."

He shook his head. "I don't believe it."

She gestured toward Melanie. "Want a ride over so you

can get it? You know you won't sleep a wink till you see it's in one piece."

"True," he admitted, the glowered at her. "But I am coming straight back here. Don't you dare fall asleep on me."

Despite the annoyance in his voice, Maggie experienced a little shiver of anticipation. He wasn't really that mad at her, she reassured herself. Maybe they could salvage the rest of the night yet. And if he was a little irritated, that just made the prospect of make-up sex more appealing.

Then she thought of Ashley and pushed her own needs aside. "Rick, wait till morning to come back, okay? I want to get to the bottom of what's going on with my sister. She'll never open up if you're here."

He gave her a skeptical look. "And you think you can do that while she's half-drunk?"

"Actually it's probably the best time. Her defenses will be down."

He nodded. "Okay, then, I'll see you first thing in the morning. I'll bring very strong coffee and pastries."

She reached up and kissed his cheek. "Thank you for understanding."

"You're giving me too much credit. I haven't understood much since the day we met."

She stared after him as he rode off with Melanie. She could relate to his confusion. She was pretty bewildered herself. But one thing seemed clear enough. Neither of them was rattled enough to run.

Inside, Maggie found Ashley at the kitchen table. A kettle of water was already boiling. Apparently Ashley had guessed that Maggie had a lot of questions that weren't going to wait till morning.

"Where's Rick?" Ashley asked.

"He went with Melanie to get his car. Then he's heading back to the B and B."

Ashley nodded. "Just as well. I have a lot of questions about what you've gotten yourself into with him."

"Save 'em," Maggie ordered as she plunked a box of tea bags on the table, then poured them each a cup of boiling water. "I'm going first."

Ashley gave her a startled look. "You have questions for me?"

"A ton of them, in fact, starting with why you're here."

"I came to check on you, of course."

She uttered the words in a way that would have convinced most people. Maggie wasn't buying it. "And?" she prodded. "That might have been part of what brought you down here, but there's more to it."

"What makes you think that?" Ashley retorted defensively. She was suddenly looking everywhere except into Maggie's eyes.

"Oh, I don't know," Maggie said. "Maybe the fact that you got drunk tonight."

"Don't be ridiculous," Ashley said indignantly. "I am not drunk. I'm under a little stress. I had a couple of glasses of wine to relax. People do it all the time. It's no big deal."

"It is when it's you. You don't unwind with alcohol. You go to the gym."

"Yes, well, the gym wasn't working for me," Ashley snapped. "Stop bugging me. Don't make me sorry I came."

"I can't give you sympathy if I don't know what's going on," Maggie told her more gently.

"I don't want sympathy. I want you to leave me alone. I can handle this."

"Whatever *this* is," Maggie said sarcastically. "Sorry. No can do. You wouldn't leave me alone if you thought I was in trouble, would you?" She paused, then feigned a sudden awakening. "Oh, wait, that's why you claim to be here, because I'm in trouble."

"Well, aren't you?"

"No, and we're not going down that road right now. Are Mom and Dad okay?"

"Never better," Ashley said, looking perplexed by Maggie's abrupt change of topic.

"And Jo's okay?"

"Our little sister is perfectly fine."

"Your love life go south?"

"Who has time for a love life?" Ashley responded wryly.

"Okay, that leaves work," Maggie surmised. "Has something gone wrong with a case?"

For an instant Ashley looked disconcerted, as if she hadn't expected Maggie to come up with that one, when the truth was that it was the most obvious one of all. Work was all Ashley ever worried about.

"I'm just a little concerned about a case," Ashley said, which in her world was tantamount to admitting she was terrified.

"Aren't you prepared?"

Ashley gave her a derisive look. "I'm always prepared."

"Then why are you worried?"

"Honestly, I can't get into it."

"It's not as if I'll blab to anyone."

"I know, but it would violate all sorts of confidentiality stuff if I talked to you about this. Don't worry. I'm sure everything will turn out just fine. I just needed to get away for a couple of days to clear my head and make sure I'm ready to go into court next week."

"You're going to knock their socks off," Maggie reassured her. "You always do."

Ashley gave her a weak smile. "I wonder if that's always such a good thing?"

"Meaning?"

"Nothing. Don't mind me." She stood up, leaned down and gave Maggie a kiss on her forehead. "Thanks for the pep talk. I'm going to bed. I love you."

"Love you, too," Maggie replied, staring after her, her heart aching. Something was obviously tormenting Ashley about this case. The fact that she'd even come to Virginia days before trial spoke volumes. But Maggie knew better than to think her sister would open up any more than she had.

She wished there was something she could do, but in an odd way, maybe she had. She'd given Ashley a chance to obsess over the relationship Maggie was having with Rick. Maybe that was just the distraction her sister needed.

If so, Maggie would just have to put up with all the annoying questions for another day or two. She just had to pray that Rick would be equally resilient and understanding.

11

"Would you mind going out to the orchard on your own this morning?" Maggie asked, when Rick called first thing in the morning.

"Be still, my heart," he said with exaggerated shock. "I surely must be imagining things. Maggie D'Angelo, the ultimate control freak, is actually giving up a chance to supervise my work?"

"Very funny. I want to spend some more time with Ashley."

Rick instantly caught the somber note in her voice. "Did you make any progress with her last night? Did she open up after I left?"

Maggie sighed wearily. "Not much. I just know it has to do with work, but that was pretty much a given. Beyond that, she won't talk about it."

"And you think she will today?"

"Probably not, but I have to give it another try. How about meeting us for lunch at the café in Irvington?"

"Sure. That'll work, if you can make it a late lunch, say, around one."

"Perfect."

"Good luck with Ashley. She's lucky to have you."

Maggie laughed. "She'd probably disagree. She's not used to being on the receiving end of so many probing questions."

"Good at dishing it out, not so good at taking it?" he said. "I can hardly wait to see if you're still speaking to each other by lunchtime. See you."

After he'd hung up, he realized he was relieved to have the morning to himself. He could use some time to absorb all these new feelings he was starting to have about her, about being drawn into her loving, if somewhat complicated, family.

Turning off the highway onto the winding driveway that cut through acres of apple trees heavy with fruit, he felt almost as if he were coming home. It was an odd sensation, one he'd certainly never experienced going back to any of the increasingly decrepit places he'd shared with his mother. In fact the only sensation he had to compare it to was the way it felt walking into Rose Cottage and finding Maggie waiting for him with a warm smile and a seductive glint in her eyes.

What the devil was wrong with him lately? He didn't do the home-and-hearth thing. So why was he suddenly going all soft at the sight of a rambling farmhouse or at the prospect of seeing a couple of old-timers he'd known only a few days? Did it have something to do with the stability they represented? Did he envy them for having lived in the same place all these years, while he'd been like a rolling stone, always on the move?

Or was it the love he truly envied? Were they the reason he was looking at his relationship with Maggie as something other than his usual lighthearted fling? No, he'd been thinking along those lines when he'd come to Virginia chasing after her. He'd just been fighting the implication of his determination to find her. He'd deliberately blamed it on the challenge she represented, rather than on the growing need he felt to be with her.

He was still sitting in the car pondering that when a sharp rap on the window startled him. He looked up to see Matthew staring at him, his expression quizzical.

"You okay, son?"

Son! How often had he subconsciously longed for someone to call him that with so much caring in his voice? That it was Matthew Keller, a virtual stranger, who imbued the word with its first real meaning for him made Rick smile. "Never better," he said. "Just woolgathering, I guess." He got out of the car and reached back inside for his camera and lighting equipment.

Matthew took a few pieces out of his hands, all the while studying him intently. "This woolgathering, does it have anything to do with the fact that Maggie's not with you? You two have a fight?"

"Not at all, though I ought to be mad as heck at her for nearly destroying my car last night." He told Matthew the story about her ill-advised attempt to drive her sister home. "Thankfully they never got out of the driveway," he said, summing up.

"Good thing one of those girls has some sense," Max said. "Not surprised to hear it's Melanie, either. She's been a real good influence for Mike and little Jessie. That child sure did need a mama's touch. Sally says she actually sits still for Sunday school now. Used to be she was hell on wheels, if you'll pardon my language."

He gave Rick a sly look. "I imagine Maggie could help a man settle down the same way, once she put her mind to it."

Rick frowned at him. "Don't start meddling in my life, old man," he said without rancor. Truthfully, it was kind of nice to have someone who gave a damn about his happiness.

"Someone needs to talk sense to you," Matthew said, undaunted. "Sally and I think you two are wasting time, when it's obvious to anyone how crazy in love you are."

"I don't know where you got that idea," Rick said, still determined to cling to the illusion that what he and Maggie had was just another fling. "I don't know the first thing about love."

Matthew chuckled. "Maybe that explains why you can't recognize it when it smacks you square in the face."

Rick flatly refused to go one step further down that road with Matthew, even though he'd been wrestling with precisely that issue only moments before.

"You going to help me get set up down in the orchard this morning or are you going to go on and on about something that's none of your business?" he asked irritably.

Matthew surveyed him with undisguised amusement. "Lucky for you, I can do both. Sally will be along in a bit, too. She has a few opinions she'd like to share."

Rick groaned. "Just what I need."

"I know you're being sarcastic, son, but it seems to me it *is* what you need, a little wisdom from some folks who've seen a thing or two. Love's rare enough. It ought not to be squandered when it does come along."

"I'll keep that in mind," Rick promised. "If you'll drop the subject."

Matthew studied him intently, then nodded. "I'll leave it alone for now," he said. A glint of pure mischief sparkled in his eyes. "Can't speak for Sally, though. The woman has a mind of her own. Says whatever's on it, too. She's a lot like your Maggie, as a matter of fact."

"She is not *my* Maggie," Rick protested halfheartedly.

"Which just proves what a fool you are," Matthew

scolded, striding past him with the gait of a much younger man. "In my day, I'd have made damn sure she was mine by now."

Rick watched him go with a mix of relief and admiration. He was having enough trouble balancing what his heart and body apparently wanted with what his head told him made sense. He didn't need a sentimental old man—or his outspoken wife—making the waters any murkier than they already were.

Maggie's gaze kept drifting toward the door of the café. Rick was late. She wasn't all that surprised, since he tended to lose track of time when he was working, but it was apparent Ashley was turning this into another black mark against him. She probably had them all listed in her day planner, ready to cite at the first opportunity. So far this morning, though, Maggie hadn't given her a minute to head down that particular road.

"He'll be here," Maggie finally said defensively, even though Ashley hadn't uttered a word.

"Whatever you say. I think we should go ahead and order, though."

Maggie was smart enough to figure out the unspoken message, that they might starve to death if they went on waiting for a man who most likely wasn't going to show up. "You order, if you're hungry. I'll wait a few more minutes."

"You could call him," Ashley suggested. "See if he's on his way at least."

"He said he'd be here," Maggie said. "If he is still at the orchard, it's because he's still working. Interrupting him will only make him later."

"Up to you," her sister said, beckoning to the waitress.

"Could I get a chef's salad, please? Ranch dressing on the side. And more iced tea when you have a minute."

"Sure thing." The waitress glanced at Maggie. "You ready to order?"

"I'm going to wait a few more minutes. We're still expecting someone. I would like more tea, though."

"I'll bring that in a sec," the waitress promised. "And if you're waiting for that drop-dead gorgeous photographer with the fancy sports car, he just pulled into a space down the block." She sighed dramatically. "What I wouldn't give to have a man like that coming in here for me."

Ignoring the wistfulness in the woman's voice, Maggie peered out the window. Sure enough, Rick was heading their way. Undeniable relief spread through her. Now maybe Ashley would quit with the pitying looks. Heck, maybe her own stomach would stop tying itself into knots.

"Sorry, I'm late," Rick apologized, sliding into the booth next to Maggie. He gave her thigh a surreptitious squeeze under the table. "Matthew and Sally were very chatty this morning."

"Oh? What was on their minds?"

He grinned at her. "You and me."

"Oh, no," Maggie said with a groan. "How bad was it?"

"Depends on how you feel about being called a damn fool as many times as I was," he said. "They think I'm wasting too much time. I have a hunch if we said the word, Sally could have our wedding planned by August."

Maggie felt her cheeks flooding with heat.

"Really?" Ashley said, looking fascinated. She shoved aside the salad the waitress had just brought and planted her elbows on the table, her steady gaze on Rick's face. "What did you say to all this unsolicited interference?"

"I told them to mind their own business." He shrugged. "They declined. It took a while to hear them out."

Maggie regarded him with surprise. "I'm amazed you didn't lose your cool."

"Why would I? I like them. And they're just interested in seeing us happy." He gave her an embarrassed grin. "First time in my life anybody's worried about me."

"As warm and fuzzy as I'm sure that made you feel," Ashley said with a bite in her voice, "you're not buying a word they said, are you? Are you just playing games with my sister?"

Maggie frowned at her. "Butt out, sis."

"How can I sit by and watch you get hurt? He's spelled it out for you, Maggie. He's not interested in anything permanent."

"Who says I am?" Maggie retorted, unhappy with the whole turn the conversation had taken. This was between her and Rick, not between the two of them and everyone they knew. "You're not managing your own life all that well lately. Maybe you should concentrate on that and leave mine alone."

Rick stared at her in obvious shock that she would take a potshot at her sister.

"Hey, slow down, Maggie," he soothed. "It's no big deal. Your sister's just expressing an opinion. She's entitled to do that."

"Well, it's an opinion I don't care to hear," Maggie insisted.

Ashley glowered at her. "Well, pardon me all to hell. I think I'll leave you two to your lunch."

"But you haven't even touched your salad," Rick said, clearly distressed by the argument.

"Doesn't matter. I need some air."

She slid out of the booth and stalked off, leaving

Maggie feeling rotten. She uttered a sigh of belated regret. "Okay, okay, you don't need to say it. I shouldn't have said what I did about her life. Sometimes that kind of remark is the only way to get Ashley to shut up once she's on a self-righteous roll. Still, I know it was a low blow, and I shouldn't have done it."

"So why did you?" Rick asked, studying her with obvious curiosity. "Is it because you're afraid she's right?"

She took a very long time before answering. "Maybe," she admitted eventually.

"Do you want to settle down?"

"Someday, sure," she said at once.

"With me?"

She regarded him with confusion. "I don't know. It's too soon."

He gave a nod of satisfaction. "My feeling exactly. So, what do you say we stop worrying about everyone else's opinion and trust our own guts?"

She gave him a halfhearted smile. "Deal, though I think you're deluding yourself if you think it will be that easy."

"Could be," he admitted, then grinned. "Want to forget about eating healthy and split a hot-fudge sundae with me?"

She felt the tension in her shoulders easing at last. If Rick wasn't uptight over all the interference, why should she be?

"No," she said at once, then grinned back at him. "I want my own."

He leaned over and touched his lips to hers. "You've got it." His gaze locked on hers. "As long as I get to lick away whatever chocolate happens to stray."

"In that case, we probably ought to have this sundae at home."

"No way. Having it right here where we can't do so much fooling around is better," he said, his expression mischievous. "A little restraint and anticipation can be very good things."

"Something tells me you've raised them both to an art form."

"Not yet," he replied. "But I'm working on it. We can consider the next half hour or so to be practice. You can decide if I'm getting any better."

Ashley came back just as Rick's tongue touched a dribble of chocolate at the corner of Maggie's lips. Ashley whipped a napkin out of the dispenser and shoved it at Maggie.

"Have you forgotten what these are for?" she asked testily.

"Oh, don't be stuffy," Maggie chided, then gave her sister an apologetic look. "I'm sorry about what I said earlier. I do love it that you care about me."

Ashley's expression softened at once. "I know."

"But I'm a big girl. You have to trust my instincts," Maggie reminded her.

Ashley sighed. "I know that, too. It's just that it's so much harder, because the stakes are so huge. Your entire future's on the line."

Rick laughed but the sound didn't have a lot of good humor in it. "Pour on the pressure why don't you?"

Ashley gave him a huge, obviously phony smile. "You ain't seen nothing yet."

Rick regarded her with amusement. "Are you threatening me, counselor?"

"Indeed I am," Ashley replied sweetly.

Maggie decided enough was enough. "Okay, you two, that's it. From now on any discussion of my relationship with Rick is off-limits." She leveled a look into Ashley's eyes. "Are we clear?"

"Absolutely," her sister said, though she didn't look particularly daunted. "*I* won't say another word."

"Good," Maggie said, still eyeing her suspiciously. "Why are you being so agreeable all of a sudden?"

Ashley glanced past her and beamed. "Oh, look who's here. And just in time, too," she said cheerfully.

Maggie's gaze shot to Melanie, who immediately crowded into the booth next to Ashley.

"The rules apply to her, too," Maggie said, instantly suspicious that Melanie had been called in as reinforcement.

Melanie looked blank. "What rules?"

"Our sister is violating the First Amendment of the Constitution," Ashley declared. "She is trying to limit our freedom of speech. We're not to say another word about her relationship with Rick."

Melanie glanced at Rick. "You okay with that?"

He grinned. "I'm loving it."

Ashley shook her head. "And I thought all you media types were great defenders of freedom of speech, freedom of the press and so on," she muttered.

"We are," he said cheerfully. "As long as it doesn't cross the line into invasion of privacy."

Maggie slapped his hand in a high five. "Good one," she enthused. She turned back to her sister. "Well, hotshot attorney, what do you have to say to that?"

Ashley held up her hands in a gesture of surrender. "You win. We will remain silent on the previously discussed topic. For now, anyway." She peered at the remains of their sundaes. "Those look decadent. What do you say, Melanie? Want to split one?"

"Absolutely," Melanie said eagerly, then gave Maggie

a sly look. "As long as they're buying. There ought to be some perks in return for our silence."

"Deal," Rick said at once. "Believe me, one sundae is a small price to pay for getting you two off our backs."

Melanie got a devilish glint in her eyes. "You may not feel that way when you see what I intend to order." She gestured toward the remains of their sundaes. "Those were nothing compared to the hot-fudge volcano Ashley and I are going to share. You in, Ashley?"

"Absolutely," Ashley said without hesitation.

Melanie placed the order, then sat back with a smug expression that Maggie thought was the tiniest bit worrisome.

When the waitress finally arrived with the dessert, she felt her jaw drop. Even Ashley, who could consume ice cream like a champ, looked stunned. Rick simply laughed.

"Oh, this is going to be good," he said. "Now remember what your mama no doubt taught you girls. You have to clean your plate."

"Not in a million years," Ashley muttered, but she gamely picked up a spoon and dug into the three-inch swirl of whipped cream that topped what must have been an entire quart of ice cream in a sea of hot fudge.

Melanie attacked the dessert from the opposite side.

Maggie turned to Rick. "I'm betting they won't eat half of that. What do you think?"

He studied Melanie, then Ashley. "I say they're going to scrape the bowl clean."

"No way."

"I've got a ticket to Paris for you that says they will," he said. "They quit and you're on your way."

Maggie stared at him with bemusement. A trip to Paris? The man definitely played hardball. She'd always wanted to go to Paris. Had she ever told him that or had he guessed? Now she had to put something on the line that she knew he wanted.

"I have a new state-of-the-art digital camera that says they won't," Maggie said. "If they do finish, it's yours."

She glanced across the table to see Ashley and Melanie regarding each other in some sort of silent, sisterly communication. Normally Maggie could read the two of them easily, but right now she was hard-pressed to say what they were thinking. Would they leave some ice cream in the bowl out of sisterly loyalty to her and to spite Rick? Would they see how badly she really wanted to go to Paris and quit? Or would they want to accept Rick's challenge and eat every bite, even if it made them both sick as dogs?

Ashley chuckled. "They've made it interesting, haven't they?" she said to Melanie.

"For themselves," Melanie agreed. "What about us? What's it worth to either of you for us to throw this game?"

Maggie frowned at her. "You're trying to bribe us?"

"I prefer to think of it as an incentive," Melanie replied cheerfully, even as she took another bite of the gigantic sundae.

She gave an exaggerated pat to her stomach. "Yum, this is good, but I'm getting full. How about you, Ashley?"

Ashley shot an expectant look at Rick. "I'm beginning to get a little full myself."

He chuckled. "Okay, if I win, you get a free family portrait, Melanie." His grin spread as he turned to Ashley. "And you get a glamour shot."

Ashley laughed. "Okay, Melanie, dig in."

Maggie frowned at them. "Hey, what about me, you

two? I'm your sister. Can you be bought off with a couple of snapshots?"

"Snapshots?" Rick said indignantly.

"Uh-oh," Melanie murmured. "Eat up before it melts, Ashley. Things are about to get a little hot in here."

"You have no idea," Rick confirmed, frowning at Maggie. "I do not take snapshots."

"Oh, that's right," Maggie taunted. "You're the world-famous fashion photographer who built his reputation on taking pictures of pretty women. How hard can that be? The scenery's incredible. They're beautiful. All you really need to do is click the shutter and try not to let the camera shake, isn't that right?"

She saw the fire in Rick's eyes and realized she might have gone the teensiest bit too far. He leaned close, his breath whispering against her cheek. She shivered.

"Take that back," he said.

Maggie held her ground, even though her stomach was doing somersaults. "No."

"Take it back."

"Or what?" she challenged.

His eyes flashed with something dark and dangerous. Maggie held her breath. Suddenly he laughed.

"God, you're amazing," he whispered right before he closed his mouth over hers.

Maggie went up in flames right there with her open-mouthed sisters and half the town looking on. She wove her fingers into Rick's hair and hung on tight as the breath left her lungs and the world tilted on its axis.

"Holy kamoley," she whispered when he finally released her.

"Ditto," Ashley and Melanie echoed, their dripping spoons still suspended in midair.

Rick gave the two of them an amused glance. "Your ice cream's melting."

"Uh-huh," Ashley said weakly.

Looking dazed, Melanie dutifully shoved another bite of sundae into her mouth. "I really need to go find Mike," she said.

Maggie bit back a smile. "Oh, why is that? Haven't you ever seen two people kissing before?"

"Sure," Melanie said. "But only once like that. It was in a movie. I went looking for Mike then, too." She stepped out of the booth. "Got to go."

Rick frowned at her. "What about the rest of the sundae?"

"Who gives a damn about that?" Melanie said. "And if you lost the bet, it's your own fault."

"I agree," Ashley said, pushing away the bowl. "I'm going home to take an icy shower."

As they walked out of the café, Rick stared after them with a perplexed expression. "How did that go so wrong?"

Maggie laughed. "Believe me, there was nothing wrong with that kiss."

"But up until that moment, they were going to let me win the bet, weren't they?" Rick asked. "They were going to eat every last spoonful of that sundae."

"That was my take on it," Maggie agreed.

"I guess you won," he said, not sounding all that dismayed about it.

"You're conceding defeat just like that?"

"You won the bet. When do you want to go to Paris?"

The question totally flustered her. She didn't want to go to the most romantic city in the world alone, and he hadn't said a word about coming with her. "I can't go to Paris right now. I have work to do."

"It's your trip. You pick a date and I'll get the tickets."

Tickets, she noted with a little leap of her pulse. Plural. "You're coming, too?"

He laughed. "You didn't think I'd let you go off to meet all those sexy Frenchmen without me along, did you?"

Maggie wanted to leap from the booth and do a little victory dance, but that would be too crass. She wanted to appear cool and blasé about the whole thing.

"Let me check my calendar and get back to you," she said. "If you're really serious, that is."

His gaze held hers. "Oh, I'm serious, Maggie. I want to show you Paris."

When he looked at her like that, when he made her knees go weak, Maggie realized there was only one thing on earth that could make this whole thing better…if they were going to Paris on their honeymoon.

12

Rick was struck by a thoroughly unexpected and way too
beguiling image of standing in the moonlight at the foot
of the Eiffel Tower with Maggie in his arms. He'd never
planned a trip with a woman before. Not that he hadn't
been with women in exotic locales, but usually it was
work that had taken them there and whatever romance
had been on the agenda had been spontaneous. This was
almost like planning...what?

A honeymoon.

The completely outrageous thought popped into his
head and refused to die, even though a part of him was
screaming no, no, no, so loudly he was surprised the
entire restaurant couldn't hear it. He glanced at Maggie
to see if she had any idea what was going on in his head.
Maybe she did, maybe she didn't, but she was looking a
little dazed herself at the moment.

"Have you ever been to Paris?" he asked, his voice
oddly choked.

She shook her head. "You?"

"Several times."

"Then you'll be able to show me all the sights."

"All of them," he agreed. But none would be more

stunning than she would be, her eyes lit up in excitement, her cheeks pink with anticipation. He wanted to book the trip right now, while they were still together. Who knew where either of them would be in a few months or even a few weeks? She could be back in Boston. He could be on assignment on the other side of the world. Parting seemed inevitable, though he was far more unhappy about it than he could ever have imagined he would be.

He met her gaze. "Let's book this now," he said with a sudden sense of urgency.

"Now?"

"Why not?"

"I have a deadline. I'm not like you. I don't get to pick and choose when I work. I have to plan vacations."

"You didn't plan this one," he reminded her.

"That's because it's more like a working vacation, which is why you're doing that photo shoot for me, remember? And speaking of that, how did things go this morning?"

"Great, I think," he said, accepting the change of subject with resignation. She obviously wasn't going to bend on the trip, at least not now. "I'm going to try to set up a makeshift darkroom this afternoon and see what I've got. It's not an ideal situation. I'd prefer to go back to my studio to do this, but I think we'll be okay."

The light promptly went out of Maggie's eyes. "If you'd prefer to go back to Boston, it's okay," she said, sounding resigned.

At yet more evidence that she was always prepared for him to bolt on her, he brought her icy hand to his lips and kissed her knuckles. "Stop that," he ordered gently. "I would not prefer to go back to Boston. The only place I want to go right now is Paris, with you. Didn't I make that clear?"

"But—"

He cut off whatever objection she was about to utter. "Think about it, Maggie. We could leave as soon as you turn the material in. There are always going to be deadlines. We'll get back in time for you to meet the next one, or you can work up an idea in Paris. Next to art, food is one of the greatest contributions the French have made to the world."

She regarded him with a puzzled look. "Is there some reason you're so determined to go now?"

He tried to find a careful way to phrase it. "If we put it off, who knows what will come along to delay the trip later? We might never go."

"In other words, we might break up."

He hated that she'd jumped to that conclusion. It was exactly what he'd hoped to avoid. "I didn't say that," he insisted.

"But it's what you were thinking," she said with obvious confidence. "Are you already planning a way to end things with me? Is the trip to Paris some sort of consolation prize?"

"No," he said, shocked that she would interpret it like that. He searched for a more palatable explanation. "It's just that I'm a seize-the-moment man."

"So you like to remind me every chance you get. But aren't you also the man who told me less than an hour ago that there's a lot to be said for restraint and anticipation?"

"Yes, but—"

Now she cut him off. "I want to anticipate going to Paris with you, Rick. I don't want some whirlwind trip that will start and end before I've even had a chance to think about it. I've always been way too impulsive. I'm trying to slow things down. I need to learn to savor what's going on in my life, not rush on to the next thing."

To his regret, Rick saw her point. Until the last couple of weeks, he'd never spent time savoring a relationship. He'd never had one last long enough for that.

"Okay," he relented. "Paris will just have to wait."

"Don't look so glum," she chided, her eyes sparkling with excitement. "That doesn't mean we can't get a zillon brochures and guidebooks and spend every evening arguing over what we want to do when we get there. For instance, I'd like to take some cooking classes. I'll bet you'd prefer to see a photography exhibit."

"Is that supposed to be some sort of big deal?" he asked, laughing despite himself. "We can do both."

"You know what I mean," she countered. "We're not going to be able to do everything. We're going to have to prioritize and compromise."

"And take all the spontaneity out of the trip," he guessed.

"No way," she said, snuggling closer to him in the booth. "We can make love spontaneously whenever the mood strikes."

He gazed down into her passion-darkened eyes. "In that case, I think I'll book a five-star hotel with excellent room service."

Maggie chuckled. "You can scrap that notion right now, Flannery. We're talking about Paris. I want to see it."

He grinned. "I'll get a room with a view."

She nodded, her expression suddenly thoughtful. "That could work."

Rick's grin spread. "How about a little of that spontaneous sex back at your place right now?"

"My sister's there," she reminded him with undisguised

regret. "And to be honest, I think we've already shocked her enough for one day."

He sighed dramatically. "Too bad."

"It really is," she said. "But she'll be gone tomorrow."

"What time?"

"Early, I imagine, since that case she's so worried about starts on Monday. I'll call you the minute she's out the door."

Rick didn't want to wait a second longer than necessary. "Call me when she's packing the car," he replied, not even trying to hide his eagerness. "I'll get a head start."

"And risk one more confrontation?"

"Why not? We've done okay so far. Besides, Ashley's not the kind of woman you want to get the idea that she has you running scared."

"You understand her very well."

"It's not that hard. Your sister is like every other ambitious overachiever I've ever met. She's totally focused and absolutely driven. She needs to learn to loosen up before that spring that's wound so tight snaps on her."

"I couldn't agree more," Maggie said. "She's the one who reminded the rest of us that Rose Cottage is the ideal place to unwind. She needs to take her own advice and spend some time here. She needs an entire month at least."

Rick chuckled. "I'll tack a week in Italy onto our trip, if you can get her to agree to that."

Maggie grinned. "Now you've made it interesting. I'll get to work on her tonight. With all these bets you're making lately, I could turn out to be a very expensive date."

"I'm not worried. You can let me know how much success you had with your sister when I see you in the morning."

"I'm very persuasive," she told him. "You, of all people, should know that."

"But I'm putty in your hands," Rick retorted. "Your sister's made of cast iron."

"Steel," Maggie corrected.

Rick regarded her quizzically. "Steel?"

"As in steel magnolia. Ashley may not be Southern like our mother, but she inherited that stubborn streak and willfulness. Did I ever tell you what an admirer our mother was of *Gone With the Wind?* Thus our names. I was named for the author. Jo's the only one who escaped. Her name came from *Little Women.* We figured that was because mother saw herself as Scarlett, so she wasn't about to name one of us that."

Rick nodded. He could see that the steel magnolia description fit Ashley perfectly. "Then I really don't have a thing to worry about, do I? Ashley will spend a month at Rose Cottage when we finally have scientific proof that the moon is made of green cheese."

"Don't be so sure of yourself," Maggie said. "I might have a few tricks up my sleeve you don't know about."

"I certainly hope so," Rick said enthusiastically. "Maybe you can show me one tomorrow."

Maggie shook her head. "Do you ever think about anything besides sex?"

"Sure," he said easily. "Photography and my makeshift darkroom are calling me right now, in fact."

"Will you have some pictures for me to look at in the morning?"

"Sure." He winked at her. "But not till after we've done some catching up."

"Catching up?" she asked, her expression innocent. "Do you think we'll have a lot to talk about less than twenty-four hours from now?"

"Who's going to be talking?" he asked, then tossed some cash on the table to pay for all those sundaes.

"Like I said, a one-track mind," she commented, as she slid past him.

Rick was pretty sure the space wasn't half as narrow as she pretended it was. She'd just wanted a chance to brush those delectable hips of hers against him. He supposed she was pleased to note that it had the desired effect. He was instantly hard as a rock.

He caught her arm and leaned down to whisper in her ear. "You're playing with fire, Maggie."

She beamed up at him, an impish gleam in her eyes. "I know. See you in the morning."

"Or sooner."

"Oh?"

"Who knows? It might be kind of fun to try sneaking past Ashley's room in the middle of the night."

"Don't even think about it," Maggie warned, looking worried.

Rick laughed. "Now look what you've done. You've turned it into a challenge."

"Everything's a challenge to you, if it suits your purpose," she remarked, then strode off in the direction of her car.

Rick stared after her. She was right. Where she was concerned, just about everything was a challenge. He couldn't recall the last time a woman had provided him with this much entertainment.

Rick spent the afternoon in the darkroom processing film and making a few prints from some of the best negatives. The photos were good, but he still didn't have the one shot that would take the layout from ordinary to extraordinary. He wanted something with both Sally and

Matthew in it, but so far Matthew had been stubbornly resistant to the idea.

Since he wasn't going to be seeing Maggie, he picked up the phone and called the Kellers. "Mind if I take a drive out there this evening?" he asked Sally.

"You'd be welcome," she said at once. "Come for supper, why don't you? Will Maggie be with you?"

"No, her sister's still here," he reminded Sally. "I think they have an evening of girl talk planned."

"Well, Matthew and I will be glad to save you from that. Drive on out now. I'll have dinner on the table in an hour. It's Matthew's favorite, chicken and dumplings."

"Sounds fabulous. I'm on my way."

By the time he got to the farmhouse, the sun was starting to drop in the western sky, splashing the orchard with a softer light than anything he'd seen so far. He regretted leaving his camera behind. It wasn't a mistake he would make again.

"Wish you'd stop trying to imagine the perfect picture and hurry up," Matthew grumbled from the doorway. "A man could starve around here waiting for you."

Rick chuckled. "I see you're in a cheerful frame of mind."

"Sally's had me moving things around again. The woman thinks the furniture shouldn't stay in the same place more than a month or two, then she gets a dang-fool notion to move it again."

Rick regarded him with worry. "You shouldn't be moving furniture."

Matthew uttered a derisive snort. "Tell that to my wife."

Rick intended to do just that. He walked into the kitchen and came to a full stop as the aroma of dinner hit him. The chicken and dumplings were bubbling on the stove, and if he wasn't mistaken, there was an apple pie in the oven. Sally was standing at the counter whipping potatoes by hand. Her face was flushed, but she gave him a welcoming smile.

"Don't you start in on me, young man. I heard what that man said to you, but it was Matthew's idea to move the sofa. Said it would give him a better view of the TV without the glare from the setting sun."

Rick turned back to Matthew. "Why didn't you say something this morning? I could have moved it for you."

"The day I can't push an old sofa around the room is the day I lie down in my bed and die."

"There's no sense in being foolish, though," Rick told him. "When help's around, there's nothing wrong with taking advantage of it."

"Oh, stop fussing about the sofa, both of you," Matthew grumbled. "If you want to worry about something, worry about Sally and her refusal to get that slippery rug away from the foot of the stairs. One of us is going to slide right out the front door one of these days, you mark my words."

Sally gave him an impatient look. "That rug is perfectly fine. It's been there twenty years, and neither of us have fallen yet."

Rick looked from one to the other, expecting to find sparks of real anger about to flare into something ugly, but then Matthew walked over and pressed a hard kiss to his wife's mouth.

"Stubborn old woman," he said gently.

"Mule-headed old coot," she retorted just as affectionately.

Rick bit back a sigh. So, this was what it was like to

grow old with someone, to know them so well that the taunting and bickering ended in a kiss, not a free-for-all.

He wondered if his mother, whom he hadn't seen in years now, had ever learned that lesson. Probably not. She'd gotten too used to arguments being settled with fists and nothing he'd ever said to her or tried to do to protect her had ever been enough to get her to change the sort of relationships she had. For years it had broken his heart, but when he'd realized he couldn't save her, he'd left home to save himself.

He glanced across the room to see Sally studying him with a worried frown.

"What's on your mind?" she asked him.

"Just thinking about things I couldn't change," he said.

"What's that mean?" Matthew asked, as they sat down for dinner.

"Don't push the boy," Sally said. "He'll tell us as much as he's willing to."

"Thank you," Rick said gratefully. "It's not something I intend to discuss. It'll only ruin our dinner."

"You ever told Maggie?" Sally asked.

He shook his head. "Some, but I've never told anyone all of it. Talking won't change anything." The beatings that had shaped his early life were a secret no one would ever know.

"But it might help a woman understand the kind of man you are," Sally insisted. "Something tells me you're an enigma to Maggie, close as you are. That's not right. If the two of you plan to be together when you're as old as Matthew and me, you have to learn to share the important things. You need to open up your heart, Rick. Let her inside."

She frowned when Rick opened his mouth to deny that he intended to stay with Maggie that long. Before he could utter a single word, Sally said, "Don't try telling me you don't have feelings for her or that you don't want a future with her, because I won't believe you. The two of you can barely keep your hands to yourselves."

"You have it all worked out, don't you?" he grumbled.

"Sally's a romantic at heart," Matthew confirmed. "You'd think all these years with me would have changed that."

"You know a thing or two about romance, old man," Sally retorted. "Don't even try to say otherwise."

Matthew chuckled. "I could give you some tips," he told Rick. "Plucked a flower for Sally every summer morning we've been married. Wintertime, I find some other ways to let her know I'm thinking about her when I come in the house at the end of the day."

"And what does Sally do for you?" Rick asked, absorbing the advice even though he'd just sworn he had no use for it.

"It's not a tit-for-tat kind of thing," Sally scolded.

Matthew's gaze rested on her face. "No, it's not, but all I ever craved was her smile and she blesses me with that every minute of the day." He shrugged. "Except, of course, when she's fussing at me."

He turned toward Rick. "Don't imagine you came out here tonight just to hear how we keep our marriage going." He leveled a knowing look into Rick's eyes. "Or did you?"

He hadn't, but it was an unexpected benefit. Rick could see that. He was beginning to think that enduring love was possible, even for a man like him who'd had so few examples to learn from.

Not that he intended to tell Matthew or Sally that.

If he did, he'd be listening to advice for the rest of the evening.

"Actually I came out here to talk you into getting into a picture with Sally," he told Matthew. "The story needs one of the two of you together."

Matthew frowned. "I'm not posing for you. Told you that from the get-go."

"You wouldn't have to. You two could go on about your business here in the kitchen or down in the orchard. You wouldn't even know I'm around. The shot will be something perfectly natural, not posed."

Matthew shook his head, his expression adamant. "No," he said flatly.

He'd left no room for argument, but Rick had one more trick up his sleeve. "What about letting me take a portrait for your kids? I'll bet they'd love that. If you like it and agree, then Maggie could also use it in the magazine."

"Come on, Matthew. Don't be an old fogy," Sally pleaded, looking excited. "Just think, we could have our picture taken by a man who's famous all over the world. The kids would get a real kick out of that."

"Don't you two start ganging up on me," Matthew grumbled. "I said no."

Sally reached over and covered his hand. "Please. For me."

Matthew returned her wistful gaze, his expression stubborn, but he finally heaved a sigh when there was no sign that Sally intended to relent. "Just tell me one thing. Would I have to wear a suit?"

Rick bit back a triumphant grin. "Absolutely not."

"Okay, then, I'll do it." He looked at Sally. "But only because it's something you want. I think the whole idea's crazy."

"It'll be something the kids will treasure long after we're gone," she corrected.

Matthew rolled his eyes. "It'll probably wind up in a drawer."

"You are such a cynic," she said. She looked at Rick hopefully. "I don't suppose you brought your camera with you tonight. We should do this while he's willing. Who knows what excuses he'll dream up by morning."

"No, sorry," Rick said. "I thought he was going to be a tougher sell. I'll come back first thing tomorrow, though." He thought of his plans to be at Maggie's as soon as Ashley hit the road. With luck, he would be able to get the shot he wanted and still be there right on time.

"It'll have to be after church," Sally told him. "We'll go to the early service and be home by ten."

"Don't bother bringing all those rolls of film like you did today and yesterday," Matthew said. "You get one chance to get it right."

Sally slapped him on the shoulder as she passed with the dirty dinner plates. "Rick will take as many as it takes," she said. "We don't want one with our eyes closed."

"It would suit me," Matthew insisted.

Rick stood up. "I think I'll leave you two to your squabbling," he said. "I'm going to need a good night's sleep. I have this cantankerous subject scheduled for tomorrow morning. I need to have all my wits about me."

"You talking about me?" Matthew asked.

"Who else would he be talking about?" Sally demanded. "You take this with you," she added, handing Rick a still-warm slice of pie wrapped in foil. "You might want a midnight snack."

"Thanks," Rick said, leaning down to give her weathered cheek a kiss. "See you in the morning."

"Drive safe, you hear."

Rick smiled at the motherly admonishment. "I will," he promised.

He left the house filled with contentment. Those two had given him so much in such a short time. Taking a perfect photograph that would capture who they were and the love they shared would be good for the magazine, but it would also be his way of giving something back to them.

13

Ashley seemed to be dragging her feet. Maggie had been so sure she'd be up and on the road by dawn, but it was almost 9:00 a.m. now and Ashley was still lingering over a cup of tea at the kitchen table.

Maggie regarded her with renewed concern. "I wish you'd tell me what's going on with this case. You're obviously dreading going into court tomorrow."

Ashley looked startled by her assessment, though why she should have been was a mystery. She'd been dropping clues since her arrival. Even her careful evasions were telling. It seemed evident to Maggie that her sister's silence was about more than lawyer-client confidentiality. She appeared to be weighing some sort of ethical dilemma.

"What makes you say that?" Ashley asked Maggie, her tone dull.

"For starters, the fact that you're still here, instead of halfway back to Boston."

"Are you anxious for me to go for some reason?" Ashley asked. "Are you expecting Rick any second? If I'm in the way, just say so."

Maggie clung to her patience by a thread. "This isn't about Rick," she insisted. "We're talking about you."

"I told you before, I can't talk about a case."

"I imagine it's something high profile enough to have been in the paper, since that's what you do. Just tell me the public information part," Maggie suggested. "Maybe I can figure out the rest."

Ashley frowned. "What's the point of playing guessing games? I'll deal with this, Maggie. It's my responsibility."

"We wouldn't have to play guessing games if you'd just cooperate," Maggie retorted impatiently. "I'm worried about you, dammit! Whatever this responsibility is, it's clear that it's too much for you."

Her sister merely shrugged off the concern. "Don't be absurd. I've handled far tougher stuff than this in my career. The case will be over in a couple of weeks, and I'll move on to something else."

Maggie shook her head. "Then let's talk about when the case ends. I think you should come here when it's over."

"Sure, why not?" Ashley agreed a little too readily. "If I can manage a few days, I will."

"Not for a few days," Maggie corrected. "A month, minimum."

Ashley stared at her incredulously. "You know that's impossible."

"Why? It's not like you don't have any vacation time," she reminded her sister. "You haven't taken one in five years. The law firm owes you."

"I have cases," Ashley protested.

"Hand them off. Isn't that one of the perks of being part of a huge firm? There are people around to back you up. Or if you don't want to hand the cases off, ask for continuances or whatever it is you lawyers do to stall things in court. You do it if it's to your client's benefit. Why not do it when it's to yours?"

"Why are you pushing this so hard?"

"Because it's obvious you're stressed out. You need a break. A real one. Even Rick noticed it."

"So of course it must be true," Ashley shot back sarcastically. "The man doesn't even know me."

"But he *is* a photographer. That makes him a rather keen observer of expressions and body language," Maggie replied.

"He sees what's in front of his lens. I doubt he sees beneath the surface of much."

Maggie regarded her with renewed impatience. "Don't try making this about Rick again. It's about you. Please, Ashley, just think about it. You need some time off. You've been working at full throttle ever since you joined that law firm. It's time for a break."

"Fine. Fine. I'll think about it. And since you think my presence here is making some sort of statement about my reluctance to go home, I guess I'll hit the road."

"You don't have to leave to prove something to me," Maggie said.

Ashley sighed. "I know. I have to leave because it's a long drive and there's a lot to do once I get home. You're right. I have been putting it off." She stood up and gave Maggie a fierce hug. "Thanks for caring so much. I'm sorry I'm being so impossible."

"You're always impossible," Maggie retorted, giving her a hard squeeze. "We all love you anyway."

Ashley linked her arm through Maggie's as they went to the car. "You have plans with Rick today?"

Maggie nodded. "He'll be over later."

"How much later? Five seconds after I'm gone?" Ashley asked, amusement finally twinkling in her eyes.

"If you're implying that you scared him off, you're wrong. He wanted me to call and let him know when you were getting ready so he could get here in time to say goodbye."

"Ah, then it's you who didn't want us bumping into each other again," Ashley teased.

"No, it's you who puttered around so I couldn't figure out when to call," Maggie responded.

Ashley's expression sobered. "Be careful, Maggie. Don't let him break your heart. I think he cares about you. I just don't think he's capable of making a commitment."

"He won't break my heart," Maggie said, even though it might be wishful thinking on her part.

"If he does, I'll hunt him down for you."

Maggie laughed. "I know you would, too. We all know you're always in our corner. Just don't forget that we're in yours, too."

"I won't," Ashley promised, then climbed behind the wheel and started the engine. "I'll call you when I get home."

Maggie stood back and watched her sister pull out onto the road. Ashley gave her one more jaunty wave, then disappeared from view.

Back inside, Maggie couldn't shake the feeling that she should have done more for her sister. But how could she do anything for a woman who wouldn't talk about what was really bothering her? She reached for the phone, intending to call Rick, but dialed Melanie instead.

"Hey, sis, I just called to let you know that Ashley's gone," she said when she got the answering machine. "I'm worried about her. Call me when you get in."

She hung up, then dialed Rick, but got no answer on his cell or at the B and B.

"That's odd," she murmured, especially given how anxious he'd been to get over here today once Ashley was out of the house.

Still, for once she didn't immediately obsess about whether he'd run out on her. Instead, she was grateful that his absence gave her some time to think about her sister.

She poured herself a glass of iced tea, then walked out to the swing facing the bay. There was a hint of a breeze in the shade, but the air was muggy. There would more than likely be thunderstorms by afternoon. She could already see the dark clouds gathering. She shivered at the ominous sight. She'd never liked storms, but it was more than that. She had this feeling that something bad was about to happen. With Rick nowhere to be found and her sister on the highway, it was not the kind of thinking she wanted to pursue.

She needed a distraction. Maybe she'd take a drive out to the orchard and talk to Sally. If she hurried, she could probably beat out the storm.

She rushed inside, left her empty glass on the counter, then grabbed her keys and purse. She considered calling first, then decided to take a chance. The Kellers didn't stand on ceremony. If they were busy, she simply wouldn't stay.

As she got behind the wheel of her car, she took one more look at the darkening skies and wondered if she was nuts to be heading out there now.

"Oh, stop being a sissy," she muttered, even though the ominous feeling was still present. More often than not, she worried about things that never happened. Surely it would be that way today, too.

* * *

When Rick got back from grabbing breakfast at the café in Irvington, he tried to call Maggie to let her know that he was going to the orchard before coming by, but there was no answer. Maybe she and Ashley had gone out or maybe Maggie was outside. He cursed the fact that she didn't have an answering machine in the house. She claimed they all thought of Rose Cottage as a refuge and that the voice mail on her cell phone was sufficient.

He tried her cell phone, but got an all-too-familiar out-of-range message. He'd just have to keep trying. He doubted she'd be away from the house for long.

Glancing toward the sky, he noticed the threatening clouds rolling in and concluded that he'd be taking his pictures of Matthew and Sally indoors. That suited him fine. They were most at home in the kitchen or at least that's where he envisioned them at the start and end of each and every day.

Filled with the kind of anticipation he rarely felt on his usual fashion shoots anymore, Rick turned into the rutted driveway at the orchard. But as he neared the house, anticipation turned to dread at the sight of an obviously frantic Matthew waving him down.

"Hurry, son," Matthew hollered. "Sally's taken a spill. Looks to me like she's broken her hip. Got a nasty bump on her head, too. I can't get her to come around."

Rick bolted from the car even as the engine died. "Where is she? Have you called an ambulance?"

"About twenty minutes ago. The rescue squad's on its way," he told Rick. "But it's bound to be another few minutes by the time they round up a crew and get clear out here."

Rick paused and searched Matthew's face. The old

man's color wasn't good. He looked as if he might pass out. "You okay?"

As expected, Matthew waved off his concern. "Don't worry about me, boy. It's Sally we need to think about."

"Where'd she fall?"

"Tripped over that blasted area rug at the foot of the stairs," Matthew said. "Told her the dang thing was a hazard, but would she listen? Of course not. She thought it was pretty there and that was that. You heard her just last night. I'll wager she wouldn't say the same thing now."

Rick's heart took a dive at the sight of Sally looking pale and far too still where she lay at the foot of the stairs. "You sure she didn't fall down the steps?" he asked Matthew, checking for a pulse and touching a hand to her wrinkled cheek.

Her heartbeat was steady enough, her skin warm enough, but she looked like a crumpled rag doll lying there. Rick felt his heart clench with something akin to panic. He couldn't lose her. One look at Matthew's stricken face and he amended, *they* couldn't lose her. If Sally had come to mean a lot to him, it was still nothing compared to what she meant to the strong man hunkered down beside her, his cheeks damp with tears.

"No, she didn't tumble down the steps," Matthew assured him. "We'd just come in from church. She was fussing about getting everything ready for you. I was coming round the corner from the kitchen and saw that dang rug shoot out from under her. Tried to catch her, but she went down like a rock." He sat on the bottom step and took her hand. His fingers trembled visibly. "Dang it, Sally. You wake up now. It's not right, you givin' me a scare like this."

Rick had never felt so helpless in his life. He knew the basics of first aid, knew enough not to try to move her, but what else could he do? There had to be something. What if she went into shock before the ambulance arrived?

"You have a blanket around here?" he asked Matthew.

Matthew stared up at him in confusion. "A blanket? It must be ninety out there today."

"Trust me, it'll help," Rick said.

"Her favorite throw's on the sofa. It's the blue one Ellen sent up from Atlanta last Christmas."

Rick found it, folded up neat as a pin on the back of the sofa. As he stepped back into the foyer, he could hear the ambulance siren in the distance.

"Wrap this around her," he instructed Matthew. "I'll go meet the ambulance."

He was about to head outside, but Matthew grabbed his hand. "I'm mighty glad you turned up when you did, son."

Rick stared at him, struck by the genuine relief and affection in Matthew's eyes. "I haven't done anything."

"You were here when we needed you. That's what counts. I won't forget that."

For the next hour there was a flurry of activity as the paramedics brought Sally around, then transported her to the hospital. Rick drove an unusually silent Matthew to meet them there.

"She's going to be okay," he reassured Matthew as they walked through the emergency-room doors.

Matthew nodded, his gaze already searching for some sign of his wife. "Has to be," he said tersely, then went off to find her.

Rick walked outside and used his cell phone to call Maggie. Yet again, there was no answer. He struggled to remember Melanie's number, but couldn't. He went inside, asked one of the clerks to borrow a phone book, jotted down the number, then went back outside to call.

Melanie answered, sounding breathless.

"Melanie, it's Rick. Is Maggie over there?"

"No. We just got in. I had to run to catch the phone. I assumed she was with you. Wait a sec, though, there's a message light blinking. Let me check to see if she called while we were out."

Rick waited impatiently till she came back on the line.

"She called about an hour ago and said Ashley had left and for me to call her at home. Obviously you tried there."

"Yes. There was no answer. I guess I'll just have to keep trying."

"Are you okay? You sound kind of shaky."

He sucked in a deep breath and tried to steady his voice. "Actually I'm at the hospital. Sally Keller took a fall. I came in with Matthew."

"That's awful. Is Sally all right?"

"They're checking her out now. She'd come around by the time we left the farm, but there's a good chance she broke her hip in the fall."

"I am so sorry. Please tell Matthew we're thinking about both of them. And don't you worry about a thing. I'll find Maggie and send her over there, okay? Would you like me to send Mike in the meantime?"

For a minute Rick considered saying yes, but he stopped himself. He wasn't used to leaning on anyone. "No, I'll be fine."

To his astonishment, his eyes were stinging with unshed tears as he hung up. For a man who'd had no one in his life a few short weeks ago, he now seemed to be surrounded by people he cared about, people who genuinely seemed to care about him. Getting emotional about a thing like that seemed crazy. He blamed it on his concern for Sally. There was no point in trying to deny that he'd started to think of her and Matthew as the grandparents he'd never known.

So this was what it was like to have his life emotionally entangled with someone else's. He'd always avoided romantic love, because he knew the heartache that sort of attachment could cause, but this one had snuck up on him. He hadn't protected himself from starting to care for these two old people.

He was on what had to be his third cup of very bad coffee and his hundredth trek between the waiting room and the emergency entrance when he finally spotted Maggie running across the parking lot. He met her halfway and swept her into his arms, clinging to her like a lifeline.

He felt steadier when he finally let her go. "You didn't have to come over here."

"Of course I did. I came as soon as Melanie caught up with me. Ironically I'd gone out to the farm to see the Kellers, but no one was there. You must have already left for the hospital. How is Sally?"

"I'm still waiting for word. Matthew is with her." He looked into her eyes. "I know I said you didn't need to come, but I'm glad you're here."

Maggie reached up and touched his cheek, her expression filled with understanding. "I know. Why don't we go back inside?" she urged. "It's hot as blazes out here, and we want to be where Matthew can find us when there's news."

They went into the crowded emergency waiting room. Maggie checked at the nurses' station to see if there was any word on Sally, while Rick found a couple of empty seats. What was it with hospitals that every waiting room was too cold and had this antiseptic smell? He'd have felt better outside, but Maggie was right. They needed to be right where Matthew could find them if the doctors booted him out of Sally's treatment cubicle, which they were bound to do sooner or later.

"The nurse at the desk doesn't know anything, but I'm going to see if I can get into the treatment area," Maggie said when she finally joined him. "I spotted a nurse going into the back who looked familiar. I think my sisters and I used to play with her when we were girls. At least she might get us some information. I'll be right back."

Rick nodded. After she was gone, he closed his eyes.

"Let Sally be okay," he murmured, not entirely sure if he was expressing a wish or saying a prayer. It had been a long time since he'd had any reason to ask God for anything, so it was little wonder he wasn't sure if that's what he was doing now. Praying seemed like a good idea, though, so he silently repeated the same words. "God, please let her be okay. Matthew needs her. And," he added, though he was still surprised by it, "so do I."

Until today, he hadn't realized how true that was. For years and years, he'd told himself he didn't need anyone. He'd gone through life with a tough attitude and a grim determination to keep people at arm's length. If a man didn't need anyone, then he couldn't be hurt. He couldn't get his heart broken. Letting people close was a guarantee that sooner or later there would be heartache.

Matthew and Sally hadn't allowed him to keep his distance. They'd poked and prodded. Matthew had butted in with advice whether Rick wanted to hear it or not. Sally had fed him and teased him and—yes, he could see it now—loved him. They'd asked nothing from him in return. They'd simply welcomed him into their lives.

As had Maggie. Of course, with Maggie it was entirely different. Her welcome had been more cautious, her trust harder to win. In fact, he was still on that particular journey, but after witnessing the glory of the love between Matthew and Sally, he was beginning to see the value of the prize.

His eyes were still closed when he felt Maggie's presence. She slipped into the hard plastic chair beside him and linked her fingers through his.

"I was right. It was Laurie. She wouldn't let me go back to the treatment area, but she went in and found out that Sally's having her hip X-rayed. Matthew is with her. He won't leave her side, mainly because she keeps insisting she's getting up and walking out of here. Her determination to leave is beginning to make the doctors a little nervous. They seem to think she just might try it, broken hip or not."

Rick smiled. "That's Sally, all right. She hates people fussing over her. She thinks she's the only one who gets to do any fussing."

Maggie grinned. "I know someone else like that. I'm a little surprised you called me at all."

"Thought you'd want to know," he said, fearing that he'd revealed far too much about his own neediness.

"I did and not just because I like Matthew and Sally."

He slanted a look at her. "Oh?"

"Because I know how important they are to you."

Rick nodded slowly. "Funny thing about that," he said. "I'm just now figuring that one out myself."

Maggie wondered if Rick had any idea at all that his emotions were written all over his face. She doubted it. If he knew, he'd have found some way to mask them.

When Matthew eventually emerged from the treatment area, his expression was grim, his legs unsteady.

"What?" Rick demanded, bolting to his side and walking with him to a chair.

"Broke her dang hip, just like I thought," he said, sounding shaken. "They're talking about putting her in a nursing home when she leaves here. She's mad as a wet hen about that. She says if I let them do that, she'll divorce me. Wouldn't put it past her, either." He regarded them with a helpless expression. "What am I supposed to do? I'd do anything in the world for her, but this is beyond me. We can't afford to have a nurse at the house, and I can't manage her till she's back on her feet some."

"Couldn't one of the kids come home?" Maggie asked, but even before she'd finished the question, Rick said, "I'll move in."

The unexpected offer surprised Maggie and clearly stunned Matthew. Hope lit his eyes. "You'd do that?"

Rick looked embarrassed. "It's no big deal. Living in a bed-and-breakfast place is getting old anyway."

Matthew turned to Maggie. "You got anything to say about this?"

Other than wanting to throw her arms around the man in question and hug him, Maggie knew her opinion wasn't really the important one. "If Rick wants to do it, I think it would be foolish of you to turn him down."

"Might put a crimp in things for the two of you, though," Matthew said, giving Rick a sly look.

"Stop worrying about my love life, old man," Rick said. "Just think of the fun Maggie and I will have trying to sneak around behind your back."

Maggie couldn't help chuckling at that.

"You're sure?" Matthew asked again. "I don't want to say a word to Sally if there's a chance you'll change your mind."

"I'm not changing my mind," Rick said, his voice filled with resolve.

In that instant, Maggie's heart did a little lurch. This caring, compassionate side of Rick was something she'd suspected he possessed. Now that she'd seen it, though, she knew she was a goner. She could build brick and steel barriers around her heart, but they wouldn't do a damn thing to protect it. The man was already inside, as much a part of her as breathing.

She watched Matthew clasp Rick's hand.

"You can't imagine what this means to me," Matthew told him. "Don't know what I'd do if Sally and I had to be separated, even for a few weeks."

Rick glanced at Maggie, his eyes filled with raw emotion he didn't even attempt to hide. "I think I understand," he said softly. "For the first time in my life, I honestly think I understand."

14

Rick had been as stunned by his impulsive offer at the hospital as everyone else, but the instant the words were out of his mouth, he'd known that offering to stay at the farmhouse was the right thing to do.

It didn't have anything to do with impressing Maggie, either. He'd wanted to be there for Matthew and Sally. There was no way in hell those two should be separated, even for a short period of time, not when he was in a position to prevent it. At least this was one time when his presence might make a real difference. Sticking around home had never been much help to his mother. If anything, he'd only served as a reminder of his father.

A week later he was settled into an upstairs room at the farmhouse. He'd spent most of the week doing odd jobs around the place to make it easier for Sally to get around once she was in a wheelchair and eventually on crutches. The offensive rug that had caused her fall had been rolled up and stuffed in a closet. Matthew had wanted to toss it in the trash, but Rick had persuaded him to put it away and let Sally decide where it belonged.

Now everything was ready for her arrival. An ambulance would be bringing her and Matthew home in an hour. Maggie was in the kitchen preparing a welcome-home lunch. After making one last check of the downstairs rooms, Rick went to join her. He slipped his arms around her waist from behind and nuzzled her neck. She smelled like night-blooming jasmine. The scent had turned into an aphrodisiac for him.

"Guess I better get my fill of you before the chaperones arrive," he said.

Maggie chuckled and took an exaggerated look at her watch. "How much do you think you can get away with in twenty minutes or so?"

"Not nearly enough," he said, his voice husky.

Maggie turned in his arms. "You're doing a wonderful thing, Rick. You know that, don't you?"

He still felt uncomfortable with the praise. "Anyone would have done the same thing."

"Their kids never even offered," Maggie reminded him.

"Because I'd already agreed to stay here," he said, giving them the benefit of the doubt. "They did come right up to visit Sally in the hospital. And their daughter seems like she really wants them to move to Atlanta to be close to her family once Sally's back on her feet."

"I suppose that's something," Maggie conceded. "Do you think they'll do it?"

Rick shrugged, not at all sure how he felt about Sally and Matthew leaving the home they'd always known. It wasn't his call anyway. "I think Matthew is considering it," he admitted. "Sally's refused to discuss it."

Maggie gave him a knowing look. "And you? What do you think?"

"It's not up to me."

"But you have an opinion. I can tell."

Rick sighed. "Actually I don't. On the one hand, it saddens me to think that they'd leave this place behind. On the other, I can see why it would mean a lot to them to be close to one of their kids, especially at this time in their lives. This may be the first major health crisis they've faced, but it probably won't be the last. They'd be closer to excellent doctors and hospitals in Atlanta or over in Charlottesville or Richmond, if they moved closer to one of their sons."

"That's definitely a consideration, since you won't always be here to pitch in," Maggie said, looking oddly sad herself.

Rick studied her curiously. "Probably not," he admitted.

"To say nothing of the fact that it's not your job to look out for them in the first place," she added. "Which makes it all the more remarkable that you've made it your responsibility this time."

"Don't go back to that," Rick said. "I'm glad I'm able to do it. It's not going to be forever."

"No, I don't suppose it is," Maggie said, that surprising hint of sorrow still in her eyes.

Before Rick could figure out what that was about, he heard the ambulance pulling up in front of the house. "They're home," he said.

Maggie gave him a fierce, lingering hug.

He studied her curiously. "What was that for?"

"To make up for the fact that we never got to fool around," she teased.

Rick laughed. "You can't make up for that unless you're willing to sneak over here and into my room in the middle of the night."

"Fat chance. There's nothing wrong with Matthew's hearing."

"Oh, I'm pretty sure we'd have his blessing," Rick said.

Maggie shook her head. "Men!" She shooed him toward the door. "Go meet them. They might need some help getting Sally settled. I'll check the chicken and be right out."

Rick released her reluctantly and went off to greet Sally and Matthew. The paramedics had already settled her into the downstairs bedroom she and Matthew had shared for their entire marriage. She beamed when she saw Rick.

"Come right over here and let me give you a kiss," she said, holding out her arms. "I wouldn't be here in my own bed if it weren't for you."

"Don't make too much of it," Rick said. "I'm here for the apple pie. Matthew said there are half a dozen in the freezer. When they're gone, I'm out of here."

"Stop it right this minute," Sally said. "Don't make light of what you're doing for us. We won't ever forget it."

Rick clasped her hand in his and brushed a kiss across her knuckles. "I'm just glad you're well enough to be back home."

She gave him a sharp look. "It is wonderful to be surrounded by my own things. Just one question—what did you and Matthew do with my rug? That ornery old coot won't say."

Relieved that he'd had the foresight to keep the rug from getting tossed out, Rick chuckled, but Matthew obviously saw nothing amusing about the question.

"Should have burned the dang thing," he grumbled.

Sally's gaze stayed on Rick. "But you didn't, did you? You wouldn't let him."

Rick winked at her. "Nope. It's in the closet in the hall."

"Thank you. I know it's silly to be so attached to a thing like that, but I brought that rug from my mama's house. I'd hate to think of losing it."

"That rug is why you're in this bed," Matthew retorted.

Sally frowned at him. "No, it's not. I'm here because I was rushing around and not paying attention to what I was doing," she insisted. "Now where's Maggie? I can smell lunch cooking, and I know Rick wasn't the one fussing around in my kitchen."

"She'll be in here in a minute," Rick promised, "and we'll have lunch soon. Since Maggie cooked, it will be delicious, though I'm no slouch in the kitchen. You'll see when I whip up breakfast tomorrow." He saw the weariness in Sally's eyes. "Why don't you take a little nap? There's time before lunch."

She gave him a grateful look. "I believe I will," she said, her gaze seeking out her husband. "Matthew, will you stay with me?"

Matthew immediately pulled a chair closer to the bed and took her hand. "Now, where else would I be?"

Rick saw the emotion in their eyes and knew they'd already forgotten all about him. He slipped from the room, quietly closed the door and leaned against it. Something that felt a lot like yearning filled his heart. He wanted what they had, wanted it with all his heart.

He could have it, too. There was a woman in the kitchen who could give him all that and more. He simply had to take the risk and ask.

He sighed and moved away from the wall, knowing that he wasn't quite brave enough yet. For too many years he'd been conditioned to run. A few weeks around a couple as much in love as Matthew and Sally couldn't completely banish the memory of a woman whose volatile relationships had never lasted, or in some ways had lasted too long. It would take more than one little streak of yearning to overcome that history.

But one of these days he would. With every day that passed, he was growing more confident of that. He'd just have to pray that Maggie was patient enough to wait him out.

"Come sit by me," Sally encouraged Rick one morning a few days after her return home. "There's something I want to talk to you about."

Rick eyed her warily. "You're not meddling again, are you?"

She laughed. "Somebody certainly needs to, but no. Not this time, anyway. I want to ask you what you think about Matthew and me moving to Atlanta."

Rick's heart immediately felt heavy. He'd known this was coming—their daughter was calling almost daily to pressure to make a decision—but he hadn't wanted to think about it. Staying here had given him a sense of family, something he'd apparently craved far more than he'd ever realized.

"I think it's up to you and Matthew," he said honestly. "Is it what you want to do?"

"Matthew does," she admitted. "He adores Ellen, and he says it's time for a new adventure."

Rick studied her expression. Reluctance was written all over her face. "You disagree, don't you?"

"Not entirely," she said carefully. "It's just such a huge step. Neither of us have ever lived in a big city. Haven't even been to Atlanta to visit, if the truth be told. Even if we had been, a visit doesn't tell you what you need to know about living in a place. I'm afraid we'll get there and hate it, that we'll feel overwhelmed. Then it will be too late."

He saw what she was driving at. Once the farm was sold, they would have no choice but to make the best of it, even if they hated Atlanta. "Would you have to sell the farm before you make the move? Maybe you could stay with Ellen for a few months to see how you like it."

"That's not an option. Her house is too small. We'd be an imposition, even for a short time." She gave him a sly look. "There is another possibility, though, one that could solve everything."

Rick wasn't sure he liked the sneaky glint in her eyes. "Oh?"

"Why don't you buy the farm?"

He stared at her in shock. "Me? What would I do with a farm? I'm a photographer. I travel. The place would fall to ruin while I'm gone."

"Then hire someone to run it when you're away," she suggested, then added, "or marry someone who'll stay right here while you're on assignment."

He stood up and backed away from the bed as if he were retreating from danger. "I knew you were meddling," he accused.

"Oh, sit back down," Sally ordered impatiently. "You know you love the woman. Stop dillydallying."

He studied her with a narrowed gaze. "I don't see how this solves your problem."

"If you had the farm, it would be as if it were still in the family," she explained, her expression wistful. "Maybe Matthew and I could come to visit from time to time. Moving doesn't seem so final. Maybe Matthew could even help you run it for a few months each year. It would be the best of both worlds, at least for as long as we're able to travel back and forth."

The whole idea was outrageous, but it slipped right past Rick's well-honed defenses and grabbed hold. "I don't know, Sally," he protested, even as he began imagining how it could work. It would tie him to these people— give him a family, in a way—forever. To his dismay, or maybe his delight, he could imagine growing old here with Maggie, raising kids, just as Matthew and Sally had done.

"What does Matthew say about this scheme of yours?"

"He says I'm not to pressure you." She met his gaze. "But I don't see this as me being a selfish old woman, Rick. I see it as giving you a chance to do what I know you want to do, whether you're ready to face it or not."

"Let me think about it," he said eventually.

Her expression brightened. "You'll really consider it?"

"I'll *consider* it," he stressed. "But please don't count on it, Sally. It would be a huge change for me. I'm not sure it's a change I'm ready to make."

"Yes, you are," Sally told him gently. "I see it in your eyes when you're with Maggie. Just listen to your heart, Rick. It won't steer you wrong."

"When are you coming home?" Ashley asked Maggie, when she finally checked in during the middle of her big trial.

"When is this case of yours going to wind down?" Maggie responded, immediately turning the tables on her.

"We should be getting to closing arguments in another week or two," Ashley said wearily. "It's been a more complicated case than I'd imagined. I really didn't call to talk about it, though. I want to hear about you."

"There's not much to tell," Maggie said evasively. She was still having difficulty realizing that she'd been at Rose Cottage for nearly two months and that Rick had been underfoot for nearly that long. She'd grown way too comfortable with the arrangement.

When she thought of work, though, there was no denying that time was slipping by. She was already working on the November issue of the magazine and had been making notes for the Christmas issue. It was hard to think about Thanksgiving and the holidays when the August temperatures were so steamy. The weather was getting to her. She longed for the rare early mornings when a thunderstorm had cleared the air the night before, pushing out the thick, humid air and leaving behind a dry, cool breeze that unfortunately wouldn't last past noon.

"Isn't the magazine getting antsy about you being away so long?" Ashley asked.

"If they are, no one's said anything. They won't as long as the pages are in on time. And to be honest, I haven't thought about coming home," Maggie admitted, surprised by the realization. There'd been too much going on lately, especially with the daily visits to the farm to help out and the time she managed to steal alone with Rick. The pace here was quieter, to be sure, but it was never boring. Even Rick seemed content for the moment.

"And Rick's still there?" Ashley asked.

"Yes."

"Still living at the B and B?"

"No, actually he's been out at the farm with Sally and Matthew," she said. "Most of the time, anyway."

"Ah."

"Ah?" Maggie echoed. "What does that mean?"

Ashley laughed. "It means that Melanie and Mike say that the two of you are inseparable. They say that love is most definitely in the air. I was hoping that was an exaggeration. They've mentioned nothing about Sally and Matthew. What's that all about?"

"Sally broke her hip—on the day you left, in fact. She didn't want to go to a nursing home, so Rick moved in to help out."

"Oh, boy. That would explain it all right," Ashley said, a gloating note in her voice.

"Explain what?"

"You falling head over heels for the guy. Sexy, intelligent *and* compassionate. That's a hard combination to ignore, no matter what common sense tells you to do."

As usual, Ashley had nailed it, but Maggie didn't want to admit to her feelings aloud. She wasn't sure she could bear the sympathy if Rick disappointed her in the end. And the jury was definitely still out on that. He seemed happy enough with the way things were, but she was starting to lose hope that he would ever change enough to take a risk on a future with her. Ashley's skepticism only seemed to confirm her own doubts.

"Don't be ridiculous," she said shortly, clinging to an old spin that might have worked on someone other than her sister. "We're still getting to know each other. That's all. Sooner or later, he'll go back to work. I'll come back to Boston and we'll drift apart. I accept that."

"I can tell from your voice that you actually believe that," Ashley said. "Why? Come on, Maggie. Why can't you trust what you and Rick have? If you don't, that alone should tell you something, don't you agree?"

"Okay, okay. I know you're right. I know I don't trust it because he's Rick Flannery, after all, the ultimate rolling stone," Maggie retorted, tears stinging her eyes. That said it all. Rick Flannery didn't do commitment. She'd known it from the beginning. She might as well accept that nothing had changed.

Still fighting tears, she told Ashley, "I have to go." As she hung up, she turned to find Rick standing in the doorway, staring at her with a shocked expression.

"What are you doing here?" she snapped, her heart hammering. How much had he heard? Too much, judging from his expression.

"I came over here to ask you something important," he said, "but obviously my timing sucks." He leveled a hard look directly into her eyes. "What the hell did you mean by what you told your sister just now?"

"How much did you hear?"

"Enough to know that you don't think too much of me." He shook his head. "How did I get this so wrong?"

Maggie couldn't understand why he was so offended. She scowled at him. "Well, it's true, isn't it? It's taking a little longer than I expected, but eventually you'll get bored with all this and go back to Boston. You'll start doing photo shoots with all those gorgeous models again, and the next thing you know you'll be involved with one of them. The Kellers and I will just be a distant memory."

He regarded her with a look that was filled with wounded pride, or maybe genuine bemusement. "Do you honestly think I'm that shallow? Do you think the last few weeks have been some sort of game for me?"

She could tell he was furious, but she really didn't know why. "Isn't that the way it's always been?"

He had the grace to look chagrined by the question, but then the fire in his eyes returned. "Before I met you, yes," he said tightly. "But crazy me, I thought what we had was different. I was starting to believe in it. Obviously you still see our relationship as some sort of summer interlude. That's *your* usual pattern, isn't it?"

She winced as he leveled the harsh accusation with dead aim, then headed for the door.

"You're leaving," she said flatly, resigned to it. No matter how many times she'd deluded herself into thinking otherwise, she'd been expecting this from the beginning. It didn't really matter that she'd been the one to give him an excuse to go. If she hadn't, he would have found another one, no matter what he said now about having changed.

To her shock, though, he whirled around, came back and dragged her into his arms, crushing her mouth under his. The kiss was laced with barely banked fury, but it still stirred her. She hated that he could get to her, even when there was so much anger in the air, even when it was all over between them.

"I'm leaving, yes," he said. "Because right this second I'm too furious to stay. But I will be back, Maggie, and we will talk about this. Nothing's over between us. Nothing."

After he'd gone, his words—his promise—lingered in the air. Maggie touched a finger to her bruised and tender lips and let the tears fall.

But rather than the bitter tears of a woman who'd gotten exactly what she'd expected from the beginning, they were tears of relief that maybe, just maybe Rick was going to prove her wrong, after all.

15

"Is it just me, or are the D'Angelo women absolutely, positively impossible to understand?" Rick asked Mike over a beer an hour after leaving Maggie's place. His fury was slowly but surely dying down, but in its wake was a mile-wide streak of sorrow and confusion.

"How is it that a man who's dated more than a few of the world's most gorgeous creatures still doesn't understand women?" Mike replied.

"Those women weren't half as complicated as Maggie," Rick insisted.

"How so?"

"They wanted to be seen in the right places and they wanted me to make sure that they looked beautiful in their pictures. There weren't all these undercurrents to trip a man up."

"Maybe the real difference is that you never cared about any of them enough to let them stress you out," Mike suggested.

"Could be," Rick conceded. "But answer my original question, is there something about the D'Angelo women I just don't get?"

"I can't speak for Jo and Ashley, or even for Maggie,"

Mike said, his expression thoughtful, "but Melanie certainly wasn't the easiest woman to read. I figured it was just me." He grinned. "Either that, or the fact that men simply aren't supposed to understand women ever, no matter who they are."

Rick lifted his beer in a toast. "I like that one. I'd hate to think I'm the only dense male on the planet."

Mike gave him a quizzical look. "Do I get to know what any of this is actually about, or did you drag me over here just so you could get some male sympathy?"

Rick wasn't prepared to go into detail, so he gave Mike the condensed version. "If you must know, I went over to Maggie's tonight with a plan. It went up in smoke."

"You asked her something and she shot you down?" Mike guessed.

Rick's bark of laughter held a note of bitterness. "I never asked a damn thing. I walked in to hear her telling Ashley that she couldn't count on anything with me because I'm just a shallow jerk."

Mike regarded him with disbelief. "She said that?"

"I'm interpreting," Rick admitted.

Mike shook his head, regarding Rick with pity. "Never do that, man. Never try to interpret or assume when there's a woman involved. It's dangerous. It'll come back to bite you in the butt every time. Whenever I took a stab at guessing what was going on with Melanie, I got it wrong."

"Amen to that," Jeff said, pulling out a chair to join them. He looked at Mike. "Are we here to commiserate with Rick over something specific?"

"He's not being that specific," Mike said. "For the moment, this is just a general discussion of female idiosyncracies."

"All women's idiosyncracies, or Maggie's in particular?" Jeff asked.

"Maggie's, if you must know," Rick said.

Jeff and Mike exchanged a look filled with barely concealed amusement. Maybe it had been a mistake to call them. They seemed to be taking a lot of pleasure in his pain. Still, he'd needed to talk to someone. If he'd gone back out to the farm, heaven knew what Matthew and Sally would have had to say. They were losing patience with the pace of his courtship as it was. For once, he hadn't been in the mood for any of their sage advice, no matter how well-meant.

In fact, what he'd wanted was a couple of drinking buddies who'd help him get stinking drunk. The fact that the idea held any appeal at all was a shock. That he'd turn to alcohol was proof of just how deeply he'd been wounded by Maggie's words. It had hurt like hell finding out that the woman he loved still thought he was little better than a shallow cad. He could have sworn they'd gotten past that weeks ago, but Maggie's uncensored comments to her sister told him otherwise.

"How about another round of beer?" he suggested, gesturing for the waitress.

Jeff cast another of those amused looks at Mike. "I'll stick to club soda, I think. Something tells me this crowd is going to need a designated driver."

"I'll join you, Rick," Mike offered. "Though two's my limit. I don't want to spend the whole night trying to explain to Melanie why I've come home drunk. To be honest, you don't want me to have to do that, either. She'll run straight to her sister. They'll commiserate, and we'll wind up catching hell somewhere along the line."

Rick regarded him curiously. "Does Melanie keep you on a short leash?"

Mike laughed. "Oh, pal, if that's your idea of marriage, I think I see why things aren't going too smoothly with Maggie."

"Explain," Rick pleaded. "I really want to get this."

"Seriously?" Mike asked.

"Yes, dammit!"

Mike glanced at Jeff. "Feel free to jump in anytime," he told his friend. "Okay, here it is in a nutshell. Marriage is a partnership. When it works, both people get what they want. Sometimes that takes a little compromising."

"Which means you give in," Rick guessed. In his experience, the only way to keep a woman happy was to do everything her way.

"The man is a real cynic, isn't he?" Jeff noted. "No, pal, compromise means both people give a little. Or you give in on one thing and she gives in on another. Things balance out."

Rick nodded, taking that in. "Okay, partnership and compromise. What else?"

"Friendship," Mike said.

"Respect," Jeff added.

Rick lifted his beer in another toast. "Respect, that's it," he said triumphantly. "That's what's missing between Maggie and me."

"You don't respect Maggie?" Jeff asked, looking incredulous.

"No, no, no," Rick insisted. His words were beginning to slur a little. He was actually getting drunk. He couldn't remember the last time that had happened. He'd vowed years ago never, ever to use alcohol as a crutch the way his mother had. "Maggie doesn't respect me. She thinks I'm a scoundrel."

"Really?" Jeff asked, fighting a grin. "I don't suppose all those stories in the tabloids contributed to that opinion, did they?"

Rick shook his head. "Haven't been in the tabloids. Not for weeks and weeks."

"Since you've been here," Mike said.

"Exactly." He was beginning to feel very sorry for himself. "Been loyal and faithful for weeks and weeks, and what does it get me? Not one thing. She still doesn't trust me not to take off on her."

"Have you told Maggie you love her?" Mike asked.

"That was the plan," he said sorrowfully. "It all went to hell."

Jeff regarded him with confusion. "What plan?"

Mike's expression filled with sudden understanding. "Tonight's plan," he explained to Jeff, then turned to Mike. "You went over there tonight to tell her you love her."

Rick tapped his beer bottle against Mike's. "And to ask her to marry me." He shook his head sadly. "Never got that far, though."

"Because of something you overheard her say to Ashley," Mike concluded. "Oh, man, you are such an idiot." He leaned forward and regarded Rick intently. "Go home. Sober up and go back over there tomorrow with enough flowers to fill the damn place. Don't cut them from the garden over there, either. Buy them."

"You really think the flowers will change the way she thinks of me?" Rick asked.

"Hell, no," Mike told him. "But they'll get you in the door. After that, start tap-dancing as fast as you can."

"I can't tap-dance," Rick said, confused.

"Not literally," Mike explained patiently. "Start talking and don't let up until you've gotten through to her. Now do you get it?"

For the first time since he'd left Maggie and let his temper cool into something that felt more like hurt, Rick felt hopeful. After all, the entire world knew what a smooth talker he was, thanks to his tabloid reputation. Maybe this was one time when living up to that reputation could actually serve his purpose.

Maggie waited for hours for Rick to turn up again so she could apologize for her possibly unfounded accusations and they could start the evening over.

As it grew later and later, though, her own temper began to heat up. How had she wound up on the defensive for merely expressing the truth? He'd certainly said or done nothing to dispel her impression that their relationship was going to end as badly as all her others. It was just taking longer than she'd expected to get to the final breakup.

When she couldn't bear staring at the walls another instant, she picked up the phone and called Melanie. Maybe her sister could offer some words of wisdom. At least she wouldn't denigrate Rick or say anything to reinforce Maggie's own insecurities. Melanie was far more diplomatic than Ashley.

"I suppose you called because you're worried about Rick?" Melanie said as soon as she heard Maggie's voice.

"Worried about him? Why would I be worried about him?"

"Uh-oh," Melanie whispered. "I thought you knew."

"Knew what?"

"That he's out with my husband and Jeff. Mike called

a few hours ago to say that you and Rick had some sort of disagreement and Rick needed company. They're drinking."

Maggie was shocked. Rick didn't drink, at least not much more than an occasional glass of wine with a meal. After being reared by an alcoholic, he was religious about cutting himself off after one drink.

"Rick doesn't really drink," Maggie said worriedly.

"Well, something changed tonight. Did you two fight?"

"I wouldn't call it a fight exactly. He overheard something I said to Ashley, and it made him angry. I pushed a few more buttons, and he stormed out of here. I actually thought he'd get over it long before now and come back, so we could sort everything out."

"He's not over it apparently," Melanie said. "I can tell you where they are, if you want to go over there."

Maggie sighed. "No. Rick needs to figure this one out on his own."

"Is he the only one with a problem?" her sister asked.

"No, but he's the one with the solution. I'm just not sure if he'll ever figure that out."

"He loves you, Maggie."

"There was a time when I thought he did."

"He does," Melanie said confidently. "Otherwise he wouldn't be with my husband right this minute trying to drown his sorrows."

"That's love?"

"It is for a man who's fighting it. Be patient, sis."

"Not one of my virtues," Maggie said. "I think we all know that."

"Then it's about time you developed it," Melanie chided. "If things aren't better by this time tomorrow, call me. Until then, hold tight."

"I'll try," Maggie promised. Even if it killed her.

* * *

It was dark as midnight when Rick got back to Maggie's cottage. He'd had a half-dozen cups of coffee after Mike and Jeff had dropped him at the farmhouse. Thankfully Matthew and Sally had been asleep. He'd sat alone in the kitchen drinking cup after cup of coffee until he concluded he was not only reasonably sober, but wideawake enough to do what he had to do. Now that he was here, though, he didn't feel half as steady as a man should when he was about to make the most important pitch of his entire life.

Maggie was sitting on the porch. He could smell the faint scent of jasmine she always wore. Maybe she was waiting for him. Maybe she was sulking. Either way, at least he wasn't going to have to wake her from a sound sleep to get this over with before he lost the last of the false courage he'd bought himself with a couple of beers.

"I thought you might be in bed by now," he said, standing on the bottom step and waiting for some sign that he'd be welcome after the way he'd stormed off earlier. Not that a lack of welcome would turn him away, but it might change his tactics ever so slightly. He might be forced to resort to those flowers Mike had recommended, even if he had to go into the garden and yank them out of the ground. Right now, he was relying solely on himself and the message he needed to deliver.

"I knew I wouldn't be able to sleep until we talked," she said.

"Then you knew I would be back?"

"You said you would be, so, yes, I believed you."

He gave a nod of satisfaction, then realized that on the moonless night, she couldn't see him. "Good. Then you do have some faith in me…in *us*."

"I want to," she said, her voice shaky.

"What will it take to convince you?"

"I honestly don't know."

"Does this lack of trust really have anything at all to do with me, or is it about your past relationships?" He'd realized somewhere between the farm and here that it was all twisted together. Did she recognize the same thing?

"Both," she said at once, surprising him with the admission. At least she could see that he wasn't entirely to blame for all the doubts she had.

"What have I done, not in the past but to you, to inspire your distrust?"

"Nothing," she admitted at once. "But I do know your pattern, Rick. I've seen you change since we've been here, but I'm terrified to trust those changes."

"Patterns can be broken—at least I'd like to think some of them can be. Yours and mine, anyway. If we're going to talk about what we want, then you should know that I want to believe that you and I have what it takes to make a whole new pattern, one we can live with forever. I want us to wind up like Matthew and Sally, together in our old age, not letting anything get between us."

The words hung in the air, and for a long time he thought she might not respond at all, but she finally whispered, "What do you mean?"

He grinned at her caution. It was plain she didn't intend to take a chance on misinterpreting. He could hardly blame her after the way they'd gotten it so wrong earlier tonight.

"In my own clumsy way, I'm asking you to marry me," he said. "Do you suppose I could come up there where I can see your face while I try to convince you about this?"

"I guess," she said, sounding doubtful about the wisdom of it.

Rick could see he was going to have his work cut out for him. That's why he'd taken a few precautionary measures to ensure his success. He'd taken them earlier in the day, but he had a hunch they were even more essential now.

Maggie was sitting in a rocker, so he took a seat in the one next to her. He set it in motion to match the somewhat agitated pace of hers.

"Here," he said, handing her a piece of paper.

"It's too dark. I can't read it," she said, clearly frustrated. "What is it?"

"A contract. I've bought a place a few miles from here."

"The orchard?" She guessed at once, not even trying to hide her disbelief and her excitement. "You actually bought it from Matthew and Sally?"

"Yes."

"Did you do it just to help them out?" she asked, that familiar note of uncertainty in her voice.

Rick wondered how long it would take before he could wipe that need for hesitance away. He had to start trying now. "Actually, I thought it would make a good place for us to raise our kids," he began, then tried to sell the idea. He leaned toward her. "We'd be close to Melanie and Mike. The rest of your family is bound to turn up here at the cottage from time to time, so it won't be like you'll be separated from them. You've been able to do your job from here, but even if you had to give it up, there are other regional magazines that would welcome having you on staff, especially if you can guarantee them that we're a team and I'll shoot all your photos at a reasonable cost."

A gleam immediately lit her eyes. "What's your definition of reasonable cost?" she demanded.

She asked in a suddenly businesslike tone that had him smiling and trying to hide it. Even though he'd sidetracked her, he could tell he'd almost won.

"I think you'll find my rate acceptable," he assured her.

"Too vague," she retorted. "Spell it out for me."

He did laugh then. "Okay, here's what I have in mind. You'll use Sally's recipe and bake me an apple pie and eat it naked with me in bed, like we did the other night." He heard the chuckle she couldn't quite conceal. "Of course, the fee I charge the magazine will be in dollars and cents."

"Of course," she said primly.

"There's another thing," Rick said, digging into his pocket. He handed her a velvet jeweler's box. "I thought this might tie the deal together."

"Buying an orchard was pretty impressive," she admitted.

"But this is sort of traditional, and something tells me that you need the traditional when it comes to the really important things," he said. "When we met, I thought you were a fairly unconventional woman, but I've found out differently. You're a lot more complicated than that."

She shoved the box back at him, and he thought for one heart-sinking moment that he'd blown it, after all.

"My hands are shaking," she whispered. "You open it. Besides, that's even more traditional."

Rick had looked at a couple of dozen different rings, some flashy, some understated. He'd settled for something in-between. He removed the simple emerald-cut diamond from the box, then dropped down on one knee in front of her. When it came to tradition, he'd come here prepared to go for broke.

"Maggie D'Angelo, will you marry me? Will you let me spend the rest of my life proving that no woman on earth could entrance me and fascinate me the way you do?"

He waited for what seemed like an eternity for her reply, but when it came, it was the last thing he expected.

"I'm wearing shorts and a T-shirt," she wailed, her voice choked with sobs. "And no…no shoes."

Rick laughed, his heart suddenly lighter. "Mind telling me what that has to do with anything?"

"I should be dressed up, and there should be candles and music."

She sounded so forlorn, he said, "We can do this over tomorrow night. Of course, it won't be quite as much of a surprise." He started to withdraw the ring.

"Oh, no, you don't," she said, then held out her left hand. "I love you, Rick. It scares me sometimes when I think about how quickly this happened and how much you matter. I know that ring isn't a guarantee of anything, but I think it's time I take it on faith that we're strong enough to weather whatever comes along, even a parade of size-two women."

"Sweetheart, they're no competition for you at all. I love food too much to spend my life with someone who exists on yogurt and the occasional lettuce leaf."

"Then it's a good thing I can cook, isn't it?"

"It was the first thing I fell in love with," he said, then yelped when she pinched him. "Okay, the second thing, but now the list's so long, I can't even count that high."

"Nice save," she commended him, then held out her hand to admire the ring that was winking in the faint light shining from the living-room window. "You have excellent taste, Flannery."

"I picked you, didn't I?"

The smile that lit her face would stay with him forever. It appeared he'd gotten the words exactly right.

Epilogue

"I can't possibly put a wedding together in two weeks," Colleen D'Angelo protested when Maggie called to tell her mother about her engagement. "Why on earth can't one of my daughters do things the traditional way and have a nice *long* engagement?"

Maggie laughed. "You should have brought us up to be less impetuous."

"So, it's my fault?"

"You're as good a person to blame as anyone. At least Rick and I are getting married in Boston, instead of in grandmother's garden at Rose Cottage the way Melanie and Mike did."

"You know perfectly well the priest will never agree to perform a ceremony on such short notice," her mother fretted.

"Then Ashley will marry us and we'll have a church ceremony later. She's a notary," Maggie said. "We want to get married at home, anyway. Just something small, Mom. It will be fine. We'll be up tomorrow to help with the preparations. I can't wait for you to meet Rick."

"I wish your father were here right now. Maybe he could talk some sense into you. Couldn't you at least wait till October? A fall wedding in New England is always lovely."

Maggie laughed. "We've already booked our honeymoon. We're going to Paris in September."

"Of course you would arrange things backward," her mother said with a sigh.

"We could forget about the wedding altogether," Maggie suggested slyly. "I hear marriage is highly overrated. Living together could work nicely."

"Absolutely not! I'll manage. I always do. And your sisters will pitch in, I'm sure. Thank goodness that case of Ashley's is finally wrapping up. This wedding will give her something positive to look forward to. She's been taking a beating in the media."

"Why?"

"Everyone seems convinced her client is guilty, but she's defending him so aggressively, it's all but certain she'll win. I don't know how she'll live with herself if she finds out too late that everyone was right."

Maggie thought of Ashley's despondence on her last visit to Virginia. She must have known then that she was going to get hammered by the media for her passionate defense of her client. It must have been weighing on her terribly. She was used to being victorious, not vilified.

"I'm sure she's doing what she feels she has to," Maggie told her mother. "Ashley has a very strong sense of justice as well as faith in the system."

"I know. I just pray this isn't one of those times when her faith is misplaced. But," she added briskly, "that's enough of that. Let's concentrate on making your wedding day perfect."

"As long as you guys and Rick are there, nothing else matters," Maggie said. "The frills aren't all that important."

"Well, they are to me," her mother said. "I'll have samples waiting for you when you get here."

"Samples of what?"

"Everything...dresses, cakes, flowers. And I think I know someone who could transform the living room on short notice. What about music? Do you want a string quartet?"

"Whoa!" Maggie pleaded. "Slow down. This is going to be a simple occasion, Mom."

"Simple doesn't mean it can't be memorable," her mother retorted. "Just leave it to me, darling."

"Please don't go overboard," Maggie said, knowing the words were falling on deaf ears. "I'll see you tomorrow."

When she'd hung up, she turned to Rick. "It's going to be a circus," she said, resigned to it.

He studied her. "Will you mind very much if it is?"

She touched his face. "Not as long as you're there beside me."

"Every second," he promised. "For the rest of our lives."

"We could elope," she suggested hopefully.

"And disappoint your mother? I don't think so. I want to start out making a good impression, not infuriating her."

"Then prepare yourself, Flannery. You are about to fall victim to a tornado."

Maggie had been right. Rick had had no idea how quickly tuxedo fittings, cake selections and all the other trappings could fill up his days. He barely managed to steal ten minutes alone with his bride-to-be at the end of the day. Thank heavens they'd decided to be married in two weeks. He wasn't sure he could have endured the pace for much longer.

Now the day had finally arrived and as he stood in

one of the bedrooms that had been designated for the groom and his best man—Matthew—Rick waited for the expected jitters to set in. Nothing, not even a twinge. All he felt was a deep sense of anticipation.

"What time is it?" he asked Matthew.

"About five seconds since the last time you asked," the old man told him. "For a man who swears he's not nervous, you seem mighty jumpy to me."

"I'm not jumpy," Rick protested. "I'm eager. There's a difference."

"You'll have to explain that one to me," Matthew said.

"It's not important," Rick told him. "Do you think Maggie will be ready on time?"

Matthew chuckled. "I think Maggie's been ready for a long time now, a lot longer than you, in fact. You were the one dragging your feet."

"That's not what I meant and you know it."

The bedroom door opened, and Mike poked his head in. He grinned at Matthew. "You need any help in getting him out here?"

"Nope. I think he'll come peacefully."

"Then it's time."

"Now?" Rick asked, suddenly overcome with anxiety.

"Now," Mike said. "Don't panic. All you need to do is get out there and keep your eyes on Maggie. Everything else will fall right into place."

"Eyes on Maggie," Rick muttered. "Right." He glanced at Matthew. "Let's do it."

He walked into the living room and took his place in front of the bay window that had been filled with baskets of flowers. He kept his gaze pinned to the stairs that Maggie would descend.

Ashley came down first, dressed in a simple, but elegant pale blue satin suit. She took her place in front of him. Then came Melanie and Jo, wearing similar suits in a deeper blue.

Rick swallowed hard as the music changed. And then Maggie was there on her father's arm, looking as if she'd stepped out of the pages of one of those fashion layouts he'd shot through the years. How many bridal gowns had he seen in his lifetime, but none had taken his breath away as the sight of Maggie did. The white satin clung to curves and dipped low in the back. It was simplicity at its very best, seductiveness at its most discreet.

She caught his gaze and smiled and his entire world steadied. "I love you," she mouthed.

"I love you," he said, loud enough to be heard by everyone. He wanted this roomful of people to know right here, right now before the vows that he had no lingering doubts. This marriage was what he wanted.

Behind him, Ashley laughed. "I think we all heard that. We could dispense with the vows."

Rick turned and grinned. "No shortcuts. I want this binding."

She winked at him. "Believe me, it will be."

He took Maggie's icy hands in his. "Then let's do it," he said softly, his gaze locked with hers. The light in her eyes burned brightly enough to fill his heart with joy. He knew in that instant why people did this, why they took a chance on love. It was for this moment when everything seemed perfect, when two hearts were precisely in tune, when faith was strong that the feelings would last forever. Maybe the rest of the years would take patience and love and hard work, but right this instant everything seemed possible.

He glanced over to the chair where Sally sat, almost

fully recuperated now, her gaze on Matthew, her eyes damp with tears, a smile on her lips. There was his proof that love could last, there and in Maggie's eyes. It was enough to make a cynic into a believer.

Rick said his vows without hesitation, his heart filled to overflowing. Maggie's voice was just as strong.

But neither of them held a candle to Ashley's firm declaration that they were now husband and wife. She grinned at her sister, then frowned at Rick. "This is my very first wedding. It had better last," she warned.

He laughed, even though he wasn't certain she was joking. "Believe me, you have nothing to worry about. We're in this for the long haul."

"Eternity," Maggie confirmed, eyes shining. "And then some."

Rick couldn't have said it better himself.

* * * * *

THE HARLEQUIN BESTSELLING AUTHOR COLLECTION

CLASSIC ROMANCES IN COLLECTIBLE VOLUMES
FROM OUR BESTSELLING AUTHORS

SHERRYL WOODS

Dream Mender

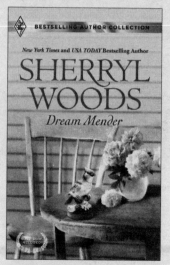

Available where books are sold.

www.eHarlequin.com

Also by #1 *New York Times* bestselling author

DEBBIE MACOMBER

NOW A HALLMARK CHANNEL ORIGINAL MOVIE, COMING THIS HOLIDAY SEASON.

What would the holidays be
without a new novel from
America's favorite storyteller?

**Available in hardcover
September 28!**

REQUEST YOUR
FREE BOOKS!

2 FREE NOVELS
FROM THE ROMANCE COLLECTION
PLUS 2 FREE GIFTS!

YES! Please send me 2 FREE novels from the Romance Collection and my 2 FREE gifts (gifts are worth about $10). After receiving them, if I don't wish to receive any more books, I can return the shipping statement marked "cancel." If I don't cancel, I will receive 4 brand-new novels every month and be billed just $5.74 per book in the U.S. or $6.24 per book in Canada. That's a saving of at least 28% off the cover price. It's quite a bargain! Shipping and handling is just 50¢ per book.* I understand that accepting the 2 free books and gifts places me under no obligation to buy anything. I can always return a shipment and cancel at any time. Even if I never buy another book, the two free books and gifts are mine to keep forever.

194/394 MDN E7NZ

Name _____ (PLEASE PRINT) _____

Address _____ Apt. # _____

City _____ State/Prov. _____ Zip/Postal Code _____

Signature (if under 18, a parent or guardian must sign)

Mail to **The Reader Service:**
IN U.S.A.: P.O. Box 1867, Buffalo, NY 14240-1867
IN CANADA: P.O. Box 609, Fort Erie, Ontario L2A 5X3

Not valid for current subscribers to the Romance Collection
or the Romance/Suspense Collection.

Want to try two free books from another line?
Call 1-800-873-8635 or visit www.morefreebooks.com.

* Terms and prices subject to change without notice. Prices do not include applicable taxes. N.Y. residents add applicable sales tax. Canadian residents will be charged applicable provincial taxes and GST. Offer not valid in Quebec. This offer is limited to one order per household. All orders subject to approval. Credit or debit balances in a customer's account(s) may be offset by any other outstanding balance owed by or to the customer. Please allow 4 to 6 weeks for delivery. Offer available while quantities last.

Your Privacy: Harlequin Books is committed to protecting your privacy. Our Privacy Policy is available online at www.eHarlequin.com or upon request from the Reader Service. From time to time we make our lists of customers available to reputable third parties who may have a product or service of interest to you. If you would prefer we not share your name and address, please check here. ☐

Help us get it right—We strive for accurate, respectful and relevant communications. To clarify or modify your communication preferences, visit us at www.ReaderService.com/consumerschoice.

MROM10R

SHERRYL WOODS

31289	A SLICE OF HEAVEN	___ $7.99 U.S.	___ $9.99 CAN.
32753	AMAZING GRACIE	___ $7.99 U.S.	___ $9.99 CAN.
32975	ABOUT THAT MAN	___ $7.99 U.S.	___ $9.99 CAN.
32976	ALONG CAME TROUBLE	___ $7.99 U.S.	___ $9.99 CAN.
32977	ASK ANYONE	___ $7.99 U.S.	___ $9.99 CAN.
32626	THE INN AT EAGLE POINT	___ $7.99 U.S.	___ $7.99 CAN.
32634	FLOWERS ON MAIN	___ $7.99 U.S.	___ $8.99 CAN.
32641	HARBOR LIGHTS	___ $7.99 U.S.	___ $8.99 CAN.
32962	WELCOME TO SERENITY	___ $7.99 U.S.	___ $9.99 CAN.
32961	SEAVIEW INN	___ $7.99 U.S.	___ $9.99 CAN.
32895	MENDING FENCES	___ $7.99 U.S.	___ $9.99 CAN.
32893	FEELS LIKE FAMILY	___ $7.99 U.S.	___ $9.99 CAN.
32887	STEALING HOME	___ $7.99 U.S.	___ $9.99 CAN.

(limited quantities available)

TOTAL AMOUNT	$ _____
POSTAGE & HANDLING	$ _____
($1.00 for 1 book, 50¢ for each additional)	
APPLICABLE TAXES*	$ _____
TOTAL PAYABLE	$ _____

(check or money order—please do not send cash)

To order, complete this form and send it, along with a check or money order for the total above, payable to MIRA Books, to: **In the U.S.:** 3010 Walden Avenue, P.O. Box 9077, Buffalo, NY 14269-9077; **In Canada:** P.O. Box 636, Fort Erie, Ontario, L2A 5X3.

Name: _____

Address: _____ City: _____

State/Prov.: _____ Zip/Postal Code: _____

Account Number (if applicable): _____

075 CSAS

*New York residents remit applicable sales taxes.
*Canadian residents remit applicable GST and provincial taxes.

MIRA®

www.MIRABooks.com

MSW1010BL